Witch Queen of Redwinter

THE REDWINTER CHRONICLES
VOLUME III

Witch Queen of Redwinter

ED McDONALD

TOR PUBLISHING GROUP
NEW YORK

WITCH QUEEN OF REDWINTER

Copyright © 2024 by ECM Creative, Ltd.

All rights reserved.

A Tor Book
Published by Tom Doherty Associates / Tor Publishing Group
120 Broadway
New York, NY 10271

www.torpublishinggroup.com

Tor® is a registered trademark of Macmillan Publishing Group, LLC.

The Library of Congress Cataloging-in-Publication Data is available upon request.

ISBN 978-1-250-81196-7 (hardcover)
ISBN 978-1-250-81197-4 (ebook)

Our books may be purchased in bulk for promotional, educational, or business use.
Please contact your local bookseller or the Macmillan Corporate and Premium
Sales Department at 1-800-221-7945, extension 5442, or by email at
MacmillanSpecialMarkets@macmillan.com.

First Edition: 2024

Printed in the United States of America

0 9 8 7 6 5 4 3 2 1

This book is for
Blake Jonathan William Bear McDonald

Witch Queen of Redwinter

Events That Have Passed

Should it have been a while since you last entered Raine's world, a brief summary of key events that have transpired so far is given below. A glossary of characters, clans and terms is included at the end of the book.

Raine was born in the High Pastures, bleak and unforgiving highlands in the far north of Harran, a kingdom that has long been ruled by their overlords of Brannlant. Even as a child, she could see the spirits of the dead, a curse that carries a death sentence if it were ever to be discovered. At seventeen, having abandoned home years before, Raine found herself besieged at Dalnesse Monastery.

Raine helped a wounded girl named Hazia into the compound, but Hazia's mind had been taken by something dark and terrible. It was only the intervention of two Draoihn, Ulovar and his nephew Ovitus—magic users, spell casters, warriors who had been pursuing her—that prevented the rise of Ciuthach, an ancient demon. During the battle Raine discovered a trance awakening in her own mind, and together with Lord Draoihn Ulovar Lac-Naithe, banished Ciuthach.

Ulovar and Ovitus took Raine south to the city of Harranir and the fortress-monastery of Redwinter, heart of the Draoihn's power. Ulovar used his power to draw a scar across Raine's mind, to allow her to cope with the things she had endured: she felt no grief, no empathy thereafter, until a cult of those who also possessed the grave-sight attempted to frame Ulovar for unleashing Ciuthach from the Draoihn's prison vault, the Blackwell. In a blazing battle with summoned demons, Raine and another of Ulovar's nephews, Sanvaunt LacNaithe, defeated the demons. Raine went on to wipe the cult out, rescued Ovitus and cleared Ulovar's name. Having proved herself, she was then allowed to train as Draoihn.

The following summer, Raine witnessed her country become embroiled in the beginnings of civil war, finding herself wielded as a pawn by the ruthless Grandmaster Robilar.

Raine soon began to read more and more from a mysterious book that told her the secrets of the dark past of the Sarathi, magic users who could wield the power of the Gate of Death. The dread spells Raine read of seemed all too familiar to her. As she found herself inexorably drawn towards these dark abilities, Ovitus returned to Redwinter from a diplomatic mission with a new bride—Princess Mathilde—and a faithful dog, Waldy. He also revealed he had advanced his own magical powers by a staggering degree.

All was not well with Ulovar, who was slowly dying, and had even diminished so far as to start losing his powers. Despite Raine's determination to save him, she failed, even as she sabotaged her relationship with her best friend Esher, and her courting by Sanvaunt. Finding herself alone, Raine allowed herself to accept her fate as one who wields the Sixth Gate, death.

Ovitus LacNaithe was revealed to be a traitor, and the architect of a coup against Redwinter, aided by a powerful Faded Lord, Sul. When faced with arrest, Ovitus callously murdered Liara LacShale, a close friend of Raine's, while Sanvaunt's true nature as a wielder of the fires of the Fifth Gate came to the fore as he fought Sul to a bloody standstill.

Having come to the terrible understanding that Ovitus's growing powers were a result of his draining Ulovar of his own Gates, Ulovar had Grandmaster Robilar kill him outside Redwinter. Attempting to head off the coup, Raine used her master's death to unleash a terrible and forbidden spell, Soul Reaper, killing hundreds of Draoihn, but was run through the chest by Sul.

Robilar fought Sul, and transported him into the Blackwell where he would be frozen for all time, and mortally wounded, turned herself to stone. These calamitous events could not have come at a worse time, as the king of Harranir lay dying. A new heir had to be chosen to take the burden of the Crown—a huge dome beneath the city, which contained vast power that stabilised the world.

Raine was accused of being a Sarathi, a wielder of terrible death magic, and Ovitus had her tied to a pyre, her only hope that someone would stand to fight a trial by combat on her behalf. The challenge was answered by Esher, who stalled the trial long enough that Sanvaunt could heal Raine and stave off her death. The trio flung themselves onto a moon horse, a gentle magical creature, which transported them to another realm, a place of myth known as the Fault, even as the king of Harranir passed on and the power of the Crown was lost.

Unless the Crown is claimed, only calamity awaits the world.

Through all of this, Raine has been watched, guided, punished and humiliated by the Queen of Feathers. Just who and what she is remains unknown.

The stories of this age begin and end with monsters, and mine is no exception.

His skin was grey, mottled as if he'd rotted from within. Mail had rusted away entirely in some places, exposed beneath the patterned breacan of a clan that had died centuries ago. Perhaps he'd been a husband once, a father. Maybe he'd been a farmer and worked the land, tilling dark earth, scything wheat. He was none of those things anymore. Whoever the corpse-man had been all those years past, he had lingered in this place of blood-red sky and broken nature, caught between life and death, observing the tedium of centuries, purposeless and lost. Half-living, half-dead, he became all dead as I put my boot against his wheezing chest and wrenched my glaive clear. It gave a slight hiss as the old iron escaped bloated flesh, a wheeze of lost essence. The creature's stare remained locked onto me, wraith-like eyes lit from within. Its shade began to flutter free. One fewer deathless monstrosity haunted the Fault now, but we were not done. It was far from over.

Around me, the battle continued.

Metal on metal. The hideous, life-hating cries of the half-dead. The sound of feet against the stones as more of them forced their way up from their dark dreams beneath the mud. Around the courtyard, the half-dead warriors of another time engaged in battle, and we smote them down again for it.

'Up top!' Esher shouted. On the courtyard battlements more of them scuttled, one dragging a leg that ended in a stump. The half-dead emerged from cracks in the black stone walls and forced their way into the blood-sky's light from trapdoors that had long since rusted shut. They emerged loping from cavernous archways in the outbuildings. They forced their way from compacted earth, unnatural, twisted things who had lost all desires but those that seeped into them from the rancid earth. Kill. Devour. War.

They made war on me now. A creature that might once have been a

mother, a scribe, a sailor, charged across the courtyard with a great, rusted
axe held high. There was only hatred in the inner lights that glowed within
her half-rotten face. I cut the axe from its path, twisted the glaive's haft in
my grip and hacked the blade through her neck. She teetered, head half-
severed, and a second strike put her down.

This was life for us—for me, Esher and Sanvaunt—in the Fault. Just
another day cutting a path through the detritus of long-ago defeats.

One of the half-dead that would have been indistinguishable from a clan
warrior skipped forward one step, two, and hurled its spear. It was a clumsy
throw, his arm stiff. Esher brought down one of her curved swords, striking the
spear from the air before it reached me. The half-dead hissed, unused throat
trying to flex and curse. They'd slept here a long time. We'd woken them. Or
something that didn't want to be disturbed had, anyway.

'Nice catch,' I said. Another of the half-dead warriors ambled towards
me, stooped as if its back had set into a rigid arch during centuries of sleep,
but the rusted, curved swords it held before it were serrated with jagged
teeth. I readied my glaive, a five-foot pole with a thick, reaping blade at
the killing end, over my head and dared it to come on. The decayed, joyless monster was manic with hate, and it swept its weapons towards me in
clumsy, half-blind arcs. Bent over and slashing like mad, it was easy prey. I
slid back from its erratic assault and made a great parting cut downwards.
It died for the last time. After seven hundred years of banishment from the
world, perhaps it would be a relief. Its ghost erupted, greenish white, thin
and insubstantial, as if time had watered it down.

'They keep on coming,' Sanvaunt grunted. He'd dealt with five of them.
Esher cut the arm from another, kicked it back against the wall and ended
its hissing decisively. She flourished her twin blades, crouched and ready
for the next.

'Too damn many,' she said. 'We need to move.'

Overhead, the sky rumbled, the thunder turning into a shuddering,
high-pitched shriek of rage. The land hated us here, but it was the sky that
voiced its ire.

'Then let's move,' I said. 'Into Gaskeiden. This has to be it.' When in
doubt, head towards the yawning, gargoyle-adorned archway leading into
the darkness. The keep reared up above us, a lightless block of history
against the blood-bruise red of the sky.

Something thumped against the back of my cuirass and fell away. Another spear. It was definitely time to go. There had to be twenty or more of them now, and by the distant shrieks and trills, more on the way. You'd think that these warriors, cut off from the true world for more than seven hundred years, might have wanted more than to cut us apart, but empathy seemed to be a finite resource. Perhaps we're only born with so much of it, and age and defeat gradually siphon it away until there's nothing left but malice.

Sanvaunt and Esher led. They cut a path through the half-decayed, age-bent creatures between us and the keep's main entrance as I warded the rear. I took another one down as we retreated forward into the keep. How many was that now? I'd stopped counting months ago.

'Doors,' Sanvaunt barked. As I backed up, he and Esher took hold of the half-arch doors and put shoulders to them, driving forward against centuries of accrued dirt. The half-dead's approach faltered as they formed a semicircle around the doorway. I levelled my glaive towards them, but their advance had ended. Jaws hung open, poisonous breath steaming beneath the crimson sky, glowing eyes watching. Lurking. I stepped through and the doors drew closed with a dull *boom*. Those twisted enemies, the outer walls and the cracked sky beyond were shut away, leaving us panting and alone in the quiet of a time-lost hall. Esher heaved at a beam on an axle and it slammed down into brackets. Locking them out. Locking us in.

We listened.

'They're gathering,' I said.

'But they stopped,' Sanvaunt said. 'For now.'

'Makes you wonder what's in here that they're reluctant to follow,' Esher said. 'They didn't come from in here. Just about the only place they didn't.'

'It shouldn't surprise us anymore,' Sanvaunt said. He ran a rag along the edge of his longsword, wiping away thick, congealed black slime. 'There's always something worse around the corner.'

'Always something worse,' I agreed. 'But we made it.'

'Getting out might not be so much fun,' Esher said. 'We got through by taking them by surprise.'

'One thing at a time, I guess,' I said. 'But let's move fast. They're hungry. The hate keeps on building. They'll find enough of it eventually.'

The snarls, half-word curses and breathy hissing of the half-dead lay, for the moment, beyond a solid door. I looked around the hall we'd made it into. Small glass globes lined the walls, filled with chips of the blue mineral cadanum, which somehow knew we were there and gave off its waxy blue-white light. We figured this place had been a border fortress once, somewhere far from Harranir judging by the unfamiliar architecture. The columns were square and decorated with zigzagging geometric shapes. Like everything in the Fault, time had eaten away at anything that had once spoken of grandeur. A dead hall, a corpse castle lying in the midst of an endless, red-skied swamp.

'Anybody get hurt?' Sanvaunt asked. His hair, grown long over six months of fear and endless threat, was tied back from his face. He'd grown leaner, cheekbones like cut-marble bricks. It was his eyes that worried me the most. He'd hardened on the outside, but that wasn't the only place the Fault was affecting him. Esher shook her head.

'I think I took a spear in the back,' I said. 'Check me?'

Esher ran practiced fingers over my armour.

'Didn't penetrate, thank the Light Above. You're good.'

'The Light Above didn't bring us here,' I said. 'And I don't think she sees into this cursed place either.'

'Might as well thank her anyway,' Esher said. 'You never know who's watching.'

'Where now?' Sanvaunt asked.

'Where do we always go?' I said. 'Forward.'

'Technically sometimes we go back even when we're going forward,' Esher said. There were few smiles to be had in the Fault, and that was one of the least funny of its aspects, but eventually you have to smile about things that will otherwise drive you mad. 'And sometimes we seem to go sideways. The only thing we never do is get any nearer to the City of Spires.'

'True enough,' I said. I rested my glaive against my shoulder. 'But onward anyway.'

The city was ever out of our reach. It had to be the key, had to hold some kind of answer to the nightmare world we'd found ourselves trapped in. Little made sense in our cursed prison. There was nothing you'd want to eat in the Fault, no clean water, but we didn't need to eat, or drink here. There was no hunger, no thirst. We sweated, but didn't need to replenish water. We exhausted ourselves, but time recharged us, as if the land wished us to return to our former state. It had not taken long to realise that we didn't need food or water to exist here, that our bodies simply kept on going regardless. For a time we'd wondered if we'd died, if this was the Afterworld, but things could still die here. What passed for weather followed no routines, no regular patterns that we could tell. The land was a ruin. Echoes of bygone days littered the endless marsh, but the city stood tall. If there was a way out, that's where we'd find it. That's where we'd find the prison that bound the Queen of Feathers.

Through everything that had happened to me, from the very first, she'd been there, haunting, watching, saying the maddening things that passed for her advice. Sometimes she'd been helpful, at others I'd thought she was leading me by her own unknown agenda. The little information we'd dragged from the creatures of this place told us that she was there, in that unreachable city. Maybe she was as much a prisoner as we were, but if anyone might know a way we could attempt to break free and return to our own world, it had to be her.

We'd thought of Gaskeiden as a border fortress, because it was squat and square and that seemed in line with military design, but that had only been an assumption. As we headed deeper into its vaults, it became apparent that Gaskeiden had been a temple. The trio of Cainags who'd sent us this way had been muddled, time having eaten away their memories as it had their hunger, and their wails were tired things, dried up through centuries of neglect. That was the story of the Fault, told in broken stone, fallen idols, decayed castles and ruined things that crawled through the murk.

Six months of wandering, of searching, of trying to find a way to the City of Spires that always lay on the horizon but never in the same place twice, had taught us a great deal about the things that had been banished here. Some of them were familiar, like the half-dead, but we'd long ago agreed that if some of these monstrosities had come from our world, history must have forgotten them. The Cainags had appeared like three sisters, though they faded to nothing below the knee, but through our brief conversation I'd figured they'd been just one person once—one of the Faded, or a demon of the Night Below, or some combination of the two—but endless, unmoving time, the toxic magic that infused this whole place, or maybe just their own despair at their endless, joyless existence, had caused parts of them to grow weak and thin, and there had been three of them, whispering and breathlessly trying to summon their lethal scream as though they were one. They'd not been keen to give us the information we needed, but we'd asked them hard, and eventually the three mouths had given us the route to Gaskeiden, and told us who lay beneath it. There was something down here, something old and powerful, and it was the powerful ones that still remembered, and could still give us answers.

The spirits and half-dead we'd interrogated called her the Dryad, but the Cainags had known her true name. She'd been called Hazel, once, or the universe had marked her so. An unassuming name for what I assumed was likely to be something fairly grotesque.

This was our life, now. We figured it had been six months, though there was no way to tell. Esher, Sanvaunt and I had ridden a moon horse right through the veil between our world and this place—the Fault. Numerous histories agreed that when the once-mighty Riven Queen was defeated by the great hero Maldouen at the battle of Solemn Hill, her enemy had activated the five great Crowns across the world and sent all the evil she'd summoned here, into the Fault. Sometimes history gets things right, but there were things here our world had never known. Or at least for our ancestors' sake, I hoped that was so. We trudged through swampland, day after day, seeking answers. Seeking a way home.

The bloody moon horse had ditched us here and vanished. They said never to ride one, beautiful as they were. That had proved true as well.

We made our way through dead halls, the hollow sounds cast by our clanking footfalls bringing more life to this place than it had seen in generations. The Faded avoided these places. The half-dead had been people once, but they'd been dead before they were banished here. We were giving them second deaths. The Faded were different. For all the passage of centuries, they'd retained their wits and their power, and we avoided them when we could.

At times we found evidence that one of the more powerful, one like the Remnant Sul, had visited. Footprints last a long time when there's nothing else to disturb them. But we were yet to see one of their lords. Where the half-dead were pitiful things, half-sentient, maddened by their long confinement, we all knew that the Faded Lords were things to be feared. But there were none here now. What lay here was very possibly worse. None of us could move stealthily through those halls. The armour we wore had been scavenged from another of these decayed sites, months back now, as we tracked time. It had a bronze-coloured cast to it, engraved and spell woven, harder than any bronze had a right to be, but it still clicked and clacked as we made our way through halls of dead memory.

'Ward room,' Sanvaunt said as the light globes lit a large chamber ahead. 'Has to be.' Esher nodded. I nodded too.

The walls were lined with carved figures, reliefs cut into the black stone. They showed people, some human, others less so, all dressed in a way that told us that they were not from our time. The carvings had been old even before the Faded were banished here by the hero Maldouen, eight centuries past. They'd been our enemies since time began, and this bitter place was their defeat, a plane of containment that lay between the world of the living and the demon realm of the Night Below. In the centre of the room, a vast table was dust-coated, but old colours showed through, maroon and white ivory inlaid against the stone. This had been a grand place once. The creatures that crawled through its bastions and beneath its buttresses were shadowed, withered remnants of the once-proud creatures who'd walked its halls. Seven hundred years and more of starvation and pain will do that even to those once thought fair.

Back down the corridor, something threw itself bodily against the door. A series of hisses and grunts sounded, muffled, beyond.

'Their fear didn't last long,' Sanvaunt said. 'Go on, Raine. It's you who needs to find the Dryad. It's your question needs asking here.'

'I don't want to leave you,' I said.

'Sanvaunt and I can hold the doorway,' Esher said. 'Besides. We're the better fighters, and you're the better ghost caller. Only thing that makes sense.'

There was no ego to what Esher said. They were both better than I was. You get over things like that fast when your lives depend on it daily. Mostly get over it. I didn't like that it gave Esher and Sanvaunt something to share, something that I didn't have with them. They'd been in each other's lives far longer than I had, but before—back when such things mattered—I'd been bonded to them separately. Esher had been my best friend, the kind of friend I'd never hoped to have. Sanvaunt and I had never been friends, he'd been ranked above me, but there had always been a hot ember waiting to catch. Maybe I'd felt that with Esher too, and just hadn't seen what was right in front of me. Now there was something new growing between them, a thing I'd cast away, denied, stamped on. It shouldn't have mattered, here in this nowhere land, but too often the ember rose to burn me.

'All right,' I said. But I looked to Sanvaunt. 'Try to save your strength. Don't go fire-beast if you don't have to. We might need that strength soon.' Sanvaunt gave me a curt nod.

'Go.'

I headed on past the decadent table, where forgotten silver goblets sat tarnished with age and draped with cobwebs, deeper into the temple. The statues watched my passage with unseeing eyes. This was not a place like any other. Nowhere in the Fault was. Each step I took seemed to smudge the floor, as if I were something altogether alien, not of this plane. Which I wasn't, I supposed.

I could hear the half-dead scratching and banging at the door as I reached the head of a stair. I glanced back over my shoulder at my friends, my beautiful, hardened, warrior friends. Esher gave me a smile and mouthed *Go* at me, and all I could do was nod and descend into the dark. I had seldom been alone since we'd found ourselves here, six months of battle, fear, and growing despair turning us harder and leaner. Taking away our fear of the strange and unusual, reforging us, scarring us, binding us together.

When we awoke here beneath the Fault's cracked red sky we'd thought we'd been through the worst. I'd killed hundreds at the foot of Redwinter's slopes. I'd been run through the chest with a sword. We'd fought Sul, the Faded Lord, we'd betrayed the Draoihn. We hadn't known that we'd only been at the beginning.

Egg-sized cadanum lights lit my path as I descended rough steps. The ceiling dripped. Everything was marsh here and little of the world seemed dry. But as I descended, quick steps carrying me further below, I smelled a different kind of wetness. It was cleaner somehow. Down and down, and I had no idea how many steps I'd descended. But she would be down here. The Cainags could not have lied to us. The creatures of the Fault were twisted and ruined, but they had rules. Laws that had to be obeyed. Some of them had come to fear us.

As I reached the base of the stair, an underground lake stretched before me, an impossible, artificial cavern whose ceiling reached up into darkness. My armour-capped footfalls cried out across the space in diminishing, rattling echoes. I couldn't see the far side, but then, the cadanum light wasn't offering me much. Just enough to make out an island across the water, and on that island, an ancient tree. The island was man-made too—or at least *something* had made it, with cut-stone blocks and a little jetty reaching out towards me, eighty, ninety feet out across the still black water.

Horizon to horizon, the Fault was a stinking, pernicious swamp. Endless, roiling hummocks of earth jutted from murky water, water that reflected the red light of the sky above. Even the light felt like betrayal, cast erratically by three moons, one red, one gold, one blue. Nothing felt real. In the right combination, splintered cracks could be seen marring the blood-bruise sky like a shattered pane of glass, or the broken surface of a frozen puddle. Sometimes the sky grew loud. Sometimes it was practically screaming. But no matter the pain in the voice of the damaged heavens, the land was still. The water held its silence. It was a dead place, endlessly dead, unless the things that lurked within the water, the things unburied, the things that had hungered for life and sound and flesh for seven centuries and beyond, emerged to enact their violence. The lake was like that too. Not a ripple marred its surface. The tree stood alone in the darkness as though it had been waiting for me for decades.

'Guess I'm in the right place,' I muttered. I could have tried shouting across the expanse of dark water, but I didn't think any ancient being was likely to holler back and forth across its own moat. I stepped out towards the surface.

Since the day that Sul had run a sword through my chest, things had changed considerably. Back then I'd drawn in a hundred dying souls and used them to fuel my failing body, to keep it moving, forcing myself to live when even I didn't want me to. But things were different now—I was different. Six months—despite the lack of day and night, Esher and I could measure time through our cycles—had changed us all. What I'd had, what I'd needed, was practice. I could never have practiced in our world. Too many doubts, too much fear of what I was doing and what I was. Too aware of the judgements of my own kind, and the fate that awaited one such as I who saw the dead, and worse, commanded them. But it was different here. Here in the Fault, I was free.

I called forth souls that I'd taken, drew them up from the cage inside. I needed fewer of the half-dead's souls than I had when I'd needed to hold my failing body together. They were denser, more potent, but I'd grown more skilled at pressing them to my will. The souls hated me with an intensity that should never have been, and that made it easier. I drew on one, a creature that had risen from the ruddy water to attempt murder with a scythe. I'd cut it down and sucked its life into me, and now, I put it back out into the world as something I could step on. Not a dignified way to be used in death, but then, death is the final indignity we all have to face. The sooner one accepts that, the less one cares.

I made stepping stones of a creature's life, and walked out across the surface of the lake. I could have kept that one as I reached the artificial island, but I felt it had served its purpose, and let it go. There were far more souls to take above anyway. My cage was already close to its capacity.

There wasn't much on the island. The tree rose stark and jagged, thirty feet tall, leafless, bark long turned grey, just as dead as everything else. A handful of offering bowls lay around its trunk, their contents long withered away. And yet, despite its deadness, the tree held fruit, shrivelled, leathery things I had no name for but definitely didn't want anywhere near my mouth.

Time was not waiting on us. Esher and Sanvaunt were dealing with the Light Above knew what up in the temple. I wasn't here to gawk.

'Dryad,' I said. 'Whoever you were. Come on out of that tree. I doubt it's more interesting in there than it is out here.'

I'd found it paid to be irreverent with the named creatures of the Fault. They didn't like it, and that made them curious at least.

The tree trunk shivered and creaked, and then midway up its trunk, something began to unfurl. A torso, its waist blending seamlessly into the tree's trunk, flexed up and towards me, horizontal with dangling arms and a face that seemed to have the semblance of a woman's with ears like a fox and spiky pine needle hair. Perhaps 'woman' was a strong term for her. She was eyeless, knife-blade gouges cutting across brow and cheekbones where the Dryad had been blinded, her hard flesh solid grey wood, but flexible enough to give her a little motion. Her fingers trailed away into thin, whippy tendrils, slithering as they unwound from the tree trunk.

I have not had a visitor in a long time, the Dryad mouthed, but the words flowed straight into my head, through the six-circles within six-circles that

I moved in at all times. I seldom released my grip on the trance of death in the Fault. The tunnel that had once filled my mind seemed little more than a backstage door. Practice can make anything seem normal.

'I am Raine Wildrose, Sarathi of the Sixth Gate, and I don't belong here,' I said. 'I've come for what you know.'

I cannot see you, the Dryad hissed.

'Do you have a name?' I asked.

No true name should be given so freely, she murmured back. *What is yours, I wonder?*

Spirits and fey beings were always going on about true names. I'd been asked for mine before, and I hadn't known it then, and I didn't know it now, if I even had one. Raine was as good a name as I needed.

'You don't need my name,' I said. 'But I know yours, Hazel.'

She hissed, a foul stench emanating into the air in a cloud of spores. I had her now. She couldn't resist me.

'I don't have a lot of time,' I said. 'There's a lot of killing going on upstairs and I need to get back up to it. But I need some information, and I'm told you're the one to provide it.'

Treacherous Cainag daughters, the Dryad hissed, and for a moment I felt her anger. Her fingers spread, the drooping, whip-like tendrils brushing the smooth dirt around her roots. But there was something behind that anger as well. Anger and fear are two sides of the same coin; twist one in the light and you'll see the other clear as day.

'They're unharmed,' I said. 'Mostly. They all live, as much as anything here is living.'

You live, the Dryad said. *Live and dead as one. I sense the tunnel. I sense what you carry within you.*

'Good, excellent, well I'm glad we understand each other,' I said. There had been a time when a thing like this would have terrified me. Today it was just another twisted creature of the Fault. She had not always been like this, I knew that. But she hadn't been anything else for a long, long time. 'I'm looking for someone,' I said. 'She's imprisoned, just as you are. She's been here even longer than you have. I need to find her.'

The Fault is a twisted place. Directions were seldom what they seemed, and no amount of walking could bring us to the City of Spires that always lay on the horizon. By the time we got closer, the light would change and it would be gone, sitting distant in some other location. But always in sight, always reminding us that it was there. Unreachable, but there.

Time means little here, the Dryad said. *Infinite time. We have always been here. But why should I help you, child of the world above? What do you bring me in offering?*

Hunger. Need. Thirst. There it was. Behind the scabrous bark, behind the timeless existence, there was always a desire to consume. It is what we exist for. Nobody, not woman, not man, not the things that dwell in the Night Below or the Fault, can pass through the world without desiring to take from it.

From above us, there was a detonation of some kind. The mildest of tremors rippled the surface of the water. That would be Sanvaunt. He was having to draw on that life-fire after all. There were even more of the half-dead than we'd thought if he was resorting to that already. My friends needed me. Time to cut to the chase.

'I'll trade,' I said. 'I'll give you a soul in exchange for telling me how I can free the Queen of Feathers.'

It was the bargain of a madwoman. I'd been a sweet child once upon a time. I'd wondered how people could fear me so much just for seeing the dead, how they could believe that such a simple gift—simple to me, anyway—could be dreaded as something worthy of stoning, hanging, burning. But I'd had my third death, and the depth to which I could delve into the tunnel had multiplied tenfold. Sul had killed me, and I'd refused it. I understood the fear now. It wasn't just some misunderstanding. I'd made life and death a cheap commodity, one that I dealt in. One that I made into stepping stones to get to what I wanted. Souls were the only currency of value to these nightmare creatures.

I had become the dealer in death people always feared me to be.

Ten souls, the Dryad demanded. Her torso flexed left and right, worming as if she sought to pull herself from the trunk, to close the distance. But she was well and truly bound. *Ten!*

'I'll give you five,' I said. 'That's the final offer. You tell me which edifice the Queen of Feathers is bound to, and that's two. Tell me how I can get there through the swamp, and that's three more. You won't get a better offer.'

Another tremor ran through the earth. To reach us so far down here, it had to be big. Something massive was happening up there. Sanvaunt didn't unleash like this for the half-dead. I ground my fingers together, trying to read something from the Dryad's face, but it was an eyeless, wooden mask.

The Queen of Feathers is gone, but remains. She is born and dies in the Fault's heart, and you will rise until you see, but break before you understand, the Dryad said. *The path is clear, but only one can show you the way to her. The child provides the means. Seek him at Avangrad.*

'A child?' I said. 'Here?'

I have answered, the Dryad said. She reached towards me, training fronds. *My reward!*

One of the difficulties with rampaging through a hellscape like the Fault is that even when you get the information you want, it seldom makes sense to you. It's not like we had a map, and even if we did, the Fault didn't respect the concept. But a deal was a deal. I reached out and took one of the Dryad's extended fingers. It was cold to the touch, brittle. I reached for the soul-cage in my chest and opened its gate a little, choosing the first soul to brush against my awareness. I remembered it dying. Esher had killed it, a squat, fat little creature with too many eyes and backwards arms. An inefficient form for something that had rabidly tried to hurl its aggression against us. After Esher split its head open and I ate its ghost, I'd felt there'd been more to it than mindless aggression. It wanted to feel something, anything. It had lain unmoving in the mire for forty years, and had been mad long before that period of torpor began. Just to feel something, anything, was what it had wanted. And it had, in a way. It was a pitiful thing, and I wasn't sad to give it up. There is no room for pity in the Fault. I'd made that choice a long time ago.

I passed the tormented soul out of the cage, which I envisaged as somewhere in my chest but obviously wasn't; down along my arm and into the Dryad's tendrils I saw the wispy green-white spirit energy flowing into her. I gave her another; I didn't remember where I'd got it from. The Dryad shivered as something long denied her rippled through her branches.

'This place, Avangrad. How can I get through the Fault to find it?'

The Fault did not believe in directions. I had come to think of it as a place alive, with an intelligence behind its changes, twists and turns. Sometimes they were too cruel not to be. We'd walked two days to reach one of the edifices, only the next morning to find it back the direction we'd come from. Maybe it was just random chance. We see meaning in coincidences because we believe ourselves to be the pinpoint around which the six circles of existence rotate. Self, other, energy, mind, life, death. That makes us creation, I suppose, the theoretical seventh sphere. Or at least it seems that way. But the Fault cared nothing for the normal rules, and we'd learned that movement, change, took different forms here.

A great palace, apart from the corruption that haunts this place. It lies on higher ground, beyond the fog. Appease the iron child, and the city will come to you. She lurched forward, stronger now with her meal of soul energy. Tiny little buds had formed across her brow, around her fingers. *Give me more now!*

I was having none of that, and I'd been ready. I twisted my glaive around and sawed across her fronds.

'Back!' I barked. 'A deal's a deal, but get control of yourself or I'll take you as well.'

That calmed her down. She retreated from me, hissing softly, leaving only one six-foot whip of finger out for me to touch. She was greedy, but in the Fault, a deal was a deal. I took the finger and fed her three more lives. Monstrous, empty, violent, tortured lives. Usually when I used up a soul it fled on into the tunnel. I didn't know what she did with them, but they didn't seem to be going anywhere.

'It's not the first time I heard that name,' I said. 'The iron child. What is it?'

But I knew the answer already. I'd fought him before, in another life, as another woman. He'd destroyed me.

More questions, more souls, the Dryad said. She was growing stronger as she absorbed them. Too strong to be questioned, maybe. The ash-grey bark was growing warmer, turning red like apple skin. She was softening, but sharpening at the same time. Souls were not a currency to be traded lightly. I teetered on the edge of making further deals and wondering just what she'd become if I fed her another ten, curiosity, some fear, but then a great blast of heat and smoke erupted from the tunnel I'd entered in through.

'Next time,' I said, and burned through another soul to make a path back across the lake. The Dryad wailed, reached for me, but I was too fleet. Now I had a name, and a direction, as strange as that direction sounded.

'Don't worry, your annoying highness,' I said as I took the stairs three at a time. 'I'm coming for you.'

Everything that could burn seemed to be on fire, but that was nothing new.

The half-dead had breached the temple's doors somehow and the bodies were piled atop each other in the corridor, but it was the millipede that had brought Sanvaunt to call on his trance. With a body as wide as a bull's, it lay in several segments in the room with the table, leaking scorched yellow ichor across the floor. Sanvaunt had calmed down now that it was dead, just the odd drip of fire from his eyes signalling the power he'd drawn on. He was breathless, and the blade of his sword was a crooked mess, ruined by the heat of his life-fire.

'Where in Skuttis did that thing come from?'

'Not sure,' Esher said. 'It just came in through the window. Did you get what we need?'

'I got it,' I said. 'Let's get out of here.'

The millipede had no ghost. It wasn't human, and never had been. Animals had spirits, but a spirit and a ghost are different things altogether. I'd wondered sometimes whether animals had ghosts of their own and I just couldn't see them. Maybe there were sheep out there somewhere who saw the spirits of dead sheep. They wouldn't have known that other sheep didn't see them, which was a weird thought.

'There are more of them out there,' Sanvaunt said. He leaned against one of the pillars. 'I can do more of this if I need to.' He gestured around at burning carpets and wall hangings, but he looked tired. No wonder. We were all tired. How could we be anything but? Finding ourselves in the Fault had changed us, but I felt it, deep in my bones. We weren't built for this place. It both wanted us, and it knew we were alien. The charred remains of a giant millipede were a stark reminder that this land hated us.

'No more fighting if we can avoid it,' I said.

'The half-dead retreated when the bug came down,' Esher said. 'But they'll find their nerve again. Do you really think they want to eat us that bad?'

'That's what this place is, isn't it?' Sanvaunt said. His voice was raspy. He straightened himself against the wall, took a deep breath. His Fifth Gate made him powerful, but even the Gate of Life had its limits. 'Hunger. Everything here is hungry. Everything lives on without food, without water, just endless existence. They're maddened by it.'

'Maybe they can eat this thing,' I said, nudging a segment of segmented carapace. The millipede looked like it had been tough to cut through. No wonder Sanvaunt's sword was a wreck.

'They don't want to eat the things that are trapped here with them,' Sanvaunt said. 'They want us because we're something else.' He closed his eyes for a moment as the last burning tears dripped down his cheeks. Light Above, what a jawline. Maybe it wasn't exactly healthy that watching my friends fight woke me up in all the wrong ways, but there was something raw and primal about it. All that was in the past now. We were warriors, we were trapped here together, and there was no time for anything else. But the feelings hadn't gone anywhere. Not mine at least.

Sometimes when I looked at Sanvaunt and Esher together, if she laughed at his joke or she congratulated him on a kill, I wondered if they remembered me at all.

'Even if we're just as trapped as they are,' Esher said, 'maybe there's a back way out. Something they're not expecting.'

'No,' I said. 'There was only one way in. How many do you think are out there?'

Esher wiped a grim fist across her mouth. The fighting had taken it out of her even more than Sanvaunt. She had her First Gate, and she was lethal with a sword, but she didn't have Sanvaunt's Fifth Gate, or my Sixth. It was hardest on her. In all the time we'd fought and tricked and lied and bargained our way across the Fault, she hadn't complained once. I loved her all the more for that, even if I just had to keep my dumb mouth shut.

'A lot,' she said. 'Really, a lot.'

I loved them both so much. Not just some puppy-love attraction, not just that glamour that comes from staring into the eyes of someone who makes your knees weak. It was the love that comes from fighting side by side with someone, depending on them, knowing they're at your back, that you'd give anything for one another. I'd seen the same love between Sanvaunt and Esher too, strange to see from the outside. It was like being born from the same forge. It wasn't romance, and it wasn't sibling comfort. It was something that few people will ever understand, and I was glad they didn't have to.

'Then we aren't going out that way,' I said.

'You don't have a Banshee's Wail in there to clear a path?' Esher asked. She didn't sound hopeful.

'I have the souls, but I'd rather not waste them,' I said. The creatures of the Fault had proved somewhat resistant to my death-powered magic. Throwing souls directly at them had yielded few positive results. 'Those bone hags actually got stronger when I hit them with it. I'd rather not make things any worse.'

'Incantation,' Sanvaunt said, his head rising and his eyes opening. They were just ordinary eyes again now. I'd grown accustomed to the fire that grew within them when he summoned his Gate; it was returning to normal that caught my breath every time.

'Here? Now?' I asked.

'Travel through fire. Like the grandmaster used to,' he said. 'We don't have to go far. I don't have anything like her skill, or her knowledge. But maybe I can take us outside of this place.'

'Do we have time?'

'We better,' Esher said. 'Sounds like the half-dead are realising the bug didn't get us. Or else the hunger is just getting too much for them.' She flexed her shoulders, the pauldrons of her scavenged armour clanking. Her hair hung in six interwoven braids down her back, its golden lustre dimmed by months without a single wash, but she looked good. She looked right. The one thing we consistently failed to scavenge were helmets. The most important part of any armour, and we'd yet to find any that fit well, and a poorly fitting helmet that slips over your eyes is no protection at all. The armour we wore had mostly come from another edifice, mismatched. Esher had started with a suit of her own, but armour gets battered and dented and piece by piece she'd been forced to replace it.

She moved across to the doorway that looked down the hall towards the piles of bodies she and Sanvaunt had made. The half-dead hovered some distance back in the gloom. They growled and slunk about, fish-like eyes swivelling and peering, but they weren't ready to cross the mound of dead to take a bite at us. Not just yet.

'I'm doing it,' Sanvaunt said. 'It won't be pretty but I'll try it.' He swept the last clutter free from the surface of the large table and took out a dagger. It was a wicked thing, made with cruelty in mind, but beauty as well, its edge serrated, its hilt the bone of a beast long since in the earth. He breathed out. 'Never was my great talent, but I'll try it.' He applied the knife's point to the marble-and-ivory tabletop and began to carve. I'd never had much talent for incantation; the pictograms I crafted more frequently went wrong than right, like the time I'd rotted the insides of a pie and terrified our teacher, Palanost. Sanvaunt moved with more confidence, but this was a new trick for him to try. Moving by fire was a big ask. Incantation rewrote the truth of the natural world around us. One wrote it into paper—metal or stone were even better—then infused oneself into it through Eio, the first trance—or in this attempt, the fifth, Vie. The incanter became one with the world, not separate, but part of the essence and fabric that made up reality. To travel by fire was not a skill I could ever learn, no more than Sanvaunt would ever learn to rip out the souls of the dead.

He really had got the better half of our heart bond deal. When we'd faced the demons my enemies had summoned against me, as my Sixth Gate opened Sanvaunt had chosen to stand his ground to protect me. That love, that selfless act, had awoken the Fifth Gate within him. We were two sides of a coin, the light and the dark, the powers forged from trust, and hope.

I moved to stand beside Esher. She was spattered with the blood of the emaciated, grey-skinned things out there. They watched her back with luminous, protruding eyes. Some of the half-dead hadn't been people at all, they'd been something else.

'Let me take them,' I said. 'Rest some.'

'No,' Esher said fiercely. 'We fight together. Don't put me to the back of the class, Raine. Just because I don't have the Gates you and Sanvaunt have, it doesn't make me any less part of this team.'

Her words spat with fire. It was a conversation we'd had often.

'Without you I wouldn't be here,' I said. 'Alive, I mean. I didn't mean the Fault.'

'Both are true,' Esher said. 'I'm not sore over it. I'd rather we were all here and you alive than back in the real world bowing to Ovitus and laying flowers on your grave.'

'Ovitus,' I said. 'It seems so impossible that everything—all of this—can come from the spite of one sad, self-absorbed man.'

'Find me a trouble in the world and I'll show you a frightened, self-absorbed man behind it,' Esher said.

I hated Ovitus with a hot, dry fury. He'd won. He'd beaten me. Not only that, but he'd taken power, taken Redwinter, even our country was as good as his. I might have escaped him at the last, but it was a meagre kind of victory. When I'd killed before, it had seemed a necessity, but if we ever escaped the Fault, I'd take my time with him.

Behind us Sanvaunt's dagger scraped against the stone as he drew. He was creating the concept in pictures and sigils, runes and symbols, but they were no particular language. I'd learned that much about incanting, at least. The language of the incantation was the caster's understanding of the world. It didn't have to make sense to anyone else. Whatever he was doing, it was complex. It was taking time; it needed more. The stone he carved it into would make it more powerful and was more likely to hold the power needed for the incantation to work, but it was slow going.

'Look! They're leaving,' Esher said, snapping my attention back. The decayed wretches outside skittered away. 'Shit,' we said in unison. Things in the Fault only flee when something bigger comes along.

'Heads up for more millipedes,' I said. I tossed Sanvaunt my glaive and drew my sword. She'd been notched and well-used before I found her, but her core was strong. Better a shorter blade in these close confines, and she hadn't let me down yet. Esher and I fell into fighting stances. I could feel the presence of something out there. The bloody sky visible beyond the portal gave a sudden howl, the cracks spanning it flaring white for a moment. And then a figure stepped into view. Not a bent-backed, rag-wearing, broken thing, but a slender figure, hooded and robed, silhouetted black against the shattered sky.

The howling ones, the scrabbling ones, the ones whose limbs had bent and twisted, the ones who'd grown new limbs where they shouldn't, the ones with foam around their mouths, the ones with wild eyes and desperate stares—they were simple. They were all so simple. And yet in its calm, dignified, neat silence, the figure out there brought fear down like a curtain of ice. Me, with all my power and all my newfound practice, me with the souls of a hundred or more of the Fault's creatures gathered within me, I was the one who was afraid.

'Sanvaunt,' I called back. 'Time to hurry.'

I set my feet, grinding dust and spatter beneath worn boots.

'Little morsels, little sparrows.' The voice came as a slight, soft whisper. 'What lovely little things you are.'

Impossibly, it sounded like Ovitus, the LacNaithe heir, the traitor to Redwinter, and the one who was largely responsible for us being here.

'Sanvaunt?' Esher added.

'Nearly done,' he called back, dagger point scraping and scoring.

'Pretty things don't belong in a temple,' that soft whisper came again in Ovitus's voice. 'Not when they have such naughty thoughts. Such confusion, such . . . feeling. It flows from you like a spring breeze.'

'Do you want to put a sword in it or should I?' I asked, but my usual vim was missing. I could hardly get the words out.

'That voice isn't making me want to kill it any less. If it comes down the corridor we take it together,' Esher said. 'Love you, Raine.'

I just nodded.

'I've been looking for you,' the figure said, black shadow against the dim light of the outside world. A slight ripple of purple played across, as if we looked at a reflection in a mirror. 'Looking here, looking there. Looking just about everywhere.'

'Well, you found us,' I said. 'Want to find out what we have?'

'A little steel,' it said. Giggled. There was a grimy, childlike quality to its rolling whispers. Some of the dark things of the world hold their poison deep, a well filled with their breaking. But this thing—whatever it was—its poison dripped from its words. It didn't move. Not at all. It could have been made of glass. 'I do not fear a little steel, young ones,' it said. Amused. 'Nothing can hurt me. Nothing has ever hurt me. I am everywhere, and I am all at once.'

'Light Above, not this shit again,' I growled. 'It's one of those things that wants to tell you all its allegorical existences. Honestly I've had enough for one day.' Glib words, but sweat rolled down my cheeks. The ones that rage, that snap and tear, those were easy. This thing was different. Had it reached into our minds, plucked out Ovitus's voice to use against us? My breathing was up and down, staccato pants. 'Sanvaunt, how's that incantation coming?'

'Soon!' he called back, hacking at the table with his knife. Scrape, clack, scrape.

The shadowed figure finally moved. It stepped forward into the waxy blue-white light and pulled back its hood. I was ready for a pale, rotten head, eye sockets filled with worms, teeth exposed through rotten cheeks. But it was just a man. He was thirty, perhaps a couple of years younger. Unkempt, curling chestnut hair, a day's growth of stubble. He smiled, a genuine kind of smile, missing one of his incisors, but that was nothing to write home about. Unarmed, unscarred, just an ordinary man.

'I can see I frighten you,' he said, and his voice had changed. It was so different, his accent strange, the words angular, but not harsh. The giggling, sick child voice was gone. 'That's only fair. This is a frightening place.'

It was his normality that was worse. We hadn't seen a living soul—not a person anyway—not in all those months. And that displacement of expectation, that anomaly in the mix, that was worse than any thousand-legged insect. Whatever this man was, he'd frightened away the half-dead.

'You're one of the Faded Lords,' I said.

'No,' he said. 'I'm far, far more than that. This small part of me is awake in this world now. I have your friend to thank.'

'Wasn't me,' Esher said. 'I didn't wake him up.'

'Nor me!' Sanvaunt called as he gouged at the stone.

'I hate these riddles,' I said. 'I am so sick and tired of riddles. Do you have a name at least?'

'The horses brought you here, didn't they?' he asked. He cocked his head at the slightest angle, his open-lipped smile showing the gap in his teeth. 'They were bound to this place, as we all were, but somehow retained the power to slip momentarily into your realm, fleetingly and painfully. That glimpse of freedom has ever caused them to seek to break their bonds. You would be wrong to place your trust in those self-serving beasts.'

'I don't feel they're the least trustworthy things here,' I said. Keep him talking. Buy Sanvaunt time.

'Their whims matter not,' the chillingly ordinary figure said. 'The days of the Fault are numbered. It's all breaking down. It's all going to change. And when it does, we'll all be right back where we started.'

'Are you mad, or just tiresomely cryptic?' I said. It seemed an attribute of everything that dwelled in the Fault that they just couldn't say anything plainly.

'I thought I was being very clear,' the man said. 'I just wanted a look at you. I thought I'd cut off any paths to this place long ago, but it seems I was wrong. I'm impressed you made it here.'

'You cut off the paths?' I said. 'Then you have some control over this place?' A mad stab of hope shot through me that this man might be able to send us on the way to Avangrad. But there was a pretty good chance it was just another creature of the Fault ready to devour us. His eyes seemed normal. Plain old human eyes, nothing to read in them. But that voice from the entryway . . .

'Some. I isolated this vestige of the past as best I could,' he said. 'In another land I was named Iddin. I'm king here, I suppose. King of the Fault. Not that there are many who care.'

'We don't care,' I said.

'That's a shame,' the man who called himself Iddin said sadly. 'It's rare I get to converse with anybody new. But my body will be here shortly, and it doesn't play well with others.'

'Your body?'

The man-like shape giggled.

The earth shook. Tremors weren't uncommon here. They came and went and fed the land up into the hole in the sky, but this—this was different. Closer. The earth heaved beneath our feet, shifting one way, then the other. I fell against Esher and she caught us against the wall. The flagstones of Gaskeiden buckled beneath us.

'What in Skuttis?'

Beyond the doorway, one of the walls surrounding the keep collapsed. A foul stench filled the air as the soggy ground bucked and heaved then burst like an erupting boil. Smoke boiled forth, black fog dense and opaque, but within it crackles of purplish lightning flickered as it spewed from the ground. The earth heaved again as the bulk of a creature of unimaginable size forced away earth that could have covered a village and the walls came crashing down over it.

'I'm hungry,' the shadow that called itself Iddin said, and there was dark, joyous malice in its voice.

'Twenty seconds!' Sanvaunt shouted. Esher and I staggered back along the corridor as even the foundations of the temple heaved beneath us. A block of stone crashed down, shards of sharp stone ringing from our armour.

'Where do you think you can go?' Iddin asked. He mirrored us, step for step, advancing into the temple's corridor, picking his way across bodies as we retreated. 'I'll only find you again.'

I glanced behind the shadow-man, the self-named king of the Fault, and the crackling, oily fog began to fill the corridor. There was something bigger, something within it, and the doorway lost its support as the behemoth cracked through the ground below it, and the arch crashed down atop it.

'Ten seconds!'

'Well, I guess the chase is on then,' I said.

Iddin smiled, and there it was, not the physical but the essence of worms in eye sockets, of teeth showing through rent cheeks, of slopping dead flesh. Whatever gargantuan monstrosity was beneath us unleashed a terrible roar that was at once deep, mountainous, and hollow, but trilled with high, unsuppressed loathing.

'Then run. There is no escaping this place for you.'

Fire bright as the sun erupted around us, and for a moment I was weightless, and then it all came down.

3

It doesn't hurt to travel by fire. It's strange—there's no denying that it's strange—but the fire isn't fire. Not really. There is life everywhere. The life-fire is part of that. It's our life force that travels through the fire, and creation likes consistency, so it just brings the rest of us along with it. At least, that's the best that Sanvaunt was ever able to explain it, and that was good enough for me.

The rush and roar faded, and we were back standing on the smooth stone forehead of a fallen titan.

There were many like it, studding the miserable, choked, motionless waterways. The pieces of fallen stone imperators and wizards provided the only stable ground. The hummocks of earth, coated with dead brown grass, dead brown reeds, dead brown dead things, were treacherous. We'd learned that to our cost when one of them began to sink in what we thought of as the night. But it was never night here. The red sky lost its corpse-skin pallor sometimes, but the intervals were irregular and neither sky, bright nor dim, changed the light. I could see the heavens beginning to turn now: a faint pink blush here and there, mottled like snakeskin. The cracks ran through it, white, like we looked through muscle to see the bone beneath.

'Everyone okay?' I asked.

Everything was quiet here, atop the forty-foot-wide face of a long-dead warlord. We'd camped atop the head of the vast broken statue a week ago. Everything around us was quiet, too. The Dryad's temple was a long way off through a dream, a sacrifice and a series of whispers. We were safe for the moment.

Relief hit me like a stone flung from a trebuchet. Not for myself, but for Esher, for Sanvaunt. We break ourselves, hurt ourselves, take the most reckless risks with who we are, what we are, but the fear for them dwarfed whatever I cared for myself. They were alive. I could let myself breathe again.

'What in the freezing rivers of Skuttis was that?' Esher demanded. 'What in damnation was it? It sounded like Ovitus.'

'The king of the Fault, or something that thinks it is,' I said. 'Whatever it is, it's going to come for us.' Esher's shoulders were shaking and she turned to stare out across the endless marsh. She got like this sometimes. We all did. Sanvaunt would go quiet, wouldn't speak for hours. I'd seen things that were worse than a lot of what the Fault had to offer, terrible though it was, and I could tell myself that I was numb to it. Esher was just the only one who let it show. Her lips had gone pale. I took her shaking hands in mine. Dirt smeared, broken nails, but still it felt like an immense privilege to be able to touch them. There was nothing tingle-inducing about it. To even think of such things wouldn't have been right in this place. It was more like when a startled cat lets you comfort it. She'd always called me Fiahd. It meant 'wildcat.' 'Here,' I said, reaching up and wiping at her cheek with my thumb. 'You've got dead things on you.'

The mundanity of it seemed to do the trick. Esher let out a surprised laugh.

'How do you do that?' she said.

'Do what?'

'Make all the terrible go away. Even when it's just a few moments.'

I gave her a lopsided smile, even though my bones were quaking on the inside.

'I am the terrible thing,' I said. 'I'm always here.'

Sanvaunt was a little way down the head. The smooth grey surface of what had once been an angry bald man's stony face was blackened in a pattern around him. Five sooty rings, and five further rings crossing each other within them. He looked back over to us.

'I did it,' he said. He wanted to punch the air, I could tell, but he had too much reserve for that. The pride was practically spilling out of his eyes. No wonder, really. He'd just pulled off something we'd only ever seen Grandmaster Robilar achieve, and she'd turned to stone now, so he had a right to feel good about it.

'You're amazing,' I said. I meant it. He was just as spattered with the blood of the half-dead as Esher was. His hair had grown longer, and his beard had come in over the six months we'd spent trapped in the Fault. There was nothing youthful about him now. He was a man, and a dangerous one. At times he could exude threat, in the way he controlled the world around him, that ability to just take charge of any situation and deal with it. But in his moments of triumph, in brief flickers, I caught the look of that boy who'd tried to run up a wall to impress me. I couldn't tell him, couldn't let him know that every day I was terrified it would be his last, that he'd meet some challenge not even his life-fire could overcome. I wondered if he knew.

'Did she have the information we need?' he asked. Straight to the point as ever.

'Maybe. I don't think she could lie to me. But what she said was mostly nonsense.'

'What kind of nonsense?' Esher asked brightly, but she was masking fear that everything that we'd just been through had been for nothing. 'The good kind, like "Dance in a river by moonlight," or the bad kind, like "Go three times left then beyond left to the left of the left" type nonsense?'

'A little of both. The Dryad said the queen is gone but remains. Something about her existing or not existing and I think maybe we need higher ground to see her. Monster gibberish, mostly. But she said we needed to find an iron child at a place called Avangrad, through that fog we always avoid, and he can show us how to find her.'

'And the catch?' Sanvaunt asked. His voice was hard and dry.

'I didn't say there was a catch.'

'There's always a catch, here.'

'Something about we have to break before we understand. But it was just prophecy type nonsense. The Dryad can't know the future.'

'The Hexen practiced prophecy,' Sanvaunt said.

'Fat lot of good it did them,' I said. 'They got wiped out. If it was all that useful, it'd be them trapped here instead of us.'

I was defensive, and I felt how obvious that was in the tone of my voice. This plan, this whole quest to find the Queen of Feathers, had been my idea. Sanvaunt had never liked it. Esher had gone along with it just because she didn't know what else to do. They had never seen her, never felt her power. They were putting their trust in me that I knew what I was doing, but the truth was I didn't. It was a guess at best, and a yearning if not.

From the moment I'd arrived in the Fault, the Queen of Feathers had not appeared once to me. I couldn't understand it. For the first two months trapped here we'd searched for the moon horses, as if they might take us home again, but they were nowhere to be found. One night we made it through the direction we called Grey to the tumbled ruins of what had been a fallon once, one of those smooth-sided, pyramid-topped obelisks that studded our country's landscape, and speared the world, like candles on a child's cake. Every fallon I'd ever seen was smooth yellow-grey, not stone or metal or earth or wood but something else entirely. But this one, leaning at an impossible angle, was not smooth, and on it, there was a carving. A depiction that could only be the Queen of Feathers, her head haloed by a floating coronet of raven's plumage and beneath her, three indistinct figures. Those figures could have been us. In fairness, they could have been anybody.

I worked a summoning spell that night, a more powerful incantation than the one I'd first worked in the Blackwell to call her nearly a year before. She had told me then that if I called her she'd find me. She'd also said that if I did then I'd beg for the Mawleth's hunger instead, so it hadn't exactly been an invitation, but I wasn't the powerless girl I'd been back then either. I needed her. Needed her guidance. When I activated the incantation within the six circles, sparks had danced around the edge. She tried to get through. Esher felt it, Sanvaunt felt it, all three of us were wracked with pain that emanated outwards from our bones and through flesh to hang as a discolouration in the air. When we regained consciousness and opened our eyes, the carving on the fallon had gone, and in its place there rested the image of a sarcophagus.

She was trapped there, and reaching out to us.

'We have to find her!' Esher had shouted, springing to her feet.

'Or she's dead, whatever she is. Or it could be a trap,' Sanvaunt had said.

Two against one, Esher and I had won out. And so we searched. It had made things easier for a time. Having a purpose had lifted our spirits for a few weeks. Sanvaunt may not have liked the plan, but he was always good with a purpose. But time had worn on, and we'd worn down, and soon we'd wear out altogether. The Dryad had been a good lead. She was said to know the unknowable.

'There was something that creature Iddin said about shutting off the way to the Dryad,' Esher said suddenly. 'That he'd tried to close the path. And don't you think maybe that means the information was good? Maybe this "iron child" can actually give us the path we want. We have to try.'

Sanvaunt sat and considered it all carefully. He took out a small leather-bound book and noted down his thoughts, gathering them before he'd talk to us. It had become a ritual for him, as though he could make sense of the senseless if only he could bind it down. Its pages were so full now he was writing crossways up through the pages, overlapping old writing in a lattice. We gave him the time.

'Avangrad, then. We might find two allies instead of one,' Sanvaunt said. He smiled, and I saw traces of blood on his teeth. Working the Fifth Gate had gone hard on him. He was exhausted, drained of the very energy he was putting out. Life had a cost in life, just as my own Sixth Gate had cost me three deaths. He needed rest.

'Maybe,' I said. 'But if he's there too it stands to reason he's her jailer.'

'If she's imprisoned at all,' Esher said. 'You don't know that she is.'

'I know it,' I said. And I did. I felt it strongly. Just as I'd felt other things more and more strongly since I'd died that third time.

I knew things I shouldn't. Things that I'd not taken the time to learn, even from the facsimile of a book. Things that had happened long ago. Spells that could do terrible, awful things. It wasn't that I knew how to cast them: I'd seen them done. The dreams that had touched me in the last year didn't seem so much like dreams anymore. When I viewed them, it was through the eyes of the great, terrible women who'd made empires and torn them down. I could taste the ash on the wind as it blew across the deserts of Serranis's youth. I could hear the nightingales in Song Seondeok's palace garden. I could feel the horror Hallenae felt when her Sarathi turned on her. Dread queens and empresses all, I knew the men and women they'd loved, saw their faces like reflections in a rippled pool. I had ridden their horses, tasted their wine, died their deaths. None of it was clear, always more feeling than vision. But it was rising. Always rising.

So many of our allies lay dead. I needed one who could guide me through this. Someone who could show me how to use the power that rose groaning within me for good. To use it to take my revenge.

It had been six months, now, and my thirst for vengeance was as edged as the day Ovitus had betrayed us. Six months of anger since I'd acted in desperation. Ovitus, who would have become my master, had been draining the life and Gates from his uncle, Ulovar, and had allied himself with Sul, one of the Faded Lords. I didn't know if Ovitus realised what he'd done—part of me wanted to believe not, despite everything. He was ambitious and utterly self-serving, but even he wouldn't risk that. Sul had planned for Ovitus to help him enter the Crown, the power-centre beneath the city of Harranir, and with that power Sul would tear open the walls between the Fault and the real world and allow his kin to slip back into reality from their long banishment. Maybe Maldouen had sent them to this place to punish them for their part in the Riven Queen's rise to power, her dreadful conquest of the world. It was too dark a fate to be born from practicality.

And so, my master Ulovar had killed himself to stop Ovitus's rise in power, and in doing so he let me perform the Soul Reaper, a spell that had cut down hundreds of Draoihn and given me their power. Grandmaster Robilar fought Sul to a standstill and imprisoned them both in the Blackwell, forever. Our great heroes were gone, lost to us. There was only me now, and what kind of hero was I? I had torn souls from my fellow Draoihn. I had shown the world my true face and it was the face of evil. And though we had beaten Sul, fleeing from a trial in which I was to be burned at the stake, Esher, Sanvaunt and I had done that which we had been warned against and mounted a moon horse. It had carried us from harm, but it had brought us here, to this desolate place, and left us here. It had brought us to the Fault, where the Faded Lords and their vassals lay maddened and imprisoned. But it had abandoned us. It had left us here, alone, disappearing, its purpose in this betrayal unknown. And now we were trapped.

I blamed myself. Who else could be blamed? I'd failed to stop Sul, failed to stop Ovitus, and in their bid to save me from the dark power I'd nurtured and grown in secret, those I loved had been transported here, to this deathless, dying, dead place.

Through drifting mists that never lifted, across barren miles of lifeless swamp, glimpsed between the fallen statues of creatures inhuman, towering across the cold deadness of the world, there lay a city. It had not been raised by people, and it was not of the earth. It was here, with me, in a place called the Fault, but so distant that its heavenward spires were little more than needles, all save a single great, central tower that thrust up and up through the sky like a black finger. At any moment I fancied it might crook itself, and beckon me towards it. I felt its draw on me, like it had been calling me all my life, and only now, here, was I able to recognise its pull.

I could have spent hours just staring towards that distant edifice. Perhaps

I had, or did. Time didn't seem to move the same way here. Distance was broken, time was broken. This was not home. It wasn't even reality as we understood it.

The sky grew loud. A cracking, breaking sound fell on us from above, as though we heard the destruction of a dried-up forest. It came from the tears in the sky, the broken lines that spanned its entirety as though it were a windowpane webbed with cracks.

'We're throwing everything we have into finding her,' Esher said. 'I know you're right about her. She's an ally, she has to be. Nothing here seems like it wants anything but to tear us apart, but she helped you before.' Her words were for herself more than me.

'She was with me for a long time,' I said. 'But since we entered the Fault, she's gone. I first saw her back at Dalnesse.' Old feeling swarmed upwards like bubbles in the marsh. 'When the people I travelled with died. She appeared to me and . . .' I hesitated. I'd never revealed this to anyone. 'Ulovar was chasing Hazia down. And me. There was an old bridge and when he stepped on it, it was like she just tore it apart and dropped him into the river below. Then she came to me. Often. She's maddening and she doesn't know as much as she thinks she does. It's like parts of her are missing, or bits of memory anyway.'

'I've never heard of one of the Faded meaning us well,' Sanvaunt said. He had begun unbuckling his armour, tossing panels of scratched and marred metal down onto the statue's uneven cheek. We needed to rest now. A fire would have been nice, but none of us had managed to get one going.

'She isn't one of the Faded,' I said. I'd told him many times, but he didn't believe me. 'She's helped me. A few times. But she also gets angry. She's proud, and didn't like being summoned in the Blackwell. And if she can be summoned into the Blackwell and not be paralysed by its wards, then she's not one of the Faded.'

'The only things here are the imprisoned Faded, demons and the dead,' Sanvaunt said. He unstrapped his breastplate on one shoulder and it fell open like a door. 'This might as well be the Night Below. If that's not what it is.'

'The moon horse brought us here,' Esher said. 'I have to believe it meant us well. Even that—that thing that called itself king of the Fault believed that. At least you two have big magic to back you up.'

'You bring plenty to the table,' Sanvaunt said, softening. Esher hung her head.

'In our world I felt special. Being Draoihn made me that. But here I'm just so—unextraordinary.'

'You are extraordinary,' I said. 'You rode into Redwinter and you fought for me. You challenged Ovitus, and you beat him. You're the most extraordinary person I've ever known.' I took her hand whether she thought she wanted it or not, and squeezed it. I took one of Sanvaunt's as well, linking us, making a chain. 'Both of you are. All of us. We're none of us ordinary. Look where we are. We've ridden a moon horse into the Fault.'

'Now it's just a shame we can't ride one out of here,' Sanvaunt said.

'Why do you think it brought us here? Why did it help us when we needed it, and abandon us to this nightmare place?'

'The moon horses respond to need,' Esher said. 'It knew I needed it. They aren't malicious. I have to believe that for whatever strange horse-reason it had, it thinks we need to be here.'

The sky groaned and creaked overhead. The breezeless swamp lay still and dark below the red sky.

'Right,' I said. 'Then there has to be something it wanted us to do. We just have to figure out what.'

But what, indeed?

Under normal circumstances, camping up on the exposed stone of the half-sunken head would have been putting oneself out in the wind, but there was no wind here in the Fault. Months back, in a ruined, half-collapsed building that looked to have once been a fish restaurant, we'd found curtains that had stayed intact, and those made our blankets. I didn't mind sleeping on hard stone. It was reassuring to have something solid beneath me. But I hated the three moons that glowed in the sky above us. They were strange, alien things. I knew, down to my core, that they weren't of my world, and they were a constant skyborne reminder that we did not belong here.

That night I lay cold against the hard stone. Esher was on watch. Sanvaunt tended to fidget, reorganising things and grunting to himself like a man thrice his age. But Esher was always quiet. At times, if I rolled over or shifted around she'd whisper softly to me.

'Try to rest, Fiahd. The light will be back soon enough.'

'I never sleep well here. If at all.'

'You do sleep,' Esher whispered. 'I've heard you snoring.'

'We don't eat or drink here,' I said. 'Why do we need to sleep? How come we sweat, but we don't take in water? What are we using for energy?'

These night thoughts worried at me constantly.

'I don't have answers for you,' Esher said. She twisted one long braid in her hands. 'I have an idea or two.'

I rolled onto my stomach, tangled in what had once been brocade curtains for Flappy's Best Fish, and rested my chin on my hands.

'Share them?'

'You should be getting rest.'

'Just tell me what you think, and I'll go back to sleep,' I bartered, like a girl sleeping over at a friend's cottage. Mama hadn't let me do that often, and those other girls' mothers hadn't wanted to have to see Mama. The invitations hadn't come often, though I craved them, even asked for them. Mama never invited the other girls back. Perhaps that was why they stopped asking.

'I don't think we're really here,' Esher said. 'I don't think this place is real. Not in any meaningful way. The Fault isn't the real world. It's hidden away somewhere. Like those cracks we see in the sky—I think that if we could fly up and through them we'd be real again. But down here we're not real at all.'

'So what are we then? Ghosts?'

'You're the expert where those are concerned,' Esher said, and I thought perhaps I caught the slightest edge of resentment in her voice.

'Trust me, you're better off knowing as little about ghosts as possible.' On instinct I clenched my inner fist around the souls I kept trapped in my chest. Fuel. Currency. Weapons. All of them had been alive at one time or another. Unless Esher was right, and none of us were real. 'We're not dead,' I said. 'That seems obvious.'

'Not dead,' Esher said. 'But maybe we've become like your Queen of Feathers. Maybe we're not quite real. Do you think she needs food and water?'

'Shit,' I said. I sat up in my blankets. 'I hadn't thought of it like that.'

Esher tried to stifle a yawn, and failed. She stretched up and out, luxurious as a cat in a sunbeam. The Fault was warm, and she was only wearing a dirty white vest that rode up over her navel as she arched her back, and for the first time since we'd come to this place I was both mesmerised and burning at the ears. Yes, we were dirty. And yes, this place was strange and foul and there was dried blood beneath even our toenails. But the arch of her back, the smooth, hard muscles of her belly set that tingle going. Just briefly, and then the reality—or unreality—came back upon me. What was I going to do, try to kiss her in the midst of this swamp?

And even if we'd come to need each other, even if she'd fought for me, I was what I was. A dark thing, part corpse myself. A sword-thrust scar still lay in the middle of my chest. I was more killer, more Sarathi, than girl now. A dirty, unclean thing that brought nothing but death.

'It's just a guess,' she said. 'It's like the things we are come from inside us. But we don't need to put anything in, like food, because there's nothing here to put in. I don't know. I'm probably wrong.'

'You're tired,' I said. 'I'm not. I'll watch. You should bed down.'

She tried to protest, but tired people are bad at resisting their beds, even if those beds are on top of fallen statues. My weariness was gone, evaporated. *'Maybe we've become like your Queen of Feathers.'*

Maybe we had. And if we were, if we'd passed into the Fault to become like her in some way—then maybe I could do what she did. Maybe there was a way to look beyond the endless marsh around us, to see into that other world we'd left. Maybe that alone could even present a way home.

4

Our rest did not last long. The land had other ideas.

It began with a howl, delivered to echo downwards from the sky, ripping from the cracks above. Somewhere between the mournful call of a wolf and the raging of the wind, it came with the flickering, fluttering of that bone-white light beyond the tears, which began to pulse. And then the upheaval began.

'It's happening again,' Sanvaunt said as he stirred beneath his curtain-blanket, sitting up and casting around. Esher was already awake, her covering swept around her like a cloak. I stood. It was dangerous to do so, up here on the side of the stone face, when the tremors began, but I was used to danger. I didn't fear falling.

We all looked off towards the City of Spires, distant and faraway on the horizon as it always was, and the vortex that twisted the sky above it.

Something like white light flowed upwards. It was leagues away from our fallen statue's half-sunk face, but it must have covered a vast span of miles. In the village of my childhood, farther north than even the High Pastures, at certain times of year we'd look north and see vivid green lights ripple across the sky. We'd thought them the spirits of slain giants or dragons, riding the sky, beautiful and terrible all at once. But it was different here. The light that rose from the Fault had a raw, bone-white hue, but it had no control of itself. It was drawn upwards towards the hole in the sky above the City of Spires, a stream of gas, or energy, or existence. It carried things with it. Now and again, if we focused hard enough through the First Gate, we might make out a tree, a boulder, and once, something that struggled and shrivelled and burned as the light drew it away.

The ground shook. I braced my feet atop the stone head, determined not to let this land knock me down, adamant that I would not bow to its wishes, whatever they were. I would not sit for the sky, or the burning light, nor Faded nor Ovitus. Not even for a thing that styled itself king. I was done bowing and scraping to anyone or anything. Within me, I smelled the centuries-old approval of queens who had died before I had ever been born. We were none of us made to kneel.

It was a good sentiment but a sudden, particularly vicious tremor nearly had me on my knees. I caught myself on one hand, and I was back up, knees bent, riding the earth's shaking. Minutes passed us by.

'It's a long one,' Esher said. Wiser than me, she'd gathered in loose items around her, my things included. She didn't ask me to help, or to look after my own gear. Perhaps she recognised that for me it was important to stand. There was more than my bloody-mindedness to it, though. I needed to see. The vortex above the city held secrets. I'd glimpsed them, not every time, but sometimes, as they ascended upwards to the howling of the sky. This time was the strongest, the clearest I'd ever seen them in its swirls. Not just the glimpse of a face, a mountain, a banner drooping in the wind. This time I saw images that settled for moments. I saw the ruin of my homeland.

Hundreds were dead. Bodies strewn across a field. They wore clan colours, blue and white for Clan LacClune, green and black for LacNaithe. Spear wounds, sword wounds, arrows jutting from corpses like rushes along a river. Here, a dying horse, one leg still twitching. There, a carrion-picker, pulling rings from fingers and stripping arms from the dead. A battle had been fought. A field had been won, but who the victor had been, I couldn't have said.

The visions in that rising light changed quickly. I had no time to learn what had happened, or why.

I saw a village burning, grey smoke forming leaning pillars as it stretched towards the heavens.

I saw Redwinter, briefly. Its walls had sustained damage. A magical battle had been fought there.

And then I saw Ovitus. He was dressed like a warrior, mailed, plated, and whatever puppy fat he'd been holding on to had drained away out of him. He looked more like Sanvaunt now than he ever had, but there was something absent from him as well, like he'd forgotten an important part of himself, left it carelessly on the lawn, never to remember that he'd had it at all. The hate burned strong within me, hot and coarse like desert sand. Around his brow he wore a circlet of silver. His familiar, the dog Waldy he'd brought back to Redwinter with him, sat a few paces back from him.

Waldy's eyes seemed to meet mine and as his tongue lolled he seemed to be mocking me.

There is no escaping this place for you.

The upheaval juddered the ground and the stone head shifted a little. I caught myself on a hand before I could go down. My concentration broken, I stared back towards that mesmerising white light and the little pieces of the Fault it carried with it up, up, away into the cracks in the sky, but the images would not return clearly, like those little bits in your vision that dart away the moment you try to focus on them.

'Did you see them this time?' I asked when the tremors began to subside, and the light ebbed back towards the endless swamp.

Esher and Sanvaunt weren't looking at the upheaval. They were looking at me.

'Just the same as usual,' Sanvaunt said. He wore a serious expression. Worried.

'What were those words you were saying?' Esher asked.

'Me? I didn't say anything,' I said.

'Raine, you've been speaking in tongues since it started,' she said. 'You don't know that you're doing it?'

'No,' I said. I had no memory of having done so.

'It sounded like a chant of some kind,' she said. 'Or a spell.' I frowned, but looked from her to Sanvaunt. He nodded gravely. I disliked their worry. It made me feel as if somehow I'd done something wrong. I flushed the feeling with anger.

'Ovitus has made himself prince regent, crowned in silver,' I said. 'There's war in Harranir. LacNaithe is fighting LacClune.'

'If what you're seeing is real,' Sanvaunt said, 'we're worried about you, Raine.'

'In this place? We don't have time for worry,' I said. 'We don't have time for any of this. We have to find this iron child.'

'I've been thinking on that,' Sanvaunt said. 'Finding a child out here doesn't sound so likely.'

'That's why it's made of iron, I guess,' I said. 'Maybe it's figurative.'

'Or maybe it's Maldouen we're looking for.'

I felt a chill at the name. I still remembered him from seven hundred and more years ago, aiming that Lance at me. It hadn't been a real lance. It was a great tube twenty feet long mounted on a swivelling platform, and it had launched a beam of fire straight into me, through me, and cast me into the Fault even as his spells banished my Faded allies and demonic servants here with me. I remembered the agony of burning alive.

I blinked, banishing the memory. No, not my memory. It was all bleeding together.

'Yes. It's Maldouen,' I said. The knowledge frightened me sometimes. At others it was like finding an old, comfortable pair of slippers, or a fact memorised from a book as a child. Sometimes it was both. This one was just frightening.

'The Blind Child,' Sanvaunt said. My friend was unaware of those memories that haunted me. I was a freak. I was strange and broken in more ways than there were to count, and being infested with other women's knowledge would only add to the list if I told them. 'Maldouen was a warrior. Why shouldn't the great hero of the Riven War, the wizard who created the Crowns and defeated Hallenae, be here? Every damn other thing out of history seems to be.'

'The Faded and Hallenae's demons were banished here when she fell to Maldouen's Lance,' Esher said. 'Perhaps he got brought along. Or maybe that was always part of the price.'

'Maybe he was Faded,' Sanvaunt said. He shrugged. The Draoihn were big on history and I'd been made to sit through countless dry lectures on the Haddat-Nir kings, and the Delac-Mir kings, and the Age of Bronze and all the rest of it. But for every tale that rises from a war there are two more that sound just as plausible, and often none of them seemed plausible at all.

I knew what Maldouen was, and I knew how he'd come to be here. I hadn't known it before I woke up in the Fault, hadn't known I'd known it until the moment his name had surfaced. But I knew of him—in some ways it felt as though I'd met him, even. He was a caustic-tongued, angry, self-serving little bastard. But he was a genius as well. He held more knowledge than even our greatest libraries. He could have ruled us, if that's what he'd chosen. I didn't think he'd intended to end up here in the Fault.

No comfortable-slipper memories there. Just the fear.

'The Dryad said that we'll find him at Avangrad,' I said. I stared away at the City of Spires. 'Maybe he can help us reach the city. It's connected to the Crowns,' I said. 'That's what the city is. It's the lynchpin. And when one of the Crowns is uncontrolled—well,' I said. 'We've seen what's happening over there. These upheavals, these cracks in the sky—it's the Fault, bleeding through into our world.'

'Then nobody controls the Crown in Harranir,' Sanvaunt said. He looked thoughtful. This kind of mental puzzle was something he enjoyed. 'After the king died, someone should have been escorted down beyond the Great Seal to claim it.'

'But there's nobody left besides me and Merovech LacClune that can enter the Blackwell to take the Keystone,' I said. 'Light Above, that's what's happening back there, isn't it? Ovitus has taken power and Clan LacClune won't accept his candidates for the Crown so it's just . . . uncontained. They're fighting it out.'

'Ovitus is cruel, and self-serving,' Sanvaunt said. For a moment I thought he might want to defend his cousin. I didn't think of them as close, but they'd lived side by side for their whole lives. But the time for pandering to Ovitus's faults as though they were excusable had passed us by. 'Even so,' Sanvaunt went on, 'I can't believe he'd allow the Crown to lie uncontrolled for so long. If the Fault is bleeding through, then that means these things we've encountered don't just exist here anymore. They're going to be appearing in our world as well.'

'Maybe that dog has given him other plans,' I said. Since he had returned from his long journey to find a princess to make his bride, Ovitus had never been far from Waldy, a faithful wolfhound that had turned out to be far more than met the eye. It was a familiar, a demonic entity that had crawled through the void to ensnare his attention. 'This is what Sul wanted. To take control of the Crown himself and tear through the divide between the hidden realm, the Fault, and our world. He wanted to bring his kin back through with him.'

'Well, we stopped him,' Esher said. Her voice was steady with resolve. 'And we'll stop this too.' She stood. 'The Dryad said we have to head to the higher ground, to brave that fog we've avoided. There's no time like the present, is there?'

'If there's any such thing as time at all here,' Sanvaunt said. He looked down resentfully at his neatly piled armour plates. 'Time to armour up.'

There was no compass direction to follow, and nor did the moons rise and fall from static positions. This would have made navigating the swamp especially hard, but we'd discovered that there *were* directions in the Fault, they just didn't follow anything you'd have thought of as convention.

There was Irk, as we'd come to know it. For some reason known only to the Fault's creator, when you headed that way everything became more annoying. Small things, irrelevant things, phrases, or sights, or even just thoughts, became increasingly agitating. None of us relished travelling deeper towards Irk. It didn't arrive abruptly, it was a rising tide that slowly swamped you over time. We'd all come to learn that if we headed Irkwards, it was best to just keep our mouths shut and try our best not to engage with each other. There were two other directions, not quite evenly spaced apart as far as we could tell. I had wondered at times whether these were intentional, or necessary parts of the magic.

The second direction, which lay clockwise from Irk, was Grey. The longer you travelled that direction, the greyer everything looked. It had taken us a good while to figure any of this out, entirely driven by trial and error. Stopping and resting for a bit—hours, actually—brought things back to normal. One time we'd been pursued by something that burrowed through the ground, something bigger than we were prepared to have a go at fighting. It had come after us relentlessly, taking us further and further into Grey until even the colourless world began to blend together. We made our stand then, and Esher still bore a scar from that battle across the backs of her hands. Nobody liked venturing Greywards.

The last of the directions, the narrowest of the three, was Slow. Over a short distance you wouldn't necessarily notice it, nor was it apparent when moving. It just all took longer somehow. Slow wasn't so bad, you just had to be prepared not to get anywhere as quickly as you might have liked.

The three directions beneath the red, cracked sky—Irk, Grey and

Slow—gave us our navigation. The City of Spires could lie in any of those directions, but always far. Always well beyond our ability to reach it. We had given up trying. But the higher ground, the mountainous terrain and the wall of dense fog that lay around it, took us mostly into Irk-by-Grey. That was probably the best combination when forced into one. Anything-by-Slow was annoying in its own right, and heading into it was dispiriting before we even began.

It was a long, miserable journey across the swamp that lasted four days—days as we called them, anyway. The first night was the most miserable, without anywhere useful to bed down. We'd moved beyond the plain of fallen statues, leaving behind the kings, wizards, priests and gods of an older world. I wasn't sad to leave them behind. They had been titans once, impossibly tall works of perfect stone. Sanvaunt said that they must have been cut from the hearts of mountains, the stone around them painstakingly hewn away to reveal forms beneath, until time, or something worse, brought them down. That seemed too much of a waste to me. A waste of time, a waste of good mountains even, and in the end they'd come to serve only as a reminder that nothing humanity does can last.

Ovitus had lashed me to a pyre and set about offering the impossible challenge, but that challenge had been answered. What did those back home think of us now? We had all wondered that frequently. Did everyone cast us out? I'd revealed myself, after all. I doubted my name was worth a great deal, except perhaps as a curse. But Sanvaunt and Esher? Nobody could accuse them of anything worse than loving me—though perhaps that of itself was a crime.

The second day saw us pass the ruins of a settlement. We gave it a wide berth, since the half-dead tended to make their dens in the tumbled ruins of past civilisations, but we were harried by them nonetheless for four or five miles. We saw them off easily enough each time. We were practised at it now, battle hardened, and Sanvaunt's abilities were more than formidable. He took the lion's share of the work, and healed the cuts and bruises we accrued with his Fifth Gate.

Anything short of death is fine.

It had become a sort of joke among us, though any smile it drew was always accompanied with gritted teeth. Although I'd died thrice now, and I'd cheated the tunnel every time. The first death, strangled by my own birth cord, had opened my eyes to the dead. The second, drowned then resuscitated, had strengthened that link to the veiled world beyond our eyes. The third, when Sul had driven his rime-coated sword through my chest, I'd used the dead to forestall my end. But I was under no illusions that the memories that came unbidden—memories that could never have been mine—were flowing back up through the tunnel, and I was the one who had opened the door.

Esher and Sanvaunt didn't know. I lived side by side with them, had gone through half a literal hell with them, and they still didn't know who I was. But then, maybe I didn't know that either anymore.

Two further days of swamp, which necessitated wading through oily, reddish water at times, brought us to drier ground, and we were none of us sad to leave the bleakness of the marsh behind. The low purple shapes of the mountainous terrain had grown steadily larger, and finally they towered high, reaching up towards those cracks in the sky. The land had been quiet of late, no upheavals, no white light tearing the Fault apart and sending it on through the vortex above the City of Spires. As the days had passed I'd begun to wonder if maybe the Crown had found a new head to rest upon. Perhaps the battle I'd witnessed had settled matters. Perhaps Merovech LacClune had won, and Ovitus's head already decorated Onebridge on a spike. Part of me hoped so, while another part—urged on by travelling into Irk no doubt—felt angry at the prospect, dismissed.

What was I doing here? I made plans as if they made sense when nothing at all did. I turned us here and there on spirit-words dragged from things long-corrupted. I dredged memories, if they were even true memories, from the evil past. I had never been less sure of myself. I was nineteen years old, and I felt the weight of at least two worlds crushing down on me. It wasn't fair. None of it had been fair since the beginning. Without needing to find a way home for Esher and Sanvaunt I might have given up on all of it. There was nothing for me to go back to. I was a pariah, hated, cursed, my name a splash of blood on the hem of history's skirt. I'd killed the Winterra, Redwinter's own, in their hundreds.

I was exactly what people had always feared me to be, what I'd feared I could become. But when that cold part of myself that had been beaten and impaled on a sword took control it felt like destiny. In its turn the weaker, broken part of me took hold and wanted only to curl into a ball and hide from the judgement of the world.

When the light faded to its darkest, we came across the remnants of an old windmill. The sails had long since tattered away. I'd read about windmills, which worked like water mills but powered purely by, well, wind. It wasn't as tall as I'd imagined it would be, and the sails were broken. There were more trees here, out of the swamp, though like most things in the Fault they were dead. But it was better here, if only a little.

A small, green-grey creature sat on the short flight of stone steps leading to the windmill's door. It was no bigger than a two-year-old child, withered and gaunt, but its perfectly round eyes tracked us. In place of fingers and toes it had pairs of smooth, clawlike digits. An ugly thing. It looked harmless enough, but looks have a tendency to be deceiving. It looked the way the Hidden Folk did in stories, a mean, hairless little goblin with watchful eyes.

'I don't think this is the iron child,' Esher said. The creature didn't move.

'Think there are more of them around?' I asked.

'I guess we check,' Sanvaunt said. 'Hey, you, little creature. Do you speak?'

The goblin cocked its head as if it were the first time it had been addressed in a while. It probably had been. I wasn't sure if it understood Sanvaunt or not. He tried addressing it again, but it didn't seem to make much difference to its intention to sit on the step, barring our entrance to the mill. Things weren't always what they seemed in the Fault. It was as likely that it would disappear into a puddle as it was that it would grow six more legs, swell to the size of a rhinar and try to make us its lunch.

'Light's going fast,' Esher said. We were all tired, but her exhaustion showed strongest. 'If it won't talk then just step around it. It doesn't seem dangerous.'

'Stick a sword in it and have done,' I said. This had proven to be the optimal strategy in practically every situation we'd found ourselves since we awoke in the Fault. 'Besides, I don't fancy sleeping with that thing crawling around outside.'

The emaciated little creature seemed to be trying to swallow a yawn. Then its dry lips parted and it let out a high, gurgling wheeze. It took it several attempts, but finally it managed to croak out some words in a high-pitched whine.

'Seventy-three, seventy-two.'

We looked at one another blankly.

'What does that mean?' Esher asked. 'Little guy, what are you trying to

tell us?' Further wheezing followed, as if the small thing was trying to in-
flate itself to get something out. I could see Esher's sympathy for it growing.
I had none.

'The roads are a mess,' the little thing wheezed. Further attempts at
communication proved futile. Eventually even Esher shrugged and gave
up on trying to talk to it. This wasn't the strangest thing we'd seen, not
by a long shot. I would have gone for the sword-first worry-later option,
only Sanvaunt currently had my sword since the Anam Teine, the life-fire
he summoned, had melted his own, and I was by far the least competent
swordsperson of the three of us. He clanked towards it, stepped around the
goblin and pushed open the paint-peeling green door. It was dark inside,
but nothing stirred.

A small tinny sound drew our attention back to the creature on the step.
It was trying to bite Sanvaunt through the armoured plates around his calf
without any sign of success.

'Off,' Sanvaunt said, but those little arms had wrapped around his shin
and he couldn't get rid of it. Maybe it was because despite being wizened and
dried out it had a toddling child's proportions that he didn't just end it, but
I was long out of qualms. I strode forward, took it by the neck and smashed
its head against the steps until there was no further danger of being softly
gnawed to death.

'Light Above, Raine,' Esher said. There was an even balance of distaste
and awe in her voice. 'That was brutal.'

'It's all brutal out here,' I snapped. I didn't like to be criticised for doing the things that needed doing. Nothing I could do here could possibly
be worse than what I'd done to the Winterra back home. Hundreds of warriors, stripped of their souls, lying dead in the grass at the foot of Redwinter's
mountain slope. It's a strange thing when one realises that they will never be
the hero, and they are the villain everyone always feared they would become.
In many ways it was liberating. No more worrying over right and wrong,
good or bad. I'd done what I'd done, and there was only one thing driving
me now.

Vengeance. Vengeance for Ulovar, who cut his own throat to deny Ovitus
his power. Vengeance for Grandmaster Robilar, who gave everything to defeat her old lover. Vengeance for Liara, who'd been slain in a moment of
abject spite. Vengeance for Jathan, and Adanost and Gelis and Colban and

all the other young Draoihn whose lives had burned away in the fire of one young man's ambition and fear.

Smashing apart another monster's head, whether it was big or small, held no significance to me.

Esher's appalled tone didn't sit well with me all the same. I'd not lost my desire for her regard, or Sanvaunt's either. They'd managed to raise walls around their gentleness, despite being trapped here, despite everything they'd had to do. But then, they hadn't entered the Fault with hundreds of lives on their consciences. Castus had given me the best advice when it came to murder: stop counting. I didn't have a choice anymore—I'd lost track long ago.

'Check the inside,' I said, wiping my glove against the steps. 'I'll set the perimeter.'

From a backpack I'd scavenged from one of the half-dead, I took out some pegs I'd cut from a dead branch and a spool of thread I'd unpicked from a wool coat. Staked out around the mill, it formed a flimsy tripwire, but more importantly we'd found a case of delicate silver bells in what had probably been a temple of some kind and those could be attached to offer a last moment of warning. Temples and castles, those were what seemed to endure the longest here. The mill was a rare find.

By the time I was set up, the others had laid out curtain-made bedrolls. The mill's interior was dry, even if the things of the Fault had long ago stripped away anything useful. It always felt like we should have had something to cook, even if we were just boiling water for tea, but there was no tea and no need to eat anything here. Until they're taken away you don't realise how much of life is formed of rituals, sometimes just intended to give you a reason to be with one another. I laid my own bedroll out on the opposite side of the main room to the others, as I always did when we had a roof. They didn't try to persuade me to sleep over on their side anymore. At first I'd argued that it was Sanvaunt's snoring that made me sleep apart, but deep down, we all knew that wasn't it. He didn't even snore that badly. There was something that kept me apart from them, even after all they'd done for me. The more I distanced myself, the closer they seemed to get to one another. If I'd let myself believe it, I'd have said that they were falling in love, but another part of me knew that was just the jealousy talking.

Or was it?

It was.

Was it?

Esher was mine. Sanvaunt was mine. They couldn't have each other, and they couldn't have me either—or at least, I couldn't have them. They didn't understand what I was, not really. Or the part I really feared, they didn't know what I was going to do. I knew it already. I just couldn't tell anyone until it was too late. To do what I had planned—there had to be true hatred in your heart to countenance it, and for all their anger, they weren't those people. Maybe that's why I loved them so much, but in the end, it was part of why I was sleeping cold and alone again.

I had a plan. If I could find a way back to our own world, I had a plan to end all this. It just necessitated a whole lot of people to die.

I dreamed of Empress Song Seondeok that night. Not as she was at the end, three hundred years old and showing every part of it, defeated and alone in her dining hall of the dead. I saw her as she was at thirty. The dark power came to her later in life than it had me. She ran a merchant's guild in lands that would one day become part of Dharithia. A prosperous woman. I watched her chide her children, trying to hide the smile from her lips at their sheer audacity. She seemed happy in that life. I wondered what had happened to change her, to cause her to rise up and break the world. She had smothered an empire with her darkness.

I looked on her children, and her love for them, and I knew that such malice can only arise from the greatest of love. I had been dreaming of these great and terrible women for more than a year now, had felt their victories, their losses, their rises and falls. Song Seondeok had become the night, and the world had suffered for it. And now she was within me, and I her, and together we would become the night once more.

6

A bank of fog, twenty feet high or more, barred our progress further Irkwards. We'd got this far before, but had turned back in the face of the unknown. Before now, in a haze of sleep deprivation from the dreams that wouldn't leave me be, I thought we'd made the right choice. The Dryad couldn't lie to us, and if we wanted to find the iron child, this was the path that lay before us. The Hidden Folk couldn't lie to you, not when compelled by a bargain of souls. Or at least that was what the stories already said.

'It's not just fog, is it?' Esher said. She'd bound all her braids up at the back of her head, looking fierce in armour and resolve as the three of us stood before vapour so dense we saw nothing beyond it. There were colours within it, fleeting glimpses of yellow and blue. But no sound. Nothing at all. After splatting the little thing at the windmill, we'd not seen a single sign of life.

'Nothing is what it seems here,' I agreed.

'We tie ourselves together. I don't want to lose either of you,' Sanvaunt said. He took out the cord that had once hanged the curtains we now slept beneath.

'I don't think I could go on if I had to face this place alone,' Esher said. She glanced to me. There was pain in her eyes. 'Maybe none of us could.'

'Tie us up and let's get to it,' I said sharply. Judging! Always judging me, always complaining that I was withdrawn or failing to live up to whatever standards it was they wanted. I resented it, and it made me want to withdraw all the more.

Sanvaunt took the lead, as he liked to do. Maybe he felt it was the manly thing to do, though the thought was unkind and he'd never discriminated in that way. The truth was, he could command his power more easily than either Esher or I, but my mind was feeling catty and it slung silent criticisms like pebbles cast into the sea, arcing but for a moment and then swallowed and forgotten. Esher went next, and I brought up the rear. I had power of my own, but I couldn't draw it from my own life force. I had a limited reservoir of other beings' deaths, and no matter what they said, my friends judged me for it. How could they not?

We shared a last glance with each other. There was nothing further to say. We stepped onwards and into the bank of hanging white vapor. Sanvaunt disappeared first, the soft golden rope pulling taut, and Esher went in after. I came up last, and the fog swallowed me.

I'd expected breathing it to taste like vinegar, or paint, or something foul and artificial, but there was a sweetness to the cloud. Not cloying, or thick, more like a brush of moorland wildflowers, or the drifting of perfume in the air. For a moment I was reminded of a day when I'd walked into a room in the LacNaithe greathouse and known that Esher had been there just moments before. Her scent had lingered behind her, and I'd stood and breathed it in and wanted to follow without knowing where it would lead me. Well, she was leading me again now. I wasn't that girl any longer, but for a brief moment, part of me wished that I could be again.

I could barely see a thing. The ground was dead brown grass and broken stone, uneven footing but nothing too treacherous. Esher was a shadow through the fog ahead of me though we were barely six paces apart. The colours, yellow and blue, were no brighter or nearer here in the fog. There was a silence here beyond anything I could have imagined, not just the absence of sound but the swallowing of all that were made. Even my footsteps were devoured by the cloud. If anything could silence an intrusive thought, this was it.

A powerful wind blew through the fog, driving it across my path. On instinct I hunkered down as it swirled and rushed by me, cold, wet, trying to cling to me as it was driven onwards. I grabbed hold of the rope, felt it taut where Esher must have been doing the same, but I couldn't see her through the white, the yellow, the blue. The sweet flavour of the air intensified, and then it was more than sweet, it became stronger, tart in my nose and on my tongue, and then worse, turning bitter like burnt sugar. I shouted something into the sudden gust, but the words were whipped away from me before even I could make sense of them. My head was spinning. I was somewhere white and blurred and orange and purple but beyond that, I didn't know anymore. I knew I was someone, but whom? I was in danger, but why? Thoughts were being torn away, carried on an impossible wind as quickly as I could form them. So I got down low, lying on uneven rocks and dead brown grass, gripping to a rope whose purpose I'd forgotten.

It was all over quickly, or maybe it just felt that way. My memory bounced around my skull a few times, slowly coming back to itself. I was patient with it as I made myself recall who I was, where I was, what I was doing here. Some of it fit together badly, like a puzzle whose pieces had been hammered into the wrong places. But I reached for them, pried them back out and slowly put myself back together. There was a length of soft golden rope tied around my middle, though it was too delicate to be much use apart from decoration. It had been cut off after a couple of feet, worn around my waist like some kind of tail. What was that for? It seemed a strange thing to be wearing. But then, so was the armour I wore. As though I were drunk, only half of everything made sense. Somehow I was surrounded by mist, and now that there was more room in my mind, I dredged up a memory from long ago. Hallenae, the Riven Queen, had deployed this on more than one occasion. No wonder my memory was getting sent spinning this way and that. Someone was using my own creation against me.

I spoke nine words of power, an incantation made of sound rather than on parchment, paper or carved into stone, words taken from the language of the Eldritch Kin, as the Faded had once called themselves. It was an incantation of banishment and control, and I put my Sixth Gate behind it and drove the fog back from me. The path forward became clear. I smirked at the fool who'd tried to use my own spells against me. Me, the queen of all the world. Me, who brought queens to their knees, and kings to the grave. My fingers curled like claws. I had more than simply banishment to deploy when I found the impudent wretch who'd sought to stop me with my own magic.

I wasn't where I'd expected to be. The fog gave way to a landscape of winter, snow lying deep across a scene that was at once familiar, and yet seemed so distant I knew at once there was nothing real about it. A peaceful village, nestled in a valley between mountains that sheltered it from the weather's worst, holding back winds that would strip flesh from the bone. The houses were simple—but I only knew that now. When I'd lived here, so many, many years ago, they'd just been houses to me. I saw the crudeness of the joins, the simple, practical nature of the rough-hewn logs, the shingle roofs. Lines of rope stretched between the cabins, hanging animal skins turned hard in the cold. There was nobody there. The crunch of a boot in the snow was the only sound all around, louder than the coarse droning of the tunnel in my mind.

'Well, this isn't real,' I said aloud. 'I've been in a dreamscape like this before, you know. There are signs. You've crafted it well, but it's too static. Too dead. My village wasn't like that.'

I waited for someone to appear, to say something or speak. But for the moment I was alone. I advanced into the dream, confident that this was little more than a hallucination. I wasn't going to get caught up mesmerised by a glimpse of my past. I'd left this place when I was a child, when Mama decided to bring what she believed to be her special skills of reading and writing to find greater fortune in the warmer lands of the south. I'd been too young to miss it. Looking at the peaceful little scene now, I felt a certain fondness for it, but there was no yearning within me to go back to it. Whoever was messing with my mind had misjudged.

'Is this what you do?' I asked into the valley's quiet. 'Try to get people all lost and intrigued by their own memories? You seem to think I'd care for that. I don't. I'm not interested in the past.'

A door creaked a short way into the village and a woman stepped forward. She hobbled, walking with two canes, each step paining her. She had dark hair worn in a bun, a face of regular, unspectacular features, and was dressed in a long black robe with white banding across the sleeves.

'Hello, Raine,' she said.

'You've got this wrong,' I said. I wasn't speaking to her. 'That's a scribe house robe. Mama didn't wear them until after we left the mountains and she took that work. You're getting it confused. We can do this a while, or we can cut to the point.'

I didn't like the thought of something crawling through my mind, pinching at threads of memory. There were a lot of strange things in the Fault, and most of them were better off dead. I wasn't worried for myself. I had resources I could draw on, and there were spells and incantations in my mind that would deal with this if I had to. I'd learned them over two thousand years ago during the Fallon War, the second time I'd first fought the Eldritch Kin.

I blinked, shook my head. No. I hadn't fought them then. That had been Empress Song Seondeok, and that was a war of another time and another people. A memory, one that didn't belong to me, had pressed too far into me. Maybe it was this dreamscape place, blurring the edges. It was alarming, more so than my illusory childhood home. There were other memories back there, waiting at the edges. Lives I hadn't lived. People I hadn't been. Dead queens lurked at my peripheries.

At least I could take from it the knowledge I needed to break this enchantment when the time was right. But whoever, or whatever, was doing this to me had a purpose. 'This isn't going to work,' I said to the effigy of Mama. 'I'm not going to get lost in my past and reveal things about myself to you. That's the ploy, isn't it? To make me vulnerable. You're playing a dangerous game here. If you've looked inside my mind, you'll know it's a busy place. And it's not something you want turned against you.'

'Another of you,' Mama said, and it wasn't her voice. It was a voice so weary with time and loss that it ached on every syllable. 'I thought we were done. But I suppose it's only right that there be one more of you, now, when it's all falling apart. Do you understand what you ask of me, by coming here?'

'Could we dispense with this?' I said, gesturing at my childhood home. 'We can do a tour of Harran's scribe houses if you like, or maybe some of the nights Mama and I slept under hedgerows when she couldn't afford a room. Perhaps you'd like the morning she told me I'd ruined her life, that was a good one. Or when I was twelve and she told me I was making eyes at her man? Or when I had cattle pox and she stayed up with me all night singing? There's a lifetime to pick from. Go ahead. It isn't going to hurt me, I already lived through it all.'

Mama disintegrated into the wind, blowing away like she was made of sand. When the voice came again, it had no visible source. It came from inside me.

'There's more in there than just sad childhood tales,' it said.

The dream changed around me in an instant, a blink and I was elsewhere. I stood on a dark hillside, torches in the distance, and on the slope below, Esher and Sanvaunt riding up towards us, but they were frozen in time. It was Tor Marduul, the first time I'd met them. Funny that I'd met them at the same time. They'd tried to arrest Ulovar, had drawn swords on us.

'Strange friends you keep,' the voice said. 'A lot of feeling within you for these two.'

'Have you bound them like this as well?'

'No,' the weary old voice said. 'They're still wandering blindly in the mist. None of this is taking much time. But time doesn't work the way you're familiar with, here.'

'It's time I don't have,' I said. 'End the charade, or I'll end it for you. I've powers you don't comprehend.'

'You're confident. I like that. But then, your kind always are. It's the arrogance that brings you all down in the end.'

'My kind?'

'Witch queens,' the voice said. 'The dark lady, the empress of night, the woman of death. You're not the first I've met. They're all here in the Fault, somewhere. It's what happens when you refuse to let go. Nothing can live forever. You spend your long lives trying to master death, but in the end you fear the tunnel more than anyone.'

'Because I've seen into it,' I said.

The scene changed again. Now I was somewhere I didn't recognise at all, a place I'd never been, and despite knowing none of it was real I flinched. A city burned in the distance. Around me, vast creatures, hunched heads hanging forward, twelve foot tall at the shoulder, rested fists as big as oxen against the churned earth. There were bodies everywhere, some human, some Faded, armour torn apart, limbs missing.

'Hallenae's creatures,' the voice said scathingly. 'How is it you've memories of the Riven Queen's time? Even with your abilities, your life couldn't have been so long.'

'I don't know,' I said. And for a moment, despite my need to free Sanvaunt and Esher from the fog, despite wanting this creature out of my mind, I was possessed with the desire to know the same. The monstrous beasts around me were toad-like, patched with fur, rubbery mouths filled with triple rows of teeth, their armoured hides pebbled with warty protrusions. One didn't seem to register the spears jutting from its back. They were demons of the Night Below.

'If I were a gambling man—and I was, very much so once—then I'd wonder if someone hadn't found a way to play with the stream of time. Perhaps you *were* there.'

'I wasn't,' I said, knowing I was falling into a discussion I shouldn't be having. But if there were answers for me here, I had to reach for them. But reaching for something can lead to a fall, and my footing was uneven. 'Are you Maldouen?'

'It's a name I'll accept,' he said. 'It'll do for now.'

'Release the dream and let us pass,' I said. I felt him shrug at me through whatever connection he'd established. 'Release me, or I'll make you.'

'Girl, I blasted the Riven Queen herself into this place,' the voice snapped. 'Do you really think you can challenge me here, in the Fault?'

'People have always loved telling me what I can't do,' I said. I opened myself further to the Sixth Gate, let its grinding, droning roar fill my mind. 'You'll find them in the cemeteries.'

I felt the building of a power then. It was not a Gate. It was something else, a magic of another place and another land, gathered protectively, not so very far away.

'Begone,' I said, 'or I'll burn you from my mind and sow your ashes across this stinking wasteland. Try me. I'm used to it by now.' The Sixth Gate yawned wider, the tunnel growing deeper, blacker as I pushed into it harder than I ever had before. I heard the shivering cries of the evil dead beyond, whining and hungering.

'Don't do that,' the voice said, and I heard the panic in his voice. 'Don't bring that evil here, not to this place. You don't know what you're doing!'

'Then *release me*!' I screamed, white ghost-light flaring from my eyes, my dirt-darkened hair billowing around me on spirit-wind, my voice echoing through the tunnel, over and over. *Release me, release me, release me.*

He released me.

7

The dream left my mind between heartbeats. I found myself alone, the wall of fog at my back, stood before what had once been a great castle, bigger even than the king's castle in Harranir. It had been covered with ivy once, though it was nought but fossilised grey now. The walls of the LacNaithe greathouse had been covered with ivy too, and for a brief moment I wondered whether I'd ever see it again. This castle was different. Instead of the greathouse's blocky, square-edged formality, this castle had been crafted in whimsy, with cone-topped towers, broad windows, fountains dotted throughout long-dead gardens. A fairy-tale mockery of a true castle, perhaps. Beyond the romantic towers, mountains drew up tall, bleak and grey, and above them, the ominous redness of the sky. The City of Spires lay distant on the horizon as though it observed a meagre victory. I'd made it to the palace of Avangrad, but the city still taunted me, unattainable and silent.

A pair of torches guttered theatrically to either side of the elaborately decorated double doors. Of the speaker, there was no sign.

I could hear my name being called, the sound turned flat by the fog. Sanvaunt and Esher trying to find me.

'I'm here,' I called back towards it. The calls continued, but growing louder, as if they sought me in a child's game.

'Raine!'

'This way.'

'Raine!'

The golden curtain rope was still wrapped around my waist, but severed. Maybe I'd done that with my incantation. Esher emerged from the fog first, strands of it clinging to her as if it were reluctant to allow her to escape its embrace. Her face lit up when she saw me and she tried to run to me, but was jerked back as Sanvaunt was pulled along behind her.

'We lost you,' she said. Her face was so full of warmth and relief. She wanted to run to me, to throw her arms around me, I could read it in her eyes. Funny, how they could both be so expressive when one of them was clouded, pearly. The rope held her back and I didn't go to meet her. I forced a smile onto my face. Sanvaunt, Esher, they both had so much inside them. They still sought out that human warmth, physical comfort from one another, from me. There was some part of me inside that wanted it to, but it was buried behind so many walls of murder, fear and confusion that a smile was all it had to offer.

'This is the place,' I said.

'Where did you go?' Sanvaunt asked, his voice curt. 'Why didn't you stay close? We thought we lost you.' Through the terseness I felt precisely that which I found hardest to deal with: his concern for me. There was love there, in his poise, the furrowing of his brow. I hated it. I hated that they both kept throwing this at me when none of it was going to do any of us the slightest good. I was going to hurt them in the end. The more they foisted this on me, the more we would all suffer when the time came.

'There were things that had to be bypassed,' I said. Looked away. 'It doesn't matter. It's done now, and we're here.'

'This is a sight,' Esher said. 'Imagine what it must have been like, when the gardens were alive. It must have been beautiful.'

'Must have been,' Sanvaunt said. He was guarded. He was half watching me, taking me in without looking directly at me. A little anger trickled through my walls. Mistrust is hard to be around. Maybe he wondered if I was me at all, whether this was some other trick of the Fault.

'Maldouen's here,' I said. 'In there. He let us through.'

'The hero of Solemn Hill,' Esher said breathlessly. 'What a time to be alive. Or whatever we are.'

We three of us stood looking towards the strange, palatial castle. None of us had found the nerve to take a step towards it. It echoed with its own death. In a place of dead things, this fog-ringed castle somehow seemed all the more dead. Esher didn't see it that way. She saw what it must once have been, and couldn't hide her awe.

'When all seemed lost to the dark, Maldouen came to the Draoihn and told them of his great work, constructing the Crowns across the world, powerful enough to bring down even the Riven Queen and banish the Faded into the Fault.'

'And yet he's in here with them,' Sanvaunt said. 'It always bothered me that we knew more about the Riven Queen than we did about the hero who beat her. Light Above, we know more about the Haddat-Nir kings before the Age of Soot than we do about him. There's more in Redwinter's library about the Age of Bronze than there is about the Blind Child.'

'Perhaps there's a reason we chose to forget about him,' I said. We'd forgotten many things that would have been valuable about now. 'It doesn't really matter, does it? We're here. Let's go and find out.'

'Stay behind me,' Sanvaunt said. He drew his sword and started forward. For a moment a ripple of heat flowed across his blade. I watched Esher tracking him. I'd seen that look on her face before. She used to look at me that way.

'Cuts a heroic figure, doesn't he?' I said scathingly, wanting to break her from that gaze. But she caught the sneer in my words. When she finally took her eyes from him, she showed me a rare glimpse of anger.

'This place gets to us all,' she said. 'But I'm tired, Raine. I'm tired of disappointments and being burned. I'm tired of having to work around your snark and your jealousy. He was there if you wanted him. But lately, it's like you don't want to be around either of us at all. We need each other. Let's try to be our best selves.'

She drew her own sword and started after him. I had no weapon, nothing to flourish. I tried to think of some kind of smart comeback, something clever that would dissolve her words and make her see that they were childish instead of ringing with truth. But the retort didn't come to me. I balled my fists and for a few moments let the Sixth Gate drown out the silence around me, grinding, droning.

'I don't have a best self,' I muttered beneath my breath. 'There's only this.'

I followed. They would not—could not—understand. They loved me. I knew that. But you don't reward love with what I was going to do. Whatever Sanvaunt said, he didn't want Ovitus flayed alive, hung from a post on Onebridge and cut off from death, doomed to live in torment for all eternity. But that's what I had planned. Death was too good for him. I would give him unending torment, and when I did, all Sanvaunt's love for me, all Esher's belief in me, anything they'd poured into me—it would rebound on them and tear them apart all the worse. I would get them home, and that was all. After that, I planned to bring nightmare.

A witch queen in truth.

Why did Esher have to turn my legs to putty with a look? Why did Sanvaunt? How was any of that fair, and what was I supposed to do, fuck them both? Sometimes I wished I could have something, just one thing for myself. But that's the rallying cry of every self-pitying wretch in the world and I wouldn't allow myself to fall prostrate before my whinging heart.

The truth was, I did love Sanvaunt. I loved him for his resolve. I loved the way he showed so much damn respect for me, even when he was angry with me, even when I didn't deserve it. I loved his ridiculous competence. I loved his secret romantic heart, his silly *novels* and his bad acting in theatre plays. I loved the hard lines of his jaw and I refuse to comment on what his eyes could do to me. I loved his power. Had I met him in another life, I would have been completely incapable of reason around him and he could have asked me for anything and I'd have spread for him like a flower.

And then there was Esher. I loved her no less fiercely, only all that love was confused and different and wrapped in ribbons I didn't entirely understand. I'd not been raised that way, but back when I got skewered and Esher rode in to save me, I gave up pretending I didn't want to feel my body pressed hot and sweating against hers. And as soon as I accepted that, it was just the most obvious and natural thing in the world. There were times when I first met her I'd thought that I wanted to be her—to be so effortlessly a *girl,* even while she showed herself a match for any of the male apprentices in those pursuits traditionally given to the boys. But I hadn't wanted to be her. I'd wanted to be *with* her, to kiss her, to run my hands through that ridiculously golden hair.

I loved them both, and we'd all saved each other so many times that counting was irrelevant now, and I couldn't bear to break them against the jagged rocks I'd ringed myself with.

And so I hung back a little, distancing myself physically as I had done emotionally. It was good that they were finding each other. If there was any possibility for someone to experience love here in this twisted nightmare land, then maybe there was still hope. I just didn't want to have to see it.

The gates of Maldouen's castle were open to us. Beyond the first set of gates there lay a great courtyard, surprisingly free of detritus, and the palace—with its whimsical towers and artistry I couldn't think of it as a true castle—lay beyond. A huge, rusted metal bust of a child's head twenty feet wide dominated the courtyard, an equally rusted blindfold forged across its eyes. It was an ugly, half-buried monument. Life-size, relief-cut statues of rulers ran fifteen feet up along the castle wall, like a frieze, across the entire face of the stonework. Some I didn't recognise, warriors in strange costume, holding long devices I had no name for.

A pair of wide double doors, patterned with bronze turned green from verdigris, stood partially open. There was light beyond. The three of us exchanged looks.

'Swords away?' Esher asked.

'I think so,' Sanvaunt said, sliding his weapon back into its sheath. 'This doesn't feel hostile. The fog seemed a pretty harmless way of deterring things.'

If only he knew. I knew that fog could do a lot more than just get in the way.

'If he leaves his doors open like this, it doesn't seem like he's scared of much that might come from out there,' I said. 'That includes us.'

Esher put her sword through her belt.

'Let's just be careful,' she said.

'Stay behind me,' Sanvaunt told us, and strode purposefully towards the open doors.

'He loves to be protective of us,' Esher said. She tried a smile on me. It was uncertain, like a fawn trying to find its feet for the first time. It was still there, that connection that had appeared so early on, a cord of—something—that ran between us. A closeness. 'It's sort of adorable, isn't it? Even if it's silly.'

I couldn't always keep myself hard and distant. Sometimes my dam failed and I let myself through.

'He loves us,' I said. 'He loves both of us.' My words sounded so old, and lost, like they belonged in a museum of the past.

'We all love each other,' Esher said. She could see I was already trying to shore the dam back up. She was reaching an arm into the hole, trying to find me on the other side. 'Let's go be protected.' I swallowed the rising tension in my throat and nodded. *Yes.*

Passing beneath the archway, I felt a tingling against my skin. Loose hairs around Esher's head rose slightly for a moment, but the feeling didn't last long. A defensive warding of some kind. Perhaps Maldouen left his door open because he didn't need to worry.

A long hall stretched ahead, carpeted in purple. There were light globes along the walls, but the light didn't come from cadanum, no bluish blush to it. Instead it tinted everything in red, the colour of the torn sky. There were doors to either side of the hall, but they were closed, while from the far end of the hall there was light beyond a closed door. We moved along warily, but calmly. Three First Gate trances drummed softly through the world, brightening colour, sharpening edges. But there was nothing moving, not even a heartbeat as we crept along the carpet. It showed no signs of age. Everything else in the Fault had been dilapidated, broken or plundered. But as I crept towards the door, I had the Sixth Gate ready. My mind would enter it in an instant. The Banshee's Wail, the Call of Night, the Spirit Choke—I had more at my disposal than the steel my companions carried. The ghosts I carried in my chest twisted and writhed for a moment, like worms exposed to light, but their prison was solid.

The door opened easily to Sanvaunt's touch, and we looked into a grand reception hall. The plush purple carpet thinned to a narrow strip, leading the way between beautifully smooth, pale columns of rose-veined marble. The light was powerful here, shining through high stained-glass windows that covered the world in vivid colour. Steam rose from grates in the floor around the edges of the hall, which were filled with the kind of pews that filled churches. On the far side of the hall, steps led up to a throne, backed with a fan of copper piping that spread like a peacock's tail, and upon it, we laid eyes on the great hero of Solemn Hill for the first time, lying back on the throne with his legs cast over one arm. His head turned towards us.

He was not a child, no matter what the stories had said. He was made to look like a young boy, ten, eleven, with a wrap of cloth across his eyes. His hair was depicted as curly, and he was dressed in a smart jacket with toggles instead of buttons, but none of it was cloth. None of him was flesh. He was made entirely of brightly polished metal, uniform polished steel. With a creak and a clang he swung his legs down to the floor. I could feel the weight of him in that sound as he levered himself up like some terrible metal puppet.

'Is that armour?' Esher asked.

'No,' Sanvaunt said. 'It's a golem. They used to be made to guard vaults in Junath, before the Age of Soot.'

'Something like that, anyway,' the metal figure said. He sounded older than the boyish metalwork suggested. His jaw opened, but didn't move as he spoke. The sound ushered out anyway. Was there a tongue in there?

'You're the one that calls yourself Maldouen?' Sanvaunt said. He continued to move forward, approaching the steel figure.

'The name's close enough,' he said. 'Be welcome. You're in no danger here.' He walked down the flight of stairs, feet that were fashioned to the shape of buckled shoes clanging against the steps. Each pace rang like a bell. Little flickers of light sparked here and there at the joints of his limbs.

'How do we know we can trust you?' Sanvaunt asked. Esher and I hung back. I didn't sense an immediate threat from this metal boy, but I looked around the edges of the room, noting the two doors that led off into antechambers, glancing back at the door behind us. It hadn't slammed shut, and nobody else seemed to be coming.

'You've wandered into my house and you're the one asking if you can trust me? The fecking nerve,' Maldouen said. 'I don't suppose you have anything to drink?'

'You want a drink?' I asked.

'I want *to* drink,' Maldouen said. 'No? Well, probably for the best. It never worked very well in this body anyway.'

Esher, Sanvaunt and I glanced at one another, trying to read how each of us was taking this turn of events. It wasn't anything we'd expected, but then, that was the nature of the Fault.

'We've come a long way to find you,' Sanvaunt said. He used his official voice, the one he brought out to address junior apprentices, foreign delegates and rival clan leaders. There used to be something about it that made me smile, because I'd seen his vulnerable underbelly and how detached this version of him was from that romance-writing, wall-running self. 'In our stories you were the hero who defeated the Riven Queen. You saved us in our hour of need. We need your help, Maldouen.'

'Help?' the steel child said. 'I can't say I've much of that to offer. The outcome can't be changed. Not now.'

'Great Maldouen, the whole world itself is in danger,' Esher said fiercely. 'We need you. Whatever happened to you, whatever left you in this terrible place—we have to escape it. We have to find the Queen of Feathers.'

'Ah, that's the goal, is it?' Maldouen said. 'She doesn't know who or what she is. She's been around even longer than I have. You can't have missed the energy flowing up through that vortex. Help? No, I've no help for you. If I could have done something about it all, don't you think I would?'

'But—' Sanvaunt started, but Maldouen waved him off dismissively.

'It isn't even my world,' Maldouen said. 'You're welcome here. Use the facilities. You don't have long. A few weeks, perhaps, but enjoy them while they last. I don't know what you expect me to do. I could have existed here a little longer—maybe a year, before it all collapses. But events in your world have woken Iddin, and he will come for you. It can't be helped, now.'

Just remembering that dark, rippling glass thing and its oily black cloud made me uneasy.

'We've fought our way this far,' I said. 'A lot of things have tried to stop us. They all go the same way in the end.'

The metallic child couldn't make facial expressions, but he cocked his head to one side. It felt admonishing.

'Iddin is a shadow of what he once was, but even so, he is greater than anything your world has to offer. He's coming for you, but he cannot manifest his full strength, not yet. But it's growing. He dreamed a tiny part of himself into your world, and so he is divided between this world and your own, and in projecting himself that way both forms are weakened. And yet. Despite that, I do not have the power to match him. Neither do you.'

'You'd be surprised what we can handle,' Esher said.

'Even if you could, what use? My Crowns have been taken, or are uncontained. I left you people one task—one task! And you couldn't even keep them contained. The Fault is collapsing into your world. You've seen it yourselves, all that shit in the sky. I have no aid left to offer, but you're welcome to dwell here until the worlds collide. It has been a long time since I had guests.'

This was not what we had expected. Maldouen's words were chilling, but I'd been told I was done for too many times to take him at his word. My friends were about to argue, but I moved ahead of them. It wasn't time. We wouldn't persuade him like this.

'What about revenge?' I asked. 'Will you help us get that at least?'

Maldouen looked up at me. His metal-tinged voice took on a hint of wry amusement.

'That, at least, I might be able to help you with.'

'Are we safe here?' I asked.

'There's an approximation of safety,' Maldouen said. 'I thought you might enjoy the whole throne thing. It seemed appropriate. But this room probably isn't that comfortable for you. I haven't had guests in a long while. I'll be honest, I am quite excited to have some new faces around, but I've waited a long time, and I expect you'd appreciate some rest and relaxation. Baths, food, that kind of thing. Don't mind the servants. They aren't really alive, and they don't speak. Are you sure you don't have anything to drink? That's the one thing that ran out centuries ago.'

'No drink,' I said. I felt myself warming to him, strange and steely though he was. We'd come looking for a blind child and we'd found one, although he didn't seem to have any problem navigating around.

'I'd take a bath,' Esher said. There was hope in her voice. 'We can have a bath here?'

'Gorgeous girl,' Maldouen said, and though his metallic mouth didn't move, there was a smile in his words. 'You can have anything you want.'

The change in our environment was too overwhelming. Sanvaunt wanted to argue the point right there and then, as though he'd persuade a talking steel statue that it was time to change the world with us all covered in bog filth, our ragged nails black with dried old blood. Hair hung around our heads in matted tangles, and though it was white underneath, my hair was so darkened by dirt it could have been brown. I had never understood how Esher's kept so clean. Esher took Sanvaunt's hand, and followed Maldouen's directions to find palace rooms. Maldouen returned to the throne and its fan of pipes and tubes. From the moment he sat down, he was immobile, staring towards the door as if expecting further visitors.

Esher and Sanvaunt didn't release one another's hands as we exited the throne room. Their fingers were interlaced, and my heart sighed heavily. There was anger inside me, though directed more towards myself than at them. Who was I to deny them this small, fleeting comfort? Who was I to try to govern their feelings when I knew there was too much going on inside me to return them? There were two halves of me, the one that wanted to just let myself be a young woman, and the one that knew what had to come. In the fog, Maldouen had called me a witch queen. There's no room for love in the heart of a tyrant. The heartbroken girl had to die if we were going to survive.

The halls were silent, but immaculately clean. We left a trail of dirty footprints in our wake, muddying up perfection. There was no damage here, no decay or rot. That metal construct had a beautiful home.

'What's in the light globes?' Esher asked. She finally unlinked hands with Sanvaunt and put her hands near to a wall-mounted sphere. 'They're not even warm.'

'Something that comes from those copper tubes, maybe,' Sanvaunt said. 'Everything here is connected to them in some way. Maybe it's feeding some kind of luminescent gas into them.'

'It's cleaner than cadanum light,' Esher said. 'What do you think, Raine?'

'I don't know,' I said. I just wanted to be on my own. I kept on going down the hall, wanting to disappear entirely. I don't know what I'd expected to find here, but it hadn't been this. I didn't know that I liked it.

Ahead along a corridor, a door opened, sliding sideways into the wall. We all stopped and fell into crouches, hands going to weapon hilts and the thrumming of Gates suddenly all around us, a habit that had formed into instinct over months in the Fault where every movement came from a threat. A woman stepped out, or an approximation of one, but she was as metallic as Maldouen. Her body was silver, her imitation of hair forged into an elaborate pile atop her head. She wore a real dress, all white, belted with green, and carried a bucket with rags slung over the sides as she closed the door behind her. We relaxed, and she walked down the hall towards us, her metal footsteps softened by actual sandals. We let her pass and she walked silently away without acknowledging us at all.

'What are they?' Esher asked. 'I don't know that I like them.'

'We should be wary,' Sanvaunt said. 'That metal child claims to be Maldouen. But we only have his word for it. This could still be a trap.'

'It's a lot of effort to go to if it is,' I said.

'There are numerous historical accounts of Maldouen from the Riven Age,' Sanvaunt said. 'And not one of them says he was made from metal. We've learned not to trust what we encounter here. Let's not get careless just because we've finally found somewhere clean.'

*   *   *   *   *   *

The guest chambers were clean, but they weren't grandiose. I'd expected four-poster beds, full-length mirrors, armoires and overstuffed chairs before roaring fireplaces. But they were simple, spartan, and instead there were just thin mattresses. Each room slept one.

'This won't do,' Esher said. 'We need to sleep in the same room.'

'It's safer,' Sanvaunt agreed.

'You two can do what you want,' I said. 'But I'm sleeping alone.' I realised what I might have accidentally implied, and saw the colour rise in Esher's cheeks behind the layers of dirt.

'Raine, if something were to happen in the night, if this place isn't all it seems to be, then it's best that we be together,' Sanvaunt said.

'You snore,' I said. But that wasn't it, not really. The thing I wanted more than anything else just then was solitude. Even if it was just for a single night, such as nights were here, I wanted to be able to lie alone with my thoughts. To remove myself from this three-pointed life. Maybe if I left them alone together they'd bed each other. At least then it would be done. I was tired of waiting for it to happen. It was hard to feel that kind of desire in the Fault, where everything was dying or dead, and if it wasn't then it tried to eat us, but it was still there sometimes. I'd seen it, in the holding of hands, in the sidelong glances, in the slow stripping of armour, like it was a show. If they'd just get it over with, I thought I could bear that more.

'I think we have to trust him,' Esher said. 'We came here to find an ally, to help us find Raine's Queen of Feathers, and he doesn't seem to wish us harm.' She looked to me with something that could have been an apology. Sanvaunt, by contrast, didn't seem pleased.

'You two sleep now, then,' he said. 'I'll stand watch.'

'If you have to,' Esher said. She placed a hand on his chest, over his beating heart, and I didn't know who I was more jealous of, her or him. 'But I think we should all rest.'

'Bath first,' I said. 'Maldouen said it was just down the hall.' I set about removing my amour, unfastening buckles and straps, letting the pieces fall noisily to the tiles. 'Get my back straps, will you?'

De-armoured, I looked down at the gambeson beneath. It had been ancient and well-patched when I first found this suit, which had failed to save its unfortunate, headless occupant. Now it was practically falling apart. Still, I piled it neatly to the side with the pieces of my armour. The prospect of a bath was so thrilling I had to stop myself charging off down the hall, and instead walked sedately away from my friends.

'Raine, be careful,' Sanvaunt called after me, but I was in no mood to listen.

'Give me some time to get clean,' I called back.

My alone-time started now. We *were* safe here. Maldouen had his walls of dream-fog to protect his castle, and I didn't think he'd allow any of the Fault's creatures through it. We had nothing he wanted, and unlike the rest of the inhabitants of this nightmare realm, he had no reason to eat us. But maybe, a little more than that, I was glad not to be following Sanvaunt's instructions for once. Yes, he was a good leader, but I didn't need to be led. Ulovar had tried to mentor me. Grandmaster Robilar had brought me under her wing. But they were both dead now, and those who tried to take charge of me had a history of dying. I didn't want to have to look upon the graves of any more of the people who tried to care for me.

The baths. Oh, the baths. I was first there. There were murals on the walls depicting low-lying hills and a night sky overhead, painted branches housing roosting nightbirds. I'd seen a place like this before, in the dreams of Song Seondeok, whose dreams were mine sometimes. Perhaps they were just the fantasies of an overtaxed imagination, but this place was very real. The bath, nearly square, was long enough that four tall men could have floated head-to-toe on its surface. A seat ran around the edge, below the water. The baths at Redwinter had been communal like this and I was reminded of happier days. A silver attendant—perhaps the same one I'd seen before, or else of identical construction—stood to one side beside piles of thick, lush towels. The water steamed gently, and when I kicked off my worn-through boots and dipped a toe, only then did I realise how cold I'd been for so long. I stripped and splashed noisily into it.

My mind went blank for a while. I'd heard that some people didn't hear a voice in their head, constantly talking to them, chastising them, working things out and, usually, reminding them of all the embarrassing things they'd ever done, but I did. That voice sounded like me if I focused on it. I didn't know what it would be like to never hear that inner monologue, how anyone could even formulate thoughts, but this had to be close. The voice went silent. Empty, nothing for a while. It was exhaustion, crowding in from all sides. My body held so many aches, was covered by so many bruises I looked mottled. The cuts and scrapes that crisscrossed me stung in the hot water, but even that I found therapeutic. The water grew darker around me. Six months of dirt, of blood, of sweat lifted free. The silver servant didn't move or make comment.

I lost track of time as I soaked my body and mind. The steam opened up my nose, and I breathed more easily. As I tried to soak the dirt from my hair I felt calm, and I claimed that calm for myself. There would be chaos and noise and blood and horror to come, but just for that time, just for a little, I allowed myself the peace of an empty head and the soothing sensation of hot, clean water all around me. I rested my head against the side. I must have slept.

I woke when I heard Esher calling to me from across the room, gently, as if disturbing the quiet of the painted nightbirds would have been an in-trusion. It was her turn to bathe, but she understood me so well, she kept a distance as she lowered into the bathing pool. I swam across to the silver golem and took a towel from her. She moved only slightly—she was alive, or had some semblance of it, after all. The towel was thickly woven, some fabric I'd never seen before. I took another and wrapped my head.

The cool of the corridor greeted me, but the room I returned to was warm. There was no fire, but a small stove was connected to more of the copper piping, which entered the wall behind it, filling the room with comfortable heat. It was then I noticed that my tattered, filthy gambeson was gone, and so were the battered and scratched plates of armour that I'd grown so ac-customed to. Hanging neatly where it had been before was a gown—a gown unlike any I'd seen before.

The fabric rippled black and midnight blue, mottled like snakeskin, but two dozen golden panels descended in twin rows down the front. Each was inscribed with symbols that seemed vaguely familiar, but they weren't magical sigils or any language I spoke. I'd seen something similar before, though, I was sure of that. It was by no means armour, and the short golden rectangles offered no protection, but the tailoring was exquisite. The hem was long, though the gown was split up the front to enable ease of move-ment. The sleeves were short, but alongside it were a pair of golden, satin gloves that would reach up beneath them, woollen stockings that were somehow bright as true gold, and black riding boots that would reach mid-thigh. A dark cloak, its shoulders rising with hard spines, was sewn with rows of clear gemstones that caught the light in rainbow colours. Were—were they *diamonds*? It was royal attire, and looked like nothing I'd seen before; not even Princess Mathilde's regal gowns could have matched it in splendour. I picked up one of the boots and looked at the sole. It bore the scrapes that told me I wasn't its first owner.

I dressed in fresh undergarments, then the stockings, the gloves, and then the rest of it. There was a time when I would have felt ridiculous as I pinned the cloak around my neck, or afraid I'd ruin it. But the outfit had been left here for me, and it fit like a dream. Eerily well, maybe. Nobody had taken my measurements, but it fit me like a second skin.

A modest wooden table provided a modest wooden comb, and it was, unfortunately, time to detangle my hair. Perhaps I'd have been better sawing it off, but instead I worked at it, making slow but steady progress, until it was long and free of its former mistreatment. It could have been in better condition, but that's what you get after six months in a swamp. I left it loose. It seemed appropriate to the black-and-gold costume I'd been gifted.

Maldouen had provided for me like I was royalty. A witch queen, indeed. I hoped he'd have a sword and a bow I could take as well. We wouldn't be staying long. The luxuries of his palace couldn't hide the knowledge that beyond a wall of fog, there lay the Fault, and all its horrors.

The others would find me when they were done. I lay on the mattress, which was less comfortable than I'd hoped. I was asleep in under a minute.

I could tell it was one of the metallic servants waking me by the sound of its fingers against the door. I slid it open, the door rolling easily on tiny wheels set in tracks. The silver woman in the white dress held a chalkboard with lines of pink in a hand so unusual I could barely decipher it.

Please follow me to the terrace.

The message didn't say *alone,* but I didn't think the invitation included Sanvaunt or Esher. I could hear Sanvaunt snoring in the room along the corridor. Snoring seemed so unfair: it was so undignified, but out of anyone's control. The silver woman began to walk slowly away, and it was follow or ignore her, and I'd already made my choice here. If there was danger here, we'd already walked into its maw. We'd had to, out of options, out of choices. My wax had melted away, my wick had burned down. We'd been in this nightmare so long now, it was trust or die. I don't know why I felt that I could trust this place of metallic people, but there were no more leads after this one. If there was nothing here, if there was no way to find the Queen of Feathers, no way to escape the Fault, we were all doomed.

The halls were ornately decorated. Whatever magic Maldouen commanded had shielded this palace from the Fault's ravages and its corrupted denizens. He was strong. If anyone could help us, it was him. His decoration favoured brightly painted statues, their eyes somewhat unnerving, like the artist had never got the hang of painting them quite right. There was little dust here, and I wondered why he would have kept this place so spotless. He couldn't have had guests often.

The messenger led me past a great ballroom hung with glittering chandeliers, and through an inner courtyard where four cherry trees grew. Beautiful, thin and crooked, each bore a raiment of astonishing pink and white blossoms, the colour a shock to my eyes. And then I realised that they, too, were statues, painted to look like trees. Whoever had found them in the stone had been a sculptor of surpassing skill. Each of the four was the work of a lifetime—for a normal person at least. We ascended stairs, past rows of paintings. Some were basic, but they grew more skilled with time, more detailed, and I realised that they were all the work of the same artist. Maldouen, I suspected. If he'd been in the Fault since the battle at Solemn Hill, then he'd been here for over seven hundred years. On the higher floors they were masterworks beyond any mortal artist's skill.

We entered a tower, and there were a lot of stairs. The servant took them very slowly, and I figured I was going all the way to the top, so I left her behind. The rows of golden plates of the gown I'd been gifted—loaned, perhaps—clicked together. There were a dozen flights to ascend, but one doesn't run around the Fault for all that time without building up their thighs.

'I trust you're well rested.'

Maldouen was waiting for me in the highest chamber of the tower. Broad windows allowed the Fault's pink-blush sky to light the room.

'I feel like I've slept for a week.'

'Nearly a day,' Maldouen said. He had his back to me, looking out across towards the swamplands. No fog obscured the view. 'You get used to going without sleep. Forget what it's like to be truly rested. Not that I rest much these days. At least, not in the same manner.'

'What are you?' I asked. I closed the door behind me. That silver servant was still on her way up, footsteps clanking faintly below, but I didn't think she was invited.

'Cutting!' Maldouen said. He turned to face me. I didn't think it mattered very much whether he faced towards me or away. He hadn't been forged with eyes anyway. 'But understandable. I'm what I thought to send of me with the Fault as caretaker, when it was first cast adrift between worlds. Which is not to say that I did that—not this me, anyway. The original me.'

'Then you aren't Maldouen?'

'I'm the Maldouen you know from your legends, daughter of Redwinter,' he said. 'Yes, it was I who won the day at Solemn Hill and banished the Faded here. They were called the Eldritch Kin back then. They only diminished after that. My doing as well, I suppose.'

'There was another you?'

'I had a maker,' he said. 'People spend their lives wondering who created them. I know who created me. It brings no additional peace, I assure you.'

I joined him and gazed out over the bleakness of the Fault. I never much cared who made us. It didn't change anything.

'You said that Iddin would come for us,' I said. 'Can he find us here? Through the fog?'

'Yes,' Maldouen said. 'He will come for you.'

'He sees us as a threat?'

'I do not think so.'

That sat cold and hard in the air. I recalled the earth heaving, buckling, as the darkness boiled forth from it. It had been bigger than any building. Bigger than a village. I knew I'd barely glimpsed part of it. Whatever it was, we couldn't fight it, any more than a bee fights a bear. But then, I wasn't any ordinary kind of bee, and neither was Sanvaunt.

'Whatever he is, nothing's invulnerable,' I said. 'What is he?'

Maldouen's metal face couldn't smirk, but by the way the steel head re-angled on its neck, I felt it anyway.

'He is the malice of ten thousand years, flushed with broken pride and the sting of defeat. He has taken many forms, and he has won great victories and been defeated in his turn. Such is the way of immortals. But that was long ago. He fled imprisonment in his old world, only to find himself here. He has made himself king of the Fault, and the Faded bow to him—whatever they have come to be.'

'How do we kill him?'

Maldouen produced the memory of a laugh. I couldn't blame him for thinking me naïve.

'We will try. The greater part of Iddin has lain dormant these past five thousand years, but as the Crowns failed, someone from your world reached out to him. A kindred spirit. He dream-bound himself into your world. And now he is waking up.'

I turned my attention to the broad circular table in the centre of the room. A map had been drawn across it.

'Is this the Fault?' I asked.

'This? No. This is your world. This bit here.' And he took a long, thin cane and tapped at a tiny spot on the map. 'This is your homeland, Harran.'

'It looks so small,' I said.

'It is small,' Maldouen said. 'Even by the standards of your world, it's a country of near insignificance. This here is the Dharithian Empire.' He

circled the stick around land masses a thousand times or more greater than
Harran.

'It might be small, but it's my small bit of country, and I don't intend to
let Ovitus LacNaithe take it for his own.'

'That's Grandmaster Ovitus LacNaithe, now,' Maldouen said. There was
something in the metal voice that emanated from his unmoving mouth.
Amusement? 'Redwinter belongs to him now. For however long your world
has left.'

'What do you mean?'

'You can't have missed the earth tremors here. The way that the Fault's
energy is slowly draining upwards into that vortex,' he said. 'Where do you
think that vortex leads? I built five Crowns to contain the Fault, binding it
between your world and what you call the Night Below. But the Fault is collapsing into your world, and soon it will be gone. Your world and the Fault
will be as one.'

'Then nobody has taken the Crown?'

'Nobody has control of *any* of the Crowns,' Maldouen said. 'Yours was
the last standing.'

I was caught in a moment, the reddish light of the Fault turning the map
before me to rose, the world caught out of time. Maldouen was unmoving, as still and silent as the mountains that backed the palace. My existence seemed to pause in a sense of profound and utter displacement. This
was what it must feel like to realise a lover has conducted a secret affair, I
thought. A certainty, a surety held so dear, broken to the shards of a dream
that had been shattered long ago, only the pieces had held their shape a
while as you never saw the cracks.

There were five Crowns. It was common knowledge. There's a surety in
numbers, less importance tied to a single epicentre of trust. How could
mighty Brannlant have lost control of its Crown? How could we? The others,
Ithatra, Khalacant and Osprinne, had seemed so distant, places that existed
only in conception. That had made them unchanging. To believe that one
could be weakened was bad enough, to know that it could be uncontrolled,
terrible. For all five to be gone was unthinkable, and yet, I had to think it.

'How can you know that?' I asked.

'I can project myself from this world to yours, just as your friend can,
though I have seldom shown my face as she does.'

'You mean the Queen of Feathers?' I said.

'It's a sweet name for a being that has wrought so much terrible destruction as she has,' Maldouen said. 'But as apt a name as any.'

'An ally of mine knew her as Ravilaine,' I said. 'Ally' might have been a bit strong for Alianna, whose ghost had ridden around with me for a day.

'True names! Your kind and the Eldritch Kin are so bothered with the naming of things. Where I came from, where I was made, they meant next to nothing. Our greatest wizards lived through all their long existences nameless. But here the rules are different.'

'But you know her. You know where I can find her?'

'Ah, well that is a complex question,' Maldouen said. 'She has existed here from time to time, and she was drawn into it when I banished the Riven Queen's forces here. Caught in the undertow, so to speak. But I suspect she's even older than I am.'

This was not news to me. I'd seen her in my dreams, in the memories of Song Seondeok, of Serranis, Lady of Deserts.

'How old are you?' I asked.

'One doesn't tend to celebrate birthdays when there are no seasons, and no days. I lost track somewhere.' He raised a hand as I went to speak. 'No, don't try to work it out. In some ways I prefer not to know. It is galling, to have lived so long, and to be so utterly powerless now, at the end of all things.'

'No end's been decided,' I said fiercely. 'Not while I'm alive.'

'But you've died three times,' Maldouen said.

'That doesn't seem to be stopping me,' I said. I was growing frustrated with his self-pitying tone. 'Tell me where I can find the Queen of Feathers. If you aren't going to help us put things right, then she can.'

'And how will you do that?' Maldouen asked.

'I'm going to escape this place,' I said, letting the heat rise in my throat and spill into my words. 'I'm going back to Redwinter, and I'm going to crush Ovitus's soul into shreds. And when I've torn him apart, I'll enter the Blackwell, take the Keystone down to the Crown and find some poor fool keen enough to wear a circlet of gold and jewels that they'll take the burden of the Crown.'

'And what then?' Maldouen snapped. 'One Crown is not enough. The Faded took control of the Brannish Crown sometime in the last year. The serpent queens of Khalacant have fallen. The Dharithian Crown in Osprinne went long ago.'

'Then we retake them,' I said.

'Do you think I made five Crowns on a whim? There must be *five Crowns* or the magic breaks. It has been a slow erosion, ever since the loss of Ithatra. How do you think Sul, the Faded Lord, managed to escape into your world? The Crowns have been bleeding out for centuries. It is over. I lost!'

'*You* lost?' I said angrily. 'We retake them. We take them back one by one.'

'It is impossible,' Maldouen said. 'I made a critical error.' He slammed a steel fist down against the table, stone breaking, cracks radiating out. 'I built one of the Crowns in Ithatra. The ley lines were right for it, but I didn't account for the shifting of the earth. Ithatra sank beneath the ocean decades ago. Every man, woman and child of that nation was swept away to drown by great waves. Even if you could put a puppet in Harranir, and three more could be retaken from the Faded Lords that control them now—and they are formidable in their own right—the fifth lies beneath an ocean. Nobody can reach it. Nobody can control it. When Ithatra drowned, the Faded Lords began to find their ways out of the Fault, and one by one they took control of the Crowns. Only Harranir's Crown remains unclaimed. Look out there. The merging of the Fault with your world will only increase in speed.' I had never thought to see a steel statue shudder, but the metal joints rattled. 'This place was once in another world, the remnant of a catastrophic war. Long after the war was forgotten, its damage continued to grow. To spread. My original form was already ancient then, and I thought I could save that world by tearing this place away and sealing it in a dimension of its own. But I had not counted on the existence of another world. In my ignorance my spellcraft placed it alongside your own. Too close! A cosmic error of pride and arrogance, and it would have consumed your world long ago had Serranis not raised the fallons, and then when they were not enough, my Crowns, to contain it.'

'The fallons are part of the Crowns?' I had seen fallons all my life, the great stone pillars that dotted the landscape. I had fought beneath one at Tor Marduul. They had been the work of Serranis, Lady of Deserts, one of the dark empresses the Queen of Feathers had stood beside. One of her failures. I had not known her reach stretched so far across the world.

'They were a first attempt to bind the Fault back,' Maldouen said. 'But they were not enough. When they failed, the Nine Devastations, great primal demons, tore free of the Fault, burying it in what you call the Age of Soot. Even then we contained it. But now? Now there are no great wizards left to you. No great powers to draw upon. It is over, Draoihn. It has been over since before you were born.'

I stood silently for a few moments.

'I don't accept that,' I said. 'The moon horses brought us here for a reason. Iddin said they want to escape. They brought us from our need, but it's their need as well. How long do we have?'

'I would only be guessing.'

'Then guess.'

'Until the Fault collapses into your world? Six of your world's months. Maybe a little less, maybe a little longer. For us? No more than weeks.'

I let his words sink in. No possibility of restoring the Crowns. Three claimed, one lost, one vacant. I wanted him to be wrong, but I'd seen the Fault tearing itself up into the sky. I knew he wasn't.

'Iddin will come for us here before then?'

'Oh, he's coming. I've felt his movement. But he does not traverse this realm quickly. Distances are longer for him here than they are for you. It doesn't make sense, I know, but then you'll have experienced the time distortions here for yourself. Time, distance, everything has always been broken here. You have a few days.'

'Then we have time to prepare. I have time to learn.'

Maldouen traced the cracks in the table, where his fist had sundered stone.

'I was never one to go down without a fight,' he said. 'What do you want to know?'

10

'Your power works through the tunnel,' Maldouen said. 'So your projection must be through the tunnel also. You'll follow the path of the dead.'

We were down in what had once been a wine cellar. It was a cellar for empty barrels and wine racks still, but anything drinkable was long gone. The floor was surprisingly clean. Copper pipes ran across the walls just below the ceiling. Some of them hummed. It was a tranquil atmosphere, hidden from the oppressive red sky. I sat cross-legged on the floor. Maldouen couldn't cross his legs—his limbs didn't bend that way—so he was sat with them splayed in a rather undignified manner.

'And that's how the Queen of Feathers does it?'

'I have no idea,' Maldouen said. 'But it's one path.'

'Do you do it that way?'

'No,' Maldouen said. 'I follow the light. There's light here, just as there is in your own world, and it's the same. No difference at all. Everything is one—isn't that what you Draoihn like to say?'

'How can it be one when we're not in the same world?' I asked.

'It's all one,' he said. 'Every one of the circles you understand. Self, other, energy, mind, life, death, and creation. They're all one thing. Nothing is different to anything else.'

I had listened to many lessons like this in my Draoihn training. When I passed through Eio, the First Gate, I spread myself into the world, made myself wider, thinner. But I only had the First Gate and the Sixth. It would have been pleasant to control Creation, but it was only theoretical, and I'd probably have done more harm than good with it. The Light Above knew, I'd caused enough suffering without it.

'So how do I do it?'

'I've seen into your memories, Raine of Redwinter. You already know. It would take months, maybe years to teach you to project yourself. But you know things you shouldn't, and I do not believe this would not be among them.'

Those memories, those invading dreams—I avoided them. I tried not to focus on them. It unnerved me—no, it *terrified* me—to find myself possessed of knowledge I shouldn't own. Sometimes they were gentle. I recalled the taste of foods I'd never seen, strange fruits with spiky exteriors and sweet, tangy yellow flesh. I sometimes smelled the breath of a lover I'd never known, hot in my face as I ground against him, or the taste of women as I explored things I'd never done in my own life. The soft weight of a cat who had been dear to me—or to Serranis, Lady of Deserts—as it slept in my lap. But it was not all gentle, or welcome. Sometimes I felt the pain of wounds I'd never taken, the fear of impending deaths I'd never suffered. The burning eyes of Faded Lords who'd broken my power, or the rattle of chains I'd been cast down in. That wasn't the worst. I remembered executing helpless prisoners in the aftermath of a battle I'd never fought. The screams of men, women and children in the sack of a city that had perished millennia before my birth. They were all there, these dark and treacherous memories, if I only let my mind go still and allowed them to intrude. Since the moon horse bore us into the Fault, they shuffled at my edges like mice in undergrowth, faint sounds noticed but keeping to their shadows.

The stakes were too high for anything but total commitment to the cause. Maybe Maldouen was right and we couldn't save the world. My heart vied in different directions. Part of me said there was no way to stop such an array of forces against us. We would have needed armies, legions of wizards and warriors. Even if they existed, there was no way to gather them. That part said to try to take pleasure in the things that were left to me. To let myself go, to love, to seek resolution. But it was drowned by the stronger part of me. I'd never expected to live forever, and revenge would have to do. Vengeance on Ovitus LacNaithe. He'd pay for what he'd done to Liara, and to Ulovar, to all of them. Perhaps we'd all die, but seeing his soul torn and dissolved to nothing would have to be enough.

I reached into the shadows, looked for the mice in the undergrowth, allowed the presence of dead memory to wash through me. I saw things there I would not repeat. They were the jumbled memories of the great witch queens of the past. Of Hallenae, the Riven Queen. Of Serranis, Lady of Deserts. Of Song Seondeok, the Golden Empress. Of Unthayla the Damned, who had tried to control Redwinter. And the smaller, gentler memories of Alianna Robilar, my grandmaster's sister, whom I had once gifted my body to for a day, and others like her, were tangled among them as well. All of them had possessed the Sixth Gate as I did. All of them had been as deep in the tunnel. I searched back through those memories, wincing, feeling cuts in my skin as if they were freshly made, until I found what I needed. Alianna hadn't known this power, but the others had. It was as different to each of them as it would be to me, but the principle was always the same. That was how incantations worked. It was more about me than about the world. But I was one with it anyway, wasn't I?

'Be careful,' Maldouen's metallic voice whispered through me. 'When you project yourself, you'll be drawn to moments of high emotion, ones that match your own.'

'Won't I just see what's happening now?'

'Close. But expecting time to run naturally between worlds doesn't make sense, does it? You're not physically moving there. You're going to travel as memory and thought, and those things don't truly exist anyway. You won't go far out of line, but you will find what you wish to. And that should make you wary.'

When I cracked open my eyes I'd been drawing without noticing it. What's more, I hadn't been using inks or a piece of chalk. I'd been gouging tears of night into the air in front of me. They weren't black, as you'd imagine, they were midnight blue and sparkling lights glowed within. I'd seen something like this before, but in the surprise, my mind didn't find the connection. Swirling circles of stars gleamed in slashes in the reality I was making. But what I'd drawn . . .

Some of it was Song Seondeok's, some of it was Hallenae's, some belonged to Serranis. But more still belonged to me. The sigils and symbols I'd cut into reality groaned with the tunnel's endless, deafening cry.

'Spirit of Mercy,' Maldouen's metal voice ushered from beyond them all. He'd backed up against the far wall, putting distance between himself and the voids I'd unwittingly carved. 'Your power . . .' He fell silent and immobile as I held the tears in the world open.

'What now?' I asked, and my voice rasped like a rusted scythe dragged across a fallen headstone.

'Go through,' he said. 'Go through. See. I'll be with you.'

* * * * * *

A woman sat by the dim light of a wood-burning stove in a small, sparsely furnished room. In one hand she had a needle, in the other, a long woollen stocking. A spool of yarn sat in her lap, the dark green not quite a match to the stocking's paler hue. She worked at it deftly, making confident, precise motions. Other patches said this was not the first time she'd done this work, and she performed the business of darning with the same surety I'd seen her use on socks I'd worn as a child. She was thin, the bulk of a long scarf over her shawl doing nothing to hide her malnourishment. Everything about her was sharp and cold despite the stove's heat.

I looked around the little room. I'd seen so many like it before. The bed was a simple wooden frame with a straw-stuffed mattress and thin blankets, no drapes hung to keep the warmth in. A nightstand held a bowl, the remains of thin soup at the bottom. A hairbrush—hard-bristled, a cruel implement that punished the head—sat alongside the stubs of candles. The chair in which she sat was the only other furniture and a pair of walking sticks, cut rough from young trees, rested against the wall. It had been many years since I'd seen her but she seemed no different at all.

'Can she see us?' I asked. Maldouen stood beside me. We were both ghostly in blue, wisps of vapour rising slowly from our spectral bodies.

'Only if you want her to,' Maldouen said. 'But to push yourself further across the boundary is rife with dangers. Push too far and you'll tear yourself in two.'

I looked at my mother, at this quiet life in a scribe house cell I didn't recognise, and I felt something I hadn't felt in a long, long time.

I'd abandoned her, back when I was barely in my teenage years, in a place much like this. She'd raised me with a whip-like tongue. I don't think she'd known how to be kind, but she fed me and taught me her skills. Mama had never tried to hide that she blamed me for twisting her bones when she birthed me. Something had gone awry inside her, and she couldn't walk or stand for more than a few minutes before the pain got too much for her. When I was little, I'd blamed myself for it too. Then when I got older I'd resented the unfairness of it. But she must have loved me, in her own way, even if she wasn't able to show it. Even if it hurt her all the more to do it.

I once thought that when I'd left her to join the sooth-sisters and their daft little fortune-telling cult it had been to make my own way in the world, to find a different life. But looking at her now, older and arguably wiser, that hadn't been true. I'd been unable to bear this life. I'd abandoned her to it, leaving the cutting words and admonishments behind me, striking out to live in a gentler world. That had not gone as I'd planned it. I'd got the sisters killed, and since then I'd broken laws, and laid waste to those that opposed me. I'd killed and killed again. For just a moment, it struck me that had I never left this bitter woman, perhaps Ovitus wouldn't have turned out the way he did. Perhaps he wouldn't have burned with humiliation. Perhaps Liara would still be alive.

No. His crimes were his and his alone. I couldn't let myself feel that way.

'If you want to talk to her, you can project a little further,' Maldouen said. 'But gently. Just a touch of you against the world. Push too hard and you'll rip down the middle—you're still in the Fault. Most of you, anyway.'

'No,' I said. In some other place, tears wet my eyes. 'No, it would only terrify her. It's best I leave her be.'

I felt the guilt crushing down on me. Before Ovitus's betrayal, I'd been living a blessed life among the Draoihn. Money undreamed of had been offered to me without thought while Mama scribed away, scraping watery soup from a bowl. My worries had been who I hadn't kissed, and how I fit into high society. I could have changed her life, if only I'd known where to find her. I'd made no effort to do so. I'd been a terrible daughter, no matter how she'd treated me.

For a moment she looked up, right towards us. For a moment I thought she was looking right at me, but the door had opened behind us. A red-faced man wearing the ring of a senior scribe raised his brows expectantly.

'The brewers just dropped off their accounts,' he said. 'Need them drawn up by morning to submit to the thail.'

Mama's eyes narrowed. And there it was, that flash of the whip beneath them that I'd seen and feared on a daily basis.

'That sot brings them here, now, expecting them done in the cursed hours? He can fry his prick. Tell him to go crap on them.'

The scribe master blew out a slow breath.

'An hour after dawn I want them in my hand,' he said. 'An hour after dawn!' He shut the door behind him.

Mama put down the sock she was mending. All the viciousness drained from her face and I saw how tired she was. How exploited. How, as she put her darning aside and took hold of her canes, she feared the walk down to her scribing desk. Nothing is as easy or one-sided as we think it is. I'd never seen this look in her eyes before. I wondered if anybody had.

'I don't remember my mother,' Maldouen said. 'I doubt anyone does, now.'

'I've seen enough of this,' I said. 'I want to see something else.'

'You're the one in control,' Maldouen said. 'What do you want to see?'

The tunnel's hollow, grinding echo reverberated around me as I found the threads of death across the world. My lips drew back, and I pressed my tongue up hard against my teeth.

'Show me Ovitus LacNaithe,' I whispered.

* * * * * *

I hadn't expected so many people. The abrupt lurch through the tunnel, the sudden dark rush quicker than I'd imagined it would be. I could feel my mind growing tired even as we arrived there, the recuperation of the bath and a solid dose of sleep already being ground away. I was in the great hall in the king's own castle in Harranir, or some spirit part of me was. At least, it had been King Quinlan's hall before age took him. It was alive with soldiers now, retainers of every rank, and a small group of Winterra, Redwinter's own armoured warriors. Mercenary captains from Kwend and Garathenia brushed shoulders with Brannish generals as they talked in small huddles or examined accounting ledgers.

Behind them all, the Great Seal that protected the Crown remained closed. Thirty feet wide, it was a disc set an arm-length down into the floor. Its face was plainer than I'd expected it to be, no runes or sigils decorating it, but a number of tools had been discarded around its edges. Blunted picks, broken chisels. A team of miners in sleeveless jerkins sat off to one side, exhausted, frustrated.

'No Keystone, no Crown,' Maldouen breathed through me. He sounded smug.

And there he was, the royal piece of shit himself. Ovitus knelt on the far side of the Great Seal. He was even thinner than he had been the last time I'd seen him, his hair a little longer. He wore robes of state, a collection of heavy silver chains around his neck and a silver circlet around his brow. His face was red, his eyes wild.

In a blaze of hatred, I reached for the power within me, the souls contained within the prison I'd made for them. But they were distant, back beyond a barrier I couldn't reach through. I was powerless here. Panic drilled through me. I'd become so accustomed to them, it was like suddenly finding myself on a battlefield and discovering my weapons and armour had been left in the camp.

'You're just a projection,' Maldouen said calmly. 'You aren't really here. And the souls feeding your rite are back in the Fault.'

'I know I can reach through somehow,' I said angrily. 'The Queen of Feathers did it. She tore apart a bridge.' She'd punished me too, once.

'Ah,' Maldouen said. 'You meant to kill him?'

I didn't answer. I hadn't intended to kill Ovitus, not here and now. I wanted to be there in person when I did it. I wanted him to face his people and all that he'd done against them, and to see all his works come to nothing. But mostly I wanted to see his pain. I wanted his humiliation. I wanted him to see that which he had always feared was true. Let him know that he was unlovable, unworthy and alone. But when I'd seen him standing there, alive and free, the rage had roared within me like a bonfire showered with sawdust, the flames fed and billowing. I remembered Liara, blasted with lightning and dead on the ground. I remembered Ulovar as Robilar cut his throat. I remembered the stake at my back as I stood waiting to be burned alive. Had I been able to reach through and tear into his throat with my teeth—

'Stop that,' Maldouen said. 'Strain too far and you'll tear yourself apart. You aren't in this world. Remember that.'

For a few moments more the power of the Sixth Gate swelled back, beyond this mortal world, trying to press through. But I knew he was right. I let my grip unfurl back in the Fault, and the Sixth Gate grew quiet in my mind once more.

'I've seen it done,' I said. 'If the Queen of Feathers could do it . . .'

'Then she was using magic that didn't rely on a supply of indentured souls,' Maldouen said. 'You're new to this. Show some caution, if you want to last a little longer.' I felt old memories pressing close, other women's memories, reminding that he was right. A busy-looking woman carrying away broken tools walked through Maldouen, causing him to ripple, vapour trails rising from his form. 'Ugh. That was unpleasant. I'd forgotten how that feels.'

I stepped around those that got in my way, until I stood before Ovitus, in the middle of the Great Seal. The scar he'd taken from a boar hunt stood jagged on his face. For a moment I was reminded of my own scar, the one running across my cheek and nose, a wrong-angle, cut by a slash of Hazia's knife back when all this began. We weren't much different in age. When I'd first met Ovitus he'd been bumbling, unsure of himself and so naïve, barely more than a boy. The man who seemed to be mere feet away from me had lost his youth to his own actions. He was hard-faced, weary around the eyes. How much of that boy was still inside him?

It was a question that wouldn't matter once I had his soul.

A Draoihn in Winterra armour approached, leading a message-runner in LacNaithe green-and-black breacan. His boots were spattered with winter mud, but his face was grave. Ovitus cast a glance at them both, reading their faces. Neither seemed keen to relay whatever it was they had to say. Ovitus's expression darkened.

'Just tell me,' he said.

'There is good news and there is bad,' the Draoihn said. Her hair was flame red, a mass of ringlets falling to her neck. I thought I recognised her— her name had been Namuae. Ovitus grimaced. His fists clenched.

'Is there ever any good news these days? Autolocus once wrote that . . . No, never mind. I'll take the worst of it first,' he said. Draoihn Namuae gestured for the messenger to speak. He wasn't any older than Ovitus and I, twenty at a push. Young, to be delivering grave news to the prince regent, but then, the world was making veterans of us all.

'My lord, Castus LacClune took Dunfenny three nights ago,' he said. 'He took it in a night assault. Garrison casualties were . . . minimal.'

'Dunfenny, lost?' Ovitus said, a little breathless. Like he couldn't believe what he was hearing. 'Councillor Kyrand was in command there. How could she lose it so easily?'

'My lord, Councillor Kyrand was the minimal casualty I spoke of.' He looked around uncertainly. 'It appears the Draoihn under her command mutinied and have joined the rebel forces.'

Ovitus went very still, but everyone in the room felt his fury. His eyes no longer blinked. His fists balled. For a moment I heard Ovitus's Third Gate, Taine, open, and crackles of lightning rippled from his eyes and down his cheeks, shivering through his body. The messenger and Namuae took a few steps back. Ovitus's chest heaved.

'That bastard. That man-fucking, callous little *shit-stain*. I'll have his head. I'll have his balls hung from the gates.'

The messenger swallowed hard. He wasn't even done yet, and he feared his lord's reaction. I was rather enjoying it.

'My lord,' the messenger went on, keen to get it all out and be able to absent himself from Ovitus's display of power. 'The rest of the LacClune and the other rebel forces are marching from Bocknain to join Castus, five thousand all told. They'll be able to attack Harranir within a fortnight, if they press the march.'

'Five thousand?' Ovitus said. A little calm returned, his Third Gate snapping shut. 'With the men we had to release for the winter we still have more than the numbers to match them. The Winterra are loyal, and Castus's army cannot match our numbers in the Third Gate.'

'That's where the better news lies,' the red-haired Draoihn, Namuae, said. 'Two further mercenary companies came in on the eastern coast, nearly three thousand men and a thousand of them are armoured horse. What's more, our Brannish allies will be here within ten days if the weather holds, with another two thousand battle-hardened warriors from the imperial frontier. We'll have more than enough to crush the rebel forces.'

So Kyrand of Murr—a member of the Council of Night and Day and one of the three Draoihn who'd presided over my Testing—was dead. It hadn't been her fault she'd been turned against me, but I didn't mourn her.

I didn't feel it when the world shook—I didn't feel anything here, adrift in an astral body—but everyone else in the room did. The ground heaved, a great rumbling began as masonry dust rained from the ceiling. Cries of 'Tremor!' sounded as officials, warriors and retainers alike took cover beneath the tables. A decorative suit of armour toppled with a crash, a great painting twelve feet wide fell from the wall and clobbered somebody beneath the frame. The tinkling of glass sounded all around as high windows shook free and trolleys of crystal cups fell to shatter against the flagstones.

'It's the Fault,' Maldouen said. Around us the chaos continued. 'It's what you've seen, the bleeding of one world to the next. It's tearing the world apart and remaking it.'

Ovitus alone remained standing, legs spread and feet spaced wide as if challenging the world to unseat him. His arms were outstretched, his Gates ready to keep him upright. He dared whatever came to bring him down. I was uncomfortably reminded that I had done the same only a few days ago, back on the stone head.

'Nobody has opened the Great Seal and controlled the Crown here,' I said. 'They can't do it. They're all at war. Merovech LacClune has the Fourth Gate, he can enter the Blackwell. It can still be stopped.' If they allowed him to. Surely, in the face of this calamity, even Merovech LacClune could have seen that a temporary alliance would have been for the best. But Harran had been plunged into strife. The Draoihn were divided, at war with one another. The whole world would tear itself apart. Ovitus stood there, making himself a rock and daring the ocean to break itself upon him. But the ocean always wins in the end.

As the earth's shaking began to subside, Ovitus let out a furious grunt of disgust.

'Will somebody blast this infernal seal open before the whole world shakes itself to pieces? Where are the Artists? We've yet to try their magic. *Something* has to work.'

Maybe it was his frustration, his loss of dignity and control that made me want to do it. I might not be able to tear Ovitus's soul free, but there was one trick I knew I could work.

I stood before Ovitus and forced my image into the world. I appeared there in the room, ghostly and blue, shimmering and spilling vapour from my shoulders. Ovitus's eyes went wide, and though the world's thundering hadn't staggered him, my sudden appearance did.

'Ovitus LacNaithe,' I hissed. 'I'm coming for you. I'm coming back and I'll tear your soul out, you filthy fucking dog!'

'Raine?' Ovitus gasped. The blood left his face in less than three heartbeats. He staggered back. Around the room, screams. Someone threw a decanter at me, and it passed through without touching any part of me.

'That's right,' I said, and I heard the Sixth Gate turn my voice to something from the Night Below. 'I'm going to rip you apart. I'm going to feed you to the things from the pit. Demons will feast on you and cast you into the freezing rivers of Skuttis for what you've done.'

'Light Above,' Ovitus said. 'Back to the Night Below, you bitch!' He raised both hands and a rope of lightning ripped from them, through me. Behind me, unintended victims screamed in agony.

I laughed. I hadn't laughed in a long time. It didn't sound like me. It sounded like the dreams of other, long-dead women, and my gown fluttered in a wind of my own rage.

'You've no power to stop me,' I said. 'Wherever you go, wherever you try to run from me, I'll find you. Have your headstone cut, Ovitus. Let it read *Here lies a traitor, despised by all.*'

'Raine!' a voice called out. But it was different this time—it was Maldouen, and he sounded panicked. I heard fast steps, the click of claws against the flagstone, and then I saw Ovitus's wolfhound, Waldy, powering towards me. He was bigger than I remembered, much bigger, his fur less aged, his jaws wider and packed with more teeth. He launched towards me, and I would have laughed—but it was only at the last moment I remembered that this was no ordinary dog. Waldy was Ovitus's familiar, or he was its, and just as those jaws closed I managed to interpose my arm against my throat. Waldy's teeth sank down and I felt the pain, in my arm and into the back of my neck as impossibly, the hound's teeth tore through the divide in our worlds and punctured flesh back in the Fault.

'Break the connection,' Maldouen said.

It's you, Waldy said, his words flowing through his teeth and into my arm, transmitting through my spirit and into my mind. *The girl from the Dryad's temple.*

'Iddin,' I gasped as the teeth dug deeper into the flesh of my neck, my arm.

You made it to the Blind Child, that terrible voice said. *Of course you did.*

I unleashed something at it, a half-remembered spell Unthayla the Damned had once used on an assassin, and one of the dog's ears was torn from its head. Its eyes spun in pain but its teeth only clamped down harder.

Everything changed suddenly. I was back in Maldouen's wine cellar, the voids in the air scattered and dissipating around me. Maldouen struck them out of the air with swats of his metal hand. And then I felt something hot on my chest, my arm, something leaving my neck.

'Oh,' I said. I felt the blood pumping out, saw its dark, sticky wash falling across black and gold. I fell onto my back, stared up at the ceiling. 'Would you get Sanvaunt?'

'That thing from the temple is Ovitus's *dog*?'

Esher was horrified. Sanvaunt still had one hand on my neck, another on my arm. He'd patched the essential bits quickly, but this wasn't the first time one of us had taken a semi-lethal wound over six months in the Fault. We were all thankful for Vie, his Fifth Gate trance of life, and none of us would have been here without it. He'd had plenty of practice, and sorting out the outside took time if he didn't want to leave a scar.

Anything short of death is fine . . .

'One part of it is, at least,' I said.

'The part of himself that he managed to force through and out of the Fault,' Maldouen said. 'You see what I meant, Raine, about tearing oneself apart?'

I'd managed to hold the wound in my neck closed just about enough for Esher to bring Sanvaunt. He'd charged into the room, throwing himself down beside me, and sealed the damage, eyes flickering with that inner fire as my veins sealed and flesh re-knit. He'd been out of breath. I'd come close. When I was stable again I'd been carried down to yet another room of surpassing beauty. A grand ballroom, filled with painted statues of dancers in costume the like of which seemed too complex to be clothing. The dancers stood immobile as if frozen in time. They waited for music to begin again, to jolt them out of their stasis as if trapped timelessly in a party game whose rules had been forgotten. It made for an odd sickroom, but that's where I'd crawled to when Maldouen got back with Sanvaunt, so that's where we ended up. I lay on the black-and-white tiles of the ballroom floor, the never-living dancers oblivious to my pain.

'I get it,' I said. 'I don't want to be a dog.'

'Then that—thing—that's been there all that time,' Esher said. 'Waldy saved Ovitus from a boar . . .'

'Sul thought that Waldy was *his* familiar,' I said. My neck fizzed and itched mercilessly as Sanvaunt's warmth flowed through his hand and into my body. 'And Ovitus thought Waldy was his too.' For a moment the flow of healing stopped and a prick of cold ran through me. 'What?' I asked Sanvaunt. He took a long, slow breath and then his Fifth Gate continued again.

'That was the thing that gave Ovitus the power to steal my uncle's Gates,' Sanvaunt said. 'Wasn't it? It gave him that worm that sucked out all of Ulovar's power.'

'Seems that way.'

I could feel a tensing in Sanvaunt's hands. He'd held his fingers softly, supple. They'd turned hard and stiff. That only happened when he was having ideas. He'd gone inward, forgotten his exterior.

'And it knows we're here,' Esher said. 'It's coming for us.'

'Unfortunately, that does seem to be the case,' Maldouen said. He glanced around at his sculpted dancers. 'What a terrible waste. They took me forty-six years to sculpt and paint.'

'Then this is where we make our stand against it,' Sanvaunt said. Hard fingers pressed into me. His voice turned to granite. 'This is where it dies.'

Maldouen played that sound to us, that record of a laugh somebody else had once made. He only had the one. I wondered whether he really felt amused, or if it was all just elaborate puppetry set in motion long ago.

'You want to fight Iddin?' Maldouen said.

'No,' Sanvaunt said. 'I want to kill him.'

'Iddin *is* the Fault,' Maldouen said. 'Bound to it intrinsically. He doesn't even have a singular form.'

'That thing that comes from beneath the earth is his though, isn't it?' Sanvaunt said. His face had taken a dark, shadowed look. 'That monstrous thing. That has a body. If we kill that part of him, it has to weaken him. That's the thing about the world. It's made for breaking.'

'Sounds like honey and wine,' I said, pushing Sanvaunt's hand away. 'But that's not what we're here for. We need the Queen of Feathers' help. We need to get to the City of Spires. Gigantic burrowing darkness things can wait until after we find a way back home, stop the approaching apocalypse, put that treacherous little shit's head on a spike and get laid.'

Sanvaunt took his hands from me. Hard as they'd been, I missed their warmth.

'I want to take a shot at him.'

'Then please do it somewhere else,' Maldouen said. 'I've spent a long time making this place habitable. Perhaps climactic battles could happen elsewhere.' He sounded exhausted by us. Maybe it was just metal fatigue. I thought that was funny, but doubted he'd appreciate the joke.

'You can help us,' Esher said. 'I know you can.'

Maldouen didn't move. He sat entirely motionless. The sounds of gears and cogs ticking inside him spread out to dance among the motionless dancers.

'It is not just art I have spent my years creating,' he said. 'I . . . do have weapons.'

Esher took Maldouen's silver hand in both her own.

'Any help you can give us. Any chance at all is better than none.'

The Blind Child's head squeaked as it fell to hang forward. Just the approximation of a human emotion, but he was well made.

'I know,' he said. 'I have to. But it won't be enough.'

· · · · · ·

Maldouen had spent seven hundred and fifty-two years inside a trap of his own devising. I could imagine the endless, nightless days, the crawling of silent, lonely moments, but I doubted that any imagination I brought forth could do them justice. In that lonely time he'd crafted works of unsurpassed beauty. I had never had any aptitude for artistic pursuits. Even the pages I worked my incantations on came out bitter to the eye. The armaments Maldouen had crafted were things I understood.

Beneath his palace, rows of armour stood in gleaming ranks, worn by the simplest stone mannequins—and yet they were works of art in their own right. Some of it was simple, practical. Some of it was ostentatious and elaborate, jutting with spikes and horns. One had been moulded with a horse's head atop the visored helm, another a snarling wildcat. They filled the hall, hundreds of them, an inert army on parade. Weapons of every type filled racks to either side of them.

'It puts Redwinter's armoury to shame,' Sanvaunt said. He ran his fingers admiringly over a perfectly smooth, rounded pauldron.

'I wouldn't bother with that one,' Maldouen said. 'It's actually made from silver. Utterly useless in a fight. I didn't really think any of these were going to get used.'

'You made them for adults,' Esher said. 'Not yourself.'

Maldouen's repeated-laugh echoed through the chamber.

'If something can damage me, nothing I made here would make any difference. I may be small but I'm hardy.'

'Why did you make this version of you to be a child?' I asked. It was a cold question, perhaps. Maldouen didn't outwardly appear to take offence, but since he wasn't able to make facial expressions, he wouldn't.

'I think I was bitter,' he said. 'I got stuck in a body like this a long time ago. The original body is even harder to kill than this one. I think had he made me in his old image, he'd have been jealous. Petty, but I never was a very good kind of person.'

'But you made all these,' Esher said. 'All these beautiful things. They're for other people.'

The silver statue fell silent at that, and Esher's face showed all the sadness she felt for him. Thinking of him, alone, friendless, day after day, year after year, forging and crafting. Empathy. She was filled with it. There'd been times I'd thought empathy to be a weakness. The Queen of Feathers had told me that I had to make of myself an island, that for one such as me, I had to be alone. I felt it. I knew it. There would come a time when I had to abandon these two people, these two, wonderful, kind, fierce, solid, determined people. I got it, now. Understood it all. When Maldouen had explained how his Crowns had fallen, the knowledge had slowly risen up through me.

The world wasn't doomed. Not in the way he thought. I had to bring about a different kind of apocalypse. And the woman who brought that down could have no empathy at all.

'These are all mundane weapons,' I said as I looked over the swords, spears, axes, bows.

'I assure you, they're not,' Maldouen said.

'I had something bigger in mind. We need the Lance.'

'The Lance and Crown that defeated the Riven Queen?' Maldouen said. There was a sense of pride in his voice. 'Yes, the Lance would be helpful here. But it's gone. It was only good for one shot. Even after the Sarathi broke apart her incanted protections, Hallenae's defences were formidable. The Lance was destroyed. They buried the pieces of it after the battle.'

'Can you make another? A Lance that can strike Iddin down?'

'Making that thing cost people their lives. It took me half a war to construct it,' Maldouen said. 'There are some things better left unmade.'

'Would have been useful about now,' I said.

'You're going to fight,' Maldouen said. 'Because that's what you know. You've no way to reach the City of Spires, and Iddin comes for you now. I'm offering what I can because I have nothing else to do. But we are not going to win. Even with the Lance. Had I the time and means to craft an incantation a mile wide, driven into the bones of the world—perhaps I might weaken him. But there is no time, and there are no means. Take what you want from this place. The Fault will suck it all up through into the sky in time anyway.'

He turned and walked down among the aisles of weaponry.

'He's not right, is he?' Esher said. She looked so fierce on a battlefield, but here, all wrapped up in fresh clothes that weren't hers, hair washed and brushed, face clean for the first time in what seemed like it had been all our lives, she just looked her age. Nineteen years old. There were some nations where she wouldn't even be marrying age yet. I was younger on the outside, but I knew that even washed and scrubbed as I was, I didn't cast that youthful glow. I was scars and brimstone. Poison and vitriol. I tried to find words. I didn't have any.

'No conclusion is foregone,' Sanvaunt said. 'Raine shouldn't have beaten Kaldhoone LacShale, but she did it. I shouldn't have been able to fight the Remnant Sul, but I gave him a run for his money. And you shouldn't have been able to sweep into Redwinter and call down a moon horse. But we're still alive. We're alive and we're fighting and I won't let the Fault take our world. We're strong individually. Together, we're unstoppable.'

'Are you sure?' Esher asked. Sanvaunt took her hand. There was no softness in those hands. They were nicked, scabbed, scarred and calloused. They were worn and hard, but there was gentleness in their touch.

'Nobody's really sure of anything,' he said. 'But I'm sure about you.'

I felt a beam of staggering, white-light pain punch right through my lungs. For a moment I couldn't breathe. The way he looked at her. The way she found comfort in his words. In his eyes. Six months. Battle brings you close to each other. You bond in ways you can never experience with anyone else. I'd seen it, known it was growing, and I'd told myself—nothing. I'd ignored it. I'd blinded myself to it.

It hurt so, so much to see it so clearly. I saw it in the fear, and the grit and the perseverance. I saw it in the momentary lingering of touch.

It wasn't fair, but I felt my anger direct towards Esher rather than Sanvaunt. She was my best friend. The betrayal—it felt like a betrayal, though I'd burned them both long ago and they owed me nothing—sang from her, not from him. *I am an island,* I told myself. *Damn them both, I don't need them. I don't need anyone. And nobody could love me after what I'm going to do.*

It was for the best. That didn't mean it didn't burn.

They realised it. Their hands broke apart, that terrible, absurd embarrassment suddenly descending as I stalked away to look along the racks. I felt my lip wavering, my eyes grown hot, some part anger and some part grief. These were good weapons. I moved to the bows. Six months of killing our way through the Fault had grown my meagre skills. I'd gone through many scavenged weapons in that time: swords, axes, spears, but bows had been hard to come by. Things of metal and stone lasted better than strings, which the half-dead had presumably worn out down the centuries. The first I saw was black wood with silver fittings, taller than I was even unstrung. Not useful. The second was recurved, and gleamed like mother-of-pearl. The third, red veined with green, seemed slick with some kind of mucus. I didn't fancy even touching that one. There were at least a hundred more in the row.

'You'll want this one,' Maldouen's hollow voice called from down the aisle. I stopped considering a bow that seemed to be pure ivory and walked down to join him. He'd lifted down a bow of white wood, the grip bound in some kind of reptile's silver-black skin. The stave was that rare white wood, cut with neat red rows of runic sigils, the same as the arrows I'd discovered in the Blackwell. I reached out to take it, but Maldouen suddenly held it back.

'What is it?'

'I made this for *her*,' he said. 'Back when I thought we might be allies.'

'The Queen of Feathers?'

'I cut the wood from a stave she once carried,' he said. 'Be careful with it.'

'We don't have long to figure anything out,' I said. I reached to take it from him, but his grip was solid around it. Trying to budge that metallic child was like trying to pull a brick from a wall.

'Time is short,' he agreed. 'Running would keep you alive longer than fighting.'

The Blind Child would have been staring at me, had he possessed eyes. But the blindfold was just sculpted steel on a sculpted head.

'I don't know why you'd expect me to have an answer for that,' I said. He relinquished his grip. I strung the bow with a cord that seemed unusually thick, woven from a braid of bark string. She fitted me well, but with a pang of regret I missed Midnight, the bow I'd stolen from the Blackwell. She'd been powerful and deadly with her string of silver moonlight. She'd known me before I was a monster.

'What is she called?' I asked.

'Weapons are named by those who take them up, not those who forge them,' Maldouen said. I thought about it for a moment, considering the gleaming black limbs, the faint odour of cold, wet charcoal that rose from them.

'This all started when I found blood in the snow,' I said. 'I'll call her Winter.' The bow seemed to purr in my hand. It approved.

'I've arrows for you too.'

'Stone-headed?'

Maldouen nodded.

'Runes and all. It sounds like you may have encountered some of my work before.'

'I have, and I found it to my liking,' I said. 'Now. Armour me.'

'You don't need any armour from me,' Maldouen said. 'Or you shouldn't. I don't understand it, but—Raine Wildrose, when you cut those sigils in the air itself—you have access to more power than the Riven Queen had. More power than I've ever seen a single Draoihn carry. You know things you shouldn't. But if you know how to scry, then you should know the Witching Skin. An armour of souls is stronger than even my creations, stronger than Draoihn artificed diamond-steel. If there's anything that stands a chance against Iddin, it's you. But only if you allow yourself to be free.'

I stood in the cold of the armoury for several moments. Thinking. Wondering.

'I'll take steel nonetheless.'

. . . . . .

I kept things light, no clanking full harness for me. Maldouen had crafted a mail shirt with rings so small and tight it was almost as consistent as a woollen blanket. Whatever spellcraft he'd wrought, it moved silently, although he'd not done anything to offset the weight. It had been intended for a larger person—although a surprising amount had been designed to fit a woman's figure, this wasn't one of them. Maldouen took it away, promising that within a night he could alter it to my proportions.

Sanvaunt seemed to be in his element. The armour he'd chosen was all-encompassing, a style I'd never seen before. I doubted anyone in Harran had. The pauldrons, gauntlets and helm were all ostentatious things, formed in a likeness of draconic fury. It was much more showy than I would normally have expected from Sanvaunt.

'Never thought you'd pick something quite so ostentatious,' I said, grinning. We were at the far end of the long armoury hall. Esher had disappeared off somewhere, leaving us alone. It was dim in the armoury, the light globes set up to cast dramatic shadows from the mailed and gauntleted statues. Sanvaunt's face was pale, distant in the strange, red-hued light.

'I never believed in asking for attention for its own sake,' he said, laying the cuirass down carefully. 'This was the best fit, and offers the best protection. It's practical.'

'Admit it though,' I said. 'It's quite fun to dress up as a dragon.'

Sanvaunt looked slightly embarrassed and made a face as if to say *Don't be so absurd,* but I could tell from the little quirk around his mouth he agreed.

'I know one shouldn't complain while counting one's acres,' he said. 'And yes, of course I'd rather have been born into the wealth and power of the LacNaithe clan, even as a wildrose. But there've been times I've wished I was less visible. That fewer people cared what I did or didn't do.'

'I know. That's why you didn't let your name out and wore a mask in *Demon Lord Croak,*' I said. 'So you could get on stage and be invisible.'

Sanvaunt smiled sadly.

'Could you?' he asked, gesturing to the rows of buckles that fastened the back of his gambeson. I began picking the metal latches apart. His shoulders had grown broad, more heavily muscled in the last months. He was losing that wolfish litheness and gaining a new kind of bulk that performed no less well for him. 'You're not wrong,' he said. 'And when I wrote those romances—of which we shall never speak again after this moment—it was the same. They weren't meant for anyone else.'

With a click the last buckle came undone and he shrugged out of the padded undercoat.

'You should have let me read them,' I said. Sanvaunt reddened but laughed a little.

'It all feels a long time ago now.'

'I snuck into your room and read them anyway,' I said. 'Does that make you feel uncomfortable?'

'I know you read them,' Sanvaunt said, reaching down to pick up his shirt.

'Not then,' I said. I caught his arm as he began sticking it down one of the arm holes. 'Later. After. I found your pages and I carried them back to my room, when you were gone.' And with his arms all bound up in the shirt, I pushed into him, backing him three steps until he came into contact with the wall. I leaned in close to see the complete and utter shock on his face. He'd been less surprised by the dead bursting from the ground than he was by my sudden aggression, my warm breath in his face, flecks of my saliva dotting against his cheek. I leaned up to whisper to him. 'How does it feel to imagine me, reading what you wrote about and imagining that I was Roanna? Imagining you were Dylaine? "I didn't save you from a witch just so you could ignore me, my lord. I'll have you as I want."'

Sanvaunt was wide-eyed, confused by this sudden change of events. But why not? Why shouldn't I have a handsome boy, why not ride him on the armoury floor? What did any of it matter anyway? It's not like he was going to be my first. I reached down between his legs and—and found a hard knob of steel where I should have found something equally hard but less metallic. I laughed.

'Let's get this off you, my brave, strong hammer of a man,' I said, a hot, breathy whisper that promised my body. It had floated into me from somewhere else. Someone else's conquest, a thousand years ago, more. But it felt right just then. I felt the surging passion and excitement of another woman, another lover, mingled with my own. I'd lusted for Sanvaunt long enough. Why ought a woman like me have to deny herself? He wanted me, still, even with the scarring, the terrible things I'd done. In fact, a part of me knew his own twisted wants. I'd killed so many people, done such wicked things, become such a terrible, dreadful creature—bedding me, holding me down and grinding himself into me, making me wet, making me open, dominating and conquering me—it wasn't just his desire. It was his obsession.

'Stop,' he said. Sanvaunt had managed to get his hands free of his shirt and he took my wrists and pulled them to my sides. Not that I was getting anywhere through his metal codpiece.

'You don't want to stop,' I hissed at him.

'This isn't it,' he said. 'Not here and now. And there's more than the two of us to think about.'

'Esher?' I purred at him. I knew I sounded like some kind of slithering, seductive monster. A Drowner, maybe. 'Who's to say I don't plan to have her right after I have you? Take the steel off. Show it to me. Put it in me. Make me weak. Make me beg you.'

'Raine,' Sanvaunt said harshly. He pushed me away. His face was reddened, sweating. 'Don't be cruel. This isn't you.'

'Oh, fuck you, and fuck her,' I said angrily. 'I'm so sick of all this *caring*. Can't I for once just not care at all?'

'Sanvaunt's right,' Esher said. She hadn't been gone so very far as I thought. 'And next time you decide you want to, what was it, *have me right after,* maybe you should ask whether I'd appreciate that? Not like this, Raine. Never like this. Your gentleness is all used up. I'm not some witch queen's plaything. Especially not one from centuries ago, whichever one you feel you are today.'

That took me aback. All the hot passion drained from me like a ruptured wineskin.

'What do you mean?'

'We're not fools, Raine,' Sanvaunt said. Esher moved to stand beside him. Their anger radiated in waves, but the world was about to end. What did I care?

I cared a lot.

Forget those idiots!

But I loved them.

But I hate everything and everyone and I'm going to destroy them all.

I'm going to destroy *everything*.

The floor beneath us shook.

I took another bath. I cried a little. I slept some more. I was awoken by one of the great, terrible tremors. From a high window I looked out across the Fault. Above the City of Spires, dead trees, a tower, bits of wall and mud and water, and the hand of a giant, fallen statue, spiralled up into the sky and the vortex whorl at the heart of its shattering. The essence of the Fault bleeding through to home.

I left my room and went to find Esher and Sanvaunt. I wouldn't be embarrassed. I refused to waste any time on that. So I'd taken a shot, and it hadn't paid off. The story was told across the real world ten thousand-thousand times a day. Big fucking deal.

I wore the gold and black again, though the metallic servant had several alternative outfits for me. I was beginning to feel like it suited me rather well. I left the stockings off. The riding boots came above the knee, and the split in the gown's front would show a little thigh if I walked like a harlot. It was provocative. Deliberate. I was well aware. I was angry, whether at myself or Sanvaunt or Esher or all of us wasn't clear, but it was there—maybe it was just fear. Anger and fear are two sides of the same coin, in the end. Maybe I feared that I'd taken things too far. I'd pushed at them, my friends. Had I really believed that Sanvaunt was going to have me in the armoury, up against a wall or over a rack of magic swords? Had I been *so* confident that Esher was gone? I hadn't even thought about it. Not consciously.

Maybe I'd known she was there. It is a terrible thing to be so uncertain about one's own thoughts. So I left a bit of upper leg on show. A man in the same situation would have left his shirt unbuttoned. And yet—when I'd looked at myself in the mirror maybe there was more to it than just taunting them. I liked the way I looked like this. Since the night a knife had cut its wrong-angle scar across my cheek, since my hair had turned from dark to ice-blue white, my place in the world had seemed so uncertain, and I'd rarely liked what I'd seen. I'd tried wearing glamours as Esher had shown me, we'd worn one another's clothes, and I'd loved how close to her that had made me feel. But I'd never felt so much myself as I did now, in decadent, ancient black and gold. Displaying a little leg made me feel powerful. Desirable, even in this wretched world of swamp and violence. It was how I was meant to be.

They didn't bat an eyelid as I waltzed into the map tower. Cowards. The cracks Maldouen's fist had made were still messing up some part of the world I'd never heard of. I wasn't the only one who'd been finding themselves in Maldouen's apparently extensive wardrobe. Esher wore a pale blue dress more appropriate to a summer evening party than another red-skied day in the Fault, with sandal straps that wrapped her legs nearly to the knee. It was not the kind of dress that a priest would approve of. She hadn't bothered to style her hair, and its chaotic tumble nearly caused me to trip over my toes. As for Sanvaunt, I don't believe anyone could have shown me another man who could pull off black leather trousers and a puff-sleeved white shirt and make it look like he cared so little. He'd left the shirt, which was patterned with copper griffins, half-buttoned.

I was not the only one who'd come to the battle-map dressed for war, it seemed. If Maldouen hadn't been all shiny chrome I'd have thought somehow he was managing to find us amusing. It *was* amusing, and frankly, I suddenly felt overdressed.

'Right then,' I said, 'since we're not doing the other thing let's talk about how we kill the king of the Fault.'

'He may not come alone,' Maldouen said. 'Iddin is the lord of the Lesser Faded. Even the Faded Lords will do his bidding—though reluctantly.'

'What do we do if he brings five Faded Lords with him?' Sanvaunt asked.

'I think we die,' I said. 'But let's at least try to take some of them down with us.'

'Iddin will not bring his Lords,' Maldouen said. 'The Faded Lords have no love for him. They do not wish for a king, they wish to rule themselves. If they believe that there's a possibility that Iddin could meet his end here they'll sit back and allow it. Iddin and I have always avoided direct confrontation. I was wrong, you see. That he risks coming here now means that he fears something.'

'What could he possibly fear?'

'Raine,' Esher said. She smiled sadly as she switched her gaze to me.

Apologetic. 'It's not Maldouen Iddin fears, he's been here all along. It's not Sanvaunt. He's heart bonded to you, and he has the Fifth Gate, but he's not the first to wield that power.'

'He commands the Anam Teine,' I said. 'Life-fire. It's stronger in him than it was even in Robilar, or Kelsen. Why shouldn't Iddin fear that?'

'It's still not enough,' Sanvaunt said. 'I was *almost* a match for a Faded Lord. *One* of them. This king of the Fault rules them. I'm not the threat. It's you he fears, Raine. Maybe not just Raine alone. Maybe it's you, and Hallenae, and Song Seondeok, and Serranis Lady of Deserts.'

'What do you know of it?' I snapped. It was the Riven Queen's temper that flared, as though mention of her name had brought her more strongly to mind. That girl had been born with a razor in her mouth.

'You used to dream of them,' Sanvaunt said. 'But I think we all know it's different now.'

'It is,' I said. I shrugged. It didn't matter if they knew anymore. 'They're with me. All the time, I think. All those great tyrannical queens and empresses, and a bunch more who got stopped before their power grew enough to make a name.'

'Can they hear us now?' Esher asked. She seemed to pale at the idea.

'It's not like that,' I said. 'They're not passengers. They're not even separate. Sometimes I feel their memories. Sometimes I feel old emotions. Yes, yes like what happened in the armoury.' I snapped that last. 'I'm not even sure how much of that was me. Some of it. Maybe some of it was Song Seondeok, or Unthayla, or Alianna. I don't know. It's like—like I'm too many people.'

'You carry the souls of the dead within you,' Maldouen said.

'But it should only be those that I've taken,' I said. 'It's different. They're apart from me. And when I remember those things from the past—I'm not always *them*. Sometimes I'm watching through the Queen of Feathers' eyes. But I still feel what they felt. I understand what they want. I can learn the things they knew, if I focus on them.'

And they could hurt me, if I let them. Not just me, but those around me that I cared for. I was trying not to think of the shame of what I'd done in the armoury. I'd never been immune to jealousy, and I could be cruel. I wasn't unaware of that. But what I'd done had gone further, into the self-destructive. I'd tried to turn my value onto my body, tried to wield it against

Sanvaunt as a taunt, against Esher as a weapon. Those long-dead queens had felt no remorse at doing such. I knew that in some times, in some distant places, they'd raised the banners of war to force men to see that they were more than just an object of lust, that they were to be feared and dealt with as beings of fire and war. But when that thought entered my mind, when I wondered if those dread witches' memories were stealing into me, I had to push the thought down. The responsibility was mine, else I was lost and but another of their playthings. That couldn't be true.

'And you understand those things?' Maldouen asked.

'Little of it makes any sense to me. But it's useful.'

'Then it's your power Iddin needs to destroy,' Esher said. 'It sure as mud isn't me.'

What she said was true, and I felt her sadness. The blue dress made so much more sense all of a sudden. It had seemed ostentatious, even to put me back in my place. She was trying to give herself value, and doing it in the wrong place, just as I had. Poor Esher. She didn't realise how much value she had. How much she meant to me, to us, and that her bravery that night I'd stood bound to a pyre—her challenging Ovitus to single combat before all of Redwinter while Sanvaunt healed me of a mortal wound—that meant more than anything. But how would I have felt, in this room of fiery-angels, witch queens and immortal golems, discussing how to bring down the king of the Fault, with only one Gate to her name? It would have been all the more terrifying. For all her deadly skill with a sword, it was a battle she would need to sit out.

That said an awful lot about our chances of survival.

'We're running out of options, aren't we?' Sanvaunt said. 'Options, and time. We have to get home. Raine has to use the Keystone to open the Great Seal in Harranir. That's the only way we can stop the Fault collapsing through into the world.'

'We have to reach the City of Spires,' I said. 'That's where the Queen of Feathers is.'

'Are you sure?' Sanvaunt said.

'She has to be,' I said. 'Maldouen. Tell them what the city is.' I'd already figured it out. It was like a part of the Fault that still stood apart from it. Present everywhere, always present on the horizon, but unreachable. Untouchable.

'It's the focal point. Where the power of the five Crowns comes to bear,' Maldouen said. 'It shouldn't even be visible. It's where I bound the Faded Lords and their vassals, and the demons of the Night Below that were running rampant.'

'And with the Harranese Crown unclaimed, its power's waned,' Sanvaunt said.

It was a logical deduction. I hadn't told them the truth, that it wasn't one failing Crown causing all of this. It was four failed Crowns, and the last being uncontained was only the final blow. I didn't correct them, and Maldouen's unmoving face gave nothing away.

'He comes, we fight, we win or we die,' Sanvaunt said.

'Iddin is the only creature roaming this hellscape freely,' I said. 'He has to come here. We have to force him to give us the path to the city. We've done it with other things. And we'd have thought those impossible once.'

'What do we do that with? Blackmail? Sanvaunt could undo more buttons, if he's inclined that way,' Esher said. She shook her head. 'I need some air.'

Maldouen rose with her.

'Lady Esher. Would you come with me? There is something that I wish you to have.'

'I'm not a lady,' Esher said. But she rose, glad to be escaping the table and its conversation of doom and disaster. Her calves looked magnificent as she followed Maldouen down the stairs. I wasn't the only one who noticed. I wondered when the thoughts of those women of the past had first started bleeding out of my dreams and into my waking world, which thoughts were mine, which were influenced by memories of other times. The dreaming had begun with the Ashtai Grimoire, the book that was not a book. I hoped it had been long after that, after we entered the Fault. After I died for the third time.

'We should plan,' Sanvaunt said.

'Here's a plan,' I said. 'Hit him with everything we have, as hard as we can.'

'You have the souls for it?' Sanvaunt asked. His face was set, dark, serious.

'I have what I have. What are you suggesting?' Ah. He didn't need to say anything. We could hunt, find me more. 'Even now,' I said, 'even here, it's one thing to take the spirits of the things that are trying to kill us. Going out looking for them—killing just to take them—I think that's a step beyond. Even for me.'

'And if we needed more power?'

'I don't like what this place is doing to you,' I said with a sigh. 'You'd never have countenanced that before.'

'Winning here is about more than just staying alive,' Sanvaunt said. 'It's everyone's lives on the line. Not just us. Every time the Fault bleeds upwards into the sky—what do you think it's doing to our world?'

'Do you want to see?' I asked.

· · · · · ·

It was a long-ago memory that had belonged to Hallenae, the Riven Queen, that showed me how to bring him along. I watched her taking a defeated enemy on a tour of his realm. The man had been a king once. She did it to show him his people under her yoke, his banners thrown onto bonfires, his sons dead in the field. Of the three great tyrants, Hallenae had been the worst. I didn't want to know what had happened to her when she was young to make such a monster of her. Song Seondeok and Serranis, Lady of Deserts, had become terrible over decades or more. Hallenae had been so young when she took the dread mantle. I couldn't believe she'd been born that way, but then, I'd not believed Ovitus could have done what he'd done either. I stirred through that memory quickly, and Maldouen's trick of latching onto my scrying wasn't so very hard to master.

Sanvaunt and I sat opposite one another atop the map table, and I drew him along with me. It really wasn't that hard. He was as surprised as Maldouen had been when I tore the star-filled gashes in the air, but once you've seen a trick it becomes fun rather than astonishing. Sanvaunt mimicked me, but where he scorched the air, he cut rifts in flame. He couldn't travel through my tunnel any more than I could venture into his sky, but as he copied my movements, I felt the heart bond between us. Together we rippled through space and time, blue and insubstantial.

'Are you sure this is wise?' Sanvaunt asked.

'Afraid to look through the tunnel with me?'

'We should be afraid,' he said. His mouth was set in a hard line. 'I don't want to have to put you back together again.'

'Can't argue with that,' I conceded. 'Seems kind of unfair that he can get at us both in our world and in the Fault.'

'May the Light Above protect us,' Sanvaunt murmured.

I hadn't taken us to anyone in particular. I'd followed the flow of the Fault's decay. The erosion travelled across the worlds too.

We appeared in darkness. I hadn't expected that. But then we were following the Fault's trail, and I suppose I'd expected what had risen there to be falling from the sky. No, I realised, looking around at the vast, domed chamber of black stone that we'd blinked into. We were beneath the ground. We were . . .

'We're within a Crown,' I said.

'How do you know?' Sanvaunt asked. He glimmered, an insubstantial blue ghost alongside me.

'I've seen into Harranir's Crown,' I said. 'Robilar showed me once. But this—this Crown is dead. There should be lights all around us. The power's been taken.'

'The Fault's bleeding through at the Crowns,' Sanvaunt said. 'Oh, Raine—is this Harranir?'

It could have been. Perhaps we were too late. Perhaps it was all over before we'd found a chance to end it. I looked to the vast disc above us, the Great Seal that should have protected the Crown. It lay open. We ran to the stair that wound around the edge of the empty dome. I could smell the charcoal, brittle-air absence of magic here. It had been taken, bound somewhere else.

'Be careful,' I said. 'Some things can still see us, even like this.'

'I put your arm and neck back together, remember?' Sanvaunt said. 'I haven't forgotten.' Ghost fingers gripped mine all the tighter.

It was not Harranir. This was not the hall of the Great Seal in Harranir's castle. But whatever relief that gave, we emerged into what had until recently been chaos, and now lay quiet but for the buzzing of flies.

Warriors had tried to form a shield wall across the great chamber. Hundreds of them. They lay where they'd died, the wall broken. Spears were still gripped in dead hands, screams had been cut off in terrified throats. These men had been heavily armoured, hardened veterans with gold arm rings and chains of station. Their colours had been orange and white before the red was splashed across them. Crusts of black insects crawled across open wounds, filled emptied eye sockets, ran riot across gaping mouths.

'It's the Queen's Palace, in Loridine,' Sanvaunt said. He sounded like he wanted to vomit. Too much horror delivered in a single moment. 'This was Brannlant's Crown.'

'They tried to hold them back,' I said. The only bodies belonged to the Brannish. Whatever had passed through here had left no dead, or had taken the bodies with them.

'I'm not keen to see what's out there,' Sanvaunt said. 'But we have to, don't we?'

I ghost-nodded. We did.

A palace that had once been opulent and exquisite lay in tattered ruins. The bodies of warriors mingled with the bodies of retainers, of commoners, and occasionally of men and women in noble dress.

'I came here once, when I was twelve,' Sanvaunt said. 'It was so beautiful.' He stepped across a fallen woman, her arms wrapped around a child. Neither of us commented on the horrors we saw. There were ghosts, here and there, green-white, wispy. Some clung to their own bodies, some to the bodies of friends, wives, children, lovers. Nobody had been spared. Some sections of wall had been blasted away, and down one corridor there was evidence that a fire had swept through. Even as a silent observer, Sanvaunt's ghostly blue face became more and more distraught. He'd seen bodies before. We'd cut a path through the half-dead of the Fault, but it was different there. Putting down a monster was like killing an animal, and intention counts. It had been us or them. Even with the warriors above the seal there'd been a sense of purpose. They'd fought, they'd trained for and known the risks of their lives. Not everyone here had fought. Some couldn't have fought if they'd wanted to.

I'd read of the sack of many a city, and I knew that within my darkest, borrowed memories, I could relive many if I'd wished to. I had never looked into those screaming, unforgiven places, not after the horrors I'd seen at Dalnesse. My mind had come close to shattering back then, and I knew that anyone who had lived through this would never recover. Everyone who'd been here when the seal broke was dead now, whether they still lived or not. The one thing we could be grateful for was that there didn't seem to have been pleasure in the ruination of these lives. They'd been taken swiftly. Just obstacles standing in the way.

We emerged into the apocalypse.

The sky was red and purple overhead. Winged, unknown things wheeled high above. The Queen's Palace stood atop a hill overlooking a sprawling metropolis, many times the size of Harranir. Across ten thousand terracotta rooftops, beyond white stucco walls too numerous to count, a harbour sat before a glittering sea that cast back the sky's unnatural hue. Smoke rose in black plumes across the city. A great aqueduct that ran on arch-divided columns down from another hill had broken in the middle, water gushing to wet the cold spring earth.

We were too late to hear the worst of it. Too late for the screaming. Something vast moved along a distant street, too far to see clearly, but it walked on its fists and its mane seemed to crackle with flame. Across the river, something serpent-like coiled around a broken cathedral spire, mottled orange and grey. The Fault had begun to spill its creatures, its nightmares, into our world.

'Look there,' Sanvaunt said. I didn't know that I wanted to. Didn't want to see the devastation that had been wrought, or anything that could possibly be more worthy of note than the death of the great capital of a nation that had squatted on our sovereignty for a hundred years. Had they heard of this back in Harranir, there would have been those that would have cheered. My countrymen might have known a name here, maybe two. King Henrith the Second. He was probably a body among the bodies now. I might have stepped over him, or through him, in the palace. It's easy to congratulate destruction and slaughter when it lies so very far away. I was close enough to smell the blood. To see the last, twisted expressions of agony on people's faces. Despite everything I'd done, the lives I'd taken, the souls I'd put to my use, whether in this lifetime or those of the others whose memories had bled into me, even I felt the horror.

When I looked to where Sanvaunt's ghostly arm pointed, I knew it would be something that I would take to yet another of my graves. Beyond Loridine's limits, a procession moved along the road.

We passed through the city to reach them. There is only so much pain and death one can recount. The creatures of legend I saw could have filled books of their own. Mawleths, working in pairs, the street around them filled with hungry locusts. Trow, monstrous giants with stony, block-like heads, sat in a park drinking from barrels of ale as if holding cups. The Sluagh, the unforgiven dead, stalked constantly, armed with javelins and short bronze swords, seeking out those who may have managed to hide. Tiny Pechs and those who'd lived on in our world as the Hidden Folk picked through the ruins for trinkets, vying with one another for plundered rings, coins, chalices and beads. I saw Racklas in blackened armour, dragging their great axes behind them with slow, plodding steps and Isthags bedecked with necklaces of glass and hands, cackling to one another. We passed between the monsters of another world, unseen, unspeaking. Sanvaunt and I held ghostly hands as we walked, as though in clinging to one another we retained some aspect of the world as it had been.

The creatures that infested Loridine's once vibrant streets were the unruled, the loners, the creatures that had never accepted a lord. Some appeared rotten, some blood-hungry, but it was the organised precision of the Faded that eclipsed them all. Loridine's survivors had been rounded up, herded together, and there was nothing but dark inevitability in the way the Faded had marched them from the city. I didn't look at their faces. Instead I looked at the Faded. They were like us, but not. There was no particular feature that indicated they were inhuman, unless they'd merged with beasts, but I could tell them apart immediately. The eyes, the ears, the shape of a skull, they were just subtly different from humanity. Banished to the Fault for seven hundred years and more, they had planned for this day. They moved with purpose, driving people like sheep. At the end of that procession, people seemed to be working the fields. But they weren't working, they were digging. Ditches. No, graves. The Faded were reclaiming the world. The only place they saw for us in it was beneath the ground.

We didn't go the whole way. I saw the Faded Lord who commanded them. He wore a mask of gold, and from around it, huge, gleaming silver feathers a full three feet long rayed out like he was the sun. His armour was bedecked with glittering precious stones, and he rode something that could have been a horse if not for its flickering, forked tongue.

'They've fallen,' Sanvaunt said. 'We had five Crowns to bind the dark and now we have none. If Brannlant has fallen, it's happened already. It's over.' There was grief in his voice. 'Even one could give us hope. But we're not even there to fight for them.' He closed his eyes, lowered his face. He took humanity's shame upon himself. 'We lost.'

I had never seen Sanvaunt look so defeated. His despair forced resolve into me. I couldn't let him be like this. It wasn't who, or what he was.

'We had five Crowns,' I said. I gentled my voice for him. Sanvaunt was tough, but he hadn't lived through what I had. Even the Fault hadn't prepared him for this. Had I possessed the Fourth Gate, I might have scarred his mind as Ulovar had once done to me. 'Four have fallen. The fifth, in Harranir, is uncontrolled. While one remains, we have a chance.'

'Maybe it's all over there too,' he said.

'Then we have to see it.'

· · · · · ·

The river ran quietly, a thick silver channel cutting through Harranir's centre. Boats, punts and ferries worked it quietly. People went back and forth about their business. News of Loridine's fall hadn't reached them here yet. It might not for a month or more. The city was much as we had left it.

'It's not over yet,' Sanvaunt said. Relief spilled from him as his ghost-hand hardened around mine. I felt that, back in the Fault, sitting atop the map, he held it there too.

'No,' I said. 'And it's not going to be.' I looked up towards Redwinter. The LacNaithe wyvern flew alongside Redwinter's red-and-white tower-and-crown.

'Look up,' Sanvaunt said. 'It's starting.'

I followed his gaze up and into the sky. Above the level of clouds, a tiny purple blush touched the expanse of blue.

'How long does that give us?' I said. 'Hours? Weeks?'

'We need someone to act,' Sanvaunt said. 'Merovech LacClune, or Hanaqin Clanless. They can open the Great Seal and someone can bind to the Crown. Even if it's not someone they want. We have to show them somehow.'

'We can appear to them, if we will it,' I said.

'Then we do that. Hold to me. I'll take us to Merovech. He's the only one I've met. Maybe I can find him.'

I waited as Sanvaunt reworked his sigils to spirit-carry us away. Merovech LacClune had always been the fiercest rival to Clan LacNaithe, even during Onostus LacAud's rebellion. That Ovitus, the self-styled king of Harran and grandmaster of Redwinter, had refused to allow him to enter the Blackwell to stop all this spoke blackly of that long-festering disdain between them. He would not be an easy man to convince. Ovitus could not be convinced to relinquish his power. He had sacrificed everything that he was, everything that he could have been, to take it. Merovech would have to bow. The thought of it caused a rippling shudder to pass through my astral body, but if that was what it took . . . I would deal with Ovitus later. For now, Harran-ir's Crown had to be stabilised. Ithatra lay beneath the waves. Osprinne and Khalacant were in faraway lands, but they must have suffered the same fate as poor Loridine. How long ago had that happened? Maldouen had told me the Faded Lords had taken them one by one over long, quiet decades. They had seen their chance to strike. Only an army of tens of thousands could retake Loridine and that we didn't have.

As Sanvaunt tried to find the threads that would take us to Merovech Lac-Clune, I watched an elderly couple sitting on the edge of a fountain, oblivious to the market trade going on all around them. They giggled, nestled closer to one another, whispering things that were for each other alone, uncared for amidst the bustle. This was what it was all for, I supposed. All the toil and struggle, all the death and bleak darkness, all the cruelty and fighting and blood on my hands. It was for them. That people should be able to live and love in peace. That when she held up an apple to him, having taken clear, purposeful bites from her side, that when he took a tiny bite back and passed it to her, that they got to make this secret language of affection between them. He leant in to whisper in her ear, and she laughed and her cheeks turned red. Two children ran up to them. Grandchildren, escaped from their parents' watchful eye, flung themselves into embraces of purest love. It all gets con-fused sometimes, between adults. We expect too much of one another. Expect each other to be flawless when we're all so heavily flawed. But children don't have flaws, they aren't formed yet, and so the love is unconditional, perfect and free. For a moment I wanted to be them, child or grandparent, it didn't matter which. Just to experience loving with such complete abandon seemed to be the point of it all.

It was not the path for me. I took a long, slow breath that didn't consume any air.

I would not let this world go. I would not let the Faded take it from us. I could not be those grandparents. I would never lift my grandchildren. I would not know that love, but I would ensure that it didn't die with them. I would do what nobody else had done. I would smite the world if I had to. I was Raine Wildrose, Raine Clanless, Raine of Redwinter, and I was going to win.

'It won't work,' Sanvaunt said. 'I can't find the thread.' He let that settle for a moment. 'He's not here.' It settled between us.

'Then he's dead.'

I thought of all the allies I could have gone to, anyone to whom a case could be made. Or those at least who were driving to remove Ovitus and his familiar Waldy, about which he didn't have the slightest understanding.

'Castus LacClune,' I said. My bonds to him were tighter than I'd realised; I'd given him part of me once before and he'd kept it safe. I didn't need to find a thread, that bond still existed between us. We travelled.

· · · · · ·

'My van, you must take horse.' A bearded, bull-shouldered old warrior shouted to be heard above the din of clattering armour, shields, the braying of horses as they laboured to drag wagons through wet-churned mud. A light rain fell.

'I won't abandon him,' Castus LacClune said. 'He may have been a cunt, but he was still my father.'

Castus was thinner than I remembered him, and he'd had scant to spare to begin with, but he looked so much older than he had any right to be. His armour was dirty and bloodied. The shield on his arm was dented and the painted blue LacClune rose on its white background clung to it through sheer wilfulness. His men laboured all around him, several hundred, a thousand at best, and they were in full retreat.

'There's been a battle,' Sanvaunt said. It was evident in the bandages, the men without shields, the wagons that weren't loaded with supplies but with the wounded, and the dead.

'My van,' the big warrior said. 'They'll be on us in minutes. We have no position. We have no fighting strength.'

'Where did they come from?' Castus demanded. His face was tear-tracked. 'There must have been ten thousand.'

'Wherever they came from, they found the men,' bull-shoulders said. 'For now all we can do is retreat.'

'To Bocknain?' Castus said. 'We'll never make it.'

'To Clunwinny. And not us. Just you, my lord. You rule the clan now. You must not be captured.'

'I'll die before Ovitus LacNaithe sees my knees in the mud,' Castus spat. He turned and looked back over his shoulder, and I followed his gaze.

Horsemen had emerged from a line of trees. Heavy cavalry, hard-armoured, horses in foreign-made barding, began to form ranks at the crest of the shallow hill. 'I guess that's going to be sooner rather than later,' Castus said.

'Now is the time to—' the old warrior began, but Castus was already moving.

'Shield wall!' he yelled, waving a war hammer above his head in circles. 'Shield wall!'

'Light Above,' Sanvaunt said. 'They're done for.'

We were students of war. We'd read our histories, had been lectured on them over dreary suppers and in cold classrooms. There had been times— many times—when a densely packed shield wall had repelled the advance of horsemen. A solid line of hardened, confident, well-drilled warriors with spears wasn't something a horse wants to run headlong into. But that was not what Castus LacClune had to hand. His men had been beaten once already, and were exhausted through flight. Half of them were scraped and bloody, and a ghost clung to one of the wagons, patting himself for wounds he couldn't feel. I'd heard Ovitus say that Castus had five thousand men, but he'd be hard-pressed to turn five hundred of what he had left into a fighting force, and what came through the woodland now numbered many times that. I couldn't even guess at a number. Thousands, at least. A glittering array of steel. There were Winterra among them too.

Sanvaunt wasn't watching the approach of the horsemen. He'd gone to one of the wagons. I didn't need to look into it to know what it carried.

'He was always a bastard,' Sanvaunt said. 'But we needed him now. Ovitus has doomed us all.'

'My lord van,' the big warrior tried again as Castus continued to yell at his warriors. He grabbed Castus by the shoulder and spun him around. He may have been a vassal, but he wanted to live. 'We don't even have enough men to form a wall.' Castus shook free of him, knowing he was right.

'We can't outrun them,' he said. 'If we have to wade through Skuttis tonight, let's do it facing the enemy. Schiltron! Form schiltron!'

The wagons came to rest. The last men of LacClune began to form into a half-circle, their fallen leader at the centre. There was nowhere to run. There was no escape. Not from the mass of horse-borne riders who even now were picking up to a canter, riding in tight-packed formation. Brannish heavy cavalry, who should have been home, who might have given Loridine a chance. Mercenaries from Garathenia, plunder on their minds. Their pennants flapped in the light spring rain.

'No surrender!' Castus cried. 'No surrender!'

'No surrender!' his captain joined him. They beat their weapons against their shields.

'We don't have to watch,' Sanvaunt said.

But I looked up beyond the encroaching horsemen, and along the tree line I dimly made out the sight of a man in a green-and-black cloak, a wolfhound at his heels.

'No surrender,' I hissed.

I began to stride forward. Out from the LacClune ranks, towards the charging horsemen. Three, five, seven thousand, I didn't care. I was going to win. It was decided. I'd be right, or I'd be wrong.

The sound of horses' hooves began to thunder, rolling down from the hillside above, a hollow drumming against the earth.

'No surrender!' the chant sounded behind me. The charge came down like a mountain gale. Five hundred paces, four hundred paces.

I forced myself to be visible. My souls, the power at my disposal lay back in the Fault, but I could be here. I could make them see me. I erupted into the world, ghost-blue and steaming with ethereal force. Some of the horses tried to swerve, but the tight-packed riders to either side kept them on track, the blowing horses behind drove them forward. I reached for my souls, reached deep into me, strove to grasp hold of them.

'Raine, stop!' It was Sanvaunt. I felt his words on the Anam Teine more than heard them. 'Raine, you're collapsing the projection. I can't hold on to you.'

'I'm not going,' I sent back through the tunnel, its iron-cog grinding drone all around me. 'I'm going to stay.'

Three hundred paces. A wave of men and steel roared towards me. I pressed forward, into the real world. I wrapped myself around all those souls back in the Fault and I dragged on them, and I pulled and strove against the separation of two worlds.

'Raine, stop! You'll tear yourself apart!' Sanvaunt sent to me, but it was the last he managed before our connection snapped and I felt his spirit cast back into the Fault.

I strained against the boundary. Maldouen had made it, and the Riven Queen had drawn from it. The moon horses traversed it, and if all my pain and sorrow and grief could move from one realm to the next then so could I. I'd seen too much. I'd seen the ruin of Loridine, I'd seen the slaughter at Dalnesse, I'd been drowned and strangled and run through with a sword of frost. I'd killed men by the hundreds, I'd been savaged by a Faded Lord, I'd been betrayed and I'd lost and I'd loved and I'd be damned if I was going to let something like the rules of the universe keep me from saving a friend.

I forced myself through. I screamed in two worlds as I felt the ripping of my soul as I tore myself apart, and carried the useful parts with me as I disposed of the trash that had only been holding me back.

13

We arrive on the battlefield naked and thrumming with streams of annihilation rippling in the aether around us.

We are Raine Wildrose; we are Hallenae, the Riven Queen; we are Song Seondeok; we are Serranis, Lady of Deserts; we are Unthayla the Damned and countless others who have gone before us. The unwanted, unneeded parts of us, the weak, the chaff, the pitying, the pitied, the crying, the whining, the fearing, the hurting, the broken and the blighted have been excised. We are a blazing moment in history, an unthinkable act, a break in reality, a cheat among creation. We ride into this world in a shadowed blast of enmity, a crack of unchecked violence, a roar of black intent. We are witch queens one and all, and the world will suffer our wrath.

The Witching Skin ripples around us. The insufferable Blind Child had been right all along. We feel Hallenae's hatred for him, and Raine's reliance on him, but we're beyond him now. He reminded us of this power, and though we've not called this armour together in this lifetime, it forms instantly, setting around us like ice. We conjure it to make them afraid, perturbed. We conjure it to make them see how vastly more powerful we are than they. We do not mould it as armour. Why should we? We dress ourselves as we did of old, Raine's will the dominant power among us. She chooses the black and gold, but we build it higher. We create a fan of spines at our back, shining metal. We helm ourselves with a coronet of raven's feathers. We make the warpaint slash across our cheeks in midnight blue, form dark pits around eyes that blaze with terrible inner light. We suck cold, real air.

And we scream.

The Banshee's Wail, but not so small a thing as we once threw against Onostus LacAud. That had been the work of a girl discovering the first edge of her power. What we cast out is woven at the gauntleted fingers of a dozen masters of the Sixth Gate. We see now that our past invocations had been crude things, piling mounds of earth where a narrow stair could have sufficed. Every soul we *dragged with us from the Fault became vastly more fuel than Raine has ever projected before she realised who we are.*

The scream blasts out. Those caught directly in front of it are hurled back up the hill, colliding with comrades behind them as man and horse are stripped of flesh, blood dissipating into the air in clouds of red steam as death comes for them all. Those at the edges feel their muscles wither, skin tearing away from their bodies. The scream does not abate. We turn slowly, channelling this massive destructive force across the lines of riders. Screaming horses are tossed into the air. Gallant men and women die howling. I kill them by the hundred. Hard-flung horses crash into others. Men are knocked from them, crushed beneath horse flesh.

. . . . . .

I watched everything from behind my own eyes. The memories ran into mine like panes of watercolour bleeding one to the next, but black only comes in so many shades.

The surviving horsemen, those lucky enough to be on the distant flanks, swerved. Self-preservation took hold, and two wings of horse peeled away. I looked across what I'd done, and I felt a glee that was deeply wrong but sensual in its embrace. The hollowness hit me, the souls emptied from me. But this was what made the Sarathi of the Sixth Gate so much more dangerous than even the Draoihn of the Fifth Gate, even Sanvaunt with his Anam Teine. His magic relied on his own life force, it bonded him to the world but his resources were finite. For a Sarathi, death begat death.

I'd never seen so many souls rising at once. The shuddering, mournful cries of those left mutilated, flayed and ruined by the Banshee's Wail filled the air, but I alone heard the enormity of the cry given by thousands of dead. I thrust my hands forward, fingers spread like some monstrous puppeteer.

'To me,' I croaked. 'To me all, to me be bound and my power feed.'

The Sixth Gate no longer ground and droned, but it howled. I saw it all around me as I took the spirits of those who had thought to trample my friend into the dirt. I ripped them from their path to the warm mists of Anavia, dragged them back from the freezing rivers of Skuttis, consumed and devoured. The field ahead of me became a convergence of green-white ghostly forms, dragged, demanded, called into me. They hit me not one by one but in packs, filling me, restoring me. They were more than I could hold and the excess swirled around me, a miasma of ghostly energy, sucking the field dry of its dead. The grass around me blackened, withered, a circle of negative power emanating around me.

When it was done I was heady and breathless. I wore a smile. The unthinkable had been thought. I looked up the hill. There were more. So many more. I saw Ovitus and Waldy up there, wanted a closer look. I opened my First Gate alongside my Sixth. Ovitus's young, fuzz-beard face came to clarity. His mouth hung agape. Beads of sweat formed on his brow. I heard his own First Gate pulsing, the steady rhythm he'd stolen from Ulovar.

'I know you can hear me,' I said. 'I'm back.'

'Raine,' Ovitus breathed. 'What have you done?'

'I'm here to destroy you, Ovitus LacNaithe,' I said.

The wolfhound, Waldy, Iddin, whatever he could be called in this place, growled. His fur bristled. His eyes pulsed with a rage that no real animal could have felt. Ovitus had Draoihn with him, two dozen in oxblood red, and his own bodyguard of Winterra in bright steel. Princess Mathilde was there too—maybe Queen Mathilde, with what had transpired in Brannlant. Her puffed silks and glittering jewellery were gone, but nor was she armoured. She wore practical campaigning clothes, a doublet of orangeand-white cheques, warm and cold against the rich dark of her skin. Every one of them wore the full reality of what I'd done in their expressions. Friends had died. Many, many friends. There had likely been Draoihn among them too.

'Sarathi,' Ovitus said. He spat. He regained his composure, struck the sweat from his face. 'Don't you know, Raine, we have a long history of dealing with women like you. They all fall in the end.'

'You're skipping ahead,' I said across the distance. 'First comes the destruction.'

I took two dozen of my trapped souls, and launched them like a crossbow bolt. Waldy howled and the air before the army rippled, and the bolt shattered against them, spilling into warped and tattered ghosts, to blow away on the wind. The tunnel spun around me, a rippling howl in reality.

I was enjoying myself, but there were a lot of them up there.

'Archers!' Ovitus said.

·   ·   ·   ·   ·   ·

Ranwulf couldn't bring himself to look at the broken, shredded mass of men and horses across the field. His younger brother had been in there. It was Unfirth's first time wearing his new spurs, his harness freshly returned from the armourers. Maybe he'd not been in the path of whatever terrible blast the dread witch had unleashed. Maybe? Maybe? Could he have been pushed out to the flanks, the more experienced warriors taking the head of the charge? That's what the great warriors of the Age of Conquest would have done.

Ranwulf knew Unfirth hadn't. So he didn't look, couldn't look. The cavalry were wheeling away, but turning back up the hill—if he returned home alone his mother would never forgive him. She'd never wanted her sons to pick up a lance. Only one of them could, now. Some men were born to be heroes, but Unfirth had never possessed that destiny.

Ranwulf had dreamed of returning from civil war with silver and titles. Had thought his armour would ward him from blows and arrows, had thought the might of the Brannish charge would scatter the enemy before any real resistance was met. The dream had shattered. The darkest night was upon them. The Riven Age would begin anew. He stared towards the tall woman, stood in a blackened circle before the last of the LacClune forces. A whirlwind spun around her, and he could see the faces of the dead within it. He looked around, found the rest of the horse had galloped back up the hill as fast as they could.

Unfirth wouldn't return up the hill. Ranwulf knew that. He knew in his heart that his little brother lay dead. That girl Unfirth had got pregnant, the one he'd paid to be his mistress, what was her name? He'd have to find her. She'd been pretty. Perhaps Ranwulf would keep both mother and child. Raise it as his own. But first, he had to do something. He saw fate before him, a dagger spinning on its point, waiting to fall. The legend that followed would be dictated by the direction of the blade.

The charger below him snorted and blew in the lightly falling rain, flicking its armoured head. Ranwulf panted, one, two, three, then clamped his visor down again. He struck well-practiced heels against the charger's flanks, and felt the mighty animal surge beneath him. Hoofbeats were muffled through the padding within his helm. Distantly he heard horns. The bitch in black and gold was staring off up the hill. Distracted. She drew back her arm and something flew from it, white and immaterial, hurtling up the hill, but Ranwulf was lost in the charge.

Some men are born to be heroes.

He lowered his lance, couched it beneath his arm as he cut across the LacClune line. His target, the demon-woman with archaic warpaint beneath her eyes, didn't see him, didn't hear him. One lance, one piercing blow and he would be the man the battle rested on. He forgot Unfirth. He forgot the mewling cries of the dead. The next Age would belong to him.

She turned and saw him four lance lengths away. Her eyes were bright white fury. Her face was young, but taut with malice. White hair flowed around her like willow branches, so thick it fell as a cloak to her knees. She was a small target, thin, but this was what he'd trained for.

She brought a hand up and spoke a single word, a word that rusted the air, a word that rose from the bones of the earth, a word he heard even through the helmet's padding and—

.   .   .   .   .   .

Rider and horse exploded in a cloud of hot red liquid and gleaming shrapnel. The ghost carried on, and as it crashed into me I snapped my teeth and absorbed the would-be legend. The memories hit me as hard as his charge would have been. Ranwulf hadn't been a good man. He'd beaten his wife if he thought she met another man's eyes, he'd swindled a nephew out of half his inheritance, and he'd wanted to fill his coffers by filling graveyards. But looking at what I'd done, the detritus of an army's pride spread in pieces across the hillside, I was hardly one to talk.

I didn't care. I didn't care about these piece-of-shit bastards. There was only me, now. There was only winning.

Ranwulf had done his best. I'd been better, but he nearly cost me. I stood blinking in the wet red haze, a whirl of spirits all around me, and then the black rain came down. An archer had loosed a couple of moments before the order was given, and his arrow alerted me to the iron-tipped storm. Hundreds of arrows descended, and I drew my soul army and formed a dome. It seemed so long ago that I'd read the words in the Ashtai Grimoire, but they fell from my lips like tumbling anvils. Arrows snapped and bounced from the shield, thudded into the grass around me.

Eio pulsed in the world all about me. I saw every arrow perfectly, saw tiny, individual splinters as they collided midair. Arrows battered down, a constant rain. I squinted through the soul-distorted air, focused on Ovitus again.

'Again!' he shouted. 'Loose at will!'

The arrows came down, and down. They tapped like stones flung against a windowpane. Every arrow sent another spirit spiralling from my control, evaporating to the Afterworld. They howled. *Tak-tak-tak-tak-tak-tak-tak-tak*

'Keep shooting,' Ovitus bellowed, riding along the line, whirling a Draoihn-made sword above his head. 'Keep shooting! Kill her! Kill her!'

Tak-tak-tak-tak-tak-tak-tak-tak-tak-tak-tak-tak-tak-tak-tak-tak

Soul after soul dissipated into the tunnel, dragged on to a more natural fate. My shield was shrinking. When it was gone all I would have left was my witching armour, and though its shape didn't matter, maybe I should have given it more practical form. My flamboyance might have been encouraging them.

'My lord, we've sent a dozen volleys,' Namuae, the red-haired Winterra Draoihn barked. 'They're not getting through!'

More of the arrows were striking the shield. The archers who'd been furthest off had adjusted their aim. I was a static target, and their misses guided their hands. The arrow storm arced high, then down onto me.

Ovitus's face was contorted with rage.

'Every arrow! Send every arrow you have!'

He'd released his First Gate, so I had no opportunity to whisper something cutting in return.

The arrows embedded in the ground grew into a thicket. Outside my black circle, there was no clear ground for thirty paces, goose-fletched shafts jutting like a hedgehog's spines. The racket of the iron rain went on, and on, and I couldn't see anything around me for the sheer number of shafts falling through the air, impacting on my shield of the dead, striking, breaking, bursting apart from the force of their own impacts. And then, just as a summer squall might start and finish—it was over.

A miniature forest with pale blossoms surrounded me on all sides.

My First Gate was growing tired. The tunnel was beginning to struggle. I looked back at Ovitus, Namuae, and that fucking dog on the hill. Someone had brought a pavisse, a wheeled shield for Ovitus to hide behind. Much good it would do him if I could get in range with something that might take his head off. Iddin was providing him his real protection. I hadn't thought what to do if that dog came at me. It could pierce the veiled world, would see me ethereal or otherwise.

I was still standing. I stood before an army: cavalry, bowmen, none of them could touch me. I remembered feeling this before, many times. Not as me. I recalled watching Hallenae on the night she discovered her greatness, obliterating rooms of those who'd sought to humiliate her as she stalked through a castle, crushing all in her wake. I remembered Serranis standing atop a chariot side by side with one of the Eldritch Kin, their magic sweeping away an army. I felt Unthayla's realisation of her own mastery as she conjured something oily and black from beneath the earth. They had exulted too. They were dead, these memories of them were not mine, but I exulted with them. I wasn't alone. I wasn't alone anymore, even if it was all just a mirage.

But there they were. I sensed them then, shadowed spirits deeper into the tunnel than I'd ever looked, like blank corpse faces looking out towards me. The Sluagh, the unforgiven dead. They wanted to return, and this massive use of power—the tunnel had stayed open too long. I had to release the Sixth Gate, and I tried to close it—but no. It wouldn't go. It held itself open, and those dead faces ascended towards me. Spikes of pain shot along my bones, in my hands, my toes. My vision was so confused, the shades of the dead were overlapping the living. I felt it pulling on me. It wanted me. I'd fed it, I'd held it open too long.

With a gasp I managed to slam it shut. I was grinning. The tunnel had its own designs, but I was still its master. The most powerful person to walk the world. Without the Sixth Gate, even with the First Gate's trance open and drumming within me, everything seemed quieter, muted.

'I know you can hear me,' Ovitus whispered from far, far away. 'I shouldn't have put it past you to try to stand alone this way. And for Castus LacClune of all people. An enemy to your own clan.' I guessed he was trancing again, but I couldn't listen so far. My pulse was growing weary.

'I have no clan,' I shot back. 'I'm Raine Wildrose, Draoihn of Redwinter, Fiahd of the north, and I'm going to save this world. Do you know what that monstrous dog is beside you? Has it told you that it's bringing about the end of the world? Loridine has already fallen. Listen to me, Ovitus. For once in your damned, miserable life listen to somebody else.'

'Listen to me, listen to me, listen to me, that's all you ever think of, isn't it?'

'Look where we are,' I hissed from within a blackened circle of arrows. 'The world is shaking itself apart. The sky turns to blood. It's the Crown, Ovitus. The Crown must be controlled. It's your duty as Draoihn to ensure the succession. And you've killed the only Draoihn who could have opened the Great Seal. Besides me. Now get out of my way and let me do what needs doing.'

'You want the Crown,' Ovitus said. 'Of course you do.'

'Not for me, you ass,' I spat back. 'Put your wife on the throne if you have to. But I have to get to the Blackwell. The world is about to die, and every action you've taken is only making it worse.'

Waldy growled. I guess he could hear me as well. Hardly surprising. His fangs, longer still than they'd been, dripped with viscous spittle.

'The world can't die,' Ovitus said. 'The Crowns were a lie to keep us under control. Under Robilar's control. And now a Sarathi tells me she has to enter the Blackwell? I'll die before I give you what you want.'

'Yes,' I said. 'Yes, you will.'

Ovitus licked his lips.

'Ready the infantry. She can't kill them all.'

But a new sound demanded my attention, and my head was pounding from holding the First Gate so long that I had to release it. It was the sound of five hundred pairs of boots tramping through the grass, breaking through the field of arrows as the warriors of Clan LacClune came to form around me.

'Didn't count on seeing you again,' Castus said as his men readied shields. His eyes were tear-stained. He looked out across the devastation I'd wrought. 'Can't say I'm sorry to have you back. Mind if I ask you one question before I consign myself to Skuttis?'

There was movement up on the hill. The last of the cavalry had pulled back. Even at this distance, the infantry forming their shield wall didn't seem to be terribly keen on trying to take us on.

'Might as well ask,' I said.

'Actually, I have two questions.'

'One's a joke you just thought up, isn't it?' I said.

'Just let me ask them,' he said, and through all the raging crisscross of emotion that must have been going on inside him, he managed a smile. 'Were you always this way? Even when we were romping about?'

'Always,' I said. 'Mostly. But there was a weak part. I left that behind. That was the part that you got all sweaty with. She's still around somewhere. Just not here.'

Castus looked relieved. He'd known me ever since that day in a tavern when he stabbed a drunk in the neck. It had seemed such a big thing back then. Laughable, now.

'Well, that brings me to my second question,' he said. He looked my witching armour up and down. 'Do you know any men who have all this going on?'

'I'm one of a kind,' I said.

'Knew my luck couldn't be that good,' he said. 'Ah well. Look, they want to parley.'

'Who are they sending? Has to take some guts,' My eyes ached like a bastard. My whole body was taut and hard with the rush of battle.

'Huh,' Castus said. 'They're sending Brannlant's finest.'

Princess, maybe Queen, Mathilde descended the hill on a white horse, the banner of her noble line hanging upside down on a freshly cut branch, the symbol of parley.

'They're readying an attack,' I said. My voice had turned harsh and raspy—that banshee scream had really done a number on my throat. I still had spirits—I had a *lot* of souls caged within me—but I didn't know if I could deal with the Draoihn, and there was Ovitus too. He had three Gates to his name and that was nothing to sneer at. Witch queen I might have been, but if he could find enough energy to transmute then a bolt of lightning wasn't going to leave much of me behind if I didn't get souls in the way fast enough. But they'd seen what I could do, and Ovitus wasn't going to risk himself. Not when he could throw lives at me this quickly. With the forest at their back, the enemy's numbers could only be guessed at.

Mathilde looked regal as her terrified horse picked its way through the field of the dead. They'd blinkered it, but it could smell the death all around.

Her hair, that amazing, tight-curled hair, was bound back. It made her face sharper, more severe. She stopped a way out.

'Castus LacClune,' she called out. 'I come to speak on behalf of my husband. And of the brave men and women up that slope, who only serve at their lord's command.'

She'd been sent because she had rank, but no magic at her command, I thought. No threat.

'Doesn't seem likely I'll care for what you have to say,' Castus called back, and I was glad that he was willing to do some of the shouting. The spiking pains had not abated and I was exhausted.

'Somebody make me a seat,' I said, looking at the warriors who'd gathered around me for the first time. By rights, they should have been terrified of me. I'd made myself terrifying, I'd done terrifying things. But it's funny how much someone can ignore about you if you're giving them a chance to live. I don't know what I expected them to do—it wasn't as if they'd brought me a chair.

'I would be honoured, my queen,' that bull-shouldered warrior said. He got down on one brawny knee, the other thrust out before him. Castus seemed highly amused by this.

'I'm not your queen,' I said.

'The reign of Queen Raine sounds good enough to me,' Castus said. 'And Van LacShale is offering you the best seat we have available.' He leaned in close to me. 'Sit before you fall over. If they think you're done, we're all going to be a head shorter come dusk.'

It was ridiculous, but those old memories of the Queen of Feathers glowed within me. Abasement appealed to them. I sat down on the head of Clan LacShale's knee. Strange as it seemed, there was no humiliation in it. He hadn't asked his men to get down in the mud. I *honoured* him by taking his knee for my seat. We were warriors all. In battle, there is no indignity in helping one another, whatever that meant. I sat side on, crossing my legs in front of me as if entirely at my ease, when in fact pain was riding along my veins.

'My royal husband decrees your rebellion to be at its end,' Mathilde called out. 'You haven't the men left to you. My lord husband is not without mercy. You will all be spared, but the Sarathi in your ranks cannot be permitted to live. You know this as your sacred duty. Side with her, and Clan LacClune will forfeit its lands.' She paused, regal as she ever was, but reluctant to speak the words that had to come next.

'Go on,' Castus said. 'I'll hear it.'

'My lord king has promised that if you do not hand her over, the Lac-Clune bloodline will end in its entirety.'

Castus's face paled. That was not our way. Clans fought. Leaders came and went. Nobody went after the children. Nobody tried to erase an entire clan.

'How does that sit in your gullet, Princess Mathilde?' I asked, and my voice had turned into a raspy, monstrous croak. I was watching the men gathering up on the hill. The Draoihn were spreading among them. They'd be better prepared this time. There were defences against the kind of Sarathi magic I could deploy, and I'd spotted Brannish Artists among them, and I had no idea what they were capable of. This wouldn't be resolved with words. Mathilde's parley was only to waste our time.

I couldn't fight the rest of them. Taking on that charge had been instinctive, but desperate. I had no spell that could deal with all the warriors I saw crowding the tree line. Not with Draoihn and Artists among them.

'I want the bloodshed to end,' she said. 'The world is shaking itself apart. This is not the way. I volunteered to speak to you because you know I have only the good of the people in my heart.'

'You share your bed with a monster,' I said, but my voice was well and truly a mess now, and I doubt she understood. Across the field, the insects were arriving. It was early in the season, but it's incredible how many of the little bastards appear when there's something dead on the floor. Crows wheeled high in the sky.

'Is it true that your marriage never got consummated?' Castus asked. 'I heard you and I have more in common than apart.'

'My bed is my business, and mine alone,' Mathilde said. Her expression was pained. 'And not for discussion in this field of hopeless death.' She did seem the bigger person just then, I had to admit it. 'This is a freely offered chance to surrender,' she said. 'I don't think there'll be another.'

Castus wasn't considering it. Not really. He couldn't be unaware of the dire circumstances we still found ourselves in.

'What do we think? Do we give up?'

As one the clansmen hammered weapons against the rims of their shields. They roared.

'No surrender!'

Mathilde swept a hand at a buzzing fly.

'Then may the Light Above care for your souls in the Afterworld,' she said. 'I'm sorry it's come to this. Nobody wants this.'

Princess Mathilde turned her mount and heeled at it until it headed back up the hill.

'Insects,' Castus said disgustedly. 'Such an indignity.'

I smiled, and my face felt stiff as glass. I rifled back through the Queen of Feathers' memories. Someone, somewhere, must have tried to do what I was about to in the last five thousand years. It was too good an idea not to. I sought memories of battles, memories in meadows and woodland much like this. There were more than a few dalliances, a great many skirmishes, fewer major confrontations than one would have thought. But there it was.

'I need two minutes, then we retreat,' I said, levering myself up from Van LacShale's knee. I took LacShale's sword and began using the finely honed point to cut tracks through my blackened circle. There was latent power there, an after-effect of my previous workings.

'I think we have to fight here,' Castus said.

'No,' I said. 'I can't promise you they'll last long, but we have allies on the way.'

· · · · · ·

Nobody would know that it was an incantation, and to many it must simply have seemed a natural disaster that halted a man-made one. It began with a man slapping at his neck, swearing at being stung. Then came another, and another after. It was wasps and bees I sent my captive souls out to. Bits of them, anyway. I tore the souls like wedding day confetti, and that was still enough of a ghost to inhabit those tiny bodies. New nests had formed up in the forest, but last year's drones had perished with the winter, and they would do. It didn't really matter whose spirit inhabited which body when they were dead. I could have forced a hundred men back into sluggish undead bodies, but those same shredded souls could make me bees and wasps by the million.

The infantry line collapsed before it ever left the trees. Necromantic undead bees, who would have thought that on such things the fate of the world is decided?

14

I forced myself through. I screamed in two worlds. I felt the ripping of my soul as I tore myself apart, and something that had filled me with hollow, weeping darkness escaped me.

I fell on my back across the stone-carved map, stared up at the ceiling. Everything felt so different. My head rolled to one side. Out beyond the broad, empty window, the red sky of the Fault glowered down, quiet for once.

'Raine!' Sanvaunt appeared above me. 'Raine, answer me!'

'I feel different,' I said groggily.

'Are you hurt?'

Took me a moment to think about it.

'I don't think so.'

'Can you sit up?'

'Of course. I'm fine. Really,' I said. As the blur of my failed attempt to break through to our world came back to my mind, I remembered Castus and his warriors, preparing to face an irresistible charge. I thought of Loridine, and all the terrible slaughter there. Tears filled my eyes.

Sanvaunt was angry with me.

'What did you think you were doing?' he said, breathless. 'You could have—I don't even know what you could have done. Burned yourself to nothing, or worse. We can't lose you. We need you, Raine. I need you.'

He pulled me close, hard limbs pressing me against him. He used to smell of horses, old leather, and some of the time, the sharp acridness of rose-thistle. Those old scents were gone these days. Now, he smelled like hot stone. I let myself be held. I breathed him in.

'It's so quiet,' I said. I rested my head against his shoulder.

'No quieter than it was,' he said. He didn't let me go.

'No,' I said. 'Inside. It's all quiet.'

And then I realised what I was saying. My mind sank down through me, reached inside me, searching for the soul-cage within me—but they were gone. All of them. The souls I'd held captive, the unquiet, restless dead had disappeared. I hadn't realised just how much I'd hated holding them there, how corrupted it had felt, how I'd violated myself. It filled me with nausea now, but there was too much going on. Those poor, poor souls at Loridine—my heart broke for the world. But despite everything, selfishly, it felt so good to be quiet again. To be clean, on the inside.

'Thank you,' I said quietly. 'Thank you for everything. I'm so sorry, Sanvaunt. I'm so sorry for everything I've done to you. Every time I hurt you. Every time I was selfish, or cruel or stupid. I'm so, so sorry.'

'It's all right,' Sanvaunt said gently. He pried back from me. 'It's all right.'

But it wasn't all right, was it? I'd been so selfish. I'd been so self-absorbed. I'd pushed foolishly close to the veil, the boundary between the Fault and our world, without the means to traverse it, and it had nearly killed me.

'I'm drained,' I said. 'Makes me wish there was food around here. I know we don't need it here, but I'd kill for a bowl of mutton stew. Even bad stew. Even just, I don't know, a cold hard turnip.' He smiled at me and let me go. I guess you can always tell someone's feeling better when they start talking about food. He gave me a smile. My apology must have hit home, because it actually touched his eyes.

'And a cold pint of beer. Just one. Just one nice, cellar-chilled pint of Bunk's dark bitter. And a pie to go with it.'

'Ham and leek,' I said. 'With extra gravy. And a sausage-wrapped egg in crumbs on the side. With yellow pickled vegetables.'

Sanvaunt closed his eyes, imagining it for a moment, but then everything we'd seen came back down on him.

'I'm sorry about Castus,' he said. 'I'm really sorry. He and I didn't get on all that well, but I know he mattered to you.' He climbed down from the table, offered me a hand to help me down too. I didn't need his hand, but it was nice that he offered it.

'You got on well with him when you put your tongue in his mouth,' I said, but there was no bite in it. On a drizzly field back in the real world, Castus's fate was sealed. It seemed only fair to make the kind of joke that he'd have made. He always loved embarrassing people. I felt the lump rise, the salt-hot pressure behind my eyes threatening to break through.

'He told you about that, huh?' Sanvaunt said. 'I'm not ashamed of it.'

'If you had to pick a man to learn yourself with, I think you picked a good one,' I said. 'It's all distant history now. It's funny, I think he'd rather be remembered for the people he kissed rather than the people he killed. And he killed a lot of them.'

Over the months in the Fault, I'd turned my thoughts all around that until they fit into a slot where I could keep them without sobbing. I'd done a terrible thing when I worked the Soul Reaper against the Winterra. I'd killed hundreds of Draoihn, no less. The half-dead didn't count, they'd already been well on their way, had half-lived much too long anyway. But when I felt for that carefully stowed memory now, it was like I was remembering something somebody else had done. Like I'd been a spectator, just as I had been to all those terrible things the dark queens of the past had done to the world.

I was still in shock, I thought. Everything we'd seen in Loridine, everything we knew was happening to the world. We'd imagined and Maldouen had told us what was going on, but seeing it up close was different. Seeing it up close made it personal.

'We have to tell the others what we saw,' I said.

'Raine.' Sanvaunt took my arm as I started for the stairs. 'We can't scry like this again. It's too dangerous. Both times you tried it—I don't know what would have happened if you hadn't pulled back this time. We need to escape this place, but properly. Safely.'

'We'll try,' I said. 'But the Faded have been trapped here for seven centuries and more. It's not designed to be escaped.'

'But occasionally they've got through,' he said. 'Like the Remnant Sul. We'll get out of here, Raine. Mark me.' For a few moments his eyes seemed to be swift-flowing channels of molten metal. 'And when we do, our retribution will be the mark of a new Age.'

·   ·   ·   ·   ·   ·

There was no bitter dark beer to be drunk, and no sausage-wrapped egg. There was just a brutal delivery of terrible, world-changing news.

Maldouen didn't flinch, but then, he was made of metal. Esher took the news about as well as anybody could. Sanvaunt and I didn't talk it through ahead of time, but neither of us mentioned the chain of prisoners on their way to dig their own graves. It already felt hopeless enough. Sanvaunt also omitted that I'd drained myself and nearly done something worse. Maldouen had been right: trying to push myself through the veil had felt like I'd been ripping myself in half.

'Well,' Maldouen said when we were done with our account. 'My Crowns held for a long time. I did some good, didn't I?'

'You did a lot,' I said. 'It's not your fault.'

'If I'd built the fifth Crown somewhere other than Ithatra, it might all have been different,' Maldouen said. 'How was I supposed to know an ocean could swallow a whole country?'

'It's not over yet,' Esher said. 'What now?' While we'd been scrying she and Maldouen had been up to something, but they hadn't offered it up. She wore her hair in a fall that covered her milky, unseeing eye. She did that when she felt self-conscious. How wonderful a thing it was, I thought, to know that about somebody else. To become close enough to know the thoughts they'd had. I'd treated her so poorly, even after all she'd done for me.

'Nothing much. Kill Iddin. Go to the City of Spires, and find our way home,' I said.

'Same old problem,' she said. 'If we walk towards it, it moves away.'

'That was the point of it,' Maldouen said wistfully. 'I thought it particularly clever. The Crowns' focal point is the City of Spires, and that's where I housed the Eldritch Kin—the Faded—and the demons Hallenae had managed to pull through the Fault. It looks like a city from afar, but it's not, really. Just an artistic sort of flourish.'

'It's just a folly? An artificial thing to look at?'

'Essentially,' Maldouen said. 'Though I never expected anyone to really spend time looking at it. The Crowns converge there.'

'There must be a back door to it,' I said. 'Surely you put something in?'

'Do you think I'd have sat around trapped here with all the monsters if I had?' Maldouen said, his metal jaw wagging up and down as if it was actually part of what made the words.

'What we need is some kind of beacon,' I said. 'Something stronger than the magic you used to keep things from getting to it.'

'That would be lovely,' Maldouen said. 'But there isn't. And tomorrow, we're expecting a visitor. You should all get some rest.'

There were nods. The news we'd shared had been too bleak. Too hard to take, even in its neutered, half-measure version.

'Before you go,' I said. I sucked on my lower lip. 'Before you go, I just want you to know that I'm sorry. I'm sorry I've been such a terrible shit to you both. I didn't mean to. I love you both very much. I'll do better.'

'We all have our burdens, Raine,' Esher said gently. 'Sometimes things just overflow in the wrong way.' She smiled. Sanvaunt smiled too.

Sanvaunt left first. Esher waited a few moments, then sighed and followed him. Maldouen was about to leave me alone.

'Wait,' I said. 'You seem to have perfected painting and sculpture while you've been here.'

'Thank you,' he said.

'How are you with music?'

'Name your instrument,' he said, and sounded like he was smiling, even though his changeless face looked as morose as an eyeless child should.

'Can your servants deliver invitations to the others in an hour? And different clothes?'

'What kind of clothes?'

'Something fit for a ball.'

* * * * * *

I was the first to arrive in that strange, statue-filled ballroom. Maldouen had somehow cleared some of the statues out of the way—it shouldn't have been surprising, given that he'd been the one to put them all there in the first place, but it was the first time I wondered how strong that small metal body had to be. The dance floor alternated in black and white tiles. Four identical metal servants stood inert up in a gallery, looking down on us.

'My dear, I have spent many lifetimes on works of art,' Maldouen said. 'But you outshine them all.'

I did. I *did* outshine them all. I'd never truly appreciated myself this way. There'd always been a whisper in the back of my mind that could only see the damage. I wore a floor-length dress of royal blue and daffodil yellow, blue and yellow ribbons in my hair. And it was *good* hair. Yes, it was weird and white, but I'd earned that, hadn't I? I'd worn a face of glamours, which had been applied by one of the metallic servants who bafflingly understood how to do them. I'd had her leave the wrong-angle scar on my face uncovered. It was part of me, all of it was part of me, this one body that I feared, this mind I'd feared. I deserved to show myself, to present my face to the sun and let its rays fall on me. I hadn't been scarred, I'd *survived,* and that's a beautiful thing in its own right.

'Thank you,' I said. 'For the compliment, and the beautiful clothes.'

'I'm glad someone got to wear them. I spent about seventeen years learning to tailor,' he said. 'Now if you'll excuse me . . .' He disappeared through a small door that was disguised to seamlessly appear part of a mural. His heavy, clanking footsteps receded.

Up in the gallery, a sharp snare drum sounded, a rattle of beats announcing a new arrival. Sanvaunt appeared in the doorway.

I'd gone for blue and white. Sanvaunt had worn a coat of deep green in a style that didn't exist in our world beyond the Fault. It had long tails, rows of gleaming golden buttons. Beneath it he wore a white shirt and a cravat in gold, grey breeches, tall boots. It was best not to think where Maldouen got the materials to craft all these things, particularly the shiny black leather. Sanvaunt had tied his hair back in a tail, and he'd shaved—the first time since we'd found ourselves in the Fault. He was gorgeous, picking his way between the motionless dancers to the cleared area.

'Feels strange wearing this after the day we had,' Sanvaunt said.

'We've had nothing but bad days for months,' I said. 'I feel like I've been painted on the inside. Painted with something thick and matte, so much of it that the outside doesn't always get into me. I don't think it's silly. We might not have another chance. If nothing else, let's use the one we've been given.'

The drum beat sounded again, and Esher waltzed into the archway.

'Light Above,' Sanvaunt and I said in unison.

Esher was sleek and immaculate in scandalous red, and her confidence in it was blazing. She'd fixed her hair in what they called a Kwendish braid. She put her back against the doorframe, stretched her arms above her head.

'This old thing?' she drawled, screwing up her nose to stop herself snorting a laugh. But she did. She actually laughed. I used to think of it as giving me a tingle, but this was something different. I positively squirmed. Sanvaunt didn't know where to put his eyes. But instead of stalking towards us like a mistcat she bounced on the balls of her feet, cackling with laughter at the effect she'd had on us. She'd always been confident, but I'd never seen her this . . . this dominant in her own skin. It was at odds with her blinded eye, still hidden by an artfully placed curtain of hair below the wrap of braid. As she hopped up she grabbed our hands and began turning us in a circle. Up in the gallery the servants raised fiddles and began to play.

'Wait!' Esher shouted. The music stopped. She looked up to Maldouen's blindfolded face, just about peeking out from the balcony. 'Can I use it straight from one of the globes?'

'Any of them,' Maldouen called back down. Amused? 'They're all connected. Just do it like I showed you.'

'Use what?' Sanvaunt asked, but Esher held up a finger to silence him, then practically scampered over to the wall. She put her hand on one of the light globes, and they all began to flicker.

'Oh,' Sanvaunt said, catching his breath. 'Oh my world.' I gave him a puzzled glance. I didn't understand what was happening.

The lights continued to flicker, dimming, pulsing back, as Esher pressed her hand to it. Then she kicked off a shoe and pressed her bare toes to the floor.

Sanvaunt's jaw hung open. He understood something I didn't.

'Now!' Esher shouted, and the music struck up again.

The dancers began to move. All at once the painted statues, the inanimate dancers around the room, lurched into life. One moment they were still, and then they were moving. They turned each other in easy, graceful circles, arms held at firm angles. Around Sanvaunt and me, two dozen pairs of figures moved in time to the music. Their footsteps were loud, stone against the black and white tiles.

'Second and Third,' Sanvaunt said. He looked at me. I didn't understand. He put a hand on my shoulder, but more to steady himself. 'Don't you hear it?' he said. 'She's in Sei and Taine at once. She's *doing* this.'

'How?' I said. But Esher was striding back towards us now, a grin spread so wide across her face I could have been dazzled by her teeth.

'Like this,' she said, and reached out and put her fingers to my cheek and Sanvaunt's. I understood instantly, far more than words could convey flowing from her and into us.

'And the *Fourth Gate*?' I said. 'How . . .'

Esher pushed back that sweep of hair. Where her eye had been clouded over, milky, it was now polished silver.

'Maldouen. He gave me his Gates,' Esher said.

We stared, agog. How could that happen? How could—and then my mind got past the shock and put it together.

'Like the curse of blood and bone,' I said. Ovitus had used such a curse to drain his uncle's Gates into himself, though by a different, darker means. And then, even though it wasn't the most important thing happening right then I asked, 'Can you see out of it?'

'Not at all,' Esher said. 'It hurt rather a lot replacing it, I think, but that's one of the many advantages of the Fourth Gate. I just snuffed that memory out of myself.' She looked around at her dancers. Their footfalls were a racket.

'He gave up his own power,' I said. 'He just gave it to you?'

'He thinks we're all doomed,' Esher agreed. 'So let's just enjoy the dancing, shall we?'

We enjoyed it. We danced and whirled as a trio. Our laughter rose louder than the stone footsteps. It was movement without constraint, with abandon, with *joy*. We arched under one another's arms, twisting in knots. But there's only so much you can do as a trio.

'You two dance,' I said, a little breathless. How Esher was managing all this, keeping the statues moving while she laughed and swore and we occasionally tripped over each other, I didn't know. It seemed to come so naturally to her, even with an eye of steel.

'You sure you want to sit out?' she asked.

'We'll take turns,' I said. And so we did.

Esher danced with Sanvaunt, and then I danced with her. I danced with Sanvaunt, then we all danced together, we danced apart, we galloped up and down the dance floor, then we went on, and on, taking turns. The music followed our moods, sometimes lively, sometimes poignant, and as I took a breather I glanced up to the balcony where the servants played.

'Thank you,' I mouthed to Maldouen. A night to feel alive again. A wasteful, pointless separation from all the terrible things going on in the world. Here we were isolated. Here we were apart from the night.

I watched Esher and Sanvaunt dancing, rotating slowly, her head resting on his shoulder. I didn't begrudge them. There was no jealousy in me anymore. That had been flushed from me when I fell from scrying on Castus, like the enormity of it had washed me clean on the inside.

'This dance is for you,' I whispered, and I hid the tears. Swallowed them down as best I could. Esher soon appeared by my side and directed me back towards Sanvaunt. It was my turn to dance slowly with him. It should always have been like this, I thought. Those times I'd let him down, when I'd been too much of a coward to go to him. Like the time I'd kissed Esher and fouled that up. It didn't seem to matter anymore. None of it did. I danced with Esher the same way. She had no perfume. She smelled like life.

'I think that's all I can manage,' Esher said breathlessly. She stepped back from me and bowed. I bowed. Sanvaunt came to join us, completing the triangle, and he bowed too. We all linked hands.

The music began to die away, and the statues turned to face one another, bowed. Then one by one they settled back into their original positions.

'That was incredible,' Sanvaunt said. He looked even better with sweat in his hair.

'It was,' I said. 'Thank you, Esher.'

'That too,' Sanvaunt said. 'But more than that. Both of you. Thank you. There was never a night like it.'

Esher breathed out slowly as if half in a daze. She looked from me, to Sanvaunt, to me, to Sanvaunt.

'Fine. If nobody else is going to, then I'll do it.'

She took me by the back of the head and put her mouth against mine. She kissed me fiercely, and sent explosions through my whole body. It was brief. She broke away and drew Sanvaunt down to her, and kissed him too. A few seconds each way.

She stepped back and rested her elbow in her hand.

'Get on with it,' she said. 'Go on.'

I turned to Sanvaunt. I'd never kissed him before. It should have been awkward, but he was far less confused and overwhelmed than I was and his tongue met mine. Explosions, more of them. A surge of life. It was every-thing. Both of them were everything.

'Good,' Esher said. 'Now if you'll excuse me, I'm exhausted and my head's spinning and I think I better sleep.'

'Yes,' Sanvaunt said. Breathless and dazzled. 'Rest is definitely what I'm thinking about.' Esher and I laughed, we were all laughing then. I wasn't the only one that had squirmed.

'We'll let you walk back last to keep your dignity,' Esher said. 'Good-night!'

She turned from the ballroom and walked away, a swirl of crimson skirts.

'That obvious, was it?' Sanvaunt said.

'Pretty obvious,' I said. I was grinning. My face hurt from all the grin-ning, but I couldn't help it. 'But good to know.'

I followed Esher, found my room, and when I lay down on the bed, I just stared upwards, all a whirl, all a flutter, wondering if life could ever be more exciting than this, or if the best thing that had ever happened to me had just manifested when I needed it most. There was too much to think about. In the past I would have lain awake, thinking about everything that needed to be done, needed to be considered, how it would look, what it meant and where anything would go. Instead I just lay there, and remembered the wonder of the world.

. . . . . .

'Raine,' a rasping, dry-throated voice said in the darkness of sleep. It was a voice filled with threat, a voice that carried the croaking of crows. I sat bolt upright.

Standing in my room, a ghost of blue-and-white vapor stood wearing the most ridiculous witch's getup I'd ever seen in my life. Her hair flowed thick and white to her knees, dark warpaint across her cheeks, a fan of sword-like spines at her back.

'Oh dear Light Above,' I muttered.

'I think,' this other Raine said to me across the veil, 'we may have made a mistake.'

In some ways, it felt that we were in the wrong places. The Raine I'd left behind in the Fault was not made for the terrors that crawled from its cracks, that lurked beneath the surface of its stinking marshes. Here she would have had people who could have looked after her, taken care of her, helped her. She needed them, the wimp. I could have worried for her, but I didn't feel like it, and I had more pressing concerns.

I hadn't known I'd left her behind, whatever she was. I'd dreamed my way back to her, but it was a waking dream, comprised of a thousand moments, and I only knew I'd been in it when the memory formed. The part of me that was able to reach her didn't lie on the surface. The thoughts that flow and run across our surface are merely the shoots and buds that break through; pretty, fragile, visible. But the surface is merely the means for the roots beneath the ground to survive.

It was all clear to me now. Those haunting memories, the ones I'd had to delve into, seeking, searching, came to mind bold and clear at a moment's consideration. The experiences of the tyrants of the past had bled into me, had become memories of my own, no longer distinct or separate. I knew everything they'd ever known. The magic at my command was great enough to break the world should I choose, should I capture enough of the squealing, pitiful dead to burn on my soul-altar. There was a draw to that, a tantalising, hungry pull at my mind. I wanted to be fed. No more shame, no more guilt over what I was. No more constraint in my heart.

Exhilarating.

I was too exhausted to enjoy it properly just then. My heart might have hungered for battle, but forcing myself back through the veil had taken its toll. Worse, there was a retreat to take care of.

Retreat. The word disgusted me.

I couldn't ride on a wagon. That would have put me with the wounded, and already I could see the change that had come over the weary, blood-stained warriors of the rebel clans. They were LacClune by majority, but LacShale, LacDaine, and numerous minor clans had a presence in the ranks. It took something monumental to bring the stronger clans together in this way, but these were monumental times. They needed to be inspired. I'd given them a reprieve from the certainty of defeat and I needed to look the part. Someone found me a horse, almost full grey but for his one dark sock.

'What's he called?' I asked.

'Ghost,' Castus said, his lip quirking. He chose to walk. Too many men were more in need of a mount than he was just then. I had never taken him for a walker.

'He'll do,' I said.

Castus looked up at me with his usual smart-arse smile, but with the battlefield five miles to our backs and the threat of immediate death gone, everything he'd been taught, everything he'd known about those like me, had to be bubbling up to the surface. He knew what this meant for him, for his clan, if anyone survived.

Castus LacClune would be remembered by history as a Draoihn who had allied with the Sarathi. There would be a name for the battle—such as it had been—back on that hillside. Or there would be, if enough of humanity survived the Fault flooding into our world. When we won, there would be a name for this leg of the fight too. I would ensure it. I planned on being around for a very, very long time.

I could have taken them all single-handedly, given enough souls to draw from. The arrow-rain had been a smart idea—Ovitus knew his military history. My Banshee's Wail had used up all my hoarded souls, but its results had replenished them and more. A Sarathi going into battle only grows more powerful the more she kills. Protecting myself from that hail of arrows had drained those resources without replenishing them. If I had enough of the dead at my command I could go head-to-head with Ovitus and all his traitors, but there were two major issues. First, I didn't have that well of power to draw on and generating it was traditionally the undoing of those such as I. And secondly, there was that thrice-cursed dog, and that, I did not think I could defeat. Not yet.

It was Iddin who stood in my way. Had it just been Ovitus and his Draoihn ranged against me, I would have taken them on. I would have snuck into their camp as mist, cut souls from bones, rolled a tide of death across them and left myself a clear path to Redwinter.

'You saved us all,' Castus said. He was grateful to be alive, but his conscience didn't feel clean. Whatever else he was—hedonist, nobleman, smart-arse—Castus LacClune was Draoihn. He'd not spoken up for me at my trial. How could he have, when I stood there, a half-corpse with a mortal wound in my chest? I sensed his thoughts.

'The Sixth Gate is just a weapon, like any other,' I said. 'You'll have to get over it quickly. We don't have time to waste on foolish traditions anymore.'

'It's not like any other,' Castus disagreed. He took a deep breath. He was locking away his old beliefs, slipping down latches and binding them into dark chests. They'd come out eventually, maybe, but for now, he needed me. 'But I'll take whatever help I can get. I thought you were dead. Everyone did.'

'I was,' I said. 'But I'm back. I'm going to take the Keystone and delay the calamity. If you have a level-headed candidate to bear the Crown, my ears are open.'

How quickly a home can be lost, changed, warped into something of threat. I would have to evade the enemy, infiltrate my former home, break into its vault of magic and then fight my way into Harranir's castle and open the Great Seal. It wouldn't matter who took it. I'd herd men and women down there by the thousand until one of them took control of it and if not halted, at least slowed the Fault's flow into my world.

My world.

And why shouldn't it be? All my lives I'd been made to exist in fear, a nightmare crafted by the small-mindedness of meaningless people. They'd had the power and made me suffer for it. The power was mine now. I could remake the world as I wanted it to be.

'Hanaqin Clanless tried that already,' Castus said. 'Ovitus refused him. They fought it out.'

I recalled through my scrying the damage done in Redwinter. Hanaqin had been a member of the Council of Night and Day, though he hadn't been seen for over a decade. After Grandmaster Robilar and my master Ulovar had died, Kelsen had followed. It had been a disaster three times over in just a day, leaving only two Draoihn capable of entering the Blackwell besides myself. One had been Castus's father, who lay now in one of the wagons.

The other had been Hanaqin Clanless, who had been gone long before I ever entered Redwinter.

Now there was just me.

'Why wouldn't Ovitus allow Hanaqin to open the Crown and have it contained? Even he must see the damage being done to the world. Even him.'

Castus shook his head sorrowfully. He'd been better at masking that sorrow, once.

'When men feel hard done by, they build a fortress around themselves in mistrust and lies. They begin rejecting truth, because it has become a currency to them, and their belief lies only in that which makes them feel safe. The world is not round as was proven by mathematicians thousands of years ago, it is flat! These people look different from us, love differently from us, are called differently to us—they're not people at all! And so on, and so on, until there's no difference between truth and lies at all.'

'What happened to Hanaqin?'

'Dead, so our spies relayed. He took a good number of Ovitus's Draoihn of the Third Gate with him, but they stopped him before he could make the Blackwell. Ovitus keeps it guarded beyond reason. He can't open the Crown himself, so nobody can. Going for the Blackwell is a suicide mission, Raine. Even seeing what you did back on the field there, do you think you can stop a dozen bolts of lightning at once?'

'The Crown must be controlled,' I said. 'I came back from the dead for it.'

That wasn't quite true, but the queens who rode with me thought it sounded better. Besides, if I told Castus I'd come back to save him, we'd both have felt lesser for it.

'Then help me regroup and fight a war with me,' Castus said. 'Let's march into Redwinter together.'

'With Ovitus's head on a spike?'

'If I leave that much of him spikeable.'

'One thing at a time,' I said. 'Keep these men moving. They're not much but they're a start.'

As Castus moved on to keep his people moving, a ghost climbed up from one of the wagons, stood and peered back the way she'd come. She patted her torso down as if surprised the pain was gone, then looked back at her body and for a moment pain warred with frustration and disappointment as she realised she was dead.

Do you want to join me? I asked silently. I didn't need to speak into the aether. They understood. The ghost looked in my direction. She shook her head. *There could be vengeance.*

'I'll join you,' she said, and before she had time to reconsider, she was drifting through the air, turning to green-tinged mist, flowing into my fingers, up my arm, into the cage of my heart. Her name had been Yanessa. She'd been born in a village near to Clunwinny and her family farmed salt. Salt farming hadn't been for her. She ran away with a boy who proved to have lied about his prospects in the city, so she left him for another, and another. They were all useless dolts. Eventually she'd found her place as a warrior serving her clan, and it had brought her contentment.

I watched the battle that Castus had lost through her eyes. They'd been confident after taking Dunfenny so easily, had marched to join Merovech LacClune's forces, had marched on Harranir itself. Their advance had gone poorly. Ovitus's forces had been led by a trio of Brannish magicians— Artists, they called them. It wasn't clear what their magic had done, why it had turned the tide so decisively, but thousands were dead, wounded or captured. We knew they could alter what was real in some way, changed what our men saw, but those subjected to it hadn't survived. Yanessa had taken a spear in the thigh, the steel gouging into bone. Her blood had gone bad. It had been a painful death. I thought I'd try to use what remained of her for something significant. Something that could make it more meaningful. That's the thing with a battle, it's all just so random. Those brave cavalrymen couldn't have predicted a wraith would turn up in the middle of the field and wipe them out with a howl. I doubt any of them had understood what was happening even at the time. The survivors likely didn't know either.

Castus led us three hours into the night. For a while we'd been followed by distant outriders, but we lost all track of them as darkness fell. We had no tents, no form of shelter, not even for the wounded. It would be a night spent beneath cloaks, for those few who had them, and dawn would tell the tale of which of our weakest had survived the cold.

'They could come for us in the night,' I rasped. My voice had suffered badly from that scream.

'The first thing to know about war is that the larger the force, the slower it crawls,' Castus said. He held his arms out and a lad of no more than twelve began helping him with the buckles. The boy moved mutely, blankly, battle-shock numbing him.

'How did they catch you then?' I asked.

'I stopped to let the men rest,' Castus said. 'It was an error. Ovitus force-marched his men to keep up with us.'

'He could do it again,' I said.

'I doubt his men have much left in them after today.' Castus grinned back at me. 'And they need to spend a while picking up their arrows if those archers are going to be any use at all. My guess is they'll make camp and try to bury what's left of their dead.' He took a deep breath. 'We're alive, Raine, and that's thanks to you.' He paused. 'You can't help but see the way my people look at you. They're grateful, but they're afraid. You have to speak to them.'

'I will, but not tonight,' I said. 'Tonight I need to eat.'

Food. For the first time in six months, I was going to eat food.

There was little food in the camp, and an army doesn't hunt well, but we'd passed farms. We'd done what armies always do and pillaged the land as we went by. This was LacDaine land, and those clansmen had tried to offer recompense as we herded away—stole—sheep and cattle. It was likely better than they'd have received if Ovitus's army came through. *When* it came through. I ate meat, and it was rich and savoury, the juices exquisite. It had been half a year since I'd last eaten anything. My body wasn't happy about it, as though old, forgotten machinery was being put to work, crusted with rust, but the rules here weren't the rules of the Fault. It tasted divine.

The next three days we simply marched for as long as the light would al-low. We saw more outriders, but they weren't prepared to attack us. I slept at every opportunity. My body was remembering what it meant to be human, to breathe real air, drink real ale. I hadn't taken a piss in six months and the first time wasn't exactly comfortable, and neither was the second. I kept these things to myself, as befits a witch queen pissing in the bracken.

On the fourth night, I agreed to speak with the command council, such as they were. Some fallen logs had been dragged to form benches around a fire.

'We need to discuss our situation,' I said, sitting opposite Castus. The surviving leadership of our small force sat as far from me as they could, save for Van Hallum LacShale, the man who'd given me his knee, a huge warrior with a big red beard and a smattering of pox scars beneath his eyes. He alone didn't seem to fear me. I hadn't known it before, but he'd been Liara's father's cousin, making him her first cousin once removed. Ovitus had accused me of her murder, when I'd been lashed up to the pyre, and it wasn't as if I'd been able to argue my side.

The youngest of them was a man with a port-wine-coloured birthmark across half his face, Dinny LacDaine, a wildrose child of Prince Caelan LacDaine, wherever he'd got to. Caelan was supposed to be first in line for the succession, but hadn't returned to Harranir when Grandmaster Robilar recalled the Winterra. He hadn't wanted the Crown. It was hard to blame him, but it probably hadn't helped. I'd heard of Dinny LacDaine, the prince's illegitimate son, but I'd thought him in his teens, not his early twenties. War made people grow up fast, I supposed.

The others had avoided me since my timely battlefield arrival. It must have been hard for them. They knew they'd be dead without me, and yet, I was anathema to their life's endeavour. Sarathi, ancient enemy of Redwinter, the reason to fight.

Draoihn Palanost had taught me to work incantations. She was still ab-surdly tall, taller than most men, dark-skinned and regal, and her face was set the way it did when one of the apprentices had tried to fool around with a spell. She didn't sit. She wore her oxblood coat, and hadn't laid down her spear. Councillor Suanach LacNaruun was bald as a fish, and despite his ad-vanced age moved easily in his Draoihn-wrought armour. Little wonder— he'd been the master of artifice in Redwinter, and one of the three members of the Council of Night and Day who'd adjudicated at my Testing. Neither he, nor Palanost, were happy to see me.

'Nice to see some familiar faces,' I said. My voice had not recovered from all that screaming. I sounded like I'd smoked a pipe without relent for fifty years.

'You know that by right, we should arrest you,' Palanost said coldly. Her accent delivered every word like a fist. I heard the grinding of her skin against the spear-haft as she twisted it in her grip. She was only a Draoihn of the First Gate, but her command of Eio was so fine, so expert, as to be inaudible. I suspected she held that trance now.

'I think the old rules died when you rebelled against Redwinter,' I said. She at least was able to meet my eye. That was saying a lot about someone's mettle, these days. 'What about you, Councillor Suanach, do you want to arrest me too?'

'The Council of Night and Day no longer exists in any functioning sense,' Suanach said. He couldn't take his eyes from me even if he couldn't meet me when I looked back at him. He'd never come face-to-face with a Sarathi before. He'd probably believed what they'd told him, that a Sarathi can look and seem just like any other Draoihn. That could have been true, but I had to admit that in my black-and-gold Witching Skin, with warpaint on my face and rasping like a pantomime villain, the case could be made that I stood out pretty obviously.

'A lot has changed in the six months I've been gone,' I said.

'Six months?' Castus said. He shared a look with the others. 'You think it's been six months since the night Ovitus tried to burn you?'

'Give or take.'

'Raine,' Castus said solidly, 'we haven't seen you in three years.'

'Oh,' I said. I'd been feeling cocky, and that did take me back a little. 'Time flies when you're . . . you know.'

'Wedding the Night Below?' Palanost said darkly. I shrugged at her and stirred up a spirit or two to make my hair blow without a wind. It made all of them flinch, all but her. She wanted to kill me. She'd been my teacher once. She was twice my age, but she wanted to put that spear right through my heart.

Time had been a mess in the Fault, but clearly it moved differently to here. Of course it had, when Slow was one of the directions, why had I expected it to align? At least it hadn't been going faster in the Fault. I could have escaped it only to find everyone had been dead for hundreds of years.

'I see. Well, everything's gone to hell in that time, hasn't it?'

'Where have you been, that you've learned these forbidden arts?' Palanost demanded. Wanted to stab me. I could feel it. Suanach reached out and laid a liver-spotted hand on her arm without looking at her.

They deserved the truth. I owed them something at least.

'I've known them all along,' I said. Fine, not quite truth, but good enough. 'But it wasn't me doing harm in Redwinter, was it? It was that treacherous bastard Ovitus. I'll tell you about his dog and what it really is some other time, but I never laid a hand on anyone who didn't deserve it. And before any more accusatory looks get slung in my direction, I'll remind you who saved all of your hides on the battlefield.'

'To what end?' Palanost demanded. She shook off Suanach's arm. 'This is not right, Lord Draoihn LacClune. Ovitus LacNaithe is power hungry and has done great wrong but this—this is worse.'

'You want to stab me, don't you?' I said. I didn't get up. 'Why don't you try it and see how that goes for you?'

'I should have known it the day you rotted that pie,' Palanost said. 'I thought you'd simply made an error.'

'I've made plenty,' I said. I held my hands out to the fire. My skin had grown icy-pale under the Fault's cold, sunless sky. 'I don't care if you squirm at what I am. I don't care if you're afraid of things that rattle your window-panes in the night. Our goals are aligned. I intend to place one of our usual puppets into the Crown, have him control it, and hope that buys us enough time to try to fix the others, or find a new solution. Brannlant's Crown has fallen and Loridine is annihilated. The Crowns of Ithatra, Osprinne and Khalacant are gone too. We have to retake Harranir to buy time.'

'Loridine fell?' Castus said. 'When?'

'The same day I saved your sorry behinds,' I said. 'You don't have to like me. You don't have to like my methods. You definitely won't. But I'm going to need your strength and your warriors. I have to reach the Blackwell in Redwinter. Without the Keystone I can't open the Great Seal.'

'I will not assist a Sarathi to breach the Great Seal,' Palanost said fiercely.

'The world is dying,' I hissed. I might have been angrier at my old teacher, but some old affection for her remained. 'Pick a side. It's me, or it's Ovitus LacNaithe. There are no other options in the time left to us.'

'What happened to the others?' Castus asked.

'Others?'

'Sanvaunt LacNaithe. Esher of Harranir. They escaped with you that night on a moon horse. I remember it clear as day.'

'Them?' I said. 'I guess they're still in the Fault.' I hadn't thought of them at all since I tore my way back into the world. I hadn't wanted to. I was so much freer now that I'd left them behind. I hadn't realised how much they'd been holding me back. I'd put so much of myself into them, had allowed too much of them to creep into me, when this was what I should have been all

WITCH QUEEN OF REDWINTER

along. Me, and the memories of the great, that was all I needed right now. I could make myself an arrow, focused, speeding towards the heart of my target. I'd shed the unnecessary weight.

My answer did not satisfy Castus, but he held his tongue for now.

'You really went into the Fault? Beyond the veil?' It was Dinny LacDaine speaking now, the first words he'd found for me. He wasn't Draoihn, so I bothered him less.

'Halfway to the Night Below,' I said. 'It's worse than you've ever imagined. But I already know what happened to me. What I need to know is what happened here while I've been gone.'

Palanost sat back, her eyes dark and gleaming. Suanach tried to look impassive, diplomatic, but he didn't like me either.

'It didn't go down well when you escaped, as you can imagine,' Castus said. 'We were divided. There were those that believed you were—well, what you are. And then there were us.'

'Sorry to disappoint you.'

'It didn't matter what anyone believed in the end,' Hallum LacShale said, his voice a rumbling roll of cavern echoes. 'LacNaithe declared himself grandmaster, and he had the support of the Winterra and enough Draoihn that it was so. There was no way to challenge him. You'd been Grandmaster Robilar's protégé, and he was the one who stood up to her. The pieces all seemed to fit neatly enough.'

'Then why didn't you all accept him?'

'Because that is not the way that things are done,' Palanost said starkly. 'And there were those of us who knew Sanvaunt LacNaithe, and Draoihn Esher, and you. And for all that she was, Grandmaster Vedira Robilar had the power of life within her, Vie, the Fifth Gate. She could never have been Sarathi.'

'And then there was my father,' Castus said. He had the look of a man on the last edge of his reserves. Little wonder, to have been bearing such responsibility at such a young age. All that danger, all the blood, it seeps into you like red wine spreading across a carpet. Even if you wipe away the spillage, a stain remains. 'Ovitus demanded my father open the Great Seal so he could put his own candidate on the throne. My father refused, insisted that the heir be elected, by tradition. Before anyone could say much else he was raising men, Ovitus was raising men, and the north was raising men but mostly to fight itself since Onostus LacAud was killed.' Castus was fiddling with a leather strap. He twisted it one way and then the other, wrapped it around his fist, spilled it out and wrapped it around the other. His grip tightened on it now. 'He laid that at your door.'

'He doesn't lie about everything,' I said. 'He lies about a lot of things, but I did kill Onostus.' I looked at Hallum LacShale. 'He killed Liara LacShale. Murdered her on a whim.'

'I know,' Hallum said. 'And I'm here beside you because you're the one who'll give me my vengeance. Was it . . .' He fumbled for the words. 'I hope she died well, with a sword in her hand.'

'Ovitus LacNaithe blasted her with lightning,' I said. 'She didn't have a chance. But she was dead in an instant. Be thankful for that. He'll wish for that brevity when the time comes.'

Perhaps they'd expected kind words. The sort of futile, meaningless bleats made to comfort someone in pain. It wasn't that I didn't know how to soften the cut, I just didn't see any point to it. Hallum LacShale would hurt all the same, would suffer just as I had suffered every loss, every slice across my skin, and that pain would turn into fury, and that I could use.

'It's been civil war,' Castus said, returning to the point. 'Minor skirmishes mostly, but costly. You remember my uncle, Haronus? He defected to Lac-Naithe's side. A lot of the Draoihn stuck with Redwinter. We had around a hundred, but most of them are dead. The sky began to bleed, and the world began to change. A town in the east just vanished into the earth. Beasts began to walk on their hind legs, mad, with rolling eyes. The wind carries voices. We bury the dead face down and chain them so they don't claw their way back out. And there are no children.'

'No children?'

'Not a babe has been born alive since the king passed. The world is dying. My father saw it, we all saw it, and he agreed to open the Crown. He had conditions, of course. A full end to the hostilities. The heir who would bear the burden of the Crown would be picked from LacAud's people, not ours, not his. And Ovitus would step down as grandmaster.'

'Naturally he refused.'

'Even in the face of the death of the world, he refused,' Castus said. 'He proclaimed my father to be in league with the Sarathi, and resumed full assaults on our holdings. He brought up more warriors from Brannlant, along with their Artists. I'll wager you haven't gone up against one of them yet. You should count yourself lucky.'

Castus may have been trying to instill a reasonable sense of caution in me, but I waved it away. I'd proven myself on the battlefield. It wasn't me that needed to be afraid.

'Whatever they are, I can promise you I've faced worse in the Fault,' I said.

'They're people, just like everyone else,' Hallum LacShale said.

'No,' Dinny LacDaine said hotly. 'They're *not* like everyone else. They're all from one Brannish bloodline and they're—different, somehow. They change what's real and what's not. They make it change until you don't recognise what's truth and what's a lie.'

'Whatever they are,' I said dismissively, 'they'll die like everything else.'

We dispersed shortly after that. There were still no tents, and I didn't need one. I didn't feel the cold anymore. Hallum LacShale saluted me—me, not Castus—and tromped off to be lordly among his remaining men. Castus and I were left alone.

'You're not as you were,' he said.

'Observant of you,' I said. 'You changed too.'

'You're harder,' he said.

'And you've softened.'

He hovered on the edge of something, a bleak precipice that he didn't want to step beyond. I was comfortable in the silence, because I didn't care. It just didn't matter. But Castus needed more certainty. He stared out from the hillside as if he might see creeping figures slowly crawling across the moor, but what concerned him was right by his side.

'You won't find the nerve to ask, so I'll just answer,' I said. 'No. You can't trust me, not completely. My goals are not to serve you, nor your clan, not even Redwinter. I'm going to take the world, because it needs taking, and that may not work out the way that everybody wants it to. But you can trust me to fight that shit Ovitus with everything available to me. And that will be enough for you.'

'And if we can beat Ovitus,' Castus said, 'if we win, and somehow we can reclaim Loridine, somehow try to take back the other Crowns. What then?'

'Why would you worry over something so unlikely?' I said. 'I've learned much, but even stabilising one Crown won't be enough. But I'll find a way. I have ideas. Some very old. Some new.'

'And you think you have the power to do that?' Castus asked. He kept his face calm, lordly. But the fear was there, like a second skin beneath the outer layer, wrapping him completely.

'I don't know,' I said. 'I'm only just learning what we're capable of.'

He said no more and walked away. I didn't have soft words of comfort. We were in retreat, in disarray. My battlefield slaughter had bought us time, but not much. It sometimes seemed that no matter what terrible, important things were happening around the world, somehow I was still dealing with Ovitus LacNaithe's wounded feelings. Only now, I had a more definite way of putting a stop to all that.

I went to one of the fires where warriors were cutting fresh meat into strips, affixing it to sticks to cook over their camp fires. I took one from a man's hand without asking, but he made no complaint. It hadn't been cooked yet, and as I walked through the camp it was rubbery, soft but un-yielding as I chewed it. Goat flesh. I sucked the juice down, revelled in it. I saw the goat's life in its blood. It had just been an ordinary, goat-like life. It hated a goose. It feared the woman who fed it for a time, but it had grown used to her. Flesh, and blood, and memories, and the consumption of life.

Delicious.

16

Somewhere across whatever gulf of time and space separated us, there was another part of me out there. She'd dreamed her way back into this world, but she could no more help me escape it than I could bring her back. I didn't know what it meant, or what I'd done. What we'd done, I supposed. Her visit had been brief, but one thing was clear: I had a foothold back in the real world, and somehow I was now fighting a battle on two fronts. I didn't know that I liked that other Raine. She seemed cold, grandiose, and as mad as it sounded, like she was keeping things from me. Things had been too perfect the night we danced for me to break the news to my friends just then. We had troubles enough.

The air was calm the morning that Iddin, king of the Fault, came to destroy us. Distantly, away beyond marsh and mountain both, we watched the Fault belch more of its essence upwards, channelling from the false city's spires up, up and into the vortex in the sky, calamities spilled upon my own distant, dying world. Everything that tore away from this place, every shred of its foulness, its bleeding essence, was a disaster, a nightmare, a horror upon my people. People can be shit to you. We're mostly bad to each other through life, and we make laws to keep one another in line because ultimately, we're rarely out for much but ourselves. I'd lived a rough life. My father, whoever he'd been, never knew I was born, and my mother had resented me as much as she loved me. I'd been used by a man who thought a girl was old enough at sixteen. I'd been used by the great and the powerful, put to work, taught for their own purposes. I'd been befriended and I'd been betrayed. Little of it was something that I would have carried forward with me.

But there's the smile a baby gives you when you touch your nose, there's the way it feels when a friend puts their arms around you, and does it matter if that tingle in your groin, your spine, behind your eyes is selfish when a handsome man runs up a wall for you, or a beautiful girl shares her strawberries?

There was joy in the perfecting of art, the bright burst of the sun through the god-lights of a cloud, the mystery and awe in the discovery of unseen places. Whatever the pettiness of mankind, whatever darkness we couldn't shake as a people, whatever bickering wasted our many long hours, at least we got to choose. At least it got a chance to exist.

I loved Sanvaunt and I loved Esher. They deserved to return, to live, to be who and what they were without constraint.

The Fault's advance into our world could not be permitted.

I wept for the people of Loridine, and I wept for the world.

She'd left me that. The other Raine. The tough, hard, cruel Raine who'd escaped the Fault. She'd left me my tears. To be unable to shed any had to be worse. She'd left me other things too. Vital, crucial, magical things that I'd been unable to let myself believe, to see, to touch. She'd left me as myself, or part of myself. She'd left me the things I wanted to be—though that other Raine likely felt the same about the parts she'd taken with her.

I sorted through the stone-headed arrows in my quiver. They were much too long—nearly five feet in length, unwieldy things, heavy at the broad stone head, too long and too weighted to fly from an ordinary bow. They were fully ridiculous, but then, they weren't made to bring down game or men on a battlefield. We all knew what this morning would bring. Not just the cold of breath steaming in that chill, nose-pinching way that only early morning can. Not just a broken sky. It brought the king of the Fault to our doorstep.

The blind, steel-made child, Maldouen, had spent millennia perfecting his skills in arts and craft. I stood upon the crenulations of his home's outer wall dressed in his finery. The metallic scales were purple, but so dark as to be close to black, so dark they drank the light around me as I stood upon the perimeter wall's battlements, a protector of this marvellous, impossible palace. Sanvaunt was all dragon-armour and rested a two-handed sword against his shoulder, a war-sword, a sword to slay beasts and monsters, as he stood down below in the courtyard alongside the Blind Child and Esher. She was blue and silver, her hair bound back in a severe braid as it flowed out beneath her helmet. I was alone up here. Part of me wanted to be down there with them, but this was the vantage point, and those stone-headed arrows were good friends with gravity. They'd want to dive. Sanvaunt and Esher turned to look up at me simultaneously. Talking about me, I supposed. The intoxication of those few scandalous moments at the end of our magical ball lingered in that look. Well, there would have been a scandal if there was anyone in this world to care about such things. But there wasn't, and we were all going to die fairly soon anyway, so the quiet smiles of assurance, the acknowledgement of our trepidation, were just what I needed. They were perfect to me, this boy, this girl. Fitting that we should all die together.

There was nowhere for us to go. A dark understanding that nobody had voiced. Whatever we'd tried for, however hard we'd believed we could escape this place, there was no way out. The land changed and shifted, presented one direction only to make it another. We could not go home. If not Iddin, then it would be something else, or else one day the whole of the Fault would pour through the widening vortex in the sky and we'd find ourselves flung back into a world that had once been ours, but no longer. A world of death, and demons, and pain.

We had prepared as best we could for this confrontation. Armour, weapons. Incantations scribed on leather, rolled and placed within our armour to soften the impact of individual blows. Maldouen had spent the night working on something larger, an incantation nearly fifty feet wide, scraped into the earth with the edge of a spade. He hadn't shared what that was supposed to be.

Maldouen's mountain citadel was still surrounded by an opaque wall of mist, which didn't dissipate or flow away, but there was movement within. The sky was burning red and gold as a series of heavy, thumping steps ushered from the white mist. The first advance of an enemy. It was beginning.

'Trow,' Maldouen declared, his metal voice ringing out. Methodical, not panicked, a captain declaring an action to be taken on his ship, a stage to undertake to get through a storm. 'He brought Trow.'

A whorl erupted through the wall of mist as it spiralled like the vortex above the city, opening a tunnel through the cloud. The tramp of great, booted feet was suddenly louder, and they emerged. I had seen Trow in Loridine when Sanvaunt and I had walked as ghosts. They had been sitting down there, drinking barrels of ale as if they held goblets, but I muttered a curse, one of Mama's curses from childhood that I'd forgotten long ago but seemed appropriate now. The Trow easily stood fifteen feet tall, some were maybe as high as twenty-five, and their torsos and arms were heavy, solid blocks. They came naked, sexless, unclad, but bearing tree branches, huge axes or swords. Four of them strode swiftly from the tunnel through the mist, coming on with staggering speed.

We all reached for our trances. I was fitting an arrow to my bow as I sought the First Gate.

I might as well have tried to put my hand through a stone wall.

There was nothing but silence in my mind. Panic spread like ink dropped into water. I sought Serenity, I sought out the Path of Awareness, guiding my mind towards that higher state of being that lay beyond the First Gate.

There was nothing. A terror I'd never known I could feel swept through me, as though I couldn't feel or move my legs, or my arms. A vital part of me was missing. I was losing control in the face of the terrors that now stalked towards us.

Down below, Esher and Sanvaunt must have opened their Gates, but I heard nothing. And I realised that I'd heard nothing the night before when Esher had turned statues to dancers. I heard no trances, I opened no Gates. I was just Raine, just an ordinary girl and that meant that if I had lost my First Gate . . .

I had not realised how much the Sixth Gate had come to form a part of me. Part of what I could do. Who and what I was. I reached for the Sixth Gate, for Skal, for the Gate of Death, sought to throw myself into that droning tunnel, but there was nothing there either. I was a prisoner within my own mind. I was just me. Just Raine. Just a powerless girl.

She had taken my Gates when she left me. She had stolen who I was, and left behind—whatever I was. The little I was.

There was no time to tell Sanvaunt and Esher. It had begun.

The first Trow hit one of Maldouen's tripwires and disappeared as a vast blossom of intense white light erupted upwards from some kind of device concealed in the ground. The Trow remained silhouetted within that light for a moment as it bellowed a deep, unearthly cry of pain. I shielded my eyes against the intensity. When I dared look back, when I could blink away the images imprinted on my vision, the lead Trow lay smouldering on the ground and the air smelled like a kiln.

The second Trow looked much like the first, only it carried a small fallen tree on its shoulder. It waved a hand, said something in the Trow-tongue which sounded like a slew of gravel pouring down a mountainside, and the remaining tripwires snapped one by one, pinging as they went. A good attempt, and it had taken one of them down at least. They weren't far from my friends. I ought to act now, knew I should act now. Fear of uncertainty paralysed me. I had no First Gate. I couldn't sense the blow of the wind, couldn't predict a muscle's twitch before it happened, I was just a normal young woman. What if I loosed my arrow badly and caught my friends in its power? These weren't ordinary arrows. My hands shook.

'We've no quarrel with you, Trow,' Sanvaunt called out. 'Stand back, or you'll burn.' He raised a hand and blue-gold fire engulfed his fist. Beauty-made-heat rippled down the blade of his sword in a wave. The Trow, murderous intent never leaving their blocky heads, slowed, then stopped. Sanvaunt, Esher and Maldouen looked tiny opposite them. Surrounded, though there were three on each side. The Trow conversed briefly with one another, all making gravel-cascade sounds simultaneously until they became a union. When the Trow spoke, their thoughts became their voices until all were agreed, and the avalanche became a harmony.

'Are you King Dunthan Haddat-Nir?' the Trow carrying the tree-club asked.

Had I not been trembling so violently at the loss of my Gates, it might have been funny.

'No,' Sanvaunt replied. His voice was strong, given what he was having to speak to. The Fault had numbed us to the monstrous beings that dwelt here to some extent but maybe—maybe I was a different person now. Maybe I'd lost the part of myself that could accept them so easily. I quivered with terror, had never felt more powerless, not when Braithe had hit me, not when the Queen of Feathers had punished me, not even when Ovitus bound me to a pyre. Part of me was missing. I watched Sanvaunt. His First Gate had to be pulsing from him alongside his Fifth but I heard none of it. I poured myself into watching him. It was the only way to keep upright. 'Dunthan Haddat-Nir died nearly twelve hundred years ago,' Sanvaunt told the Trow. 'I'm Sanvaunt LacNaithe, Draoihn of—'

The Trow did not care. It looked at Esher.

'Are you King Dunthan Haddat-Nir?'

'Yes,' Esher said. 'That's me.'

It was a bold move.

'You encased the Mother of Trow in stone and hid her from us,' the lead Trow said, a grinding rumble. 'For that we will do the same to you.'

'It was worth a shot,' I muttered to myself. But whatever nonsense had taken place in the distant past, I needed to act, to do something. One did not sword-fight a Trow, any more than one tried to wrestle a woolly rhinar. The trembling sound of the Trow's feet against the earth had not subsided even when they slowed. I realised it didn't come from them. It was something else. Something bigger, beyond the fog.

I had no Gates, but I was still Raine of Dunan, Raine Wildrose, Raine of the High Pastures, Raine of Redwinter. Maybe not the latter so much given all the death magic. But in those other lives, I'd never expected to rely on magic to get my work done. I brought back the string of Maldouen's white-wood bow, her draw far too easy for her size, enhanced through some kind of magic, felt the distance to the Trow as best I could and loosed. The heavy-headed arrow lashed down from the wall, blurred the air with heat where it passed. I missed the Trow I'd aimed at, but close-by was good enough.

The stone-headed arrow erupted in a blaze of black smoke, purple and green arcs of writhing energy. Two of the Trow began convulsing, dropping their huge weapons as the lightning seemed to latch onto them, wrapping them and intensifying. The one remaining giant raised its axe and bellowed an avalanche as it stomped forward. Sanvaunt cut out with his great sword and a wave of blue-and-gold fire left the blade, arcing into the Trow and shearing off one of its arms. Esher had moved fast. Maldouen had gifted her three further Gates, and his knowledge of how to use them. He'd gifted her centuries, and there had never been a Draoihn like her before. A curved sword in each hand, she slashed through the Trow's hamstring as if carving meat for a winter feast, then the other, bringing the giant down. Sanvaunt thrust into its head. Esher climbed its back to drive her blades home. She hopped down from it in a clang of metal.

The Trow who'd been in the arrow's blast only needed a quick mercy killing. Poor bastards. They'd had the worst of it.

'Is that all you have, Iddin, king of nowhere?' Maldouen called out. A bit cocky, given he wasn't doing any of the fighting. I was selecting another arrow from the quiver—I had seventeen of them, a good number—when the voice ushered from the tunnel carved through the mist.

'. . . No . . .'

Iddin had brought plenty.

We'd heard of the Flayed Men, Faded who'd been skinned alive and cut in half so that their pain fuelled their magic. They were legless, ripped torsos dragged slithering behind them on over-long arms. They dragged tattered entrails like tails, and they wove spells we'd never heard of. I wasted two of my arrows on them as they countered the magic before it got to them, but Sanvaunt and Esher fought through waves of pain sent rippling their way and put them to the sword. Whiplashes of energy cut at them, and by the time they'd finished the skinless men Sanvaunt's life-fire was needed to stem flows of blood. Maldouen's armour protected them from the worst of the enemy magic but it couldn't stop everything.

Iddin sent his creatures at us in waves. Trow, Flayed Men, they were only the beginning.

The half-dead fell in droves. Dozens of the Faded fought, and died with human-like screams and bestial howls. Next came Isthags bedecked with long beads of glass that whined with captured souls, insect-like Skweams chittering and clacking, and Racklas in scorched black armour, which stood up even to Sanvaunt's blazing sword for a time. Iddin sent his horrors, death-wailing banshees, toad-like Dulchers, even little Pechs, but we put them down, time after time. I loosed arrows into the enemy as they emerged, blasting them apart with fire, with lightning, with gravity, with sound. All the while, rumbling tremors continued to pulse through the ground. Small stones juddered and danced. The wall felt a lot less safe than it had before that sound began.

I saw no ghosts; my grave-sight had gone with my Gates. I gurgled a wail of frustration, furious at that other part of me that had stepped through the veil and stolen who I was. I'd started crying at some point, my face wet.

Before the waves of minions stopped coming, it became obvious that none of them were meant to stop us. They were tests for us. Observations, to see the limitations of the powers we held. Perhaps to wear us down a little. All fighting is tiring work. There were five Gates down there keeping my friends going. I had the easy job. Without magic, they'd have been exhausted and done long before Iddin came. A single Trow would have been enough.

'How long do you plan to play this game for, Iddin?' Maldouen demanded. He poured his scorn, his condescension into his words, his hollow voice ringing loud into the mist. 'How long do you plan to *cower*?'

I still had seven arrows left when the king of the Fault decided to make his appearance.

There was a darkening within the tunnel of mist. Somewhere distant I heard the sounds of a droning, mouthless choir, as if this being's movements through the world were lauded and required heralds of demonic nature to announce them at all times. Perhaps, beneath the Fault, down in the Night Below, the creatures of fear and pain sang his praises, or maybe it was merely this twisted world retching as he walked. For a moment I craved the droning of the tunnel that led through the Sixth Gate and reflexively I reached for it to drown it out. I grasped into emptiness.

Tears rolled down my face. I was as hollow as Maldouen. Sanvaunt had argued that it was me that Iddin feared. It was me he came to destroy. And now I stood here, powerless and useless. My friends didn't even know how weak I'd become. I'd held back from reaching for my Gates after I tore myself in two, like I'd been savouring the time simply being myself. I hadn't known what I'd done but there'd been relief. So much I hadn't wanted to be had simply let go of me. Only she'd taken more than I'd been willing to give, and now I was useless.

The darkness seemed to emanate from the mist-tunnel, reversed light, overrunning parts of the world. The dull red sky of morning gave way to a deeper shade of purple and even atop the wall, I heard the susurrating hiss of ancient voices muttering to one another, a reedy, malevolent accompaniment to the choir. There were no words, only concepts. And then Iddin stepped through the mist. Nothing so special to see, an ordinary man, or woman, hard to say, with an ordinary face, a tousle of mousy hair around his head. Perhaps he had chosen the most average possible visage. There was nothing I could have called a distinguishing feature there. But then, I was far above him, perhaps this was just what my eyes were like now. I should have opened Eio and intensified my vision five-hundred-fold. Instead I just saw the ordinary man, swathed in black robes, walk out of that tunnel.

Iddin glanced at the field of dismembered bodies, some still bleeding, others dissolved into puddles of ichor.

'Blind Child,' Iddin said. 'What have we here? This is not part of our truce.'

'Just travellers passing through, king of the depths,' Maldouen said. He took a few heavy, clanking steps forward, putting himself ahead of Sanvaunt and Esher. 'I didn't find your monsters to be part of the truce either.'

A truce? Maldouen had omitted that. The sudden fear of betrayal ran through me, but I quashed it down. Why help us, arm us, gift Esher with his own power if he meant to turn on us?

'We both know this is a lie,' Iddin said. 'They seek our doom, Blind Child. They want us bound and trapped here for all eternity.'

'Where we ought to stay,' Maldouen replied. 'We had our time, and our world. Our war should never have spread. It was my folly that bound us here. It will be my planning that sees that we do.'

Iddin cocked his head suddenly, abruptly, like a bird. His nose twitched, snuffling at the air.

'You are lesser,' he said. 'Your power . . .' His head swivelled towards Esher. She shifted, armoured feet grinding against sand as she readied into a fighting stance. 'Why? Why spread yourself thinner than you already had?'

'Because you need a lesson in humility, Iddin,' Maldouen said. 'Your kind always did.'

'My *kind*,' Iddin said, and the guise of playful whimsy, the tone of delighted curiosity, cracked. Just for a second. Just a moment. But in that moment, for the first time, I felt a surge of hope. Because if we could annoy him, maybe we could hurt him. 'There was never any other like I. I have no *kind*. I am king of this place only by virtue of your entrapment. A new world awaits me, a world where I reign as the undisputed god of all things.'

Maldouen laughed that singular laugh, the steely resonance bouncing back from the surrounding wall of mist.

'And yet I recall a time when you were forced to bend your kingly knee to an emperor. And I recall the Bright Lady making war against you, and through all the centuries that followed. No king stands forever. No queen can claim eternity.'

'And yet,' Iddin hissed, his head rotating sideways on his neck to an obscene, bone-cracking angle, so far I thought it might begin turning upside down, 'I endure. And your mortals will not.'

I'd heard enough of this. There's a time for posturing, and a good showdown is always going to start with an exchange of words. We're warriors. We can't help ourselves in that regard. But I didn't see a need to hear these immortal old beings discussing their distant past. Someone would reveal they'd been married next, or that their children would avenge them, or they'd been around since the dawn of time, or time was meaningless—but honestly, it was time for arrows and that was about it.

I loosed one of the absurdly long shafts from the white-wood bow. It hit Iddin in the chest, punching through, as long as a javelin. He looked down at it.

'I see you're through talking,' he said. And then the arrow detonated within him, tearing him apart, vaporising him in a vortex of swirling yellow and green gas that burned the air. One foot remained, booted with an absurdly curling toe. The air itself seemed to ache in the aftermath of the detonation, but Iddin was gone.

For a very, very foolish moment, I believed I may have just destroyed the king of the Fault.

'Bit of a waste of an arrow,' Maldouen called up to me. The yellow-green gas drifted into the mist-wall, spreading like a drop of ink in water.

'That didn't do anything to help us, did it?' I called back down.

'Nope,' Maldouen replied. 'His actual body will come here now.'

'His actual body?'

'What do you think that rumbling through the ground is?' Maldouen called back. 'I thought this was obvious.' Esher looked up at me, her face solemn and pale beneath her helmet, her silver eye burning brightly. I didn't need a Gate to see her fear. I wished I could have hid mine from her.

The choir droned. The dead voices rustled like wind through reeds. And then the mist began to darken, to swell. The quaking of the earth grew heavier. With a breaking sound, a great crack ran up through Maldouen's wall not ten feet distant from me, splitting the battlements. I gripped onto the nearest crenulation, but I didn't think any of this was going to stop.

'Whatever this bastard is,' Sanvaunt called, loud as he could, only just loud enough to be heard over the rumbling of the earth, the quaking of stones. 'We send it down into the Night Below. We destroy it, here and now. We end this!' He gripped his six-foot sword in both hands, allowed his inner flame to ripple across the blade.

Iddin seemed too small a name for the thing that emerged through the mist. Any name would have. It wasn't a person, or a beast. It was barely even a thing. It was our death, come to harry us on to the next world.

A wall of slick black flesh and smoke, high as the castle wall, wider, slithered and rolled through the mist, dissipating it with a touch. Long, glistening, oily tendrils reached forward to clasp at hummocks or boulders, or just drove into the ground to drag it forward. It was a mass of bleeding, splitting, reforming, spewing impossibility. No truly living creature could have taken such a form. Iddin was as much magic as he was flesh. Part of him seemed to be below ground, reaching up, emerging and then merging again as if he wasn't required to form one single creature. The ground shook at its advance. No sign of a head. No sign of eyes, but plenty of mouths, loosely circular, rows of teeth leading into dripping warrens.

It was the size of a fucking castle. A lump caught in my throat.

'We're supposed to fight that?' I said.

I SEE YOU'RE THROUGH TALKING, a massive voice intoned, no word spoken, but I felt its meaning in the trembling of the ground, the rumbling of the world. *I SEE YOU'RE THROUGH TALKING. I SEE YOU'RE THROUGH TALKING.*

'You're damn right I am.' I had six arrows left. I drew one back—a stone-headed arrow, an arrow of white wood carved with runes as red as blood—and loosed it at the behemoth. First Gate be damned, a child could have hit it wearing a blindfold. The arrow sped into Iddin, struck glistening, leathery wet flesh and there was a flash of light, and a good amount of black monstrosity detonated out. There was a squeal, a roar, something of the two combined that radiated out into the world with enough force to send me ducking behind the battlements. When I looked back, the massive thing hadn't slowed. Purplish slime, maybe blood, maybe something else, pulsed from the hole I'd put in it, but it wasn't slowing.

Maldouen's trick came next. He hit it with more of his buried devices, a series of powerful thumps sounding as he somehow activated them, stray flares of light spitting out from beneath Iddin's true body. More furious wailing, but that didn't slow it either. The fifty-foot incantation flared as Iddin crossed its centre—but it ruptured and died. The loose earth couldn't hold the power Maldouen had tried to incant into it, and it sputtered meaninglessly.

I looked down at Sanvaunt and Esher. Swords. They'd brought swords to a god-fight. I was glad that neither of them looked up at me as they backed away from the advance of eradication. They were counting on me. Unspoken words, but words that should have been said, words that told me that I was supposed to be the one with all the power. I was supposed to be the one who could stop this thing. But Maldouen had been right. There was no stopping something like this. Nothing in all the world could have brought it down.

The tentacles reached for my friends, human-shaped hands emerging from thick stalks to clutch and cling, birdlike talons reaching and grasping. The leading limb wrapped around Maldouen, raised him up into the air. His small metal body creaked within the grasp of the tentacle.

I RESPECTED YOU FOR TOO LONG. The massive voice trembled through the earth. The almighty rumbling paused momentarily as if considering him. *I ALLOWED YOUR EXISTENCE HERE. I BELIEVED YOU HAD SOMETHING LEFT, SOME TRICK, SOME MAGIC UNKNOWN.*

'It was never for me to destroy you,' Maldouen said. 'I'm not even a person.' That damned, one-time laughter rang out from him again.

The black mass bellowed, its tentacle flexed, steel protested, and then Maldouen's body buckled in its grasp, crumpling and breaking to pieces. But instead of victory it was a roar of rage that Iddin had let out. Somehow its focus was now behind me.

That great, rusting metal head we'd seen on the way in, twenty feet high, was pulling itself from the earth.

'Oh, shit,' I said, realising that I was between Iddin and what seemed to be a titanic metal twelve-year-old boy heaving itself out of the ground. Like Iddin and his mouthpiece, Maldouen had never been a boy with a statue, it was a statue and the boy who spoke for it. The vast rusted golem had no hinged jaw to speak with. It wasn't an artist: it was a war machine. Its fists could not uncurl into fingers as it heaved itself from the dirt, they were hammer-like blocks of metal. Time to get out of its way.

I ran.

'Shit, shit, shit, shit,' I cursed as I dashed along the battlements. A long, thin black arm lashed out towards me but I ducked behind the parapet, saw its barbed coils wrap around stone and with a jerk, tear it away. The metal giant didn't try to clamber over the wall, it simply walked into it, smashing through the stone, raising one of those gigantic fists to come down upon Iddin. Maldouen was a tricky little bastard. He'd had something up his sleeve all along. Maybe we'd only been bait to lure Iddin here, where he could bring this monstrous war machine against him. Some kind of pulse of blazing light-magic leapt from Maldouen's face to blast holes in Iddin. Iddin surged for him. Absolute madness.

'Moon horses,' I murmured. 'We need you again now. If you want us to get you out of the Fault we're going to need you right damn now.'

They were nowhere to be seen.

I went for the stairs. No point being up high on a wall when what slowly ground towards us was better described as a living wall than it was a creature. Smoke coiled from it where Maldouen's buried fires had scorched it. Sanvaunt and Esher were retreating from it, but slithering, questing tentacles reached towards them. Swords cut and spun, leaving severed, pulsing onyx limbs as thick as trees in their wake as they retreated back to the wall. They ducked as one of Maldouen's vast, rusted sandals passed over them and the two great powers collided. Steam belched and hissed from the limb joints of the child-shaped statue, great clanking groans sounded as cogs, springs and valves moved within. It stomped down on sticky, pawing limbs and then brought a hammer-fist down on the thing that was Iddin. The fist buried deep, pulverising whatever it was that made up the king of the Fault.

I neared the bottom of the stairs, but the ground heaved and shook with the forces the titans were unleashing on each other. I lost my footing, fell head-first. Time stands still in those moments, thoughts running faster than ever they should. My first thought was how embarrassing it was to fall down stairs as an adult. Secondly, I hoped I wouldn't break anything; people died this way. I caught myself on my forearm, somehow rolled over and sprawled in a winded heap at the bottom. My foot hurt but otherwise intact! I climbed to my feet, picked up arrows that had fallen from my quiver, and made it around the gates just in time to see something terrible.

Esher had been caught. She was dragged across the ground, hacking at the rope-like limb, but others came to join it. My eyes grew wide, wide as the earth itself, but the scream caught in my throat. No. No. No, it couldn't be this.

On Iddin's pulsating body, a bleeding cave-mouth opened and the tentacle dragged her towards it. She abandoned her swords, pressed her hands against it and perhaps she tried the Third Gate, but whatever she tried it did nothing. The mouth closed over her, and like that, my friend's scream was cut off, and she was gone.

Sanvaunt roared with horror and fury. He launched himself from the ground. For a moment I saw wings of fire erupt from his back, propelling him across the ground like an arrow loosed from a bow, wrapped in fire, sword ready to cleave into the Fault-king's rippling form, a trail of Anam Teine trailing in his wake. And then at the last moment, before his sword cut could connect, Iddin's body let fly a jet of something murk-green, somewhere between liquid and solid, a spray of bile that slewed against his advance, smothering him and covering him. Hungry limbs descended upon him, dragging him into Iddin's body, absorbing.

They were gone.

It seemed a long time ago that Ulovar had cut empathy and grief from my mind. Something similar happened to me then, only it was of my own making. There was too much emotion. Too much pain, too much grief ready to roar into my mind. I couldn't bear to accept it, so I didn't. I became a void, a space in the world where feeling and emotion couldn't touch. Someone else was controlling my body, and I watched from afar. How could I be in my body anyway, when my heart had been torn out twice? The worst fate imaginable, and I'd broken myself. I knocked the last remaining arrows, one after another until all six were fitted to the string. I didn't think they would do much good. A golem over a hundred feet tall was punching holes in the thing, but Iddin had already bound up one of its arms. The impassive, blindfolded face could give no expression, but it knew it was going down. It was doomed, as we were all doomed. I might as well throw everything I had left at it.

Funny, the string was harder to draw with all six arrows on it, as if it felt the weight of its archer's breaking added to the load. But she drew them, watched from afar by me, and the white-wood bow that had been cut from the Queen of Feathers' stave readied them with power. She let go of the string. The arrows became blurs of light as they launched, impacting across the tide-wall of bubbling, re-melding flesh, and then they did their things. Some made it past the outer skin, some didn't. Blubber and writhing unflesh billowed into the air like blossoms blown from a tree in a series of flashes and blasts. The cacophony echoed out across the Fault, a harrowing din of thunder and blaze.

It wasn't enough. It could never be enough. Iddin didn't have a body. He just had *mass*. A chunk of him splattered against the cracked castle wall, slithered down. A malformed, clawed arm groped from it, reaching towards me.

I dropped to my knees. That was it. That was all I had left. Magic arrows, gone. Friends, gone. Even the golem, Maldouen's last trick, was no more than an arm and a head now, smothered and absorbed, billowing smoke and steam together in jets of black and white as its carapace cracked apart. I found myself back inside me, but I'd never truly left. I'd just wanted to. I had some ordinary arrows left but they were just arrows. How I'd failed. My eyes burned, brimmed, spilled over.

A voice, whispering into my mind.

You cannot defeat him here, Maldouen said. *He is the Fault. He has become misery incarnate. Take the fight to him in your own world. Do not let my error end it all.*

'But I'm alone,' I said. The statue, half-fallen, half-smothered by Iddin, had fallen still. One arm was still raised as if poised to strike, but I could see it was done. I contemplated how best to die. I had a sword, a beautiful, master-worked sword. Better to kill myself than be devoured by that thing. But part of me couldn't go through with that. So I stood, and waited for the end.

A jet of blue-gold fire lanced out of Iddin's body. Another, and another, blasting through and out from the inside. And then Sanvaunt burst forth, a holy being of life and flame, four majestic wings spread at his back blazing with his inner fire. And in his arms—*Esher!* Light-a-fucking-bove. Iddin's flesh lunged after them, tried to catch them, but Sanvaunt burned an arc through the sky, eyes and hair aflame, an angel of fire as he brought Esher back to me and my heart reawakened, my despair burning in his fire and turning to ash.

He landed heavily beside me.

'Raine!' Esher cried. Her armour was covered by fang-drawn scratches beyond counting but it had held. It had held long enough.

'I'm sorry,' I said, my voice spilling my grief and emptiness like vomit. 'I can't do anything. I've no power here. I've nothing.'

'Raine, we can go,' Esher said. Her silver eye seemed to swirl, gleaming in its socket. Sanvaunt's fire shimmered across her but without heat. He was breathing hard as his hair went back to its usual black, casting a glance back over his shoulder towards the leviathan. We were momentarily forgotten as it grew upwards, consuming the last of the Blind Child. Maldouen's silent, unseeing steel face slowly disappeared into Iddin's bulk.

'Go where?' I said. 'There's nowhere to run.'

'No,' Esher said. She wasn't just alive, she was jubilant. 'I used the Fourth Gate. I tore into Iddin's mind and he couldn't stop me, not from the inside. I know her name, Raine. *I know the Queen of Feathers' true name* and it's a light-damned *beacon*. It takes us to her. It takes us to the City of Spires.'

'We'll never outrun that thing,' I said.

Sanvaunt was breathing heavily. Life-fire leaked between the plates of his armour.

'We don't have to,' he said. He nodded behind us. 'About time those bastards turned up.'

Afraid to turn my eyes from the black wall of hate that ground onwards towards us, afraid to hope, I turned and looked behind me. Three of them appeared from their silent observance, glimmering silver and gold in the Fault's blood-light.

'We're still your best hope of getting out of here, huh?'

The greatest of the moon horses stared at me with silvery eyes. They hadn't given up on us yet. It lowered its head and bent a leg.

Not dead yet.

17

War is not a swift business, and decisive actions are rare. We pulled back from Ovitus's advance, and he followed us for a time, but our outriders finally brought the news we'd been waiting for.

'They're pulling back,' Dinny LacDaine said, a message scroll crumpled in his fist, his voice thrumming with excitement. 'He's given up the chase and they're returning to Redwinter.'

I was fond of Dinny. He was fresh and his spirits seldom dipped. He kept Castus upright, too, though I suspected Castus would have preferred him horizontal. Things were bad. There was no doubt that they were bad, but it doesn't hurt to get excited about the little things.

'That makes no sense,' Castus said. It was midday, and we'd taken the time to pause along the road to distribute what remained of our foraged rations to what remained of our rebels. Dinny looked bright, eager, his port-wine-marked face all clean and youthful. Castus wasn't even twenty-five, but the weight of command had hollowed him out. I wondered, had his hair been dark instead of fair, would we have seen threads of white here and there? Mortals faded so quickly. 'He should press us all the way to Clunwinny,' Castus went on. 'Night Below, he should lay siege to us there. We haven't the men or supplies to hold out long.'

'Perhaps not,' Dinny said. 'But Raine is with us, and I doubt he's eager to tangle with her again soon.'

'Such a charmer, Dinny,' I said. I enjoyed the praise. My name had spread. I was the woman who'd defied the usurper, the woman who'd defeated the impossible challenge, who'd decimated our enemy on the field. Men looked at me with awe now. For the first time in this life, I was someone to be feared. I'd missed that feeling. Some will try to govern through respect, as Ulovar LacNaithe had. Respect is a powerful tool, but its fatal flaw is that one who does not harbour respect for anyone feels nothing from you. Grandmaster Robilar had ruled through position, and had done so well, until that position was declared void. It had been built on acceptance, on norms, on tradition. When all that had been taken away, she had been left with nothing but her own will. Love is no bedrock to build upon at all, nothing is more fickle or changeable. And that left fear, because as long as you make them fear you, you control minds, and deeds, and never let yourself forget that it is you that drives the world around you.

'We'd be lost without you,' he said. I could see that he, like many, was struggling with how to refer to me. I even saw it in Castus from time to time. Did we call ourselves Draoihn, now that Redwinter was no longer ours? I had to do something about that.

'It's more than just my presence,' I said. 'Ovitus has a creature in his army—or perhaps it's the creature that has Ovitus in *its* army. It doesn't fear me, though I managed to hurt it once. No. They retreat because they don't need to challenge us here. The creature is named Iddin. It's not a Faded Lord, it's beyond even them, though they serve it. It wants the Great Seal and the Crown that lies beneath it. They don't need to destroy us, they only need to stop us taking it from them.'

'We made war and we didn't even know,' Castus said bitterly. He gestured towards the clusters of soldiers, mud spattered up their calves, holes in their surcoats, dried blood beneath their nails and bruises on their faces, as they chewed at spoiling meat and tipped the last of their water into their mouths. The river Speye was still some ten miles on. It was going to be a thirsty march. 'Sometimes I look across all this, and wonder just how little any of us knew before it started. The forces that were at play, the powers behind it. I'm half expecting the Riven Queen to emerge and stake a claim at some point.'

'Probably more likely than you imagine,' I said, and I smiled. Not many smiles went around our camps, and when they did, they were from relief rather than joy. I mustered more than most of them combined.

'I'll keep the outriders at a distance of three miles,' Dinny said. He bowed. 'Van Castus.' He bowed to me. Hesitated.

'Sarathi Raine,' I said. 'Let's not call a stallion a mule anymore. If your people are going to follow me, let them know the truth of it. They'll have heard of my work on the battlefield.'

'They won't like it,' Castus said. Uncertain. Distrustful?

'People will follow whatever gives them hope for the future,' I said. 'And right now, I'm it. Go on, Dinny. I need to talk to with Castus.'

He seemed glad to be going. Castus watched him go, frowning.

'"Sarathi" isn't a word we used to throw around easily,' Castus said. 'I'm still Draoihn, Raine. Whether the usurper makes his bed there or not, I swore an oath. So did you.'

'The Draoihn tried to burn me,' I said. 'And I've killed more of them than any foreign war has managed. I won't claim to be something I'm not. Not anymore. I need the word to spread. I need them to come to me.'

'Them?'

'Others like me,' I said. 'I might need them.'

'The Night Below knows, we could use more of you,' Castus said. 'Is it all right if I tell you I'm not comfortable with it? With any of it? You take their souls, Raine. If we win . . .'

'Worry about what I'll do if we win when there's a chance it will happen,' I said. 'I'll escort you to the Speye, and that town that sits on its banks. You can hold the bridge there and establish a staging ground for the counteroffensive.'

Castus looked at me like I'd lost my mind. I had to admit, it wasn't something I could entirely blame him for. It was a mind-losing kind of time.

'I have nine hundred and seventeen warriors in what I used to call an army,' Castus said. 'I lost *four thousand*, Raine. Good people. Of those left to me, five hundred and forty-three report strong enough to fight. There's no war to be had. Not without a miracle.'

'Then strip your lands bare of every woman and boy who can hold a spear. Empty your coffers to bring in mercenaries from Kwend and Hyspia. Bring the Murrish Bronze Guard for all I care,' I said coldly. 'Just get me men.'

'Get *you* men?'

'This all rests on me,' I said. 'I'm the only one who can enter the Blackwell. If I don't make it beyond the Great Seal, all of this is for nothing. We must retake Redwinter.'

Castus scratched at the dried-on mud that speckled the front of his armour.

'Were I able to conjure twenty thousand men, I couldn't do what you're asking,' he said. 'Our only hope is diplomacy. To make Ovitus see sense, and bring him back to our side.'

I made a sound in the back of my throat, a grating growl of disdain. A memory floated to the surface. I'd made a similar sound on the eve of battle, the night before Solemn Hill, when the Queen of Feathers had stood beside me.

'The remaining Draoihn are few but they're strong,' she'd told me. 'Maldouen has some new weapon. A Lance, crafted with lives and powers from beyond our world. He could topple you.'

And I'd growled, and I'd been wrong. It was my defiance that made that noise, but it was Hallenae's as well. They were all with me, all the time, just memories, though sometimes I thought them more than that. It didn't matter. We'd become something new, perhaps. But Hallenae had never been defeated until that day, and I'd known defeat. I tempered her disdain.

'That night-damned dog has Ovitus licking at its paws. He won't turn. Even when news of Loridine reaches them, he won't do it. No. It has to be me.'

'We've rested long enough,' Castus said. 'Whatever we decide to do, these people need food, and at least a pretence of safety. Until we have that, we have nothing.'

· · · · · ·

The town of Aberfaldy held two banks of the Speye. It was not built to accommodate a thousand soldiers, its buildings stern domiciles of dark grey granite, its people nervous and dismayed. Nobody could blame them for that. Ours was a dismaying kind of procession. But to the warriors I'd saved on that drizzling field, it was salvation. It was succour. Aberfaldy had no defensive walls, no battlements or ramparts, but it had a big wet river with just one stone-supported bridge, and the two wooden ones could be torn down. It was a barrier between us and them. Word of Ovitus's withdrawal from the chase had meant little to the warriors. Their dreams were filled with bloodthirsty Draoihn and the howls of dying comrades, while mine were flush with revenge.

War remained slow. Information was scant. We knew nothing of what the enemy were doing now that they'd retreated. I had to assume they'd return to Redwinter. Iddin would hold the Great Seal against us. He didn't need to enter the Crown—uncontrolled was as good as corrupted for his purposes. Men were housed in ones and twos in spare rooms, by tens in barns and outbuildings by the score in the houses of the wealthy. There were a few protests, but there's little words can do when an army sets up in your house. Over the following days the grain bins were emptied, flocks were driven in from the surrounding country and put to sword and salt. The church had some decent gold and silver in the form of its chalices, plates and idols, so we had those too—war is an expensive business. The priests cried more for those than they did for those of the wounded who expired on their pews. Some of the townsfolk wanted to join us, somehow drawn to the tragedy. Some of them were required to join us. Recruiters went out to the farmsteads with lies of silver coins on their tongues. We couldn't afford honesty.

I rested, and I plotted.

I was surrounded by more people than I had seen in six months—or three years, as the months had moved in this world. And yet, I stood apart and alone from them. People stared wherever I walked, and in fairness, my outlandish Witching Skin drew the eyes. When I walked among them, people cowered and fled. They'd heard stories. But as the account of those who'd stood on that field and watched me break a thousand men was told over every alehouse table, every tradesman's counter, across each shop floor, in every marital bed, and down into the crofts and farms and what passed for villages, it took on a life of its own. It didn't matter how I'd saved them. What mattered was that I had. Any weapon will do when it comes to life or death. They saw me for what I was, at last, in truth. I was Sarathi Raine, the power that opposed the hated betrayer. Old clan rivalries emerged in bitter stories of grandparents who'd brawled, of great-grandparents who'd warred, and Harranir became a word smeared with grime.

Sometimes I walked out on the streets just to see how people looked at me. All of Raine's life, my life, our life, I'd been afraid of being who and what I truly was. I'd hidden it from Mama. I'd seen the sooth-sisters slaughtered for it. I'd been misled and betrayed for it by Kaldhoone LacShale and Those Who See, who saw nothing at all. I'd hidden my nature from my friends. I'd delved into the secrets of a book that didn't exist in order to seek the truth. And I'd been tried, judged and nearly executed for it. Only my friends had saved me.

Friends. The word sat strange across my mind now. I thought of them sometimes, but not as often as I'd expected. They didn't need me just then. They still had that piece of me I'd left behind, the sad, trembling version of me that wasn't fit to do the job. I needed them all—I knew that without them my plans couldn't come to fruition—I just wasn't sure why I knew it. I didn't like to think on that other Raine. All that weakness, all that desperate desire to be loved and to belong. It felt like something that had been foisted upon me, when I should have been these other women all along.

I tried to rest, but the desire to move, to fight, kept my mind writhing. I hungered to begin the march on the Blackwell, but Castus was right. What was left of his rebellion was tattered and bloodied. I didn't know how long we could wait. Would the creatures I'd seen in Loridine take up there as though it were their own realm, or would they march against the rest of humanity? Perhaps they served the king of the Fault, or perhaps that golden-masked Faded Lord's allegiance to him ended when he entered our world. Perhaps they would fight each other. Dismally, I had to hope our world would become a battleground for the monsters. At least it would buy us time.

There were no books on the mystic powers to read in Aberfaldy, and few enough who could understand what I needed. Instead I walked through the town, and sometimes out into the countryside, trawling the memories of the women who'd gone before me. It didn't matter why I had those memories, why the Queen of Feathers had gifted them to me as their constant observer. What mattered was that she had given me a great and terrible gift. I'd seen the magic of other times, I knew how to wield it in ways that should have taken me years, decades, even centuries to learn by myself. I thought often of Maldouen's Lance. He'd brought it to bear against Hallenae at the height of her power, shattered her and locked the veil down beyond the Crowns. If I had a weapon like that at my disposal, I could have taken the fight to that hell-born dog directly. Iddin had to know that as well. He'd had centuries to prepare. If he knew where it had been laid to rest, he'd have destroyed it already. Perhaps he had. But I didn't think so.

It all came to me rather suddenly. The plan. The way to win the whole war. Or at least, the best chance we were going to get. I laughed when I thought of it. It was certainly audacious. Maybe not even possible. It would take a lot of luck.

I sought out Draoihn Suanach, formerly master of artifice in Redwinter. He had three Draoihn at his disposal, and two of them held the Second Gate. Of all those in Aberfaldy, it was the Draoihn who disliked me the most. I could see their discomfort in their refusal to meet my eyes, their masked words, their distance. Suanach had commandeered the small collection of workshops that the townspeople called a district, and a city would have named half a street.

'Raine, to what do we owe the pleasure?' Suanach said. He wouldn't refer to me as Draoihn anymore, but he couldn't bring himself to say *Sarathi* either. His bald head was shiny with sweat from forge heat.

'I need some things made,' I said.

'We have precious few resources to us here,' Suanach said. He gestured to a pile of mail hauberks, each one tagged with something so that its owner could find it again. He and his artificers had been reduced to assisting the smiths with common repairs. It was a fall for these men and women who'd once blended diamonds into steel and honed blades that would never dull.

'I don't need old,' I said. 'I need new. I need thunder-stones.'

Suanach put down the weighty mail coat he'd been holding. He was an old man, in his seventies, liver-spotted, and most of the hairs he still owned were on his brows. He'd served on the Council of Night and Day, a man whose authority had carried the utmost prestige and respect. He was unused to dealing with a slip of a girl like me.

'Those have not been forged for many, many lifetimes. There were two in the Blackwell, I believe,' Suanach said. 'But they were deemed to have been crafted through means . . . questionable. Devices with the force to crack stone, that even a common man could activate. I am afraid I cannot help you. Grandmaster Robilar deemed them too volatile, too dangerous to forge.'

'But could you make them, if I told you how?' It didn't help that my voice sounded like I'd been inhaling smoke all day.

'From what I do know of such things, they were as dangerous to those that carried them as those who trod on them,' Suanach said. 'Most were taken from Redwinter when the Draoihn were betrayed by Hallenae.'

I leaned against a mannequin that held a coat of mail which hadn't saved its former owner from a spear thrust. The Draoihn of the Second Gate who'd been in the process of re-linking it together, a broad-nosed woman with a complexion that spoke half of Murr and half of home, abandoned the work and took a few steps back from it. She bowed her head reverently. Suanach scowled at that.

'I need as many as you can make. If I told you the pattern, could you make them?'

'I don't know,' Suanach said. 'But I don't know that I'd be willing to try, either.'

'You don't get it, do you?' I snapped. 'The old days are gone. The old rules are gone. There's no right or wrong anymore. There's only survival. I know how they were forged. The Riven Queen used them, and yes, they were for her killers. But we need killers now.'

'I'm sorry,' Suanach said. 'But there are lines I won't cross, Raine.' He shook his head sadly. 'What have we become to consider such things?'

'You'll become what I need you to be,' I rasped. 'You all will. Because if we don't, then there'll be nobody left to judge us anyway. This is the apocalypse, Councillor. This is the end of all things if we don't win. The world is falling apart and we're all that's left to save it. Think on that, before you refuse me.'

'Thunder-stones and other such indiscriminate weapons are better left to the horror of legend, as is their maker,' Suanach said firmly. Was there a barb in there? He knew more about their construction than he was willing to let on, I thought. 'I have good work to do here. Honest work. I cannot help you.'

Well. That had gone poorly. I hadn't been refused anything since I came back into this world, and it burned within me. I knew how to craft the thunder-stones—I, we, had invented them—but I lacked the Second Gate needed to blend the sulphur with the charcoal and bat guano safely. I stared angrily for a few moments longer, and then stalked away in a whirl of Witching Skin.

Angry, denied, I went to the central square. A great number of our warriors were lounging at the tables of three alehouses that faced the river. They saluted when they saw me, and that pleased me, so I went to sit among them. They cleared a space, gave me a table, and watched me with the eyes of those who live in awe. They didn't carry Suanach's devout disgust at what I was. I'd saved them. That was what counted here.

'Is somebody bringing me a drink or not?' I demanded crossly when no servers had emerged. One of the warriors managed to ask what I desired, a formal sort of request more befitting a court. 'Whatever you're having will do me. I was born in the High Pastures, not some high hall,' I said. 'Share that jug.'

It was like I'd lit a little candle for him. He poured for me, splashing ale over the brim with a trembling hand. It was how I used to feel standing before the grandmaster. I'd become to them what those above had always been to me. The fan of spines rising behind my back did kind of mark me out, in fairness. Some of the drinking warriors cast sheepish glances when they thought I wasn't looking. Some of them listened in when someone made conversation with me. Those who dared to offered only assertions of their thanks, or asked me about logistics and strategy, things I'd given little thought to. There was a ghost among them as well, an old woman who'd died some years before and haunted the alehouse still. I could have drawn her in, but I didn't think it fair. This wasn't her war, after all.

They were afraid of me, but they worshipped me for what I'd done. There was lust there as well, strange though that may sound. I was exotic, I was beautiful, terrible and incredible. I touched something inside men and women both. Not all of them wanted to touch me, some of them wanted to be me, but none of them would have dared to do either. That impotence made some of the men angry, but weak men are always getting angry with women they can't have.

Over the course of that afternoon, only one person dared to take a seat at my table. She came wearing a cowl, though her oxblood coat gave her away when her cloak flapped open in the wind.

'May I sit with you, Sarathi Raine?' she said. Daring to use that word had my attention at once, despite five cups of ale. It was Suanach's apprentice, the half-Murrish woman with the broad nose. She was in her late thirties, perhaps older.

'You may,' I said. 'Your name?'

'I am Draoihn Ranitha, of the Second Gate,' she said.

'Escaped from under the nose of old Suanach and come for a pint?' I said. I knew she hadn't. As had been the case all across the afternoon, the warriors around were listening in, eager to recount what they'd heard me saying.

'No,' she said. 'He doesn't know I came here. I don't want to be an artificer anymore.'

'We're all what the world made us.'

'I know,' Ranitha said. 'And the world made me like you. That old woman over there, for instance—I see her. I've always seen them. I want to serve you as Sarathi, if you'll teach me.'

It was something I'd never thought to hear in my lifetime, even being what I was. A Draoihn, publicly stating she saw the dead. The old superstition ran deep through Harran. Even our warriors who'd been so keen to be close to me bristled at the concept.

'There's no harm in seeing ghosts,' I said, bellicose and loud enough that nobody would miss it. 'It's as natural as seeing fish in the river, for those who have the eyes for it.'

'Aye, my lady, I always knew it.'

Ranitha had a stern face, not much humour there. Why would there be, when she'd lived a life akin to mine?

'How many times have you died, Ranitha?' I asked.

'Died?'

'The grave-sight comes from misfortune. If you have it, then you died and came back.'

Ranitha nodded. A secret long held, about to be brought into the light. She must have been frightened. The sheer nerve it took to ask this in public. To be *seen* in public, to be *heard*. Not to be stoned to death on the spot. But she was hard-souled, used to respect. There was no tremble in her voice.

'I began seeing the ghosts when I was twenty-two,' she said. 'I was already Draoihn. I had the measles, and was very sick. Grandmaster Robilar healed me, but after that, I saw them. The dead.'

'You must have been crossing over when she pulled you back,' I mused. 'Tell me,' I said. 'How would you feel about a second death?'

My fingers were wrapped through a mane of stars and wonder, ephemeral and burning, as my legs gripped the wide body of this creature of legend, and she ran headlong up mountains, leapt across lakes, danced through the branches of withered trees. As what passed for time passed I became aware only of the rushing of the world on either side of me, the City of Spires ever ahead of us. I forgot my companions for a time, though I was aware that they were with me, their steeds bearing us faster and more surely than any beast has ever strode, any bird has ever flown, and any star has ever fallen. The moon horses were the essence of movement, otherworldly even here, silent on the hoof, determination and power and beauty encapsulated in their pale, shimmering stride.

The City of Spires lay ever ahead, and though it grew no larger on the horizon, there was a sense of journey, of progression we had never found in the Fault's foulness before. They carried us in a lost fourth direction. Irk had no power over us, the colours of the world defied Grey, and if Slow sought to deny us our progress the moon horses ignored it. We rode through the ruins of an ancient world. Sanvaunt rode at my left, and he was a godly thing now, that inner fire never quite leaving his eyes. Esher's focus was locked to that distant city as she willed us onwards, guiding our mounts by her beacon, by a stolen name that served as our guide and road. She had not spoken the name aloud. There had been no time. Time seemed to mean something different here, hurtling through marsh, soaring over stone.

On one side, a vast crater, a mile wide, silver-surfaced and glistening, appeared and was gone in less than a minute as hooves skimmed the earth. A city whose name we would never know lay half-submerged, its pyramidal structures and great statues of inhuman beings long since drowned and overcome by the Fault's misery. I caught glimpses of creatures who'd lived there once, long, long ago, not even the ghosts I could no longer see but flickers of memory, as if time itself wasn't certain here. The inlaid lapis lazuli eyes of a stone gatekeeper seemed to follow us as we passed, some ancient spirit lingering, its purpose without relevance, its duties forgotten. The pieces of some great machine leaned over our path, vast metal coils and girders hundreds of feet long arcing over our heads and leaving us in shadow as the moon horses bore us beneath them. We saw the creatures of the Fault, caught in glimpses only as our steeds bore us on. A lone giant walked with plodding steps, and twice I caught sight of sinuous dragons, curled and sleeping, as if the endless, impossible trek to the city had exhausted them. A whole legion of Trow walked in rocky unison, their march shaking ground we barely touched, striding as if they had but one purpose, and that purpose was escape. The Faded were there too. We saw their scattered camps, where they sat uncaring, trapped and bored in the endless, tedious torture of unchanging, meaningless existence. Maldouen had banished this terrible place from his world, and the remnants of its glories and its creatures lay desolate and decayed across it. But ever it was the city we pursued, and by the end of the first day of riding, it was closer. So marginally, so slightly, it would have been imperceptible had I not spent months staring after it. Something was different, and Esher was sending us onwards. Above the city, the stream of ghostly white vapour was constant now, flowing like an inverted waterfall up towards the vortex in the howling red sky above.

How long that first ride lasted, I couldn't have said. Time wasn't right here anyway, so did it truly matter? I could have clutched to that glorious, moon-silver mane and ridden on forever. I buried my face into its softness. I had not been safer in many long months.

We had to stop eventually. The moon horses were mystical creatures but their glorious charge slowed after we passed a pair of Faded warriors who had been locked in weary combat with one another for centuries, and then groves of trees that had somehow struggled free of the swamp to bear fruit. They brought us to the centre of a glade, stopped, and waited for us to dismount. I was reluctant. The fruit on the trees, warm yellow-orange plums, had a soft luminescence of their own, and a sweet, cloying smell filled the air. The horses evidently believed this was safety of a kind. I swung my leg over and dropped to the ground. Sanvaunt seemed the most reluctant to leave his steed. He'd always loved horses, had carried their smell around with him, the way he did ink and old leather. Finally he leaned forward and kissed the back of the horse's neck, then slid from her.

The moon horses shot away to wherever they felt they had to go.

'Don't worry. They'll be back,' Esher said as we watched them disappear into the haze.

'Tomorrow?' I asked.

'Do we have todays and tomorrows?' she said. She smiled, and her gleaming, silver eye pulsed. It wasn't just three Gates that Maldouen had deposited there. She knew things now. Esher seemed older, wiser than she had been. Calmer. 'They came because they need *us*. They'll be back.'

'Where are we now?' Sanvaunt asked.

'Somewhere towards the City of Spires,' Esher said. 'I know the way, and I told the horses. They'll get us there, eventually.'

'I thought I'd lost you,' I said, and I flung myself into Esher. Hard edges of her armour jarred against me as I tried to crush her in my arms. 'I thought you were eaten. I thought you were dead.'

'Me too,' Esher said. 'It didn't look good.' She pushed me back by my shoulders, placed a hand to the side of my head, then leaned in and kissed me lightly, momentarily, on the lips. 'But there's a reason we keep him around, isn't there?' She looked to Sanvaunt then, and all he needed was a smile. There was no need to balance kisses and love. Not anymore. 'Thank you,' she said. 'Nobody could have asked that.'

'Of course. I love you,' Sanvaunt said, as if that were all the explanation that was ever going to be needed for flinging himself sword-first into a wall of oblivion, and the truth was, nothing more ever could be. He looked to me as well, and we both smiled, and it was all true and it flowed between us like raw power, like the unstoppable force of a river in flood. It was weird, of course it was weird, but this place didn't abide by the normal rules, and somewhere along the way we'd decided that neither did we.

No rules, and no dark women in my head, whispering and cackling, pressing their wants into me, their past experiences. To be free of them didn't feel like a loss. Rather than being emptied, I felt instead that I'd become full. They'd been pressing into me, and there could only be so much person. Where they'd intruded, I'd been crushed, pushed down to share the space. But now here I was. Just me. Just Raine.

I was Raine without her Gates as well. They'd been part of me. It was only their loss that gave me a sense of shame. In some ways I'd been more, before. Now I was less. But I was also more myself than I'd been for a long time. I was powerless here without them, but as I'd expanded back to fill my own place in the world, silently I was exultant. They were gone. I didn't have to be that anymore.

We sat for a while. We had the usual things to do: the unbuckling of armour, the tending of scrapes and wounds. I was mostly fine. The most I'd been hurt was when I fell down the stairs—utterly embarrassing—and even stranger, the only part of me that I'd managed to hurt was the big toe on my left foot. It was swollen, tender and wasn't up for moving for a while. No idea how that happened, but there it was. Sanvaunt and Esher should both have been torn to pieces when they were eaten, but Maldouen's armour had proven it was worth more than regular metal. Sanvaunt needed rest before he opened his Fifth Gate again. I couldn't hear it anymore, but I could see it in his lack of grace. He usually moved with a catlike deftness, every movement precise and chosen, but he nearly tripped over a stone and I figured my throbbing toe could wait a while.

'Why did the moon horses come?' Esher asked. 'They took their precious time in throwing in with us.'

'They waited until you found her name,' I said as I watched Sanvaunt using his sword edge to slowly saw away some of Esher's hair. The braid that had protruded from the back of her helmet had not fared well inside Iddin, the usually glossy golden strands sticky with brown-black oil. The braid came away, and I was sad to see it go. It wasn't Esher, she was more than just hair, but I'd always loved it. 'They want out of this place. They're not Iddin's creatures. They let us fight, and waited to see whether we were still worth risking themselves for.'

Esher put a hand to the back of her head, feeling the change in weight.

'I tore it from him,' she said. 'It wasn't what I was looking for. I was looking for *his* true name. I was enclosed, being crushed on all sides. Panicking. I thought if I found his true name I could command him to spit me out again. But he doesn't have a true name. It's just . . . a void where *being* should be. This creature called Iddin was never truly a person. He's more like a concept. Like hatred, or oblivion, or cruelty. Malice. That's the best translation I can give. He's just malice.'

'So, her name?' I said. Esher knew I wanted that answer. Of course I did.

'I can't tell you,' she said. 'I just have to know it.'

'Can't tell us?' I said, aghast. 'Why can't you tell us?'

'Seems like something we should know,' Sanvaunt said. He tied the sticky braid into a ring and tucked it beneath a rock. 'Now's no time for secrets. We don't have secrets.'

'It breaks the past if I tell you the future,' Esher said. She shivered, hands gripping her arms as she drew herself in close. 'I opened the Fourth Gate inside something that's as close to a god as we'll ever behold. I saw his other world, or his memories of it. He'd been fighting a war there for thousands of years. There were other gods there too, and they were all terrible, evil things. But he knew things—such things. Cosmic things. Things that exist beyond the stars, that exist in the realms below us. He dwells half in and half out of the Night Below, beyond even the Fault, and he brought even more of the Night Below's demons here to the Fault to try to swell its power, to break free. We are not in time here. Not the time of our world. Maldouen—the real Maldouen, not the metal simulacrum he sent with it—ripped the Fault from its own world and cast it adrift. We don't exist anywhere. This place isn't anywhere.'

I sat on one side of her, and Sanvaunt sat on the other, and we put our arms around her. Esher didn't cry, but I felt she was weeping nonetheless. She wept for a simpler life and a simpler time, but her tears were only the words she shared with us. These things she'd torn from Iddin's mind—they weren't meant to be known.

'The Queen of Feathers asked me for my true name once,' I said. 'I refused, and gave her a favour instead. And she made me use that favour to live. She kept me alive. She can be a royal bitch when she wants to, but she was here with me. Inside me, somehow, for a time. I have to know, Esher.' I swallowed. 'Do you know what she is?'

Esher had been expecting the question.

'Yes,' she said. 'I know now, and I know when and where she was born. A long, long time ago. You'll understand it too, but only when we reach the City of Spires.'

'Why then? Why not now?' Sanvaunt said. Ever practical, ever the one to draw the hard line, he pursed his lips and then said, 'What if we lose you?'

'You won't,' Esher said. 'Like I said, time doesn't work that way here. I saw forward as well as back. We make it to the city. And that's where you understand her name. It can't be any other way.'

'That sounds a bit like bullshit to me,' I said. I was annoyed. I wanted to know. But there was too much knowledge in Esher's silver eye. Too much deep-knowing. And who was I to challenge her? I'd broken myself in two through careless magic, and I'd lost my own powers into the bargain.

'I lost my Gates,' I said.

The focus was all on me then. It wasn't pleasant, but I had to tell them.

'Lost them?' Sanvaunt said.

'Raine, how?' Esher asked.

'When we scryed on Loridine. Whatever I did. However it happened. There's another version of me back in our world. Only she's not like me. She's different, but she took my Gates with her. I'm just a regular person now.'

'There's nothing regular about you,' Sanvaunt said. 'And there never was, or will be.'

'Forward and back,' Esher said dreamily. 'Now you're getting it.'

We talked for a time. There wasn't much to explain. I no longer felt the First or Sixth Gates. I couldn't hear them, open them, pass through them. All that training, and it was useless to me now, like a runner missing a leg.

'This other version of you,' Sanvaunt said, frowning as he struggled with the concept. 'She's also you somehow? You can talk to one another?'

'Not exactly,' I said. 'I think she dreamed herself to me. Only the dream was taking place over hours for her, and moments for me. She—she's not *like* me, somehow. She's different. But she intends to win the war back home. She's holding the line, buying time for me to do something. And I'll do it, even if she took my Gates with her.'

'Gates or no,' Sanvaunt said eventually. 'We're getting out of here one way or another.'

'We should sleep,' Esher said. She was already drowsy. She was different too somehow, as if learning the Queen of Feathers' name had changed something monumental for her. 'The horses will be back for us. Holding on to them is tiring. They want to escape as much as we do.'

We picked watches, settled down among the softly glowing, never-to-be-eaten fruit, and tried to find sleep after the terrors we'd seen.

·   ·   ·   ·   ·   ·

Each day we rode, and after more than a dozen hours of headlong gallop on a beast of silver starlight, the City of Spires inched closer, closer. A barely perceptible change. Days wore on, and my thoughts rested on my own world, and the question that sat always at the edge of thought: Were we too late already?

19

The morning had begun with a great tremor running through the ground. The weather vane fell from the roof of the church and became lodged in the gutter. A series of fences collapsed, and for several hours pigs milled and oinked through the streets on the south side of the river. Two houses collapsed as the shaking lasted more than six minutes. There was a sound beneath the earthquakes, a twisted metal groaning as our world suffered and the sky bled drips of purplish rain.

'All men must die someday, I suppose,' Serranis, Lady of Deserts, said coldly. Her skin was warm, and rich, and her eyes were heavy with glamours.

'They made their choice,' I said as we stared out across the broken rooftops from my bedroom's balcony. 'How many times did assassins come for you?' I was used to things wanting to kill me, but for men to sneak into a town by night, blades loose in their scabbards, murder in their minds, is not something you grow accustomed to.

Serranis sighed. She seemed wistful, always sighing and being wistful.

'More than these memories hold, I expect. The worst was when my consorts banded together to try to unseat me, five nights before I crowned myself. Through all our hardships, it's when we allow ourselves the weakness of love that we suffer the most.'

'They hated each other,' I said, remembering with her. I saw the opulent palace, cut into the cliffs above the joining of two great rivers that sliced through a desert far, far away. I'd never experienced heat as I did in her memories, and was glad of it.

'They did. But still, they came together, and launched their coup when they thought I was tired. I only have myself to blame, I suppose.'

'But you had friends then. They were the ones who discovered the plot.' The faces of the old woman and her young husband floated before us in the morning chill. There was sadness around them. Serranis had ordered their deaths in the end, too, but that was a recollection she'd chosen to forget.

'I did things for show, back then,' Serranis said. 'After I broke their army, I had them beheaded, and their mutilated remains quartered and sent to the corners of my domain. There is a special power in the deaths of traitors. The old things of the world prefer their souls to all.'

I blinked at a knock on the door, summoning me. I was quite alone. Old memory faded away, leaving only the impression of scorching, arid heat on my face and hands and the cries of those who had died echoing at the back of my skull.

'No traitors today, just assassins,' I said. Nobody heard. The old memories didn't hear me.

Aberfaldy was not a place used to public execution, and our impromptu event had drawn a crowd. The practice was frowned upon even in Harranir. We were better than that, weren't we? That was the idea. That's what we'd hoped. Only we were at war now, and it begins to make less and less of a difference whether your killing is done in public or private. Ovitus may have withdrawn the bulk of his forces, but he wasn't done with us, not by a long shot.

Hallenae, the Riven Queen, whispered that she had performed her executions on the rack. We all have our peculiarities, I suppose. My methods were to be positively humdrum by comparison.

Five were destined to die, three men and two women. Two were Draoihn, though not people I'd known. They had the hardened looks of killers, which indeed they were, and I figured them for members of the Winterra, Redwinter's battle-arm. The other three were no less killers. I didn't need to check beneath their fingernails to know that other men's blood had dried there more than once. They awaited their fate beneath a vast tree in the market square's centre. It was old, and it had seen the people of this quiet trading town come and go over hundreds of years. They called it the Lover's Tree, and its bark was covered with faded indentations declaring love for this person or that. Some of them would be very old now, if they'd been lucky. Some of them were dead for sure. I wondered how foolish those lovers felt when the love turned sour, when adoration faded to affection, and then to nothing. When one lover found passion in the arms of another. They had to pass by that tree every day, knowing that all they'd wanted had come to nought.

'As van-in-waiting to Clan LacClune, I always knew I might have to order it,' Castus said. 'I just never thought about it that hard. Seems different when they're not trying to kill you, somehow. Or maybe it's just the same. We lose track, Raine. We lose track of all of it, in the mire.' He and I stood with the rest of the rebel leadership in an area of the central market square we'd roped off for the occasion. The crowd were held back by Castus's men. The common folk showed a mixture of uncertainty, anger, fear, and shock that this day had ever come to their peaceful river town.

'You killed a dozen people to take revenge for your boyfriend,' I said. 'And I saw you knife a drunk because he was being a prick once. However it's done, it's all the same.'

'Sixteen,' Castus said. He looked across the square to the roped men and women. They were bloodied and bruised, missing teeth they'd still chewed with the night before. 'Sixteen people,' he said, his voice quiet as a sigh. 'They made us this way, Raine. But we don't have to like it.'

'When Ovitus LacNaithe stops sending assassins, I'll ask myself whether I care,' I said.

'You think he'll stop?'

'He won't,' half a dozen unwanted memory-witches whispered in unison.

'He'll stop when I've buried him,' I said. I waved to Van Hallum LacShale, the big clan lord who'd given me his knee to sit upon on the battlefield. That man loved me with a passion that was surprising even to me. Not romantic love, nor lust—he loved me like I was a fall of rain after a drought, or a living martyr. I was his hope, and his vengeance all tied into one. Hallum bowed to me—we didn't do a lot of bowing in Harranir, but he was up for it—and then barked words to his warriors. They led the five roped-together would-be assassins into the centre of the square. Someone had the good foresight to create the sense of occasion by striking a drum with slow, dolorous beats. I liked that.

A bystander threw a rock from the crowd. The people of Aberfaldy hadn't had time to gather the usual array of rotting vegetables, but they had stones and they pelted the prisoners. Throwing a stone at someone is actually quite hard to land at thirty paces, though, and few of them managed it. The youngest of the captives, a man no older than I was, winced as one of them caught him in the jaw. I remembered watching a woman being stoned to death just a year or so before—no, I corrected myself. Four years before, as the world would have it. Her name had been Nairna LacMuaid, and I'd sworn to myself I'd never forget it. I wouldn't forget it now.

'Someone has to say some words,' Draoihn Palanost said. I'd not seen her smile even once since I returned to the world.

'Maybe you want to say them?' I rasped. 'I seem to recall you standing idly by when I was strapped to a pyre. You've more experience in execution than I have.' Palanost glowered at me. She'd probably still have burned me, given a chance.

'It should be me,' Castus said. He'd been drinking the night before. He'd washed up, found some fancy clothes that fit him reasonably well, but I knew what a hangover looked like on him. For a moment, a brief moment, one so small it could have been lost through the gaps of the world if it hadn't been so surprising, I felt a pang of regret that those days were gone, and I'd never share those mornings in his bed again. It hadn't been love. It hadn't even been pleasure. We'd just been looking for something, for anything, to take away our unhappiness and briefly we'd found it in each other's arms. The sex hadn't been important, but every other part of it had been.

'Then go to, Van LacClune,' I said.

Castus walked out in front of the crowd. There'd been no time to create a raised platform, a scaffold, not even a headsman's block. Aberfaldy was woefully unprepared for public execution. Hallum LacShale looked ready enough, though. He'd brought a long-handed axe, was hoping he'd be the one to be given the honour. He probably should be.

'All right, calm down, you lot,' Castus said. An errant stone whistled past him. 'Hey!' he barked, pointing an angry finger into the crowd, but fortunately for the thrower, they'd not been spotted. 'Calm down, will you? We have to do some shitty business here. Let's do it with something like decorum.'

The crowd did calm down. If they'd gone on being noisy there was little that could have been done, but they'd abandoned their morning labours to watch some people die and they had work to get back to. It was cold, as most mornings in Harran are cold, and that goes for most of the afternoons too, and most of the year. The year I'd left had been an anomaly, a burning heat wave washing over the land, turning tempers to hammers and spirits to fire. But it was cold enough that breath was steaming, and the last fog still clung to the tops of distant hills. Nobody was a stranger to it, but nobody wanted to stand around here longer than they had to.

'Two hours before dawn, the men and women you see roped up here entered Aberfaldy after slitting the throats of two good men. Oscan of Clan LacClune, and Frinda of LacGilfry. They beat a stable boy unconscious when he spotted them. There was a woman,' and clearly Castus had forgotten her name, 'who'd got up early to do laundry and for some reason they stabbed her too.'

Castus was not a particularly good orator. He'd not cared much for his public-life duties, and so he hadn't bothered to learn. Still, he was very handsome, and that counts for quite a lot.

'They came by night to do murder,' he continued. We weren't totally sure of that, but it seemed very likely, given the Draoihn-made blades two of them had carried. Suanach had identified them as witch-killers, weapons designed specifically to target somebody like me, and one of them had an amulet I couldn't bear to be within twenty feet of. 'They brought weapons of magic, intended to do great harm. They came at the behest of the usurper, Ovitus LacNaithe, the Traitor of Redwinter.' I'd had the priceless weapons and the witch-ward amulet tossed into a forge. I'd wondered briefly what would have happened if I'd been stabbed with one of the blades, but I'd only heard about all this after the assassins were intercepted, beaten bloody, and I'd decided it was best I never even lay eyes on those cursed daggers. Better that they be destroyed here.

'Make them pay!' someone cried out. The crowd weren't bothered about why the assassins had come—they'd murdered a local woman. That was reason enough. The ordinary people of Aberfaldy, some of whom had sat around watching me drink just a week before, wanted resolution. Some of them wanted to see heads come off. Some of them were just curious, unable to look away.

Castus looked from the assassins—none of them looked particularly impressive now, though they were still physically powerful enough to have some danger about them—and then back to the crowd. He seemed to want there to be more pomp to all this, more law perhaps, though he'd seldom cared for the law in the past. He'd once told me that we could do whatever we liked without repercussions, but he was in charge now. He was a leader, a van of his clan, and however few warriors we had left to us, he led the rebellion. Leaders have to do things a certain way. I'd seldom seen Castus get lost in what he was doing.

'You should nail him to the Lover's Tree,' a memory of Song Seondeok told me. She skipped through the crowd, drifting like mist.

'I don't think they'd appreciate that,' I said. I didn't find my remembered queens particularly tasteful, or pleasant to be around, but they had made all this familiar. Had Raine Wildrose done this before? No, not at all. Not exactly, anyway. But the Queen of Feathers' eyes had seen more than enough heads come off for twenty lifetimes. I moved out to join Castus. Palanost hissed at my back. She really did hate me.

'Messenger! Messenger for Lady Raine!' Dinny LacDaine called out, interrupting our display and bringing proceedings to an abrupt, skidding halt. He had a bunch of his warriors with him, and they were escorting a man who bore a fresh-cut branch with an upside-down Brannish flag upon it, orange-and-white checks hanging limp. He was a huge man, six-ten if I guessed right, and I recognised him. He was Princess Mathilde's bodyguard, a man with a dour, clean-shaven face, his hair cut as if a bowl had been stuck on his head and scissors run around the edge.

'Here to beg for their lives,' Castus muttered. I didn't see this going their way no matter what they thought they were doing sending this man into Aberfaldy, so I was prepared to hear him out. It all added to the show.

Dinny LacDaine and his men had spears at the ready, but they didn't need them. Mathilde's killing-man was huge, but he came unarmed, and as far as I'd ever been aware, he didn't have any magic. The bodyguard kept his face utterly blank and sombre. He probably hadn't expected to be speaking in front of a whole throng, but that's what you get for siding with traitors.

'Go on then, I'll hear it,' Castus said.

'The message is for Raine Wildrose,' he said grimly. I could see Castus was taken aback. He was still in command here. His army might have been trounced, but five hundred men is still an army, technically.

'I'll hear you out,' I said. 'How's your mistress?'

'Queen Mathilde is in good health,' the bodyguard said.

'And how's her piece-of-shit husband?'

'The king is displeased,' he said.

'So it's king now, is it?' I shouldn't have been surprised. 'How about you? Are you happy, keeping us from stabilising the Crown?'

'I am a loyal servant of Mathilde of Brannlant,' he said.

'You have a name?'

'Willdem of Thurstown, Lady Raine.'

'Willdem, I'm going to hear your message out,' I said. 'But you felt all that shaking and quaking this morning, and you can't be blind to the purple rain. When you go back, you need to tell them all that your king's wolf-hound is a creature of the Night Below, and Ovitus is letting them take our world. That's why we're rebelling, you see that?'

'I do not think that King Ovitus will hear the words of a self-admitted Sarathi, Lady Raine,' Willdem said. 'Nor do I think he will treat with you.'

I had to admit, Willdem was a brave man. His king's assassins were strung out on ropes awaiting their fates not ten yards behind me, and given what I had revealed myself to be—and my Witching Skin was still might-ily playing up to that role—I was nothing if not dangerous. A childhood nightmare. A witch from ancient times. And let's not forget how men hate women who have the power to destroy them.

'If Ovitus didn't send you then I guess Mathilde did?'

'Queen Mathilde seeks an end to the bloodshed,' he said. 'Harran and Brannlant should stand together. This warring serves nobody, and peace must be found. She would speak with you herself. She gave me this to show you and said that Draoihn Suanach would know what to do with it, if he still lives.'

He reached into his bag, and spears were levelled instantly. Willdem's hand stayed where it was.

'Calm down, all of you,' I said. 'I'm sure he's not on a suicide mission.' I flicked my chin at him. 'Proceed.'

This all had to be fairly aggravating for the prisoners, whose final story was being interrupted, but it was probably their best chance at a stay of execution.

Willdem produced a hand mirror, not so dissimilar to one I'd owned back in the LacNaithe greathouse. For a moment I felt a flash of nostalgia that it was gone, that I'd never sit at that unnecessary dressing table and fix my party face, or brush my hair, or try on stupid, unnecessary dresses. Maybe it was the unnecessary things that made us feel ourselves. The things we have to use aren't choices after all. Willdem went to one knee—he was still massive even then—and offered it to me. I took it from him. Silver, with vines and little metalwork roses across the back, and garnets set into the handle, it just seemed a mirror. Suanach was already on his way over.

'I believe this belonged to the grandmaster,' he said. He didn't like that. He began to explain how it worked to me, but I didn't really need to know. It seemed obvious enough how it would work. He stroked the back and the mirror surface rippled. Dimly I recalled the Queen of Feathers watching another woman with one of these, but the memory was muddy.

Mathilde appeared in the glass. I shouldered Suanach away. I should have received this communique in private, perhaps, but Castus's little command council didn't trust me much to begin with, and I hadn't been in the mood to delay things. But when I saw Mathilde appear in that mirrored glass, I felt something new and different, something I'd not felt since the moment I appeared back in this dying world. I felt I was looking into the eyes of an equal.

Mathilde had always been beautiful. Her flawless, rich, dark skin was perfect against the white lace of a gown that exposed her shoulders. Black hair was coiled in dozens of entwined braids, falling in ropes to her left. Her eyes were wide-spaced and bright, but it wasn't just her worldly beauty that struck me like a hammer against the gong. It was part her dignity, part that natural air of authority, but how she stayed so serene and devoid of expressed pride amidst all her own position and beauty—that was her magic.

'Draoihn Raine, thank you for speaking with me,' she said. I was disappointed by her deference. I wanted to talk to someone I could admire. Maybe she sensed that, because she gave a very good impression of trying to quell an unimpressed smile. 'Or should that be Sarathi Raine, now?'

'I'll go by either, Princess,' I said.

I was aware of just how many eyes were on me, and how odd I had to look speaking into a hand mirror. Willdem had stepped back to give me space, putting himself back into the hands of the guards. Good dog.

'They call me queen here now,' Mathilde said.

'You don't sound convinced. I assume your husband put you up to this. If it's begging for the lives of his assassins, it's a wasted ploy.'

'I believe this has gone far enough,' Mathilde said. 'I think it did years ago. The Crown matters—all else is dust. You believed that, when you wore the oxblood of a Draoihn once. We feel the shaking of the earth. The Crown *must* be contained and you are the only one who can enter the Blackwell.'

'How did that go for Hanaqin?' I said.

'Mistakes have been made by all sides,' Mathilde said. So diplomatic. A whole bunch smarter than her husband. 'The world is tearing itself apart. A week past, a flock of winged rats descended on Harranir, tens of thousands of them. Two towns in the eastern marches have been abandoned because a creature with nine heads terrorises them by night. The world is burning, Sarathi Raine. We need your help.'

'The last terms you offered me were not acceptable,' I said. 'Is my time being wasted here?'

Mathilde smiled, close-mouthed. She was radiant, gloriously perfect. Tingle, tingle. Deeply inappropriate.

'I would like to hear your terms.'

'Can you offer me safe passage to the Blackwell?'

'My lord Ovitus has declared you an enemy of the people, and blames the world's cataclysms on you,' she said. 'They began the day after you escaped Redwinter—which coincided with the death of King Quinlan. There is no safe passage, not now. He has the Artists of my country strung out across Harranir, backed by what is left of the Winterra. They move in small groups, hunting you. They know you will try for the Blackwell.'

'Then why tell me?'

'You caught them all off-guard on the hill,' Mathilde said. 'But Ovitus is not a fool, whatever else he might be, and he has some source of knowledge that goes beyond what even the Draoihn archivists could tell him. They have ways to counter your power, now, just as Draoihn did when they fought Hallenae. You won't find them such easy targets. But he knows you'll come for the Keystone. He garrisons himself there, along with his best Draoihn of the Third Gate. If you attempt it, you'll die.'

'And I bet that miserable dog of his is there as well,' I said.

'Yes,' Mathilde said. Her eyes, her mesmerising eyes, flashed. She knew more than she was saying. 'That dog is ever at his heels.'

'Without the Keystone, without the Crown under our control, the world burns,' I said. 'Convince your husband.'

'I do not think he'd listen to me. Nor do I trust you, Sarathi Raine.'

I liked her even more.

'Then why warn me?'

Mathilde glanced over her shoulder. She'd heard somebody coming. Either she was working in secret here, or she was doing an excellent job of deceiving me. She spoke urgently.

'Because even if I don't trust you, you and Ovitus may have to one day work together. You war with each other now, but neither of you want the world to be consumed by demons. I have to believe that.' She turned her head sideways, the mirror falling down and away, as she began to speak to somebody, and the mirror turned into nothing but reflection again.

Not the news I'd wanted to hear. Maybe it was lies. Mathilde was playing a tricksy little game of her own, whatever it was. I remembered her speaking out, back at the impossible trial, when Esher had challenged Ovitus to fight her sword to sword.

'Fight her, my beloved,' Princess Mathilde had called. *'Fight her fairly. Prove what kind of man you are. No trances, no Gates. Just steel.'*

There'd always been more to her than lay on that flawless surface. All that silk, those glittering jewels, they were her armour as much as the witching skin was mine. There was a lot more in the depth of those eyes. And what eyes they were. I felt a twitch of a smile. It sounded as if my plans were largely ruined, but I didn't feel so terribly bad about it. I could make new plans, I just needed some time.

'Well, that was fun,' I rasped as I gestured for Dinny to escort the huge messenger out of Aberfaldy. 'Time to get on with it.' I walked out in front of everyone, standing sideways so I could be heard by the crowd. Castus went to signal Hallum LacShale to get that big axe into motion, but I waved him back. I stalked up to the first of the would-be-assassins, took him by the hair and pulled his head back.

'Ovitus LacNaithe sends killers to your town,' I called to the crowd. 'Indiscriminate, murderous, treacherous shits of men and women. In this land of Harranir there is no room for such people.' There always had been, and they'd been called Draoihn. 'We do not tolerate their callousness.' I'd seen them tolerate Castus's, and more. 'Justice will be done.' It seldom was. 'Ranitha? Where are you?'

'I'm here, mistress,' Ranitha said, pushing through the crowd. The artificer wasn't wearing her Draoihn coat. Instead she wore a heavy leather coat that had a mottled black-and-blue pattern, something akin to snakeskin. Poor Suanach paled when he saw it. Palanost's eyes widened. Of everyone, only they knew what it meant. Castus had never been one for history.

'Then watch carefully. You'll not get much of a better demonstration than this.'

The Sixth Gate opened within me. It was cold, and empty, and wonderful. What I'd always thought of as a grinding, mill-wheel droning seemed more like a chorus of perfect voices now. Voices that called my own name, overlapping, overrunning, filling me, filling the world as the tunnel rotated all around us. We'd each go down it someday. Why fight it so very, very hard?

Through the tunnel I saw the spirits of the captives, bound to their flesh, unaware that there was any separation between body and ghost. There wasn't. Not for another few moments. And then I held a hand in front of the first assassin's face, fingers clawed, and I opened the tunnel wider for that unfortunate man as I dragged the soul from its confining flesh.

The man screamed as no man had screamed in hundreds of years. I was breaking the rules of the world. His beating heart was the lynchpin, the binding point, the anchor which held him together. His ghost unravelled from sinew, my mind slipping along his bones like a knife, severing as I cut him away from what he'd been. Green, white, vaporous, he flowed from his body and into my hand, up my arm, and into my own heart.

I allowed my own eyes to glow the colour of fresh spring leaves for a few moments as I breathed him in.

Ranitha watched attentively. She was keen to learn. I dumped the emptied, silent, withered corpse on the ground and went to the next. The prisoners tried to flee, but their guards were too afraid of me to permit them, and everyone likes to see an enemy come to a bad end. I devoured them one by one, eating their ghosts. My new apprentice watched wide-eyed. She'd asked to be part of this. Better she understood it now, at the beginning, as I never had.

I left five corpses on the earth. I left the audience stunned.

'Such is the fate of murderers,' Castus said, but his tone was blank. I saw the way he was looking at me. I saw the way Suanach and Palanost hung their heads in shame. I'd have to watch my own back before long.

I knew they'd turn on me one day. To be a witch queen is, ultimately, to stand alone.

20

I'd been dreaming. Nonsense dreams, the kind where you're writing on a chalkboard and the words won't come out right. I had to write a recipe for an eyewash, one that Mama swore by. Everything I wrote down was silly, like kite string and mud-lumps, but faceless, nameless people kept agreeing I was right. In the dream I thought I was. I used to dream of the dark queens of the past. The time spent in true dreams was beautiful by comparison.

I shook off the last hold of sleep. Stiff, my foot hurt more than it had all the long ride of the previous day. The white-wood bow wasn't far from my hand, its arrows alongside. Just ordinary arrows, or as ordinary as Maldouen made them.

I moved to the edge of a tumbledown wall. The moon horses had left us at a villa, its walls and the lines of columns around the central courtyard cut from the same white, rose-veined marble as Redwinter's walls. For the Fault, it was unusually clean and undisturbed. It couldn't come close to Maldouen's palace, but since that palace had likely been levelled now, perhaps it was the cleanest place in the Fault. Someone, something, had been living here, Sanvaunt had said. Care had been taken. I imagined that perhaps it had been home to one of the Faded Lords, abandoned as he ascended from the Fault into the world above. Whoever had taken it over, they were gone now. It was ours on borrowed time.

The City of Spires was closer than it had ever been, but still days away. Maybe weeks. The horses came, they left us to sleep, and returned when they would. I should have been on watch, but I'd dozed off. It could be hard work, holding on to those incredible animals—if that's what they even were. Nothing seemed to have eaten us in the night.

Esher and Sanvaunt slept within the villa. That's what Sanvaunt called it, anyway. He'd seen similar things when he was younger, travelling down to Kwend and Hyspia, where they grew citrons and olives and everyone slept through the middle of the day. It seemed funny to me that the Fault, ripped from another world and cast between them, should bear resemblances to our own world. Nothing here came from there. But people were people, I guessed. There were only so many ways to put brick and tile together if you wanted to live in them. Across the floors those alien people had put together mosaics of astonishing intricacy. Some of them depicted places that had perhaps been notable in those lands, some showed what had to be script of some kind I couldn't read—it didn't even look like our letters. The builders had crafted their myths and gods there as well, a holy woman wreathed in fire reaching up to touch the sun, a green-skinned woman with a fish's tail beneath the ocean, a starfish in her hand. The villa's former owner had cared for them, had pressed the small tiles back into place where they'd been scattered. Some of the mosaics were incomplete, their pieces lost to the swamp.

Esher had changed the villa, altering it as she did every ruin we found to rest in. She reshaped it with her Second Gate, re-forming stone in ways that pleased her, blasting dust and debris from chambers with gale-force wind. Her mastery of her new Gates was absolute, beyond anything any living Draoihn had ever imagined. She had inherited not just Maldouen's raw power, but the knowledge of the centuries through which he'd honed it. Transmitted from one to the other, she would have been the greatest Draoihn of our age in another life. She delighted in her tasks, but as ever she would have, performed them in peace. She drained power from the Fault itself to fuel the energy of the Third Gate, dragging a perfect sphere of marsh water upwards, then letting all the dirt and impurity pour away from it. She heated it, and we could wash, and launder, and sleep in beds free from the Fault's taint. She'd done the same to the villa.

I loved to watch her work. She took such pride in making the world around us livable. Each adjustment was made with care, with passion, because she knew she could keep our spirits high if only we had clean floors, clean bedding, clean bodies.

While she worked, Sanvaunt took me through swordsmanship lessons. I didn't need them, not really, but it gave him something to concentrate on. When he could, he fetched and carried things Esher wanted to build with, carried out baskets of dust and dirt she'd scoured from indoors.

Esher had reached out into the world and mended the frame of a large bed. She'd rebuilt the blankets, the threads twining and finding one another. She firmed up and cleaned a mattress that had been stained, threadbare and flattened by the years until it was lush and plump as a prince's pillow. I wished I could have heard her Gate while she worked at it. It had taken her nearly an hour, but when she let us see what she'd done, the room was as clean and decadent as one of the rooms in Maldouen's palace. Compared to making the statue-dancers whirl and cavort, giving us a comfortable place to sleep was child's play.

'I didn't make it permanent,' she said. 'It will just last a day or two. It will all remember its proper shape after we're gone.' She sounded sad for the villa but like either Sanvaunt or I truly understood how any of it worked, like the knowledge could be easily assumed. She saw the world differently now.

I shouldn't have fallen asleep while on watch. I checked on them, found them sleeping peacefully, Esher pressed up against Sanvaunt's back like an old couple. We'd had to grow up here, I thought as I watched them breathing. We were too young for any of this, and too old to go back now that we'd seen it. What a colossal failure all of those adults had been, to leave the world to us. They'd tried. They'd done their best. I wondered at what age they'd begun to feel like they were done getting older, or if they ever had. Maybe nobody ever feels like they're an adult.

I ventured back outside and sat on a low wall. Our turns at watch didn't have time to them, since there was little way to measure it. I should have ended mine when I grew tired, but guilt gnawed at me. I'd stretched myself too far, cracked myself down the middle, and now I was useless to them. I was a burden, a Gateless, powerless, ordinary young woman with too many memories she didn't deserve. I'd slept, and I didn't want to sleep again. The least I could do for them was let them sleep a while longer.

The moon horses were out there, across the uncaring marsh, five of them stood in a line. Watching. I wondered what they were, what they'd been, how they made those trips back and forth into our world.

'The horses have their own reasons for bringing you here,' a soft, deep voice said from beside me. I didn't turn my head to look in her direction. I was afraid that if I did, she might suddenly vanish and leave me alone again.

'They want to be free, don't they?'

'Their world is collapsing,' the Queen of Feathers said. 'Half of it, anyway. Like me, they've been able to scry out of this poisoned prison. Sometimes they can even affect our world. But the horses are bound here, and when it's all gone they will be prisoners in the nothingness.'

'You've been gone a long time,' I said.

'I'm not really back now, am I?' she said. 'You're dreaming, Raine. I'm no more here than you are. None of us are really here. Not in the way any of us really understand it.'

I laughed at that.

'Even in my dreams you're cryptic and nonsensical. Just for once, just one time, I'd love it if one of you mystical beings could say "By the way, just turn left over there and go down that hole, this is how it works." But you won't, will you?'

'Not here,' the Queen of Feathers said. 'But then, you're still sleeping, I'm not real, and this is only your imagination at work.'

'I'm not so sure,' I said. 'You feel real to me. Kind of.'

I turned to look at her then. She was younger than she'd ever seemed before, but no less beautiful or majestic. Not much older than me, I supposed. Her hair reminded me of the way Grandmaster Robilar had styled herself at times, the dark trailing off into white and gold. No warpaint on her face today, but the wreath of corvid feathers circled her brow.

'Few things are real here,' she said. 'Distance. Time. It's worth holding on to the ones that you can touch for certain. There are things that must be done in your world. But you know that already. It's why you let her go.'

'Let her go?'

'The Raine who has to do it,' the Queen of Feathers said. 'You had to give her your Gates. You had to set her free, to do that which you couldn't.'

'You make me sound weak,' I said. I watched a moon horse flicking its tail as if flies bothered it here, but we'd seen no insects since we arrived. They were too small to exist here.

'Who is weaker, the woman who dies protecting her babe, or the woman who kills her from spite? There is too much thought on strong and weak in this world. There's only doing, at the end of all things. Which we're approaching so quickly now. It is you, Raine. The one I've been waiting for. This time, this attempt—this is it. It has to be, as there's no other time for it if you fail.'

'I'm not some prophecy,' I said bitterly. 'I just wanted a life.'

'If there's any prophecy to you, it's only one you made for yourself,' the Queen of Feathers said. She looked older now, as old as Grandmaster Robilar had been in her crone shape. 'Or one you'll make in the future. That's the thing with prophecy. The concept itself defies time. It requires knowing. I never said I could predict the future, only that I know that someone has to make it all happen.'

'Enough, enough,' I said. 'If this is a dream then I'm just talking to myself. These are just tangled, nonsense thoughts.'

'Then they're your thoughts, and there's no need to fight them,' the Queen of Feathers said.

'Maybe I'm tired of thinking,' I said. 'I'm so tired. Tired of the fighting. Tired of the fear, and the grief, and this burden that somehow has landed on my shoulders. Only I've shed the burden to some other form of me, and I still feel responsible for it.'

'Of course,' the queen said, and she stepped lightly along the wall, arms held wing-like for balance, as she skipped past me. 'You may be divided, but you're still one thing in the end. Everything is one, Raine. Even without your Gates, you should still remember your lessons.'

'I just need there to be some light,' I said, rising. Frustrated, worn thin at my core, emptied out and hiding from the dreadful things I'd come to know. 'What I saw in Loridine—it's all already happening. We can't reactivate five Crowns. One of them sank beneath an ocean! The creatures of the Fault are flooding into the world. Demons, the Faded, all the Hidden Folk we never wanted to see. They're taking our world for themselves. What can we hope to do? Even our best hope is to re-stabilise Harranir's Crown. What then? We hold them in check while we fight unending wars to reclaim Brannlant's Crown, and the others? The world has already broken.'

'Then break it again!' the Queen of Feathers laughed. Her dream-wings spread wide, for a moment blotting out the bloody sky above me. Her eyes remained in the great shadow, pale and flickering with witch-light. 'You've come this far. You've given up this much. You've become what you had to, and more. Raine, you are great, you are terrible, and you have carried the knowledge, the victories and the errors of five thousand years of witch queens with you. Stop doubting yourself. Take what you need, become what you have destined yourself to be. Break the world. Change the world. Have what you want.'

Towards the distant City of Spires, the sky creaked and emitted a shivering howl that echoed out across the land. A great surge of glistening, satin-white energy slid upwards into the vortex rift. It should have woken me, but I held to my dream just a little longer.

'I know what you're for,' I whispered. 'I know why you exist. I just don't know how.'

The Queen of Feathers smiled, but it was only me, dream-smiling back at myself. I took a deep breath, the rancid air of the Fault filling me. There was a coolness to it just then. I wondered, if I could speak this way to myself in the dream world, perhaps I could speak to my other self. The Raine who'd escaped into the true world. I was jealous of her, envied her that she'd found her freedom, but I would never have gone. I could never have left Esher and Sanvaunt, not even to save Castus. He was my friend, but I didn't love him the way I did them. I was entwined with them, like three strands of burning flame coiling together in a braid. I had no Gates, no powers to draw on, and the Queen of Feathers had never really been here. This was just a lucid dream.

That didn't mean she wasn't right about some things. Time and distance obeyed few rules here. Perhaps I didn't have to either. *Everything is one.* The first lesson the Draoihn taught. Everything was one, and the gaps between the world were only in our mind. What is a gap except nothing?

Where are you? I asked my other self. I felt the thought ring out into eternity, rebounding from the edges of the impossible Fault, reverberating from the deaths of distant stars, echoing from dawns I'd never seen.

You're still alive? she answered.

Just about, I said. *How much time has passed for you?*

A month, she said. *You?*

A few days. Are you close to retaking the Crown?

I caught a glimpse of where that other Raine was, then. A comfortable room, darkness at the windows—true darkness, night. Only a pair of candles lit the room, and she too was alone. She must have been dreaming as well for this to happen, fallen asleep in a chair beside the fire.

I can't reach the Blackwell, she said. *Iddin is here.*

You can't match him.

No. I felt my other self's frustration, her anger at that.

Even if you could, it's not enough, I thought to her. *One Crown is not enough. We have to have more.*

One would be a start, she dreamed back. As our minds crossed paths with one another I breathed in what she'd done, what she'd become in my absence. I suppressed a shudder. There was pride there, and rage, but an empty, aching sadness as well. She'd taken so many lives. We had taken so many lives.

I have a plan, I said. And it had formed, somewhere in a dreamscape. *You have to draw Iddin away from Redwinter,* I thought. *You have to take him from the Crown. The others will be easier.*

We don't have the power for what you're suggesting, she dreamed back to me.

Not yet, I thought. I felt all the sadder. *But you will.*

The other Raine smiled in her sleep too. We were different. We'd split the parts that could stay and could go, and it had been an error, and it had been essential, I realised now. I couldn't have done what she needed to do, and she couldn't have played my part either. One of me hadn't been enough for the world. The irony was not lost on me. I'd almost felt like one of me had been too much.

I left you my love for them, she told me. *Use it. Don't waste it.*

I won't, I thought. But the dream was over, and I was blinking awake in the hellish realm of the Fault, and distantly, the moon horses had kept watch over me. Just as they'd been in my dream. One of them lowered its head, but there was nothing for it to crop at. They walked across the stagnant water, their hooves leaving no trace across the surface. It wasn't time to go yet. Sometimes they just knew things they shouldn't. They responded to need, and they knew what I needed. What we all needed.

I turned towards the villa. Esher stood in the doorway, her much-shortened hair ruffled and messy from sleep as she leaned against the frame. She wore loose pantaloons and a sleeveless nightshirt. Dishevelled had always been a good look on her. But then, everything was a good look on her.

'Don't worry,' she said. 'I watched for you.'

'The horses kept watch,' I said. 'But I don't mind you watching me anyway. I wasn't sleeping. Not exactly.'

'It sounded like you were sleeping,' Esher said. I smiled at her, standing there in the doorway, so relaxed it sent a ripple through me.

'There's something I need,' I said. 'But I need Sanvaunt for it too.'

'We're so far past the point of individual need,' Esher said. 'The fighting in Harran. The trial, the moon horses, and everything we've done here. It's so different now. Like ownership. I'm wearing this shirt but it might as well be yours, or Sanvaunt's.'

'Exactly,' I said. 'Go back inside. I just need a minute.'

Esher watched me from behind a sweep of hair. Her lip curled a little. She understood. She always got me, just a little ahead of when she was supposed to.

'Take as long as you need,' she said. 'Should I wake him?'

'No,' I said. 'I don't think so.' Esher smiled and headed back into the villa. She'd left a stone basin of clean water outside. I splashed a little on my face. I dipped my hands and stroked up and down my arms, shivering at the cold, but enjoying the alertness it brought. I let the water settle, and considered my reflection.

The old scar, the wrong-angle Hazia's knife had made all those moons ago, was still stark against my cheek, my nose. My hair was fine, as white as the day that Ciuthach had risen. Funny, that those were the things that still marked me, when by comparison they seemed such lesser events in my life now. The Raine back then hadn't known she could open Gates, or traverse worlds. She hadn't met a hero of legend, or seen the world betrayed. Behind the white hair, behind the scar, behind the eyes that had seen too much for such a short life, I looked for the girl who'd lived before that. I couldn't find her anymore. She no longer existed. We're made of the things that happen to us as much as we are our father and mother. Bits of the world embed themselves, become prints against our skin. They become scars on our bones, words that we speak and the shadows beneath our eyes. We're all of those experiences, good and bad, and they make us anew with every dawn and leave us changed with the setting of every sun. I splashed the water, disturbing my image in case I left another piece of me behind. I'd cast off enough that I didn't want. The rest of me I got to keep—or give, as I willed it.

Esher had turned the villa's central chamber into a work of art. Murals showed only forest scenes and roses that had wilted centuries or more in the past. Beauty, captured on the wall, given fresh colour by the lick of a trance. But they were nothing, not compared to Esher, who sat with her back against the headboard. She'd disrobed, the covers tucked beneath her arms, and her shoulders were lean, hard-muscled, a gift to my eyes. She smiled at me, and even now, even though this had been inevitable, and we'd wanted it and been too uncertain and too fearful to approach it, there was still trepidation there.

I had none. I was more certain of this than I'd been of anything in my life.

'Sanvaunt, wake up,' I said. He stirred quickly from sleep. His sleepy-lidded eyes blinked open and he saw me. He glanced to Esher. He was the last to know, and that felt fair somehow. I reached to the ties at the front of my shirt and began unlacing them.

'What's happening?' Sanvaunt asked. Cautious. Nervous. He was a little older than either Esher or I, and doubtless more experienced, but he seemed to be the only one unsure. I pulled my shirt ties free, standing at the end of the bed, and then pulled it over my head. I slipped the rest of my clothes down my legs. It wasn't just the hair on my head that was white—beneath my arms, down there. I hoped they wouldn't mind. I knew they wouldn't.

'Don't think on it too hard, my love,' Esher said. 'Raine?' She held a hand out to me, and I crawled up onto the bed. The distance seemed much greater than it should have. Somewhere in time, my heart had started beating with a rapid urgency. Heat filled my face, but I continued my advance. Esher pushed back the blankets from herself, dragging them from Sanvaunt and cast them aside.

'Are we—are we doing this?' Sanvaunt murmured. He sat up, knelt with his legs beneath him. His body's reactions suggested he very, very much wanted to do this.

'We all want to,' I said. 'We love each other. This is the way it has to be.'

Esher caught me, and we kissed. She tasted like travel, and sweat. My hand found the small of her back. When I broke from her to regain my breath, Sanvaunt was facing us. He was ready—he was extremely ready—but one last spark of gentleman held him back.

'What does it mean for us all, if we do this? What are we to each other?'

'There's nobody else here to judge us,' Esher said. 'We can be whatever we want.'

'We don't have to think about anything else tonight. I don't care about anything else, just for tonight. I just know that I want you, and I want Esher. I want both of you. I want to love you, and I want to be loved back. We deserve this. We deserve to make love to each other and for a time, there's nothing else.'

Esher understood it so clearly. It was easier for us, I think. She took Sanvaunt's hand and put it to her cheek, kissed his palm. I took his other hand and still surprised myself with a little gasp as I directed it somewhere else. Sanvaunt looked from Esher to me, and back. He laughed, and it was a laugh of intimacy, kind, self-mocking.

Whatever tremor of gentleman had been holding him back, he wasn't very gentlemanly from then on.

I had never made love so freely before. Always there'd been something that held me back from being me. My first lover, Braithe, hadn't seen me. I'd not been a person to him, not really. The same had been true for Castus, and though that had been pleasurable, we used each other's bodies to take refuge from our pain. But with Esher and Sanvaunt—we mattered so damn much to each other. Sanvaunt was gentle with me, until I laughed and spat in his face and told him not to be, and when he took me, fiercely, I exploded with the urgent, demanding roughness of his desire for me. I had Esher as I wanted her, worshipping her, hand and mouth, doing things I'd never imagined possible. She gave me no less in return, and when I needed to catch my breath I lay back and watched my lovers pour their ardour into one another. The way they made love was different to the way I did with each of them, but there was no comparison to be made. We joined together in different ways, that was all. Why would one love be the same as another? We made love. We fucked. We laughed, and I hadn't expected there to be so much laughter. Why shouldn't it have been funny? But there was an unleashing of lust, a flush of admiration and desire, a gentleness of care, a roughness of need. It was fast, or slow, it was sticky, sweaty, thirsty, and it set a booming through my body time and time again that was new, but felt like something old. It was everything. It was all I could have imagined, and so much more.

For ten hours, the Fault didn't exist for us beyond the confines of those walls. Neither did the people of Harran, and their struggles. Nor my other self, or our struggles, or any of it. We let ourselves go. We taught each other how our bodies worked. We played. We exulted.

'Light Above, we have to hang on to moon horses again soon,' Esher said, sprawled down the length of the bed. Gloriously naked. Perfectly Esher.

'My thighs are already protesting,' Sanvaunt said.

'*Your* thighs? Pfft.' I was giving him no sympathy. I was equally not looking forward to horseback.

'I love you both,' Sanvaunt said, laying his head back and closing his eyes, 'but is it wrong for me to say that you're both more scorching than summer?'

'It's right that you say it,' Esher said, feigning primness. 'Because it's absolutely true.'

'Just give me a month to recover,' Sanvaunt said. 'And I'll show you how much I mean it.'

'You're going to need more stamina than that,' I said. 'If you're going to keep up with us.'

We talked like we were on Silk Street for a bit. It was fun. So many old repressions seemed to have fallen away, dropped on the road. How glorious, just to get to *be*. To exist and love and be passionate without fear over what some old man once wrote in a book. I was a little sore, but the aches felt like victory.

A soft whickering sounded outside. The horses had put up with us doing each other long enough. They were eager to get on. We dressed quickly, helping one another to locate undergarments, to don gambesons, to buckle armour. We didn't speak during the dressing. My armour was the simplest, and I was first outside to where the moon horses waited for us. I walked past them, and looked out towards the City of Spires. Closer than ever. Maybe we'd make it there today, maybe it would be a week. Maybe a month, there was no way to tell. Magic bled upwards into the vortex in the sky. I found my gaze unfocused, looking past the city to horizons untold.

'Even if it was just this,' I whispered. 'Even if this is all of it. Even if I never get to have another thing that I want in my life, I got to have this. I got to be with them. I got to know love, and be loved. Which means it was all worth it, even before the end. I can die now. I can die happy, because I've had everything I ever really wanted. Thank you.'

I don't know what I was thinking. I'd given up on believing in a Light Above long ago. The only celestial mother watching over me was somewhere in the City of Spires, and she didn't care who I loved. Maybe I was speaking to myself. Maybe to destiny. Maybe it was just the universe, or creation in its most primal force.

It didn't matter. For the first time that I could remember, I was happy.

I knew it couldn't last. I knew what we had to do would sunder every-thing. But I'd been happy once, and I could go into this last fight knowing what that meant. That counted for something.

21

I was asleep when it happened. In the deep of night, the Lover's Tree tore its roots from the earth and tried to walk free of the market square. It didn't get very far. The tree had stood there long before Aberfaldy had been named, and its roots were driven deep beneath the ground. So the tree, this tree that now seemed to be possessed by a malignant entity, settled for bringing its branches down on the buildings it could reach. An inn lost a lot of roof shingles and the hoarding above the central well was smashed into kindling, but after that it could reach little else, and so by the time I arrived it was waving its branches to and fro in impotent fury. Ridiculous.

'The Fault bleeds through,' I said. I was displeased at having been roused. My voice was even more gravel-scratched than usual.

'It's absolute nonsense, is what it is. What do we do with it?' Castus asked. He looked suitably rumpled, though somehow he made his half-buttoned shirt and bed-hair look dashing. Some people are built to be alluring no matter what state they're in.

'One of the Night Below's creatures crawled up inside it,' I said. 'I doubt it has anything pleasant in whatever passes for a mind in there. Chop it down.'

'Nobody can get close enough to stick an axe in it,' Castus said. 'And cutting that down would take hours. Can't you just—you know.' He wiggled his fingers as if to suggest that I did something mystical. A number of his men had actually brought axes, as though they might give it a good chopping up, but Castus had a point. A blow from one of those branches would turn bones to so much incombustible kindling. It waved them furiously, impotently, black shapes crossing back and forth over the stars beyond.

'Doesn't seem to be hurting anyone,' I said. 'Whatever demon forced its way into our world it's better it get stuck there than popping out somewhere else. I'm not wasting souls on that.'

'If anyone goes too close, those heavier branches will make a quick end of them,' Castus said. 'I'm not volunteering, but it feels like we ought to do something at least.'

'Put a rope around the square,' I suggested.

'And the inn?'

'Easier to rebuild an inn than cut that thing down. The same story's true all across the world now. Things are making their way through. Hammer one down and another plank breaks loose. We're a ship taking on water, and we can't patch and bail. We need to get out of the ocean.'

'Easier said than done.'

One of Castus's men had lit a fire arrow. He shot it into the tree's trunk, where the pitch-soaked rag sputtered for a few moments before guttering out. It had been a dumb idea, and the tree seemed oblivious.

'Put them all back to bed,' I said. 'I want us on the road an hour after dawn.'

'I never agreed to that plan, Raine,' Castus said.

I yawned, and went back to bed. Castus hadn't agreed, but he'd have the men ready to move an hour after dawn.

Too much time had already slipped by. Ovitus didn't understand it yet, but when he sent his assassins he'd inadvertently passed me the one thing I needed to know. It had all come together in my head in a glorious, instantaneous moment. I had some dim recollection of speaking to myself somehow—that weak and powerless part of me I'd abandoned back in the Fault. The conversation had emerged very slowly over the course of several days, as if that other me's responses were so slow that I could only hear them in the background of my mind. But one day I'd awoken and I'd understood what she did. We both had a part to play, I just couldn't understand what part that other self could possibly be needed for.

I held the assassins in the cage in my chest, and I'd plundered their memories for those that were useful to me. Mostly it was dross, the humdrum of living, and their deaths stood out large in the pools of their recollections. But one of them had been pulled from his duty at the last moment.

'I'm sending fifty men north,' Ovitus had said, worrying at a heavy ring that was stuck on a swollen finger. They'd been in the king's own bedroom in Harranir castle. I'd seen it once before, when I'd been summoned in smoke by Robilar and Kelsen. Ovitus had made it his own. 'I want you leading them.'

'My place is with you, my king,' Helden had said. Helden had been Winterra, Redwinter's warrior-arm. He'd served with Prince Caelan, back when Caelan was supposed to be the Crown's heir.

'I need someone I can trust,' Ovitus said. 'And who can I trust in this damned place? I'm surrounded by incompetents. By fools!' He slammed his fist against a silver dish, bending it. There was Gated force behind that blow. Helden flinched.

'The Sarathi must die, my king,' Helden said. 'I've four good warriors picked, as you told me. I can do this. We have the weapons. We'll enter the town by night and see her dead by morning.'

'If even Draoihn weapons can kill her,' Ovitus muttered. 'My special advisor has imparted to me that there's a weapon that might destroy even her. I don't deny the bitch has to meet her end—she's going to try to reach the Blackwell and take command of the Crown herself. If we think the land is haunted now, if she makes it there—if a Sarathi were to take the power of the Crown—our current troubles would look like an equinox dance. She has to *burn,* Helden. I fear we need more than sharp swords and stout hearts to stop her. We need to find the Lance of Maldouen.'

'The Lance was destroyed when it pierced the Riven Queen, lord king,' Helden had said. 'And the Sarathi does not have the Riven Queen's power.'

'She doesn't?' Ovitus snapped. 'Perhaps tell that to Astorian, Blair, Calda or Swintheff. You can't, can you? Can you? Because she wiped them out. Them and all the rest.'

He shivered with grief, or perhaps it was rage. The two so often mingled where Ovitus was concerned. He didn't know where one feeling ended and another began. It was what gave him such colossal conceit. Every feeling was righteous to him.

'I can kill her with Draoihn steel, lord king,' Helden had claimed. 'Send Eiden north in my stead. He'll perform better than I. And perhaps I can end this in days rather than weeks.' He cleared his throat, uncertain.

'Out with it.'

'My lord, we have heard of this special advisor time and time again . . . but who is—'

'If I wanted you to know, I'd have told you,' Ovitus snapped. 'Fine. Go then. Try your blade. See what good it does us!'

I don't know if Ovitus truly looked the way he did in dead Helden's memory. He looked tired. Greasy, as if he'd abandoned bathing. Swarthy as if a razor had become alien to him. Hollow, as if he knew he'd doomed everyone but was too bloody-minded to change course. Did he know? Was it possible that Ovitus LacNaithe, despite his usurpation of Redwinter, his claim to be king, had the slightest misgiving?

There was no point in pondering on it. It was just a memory, and memories are prone to become warped, fixed into moulds they were never formed in.

The prospect of swift victory had proven persuasive, and Ovitus had relented. But I knew now what even Iddin, king of the Fault, feared could unmake him on this plane of existence. He was stronger than I was—his fangs had shown me that, and he'd withstood my power more than once. But the Lance—it had brought down Hallenae, the great Riven Queen, and cast her and her legions of deathless corpses, her summoned beasts and demons of the Night Below, down into the Fault. Even now, even as his fist closed on victory, Iddin had to wonder: *Could the Lance do it again?*

And so I had formed a plan of my own.

Maldouen had told us the Lance had been buried after it felled Hallenae. My own memories of the event were clouded. The Queen of Feathers hadn't seen that moment. She'd known it was coming, and had fled, rather than be caught up in the power it had unleashed. Nor did those other memories I carried tell me what had become of the Lance save that Draoihn had borne the steaming pieces of it away to the north to bury them.

I needed to go to a place called Draconloch. That's where this would happen.

On the morrow, I was going to take what remained of Castus's rebellion, and we would march north. To divert even part of his strength now, when all he had to do was hold the Blackwell until the Fault had fully collapsed into our realm—Iddin *feared* that weapon. Maybe not a great deal. Maybe not so much that he'd go seeking it himself. But a little. And a little was all I needed.

Dawn was nothing more than a fire-red stain on the eastern horizon when I rose from sleep. I brought the Witching Skin around myself, styling myself as close to Hallenae as I was able. I took the silver-backed mirror and walked out into the dawn light, positioning the rising sun at my back. Never underestimate the power of dramatic flair. I'd watched Suanach activating the silvered hand mirror, and tried my luck, running my fingers over silver-wrought flowers. The mirror's surface changed from casting my face back at me to showing me darkness. Likely its partner was in a box, or had been covered over.

'Whoever is there, speak with me now,' I said. Nothing happened, so I repeated myself. Then when I was receiving nothing in return, 'Answer me!' I'd grown unused to being disobeyed.

There was light at the other end of the mirror as a lid was raised. The world within lurched as I lifted it, and then I saw Mathilde. If she'd been sleeping she hid it well. I saw her for the first time without a decadent, queenly gown and sparkling stones at throat and ear. Her hair was still bound up in those rope-like braids, falling to one side of her head, and as I appraised her I wondered what clever person had worked out how to do that with something as common as hair.

'Sarathi Raine,' Mathilde said. 'I'd not expected to hear from you.'

'But you hoped to, didn't you?' I said, allowing a somewhat malevolent smile to spread on my face.

'What I hope for is peace,' she said.

I'd considered telling her everything. I could have told her about Loridine and the nightmares that had flowed through it, the slaughter of its people, but to what end? Word would reach them before long. Loridine was a good month's travel from Harranir—a desperate, horse-killing messenger might make it in three. But no word had come. Was there anyone left alive down in Brannlant to bear that dreadful news? They must have heard something by now. Nothing that big stayed silent for long.

I'd thought of telling her about the dog named Waldy, the beast that had attached itself to Ovitus at the picnic where he'd saved her from a charging boar. Only if she knew the truth, if it were spoken aloud, then what would Iddin do? He'd tear her throat out. He needed Ovitus, but he didn't need a queen who refused to consummate her wedding vows. She was useful only in holding the loyalty of the sizeable Brannish retinue supporting Ovitus.

If she knew the truth, she would act. She'd have to. But there was only one person whose actions mattered now, and there was no sense in seeing attractive things broken along my road.

'Is your husband around?' I asked.

'We do not share quarters,' she said. There was a hint of primness there, as if the idea insulted her, but she was the one who'd gone ahead and married him. She sighed. 'He sleeps no more than three hours each night, and only then it's when he's soaked himself deep enough in cider to let dreams find him. He's not a well man, Sarathi Raine. This war has drained him. He carries the weight of his warriors' deaths like anvils on his shoulders.'

'That's Ovitus,' I said. 'The weight of the world on his shoulders while he blinds himself to his responsibilities.'

'You were friends, once,' Mathilde said.

'Aye. We were friends, I suppose,' I said. 'Though I don't know if a narcissist like him can ever truly be friends. There was always an angle. He was spinning lies about me even while he asked my support. He told me he loved me once, and that was a lie too.'

'He's just a child,' Mathilde said.

'A child who murdered Liara LacShale in cold blood,' I said. 'He insulted her and burned her with a flick of his hand. He stole his uncle's Gates, killing him from the inside. He's rotten, darling queen. He's been rotten since he slithered from his mother's womb.'

Mathilde sighed. In the dark of her chambers, she was mostly shadow, but her eyes were startlingly white.

'Are you really any better than he is?' Mathilde asked. 'I was there. I saw what you did to those people. And you're Sarathi, unashamed of what you are. You call the dead and bid them answer.'

'Your husband tried to have me assassinated.'

'All of Harranir lives in fear of you,' Mathilde snapped, her regal calmness swaying out of view. 'We know what comes next. History does not lie. You'll raise an army of the dead. You'll force men to cut down fathers who died a decade ago. You'll pit dead brother against living sister. Whether you ever intended to be, you've become what the Draoihn always feared. You've become a dread queen of nightmare. You don't even try to hide it.'

'Hide it?' I said. I found a broad smile had spread. I enjoyed Mathilde's bantering. 'Why should I hide what I am? From fear? I'm not afraid.'

Her face darkened even further. There was no magic in Mathilde, but there should have been. What a lieutenant she would have made!

'Last night, the river ran black. Those who were aboard punts and small boats were changed by it. They became rotten things. Still living, but rotten inside and out. They staggered home, their own skin falling away in wet tatters, their gums running blood, fingernails left in jagged shards along the road. Most of them were put down out of mercy. Some of them the families have locked in cellars, demanding a cure. A cure! What you have done—what you mean to do—is monstrous. Tell me I'm wrong, Sarathi Raine. I'd rather be wrong.'

'I thought I'd be the one to bear the blame for these things,' I said. But I couldn't correct her. Not without endangering her. Did it matter if I did? Why was I even speaking to her this way? Ah yes. I had a message for her. I supposed I should get to it.

'I have a message for your lord husband,' I said. 'I thought you could take it to him.'

She regarded me through the mirror, bright whites of her eyes unflinching. 'Speak it.'

'Tell him the dog days are finished. Tell him I know how to lance the boil that's been holding me back from taking Harranir. Can you tell him that?'

'Just that?'

'Exactly that. Word for word.'

'You're using me,' Mathilde said.

'Obviously,' I said. 'But he'll want to hear my words all the same.'

She fell silent, committing those exact words to memory.

'We have hundreds of Draoihn at our command,' she said. A threat. 'We have an army. We have Draoihn of the Third Gate, who could lay waste any army of the dead you summon. I have Brannish Artists at my disposal, and you've not met their like. You won't even know they're among you until they take your head. And my lord husband is more powerful than ever. I'm not afraid of you, Sarathi Raine.'

I grunted. A smirk.

'You should be, beautiful queen. Just give him the message.'

I stroked the back of the mirror and the image faded, leaving me looking back at my own reflection, my eyes lit from within. I was strange-looking, no doubt about that. But I liked what I saw. I killed time running through the Queen of Feathers' memories, the stories of the women who'd gone before me. I was certain. I had to be. I'd come up with something truly monstrous.

An hour after dawn, I mounted a white horse and rode out to see the arrayed strength of Clan LacClune, Clan LacDaine, and all those minor clans who'd been able to spare their young hearts. Our numbers had swollen over the weeks we'd spent in Aberfaldy. We had just over a thousand men. Not enough to challenge Ovitus directly. Certainly not enough to take him to battle, and too few by thousands to assault Redwinter.

'Well, looks like you were right,' Castus said. He looked rather fine atop his horse. He shook his head ruefully. 'I've amassed everyone here. Where are we going?'

'North,' I said. 'I need a weapon. We're going to find it.'

It grew colder, as though we rode into winter, and our long journey to the City of Spires was done.

I cannot say how long it took to reach it. But that was my time, and Esher's and Sanvaunt's, and it was our time then and forever. There were times when I didn't want the journey to end, but a darkness was growing at our backs as we rode, distant on the horizon, and it was spreading. We did not have forever.

The horses had slowed to a walk. Even they could tire. But we were close enough now that the city rose before us, and with every fall of a hoof, frost crunched. The marsh was glazed with ice, thick enough that it could bear the moon horses' weight, rider and all. The cold had become a shroud, dense, thickening the air, turning breath to cloud even within our mouths. We wrapped blankets over our armour, fashioned them into makeshift hoods and scarfs. The moon horses didn't seem to notice.

We had formed no bonds with the creatures. There was an intelligence among them that ran without words from horse to horse as if they shared some parts of their minds, speaking to one another in ways we couldn't fathom. They were using us, just as we were using them. The City of Spires reared above us, reaching towards the heavens, its flow of misty white energy a constant stream filled with rocks, trees, and things both living, unliving, and those halfway between the two.

'It's not a city at all,' Esher said. She gazed towards the titanically rising blocks of mute yellow-grey stone, the swathes of ice that blanketed and sheathed them. 'It's just the pieces. A grand façade. A folly.' She looked over that frozen target, our goal for so long, and she saw things I didn't. Maldouen's Gates had changed her in ways I would never understand. She saw the joins between the things that made up the universe. A radiance of colours, she'd described it as once. I could never see that radiance. For me, there was only grey and grey's absence.

'Those aren't buildings,' Sanvaunt said. 'They're fallons.'

It *looked* like a city, only it never had been. The standing stones were vast things, stretching hundreds of feet tall, impossible in height, but there were gantries and walkways that ran between the higher levels and dark holes that mimicked doors and windows.

It was more a forest than a city, a forest of that strange material that was neither stone, metal nor wood, but it was not devoid of travellers. Most had not made it. They stood frozen, both in time and actuality, by great planes of ice that dominated the City of Spires from its outer reaches to the great tower at the centre as it thrusted spearlike, thrice as tall as any of its compatriots, into the vortex of the sky. Thousands of feet tall, it rose far beyond anything mankind had ever crafted. Bridges and stairways linked each tower, each square block of stone to the other, walkways through the sky. I do not have to tell you how small it makes you feel to be creeping into a fake city, seeking out a spirit whose name you don't even know, on the smallest chance that it might take you home.

'You're certain she's here?' I said. 'The Queen of Feathers is somewhere in this ice palace?' My breath clouded, formed painful ice crystals on my lips.

'As sure of anything I've ever known,' Esher said. 'She's in there. Right at the heart of it all. She's locked away. In a tomb.'

'It was always going to come back to a tomb in one way or another, wasn't it?' I said.

'But she's not dead?' Sanvaunt said.

'No,' Esher said. 'But she's not alive either. Not now, at this point in time. Time's a mess, here. The distances we've crossed, the disconnect from the real world, all of it comes from a confusion in time. This place doesn't know when it began, or when it will end. It doesn't require that we eat, because it doesn't remember when we last did.' She tore her eyes away from the glistening, frozen edifice. 'Same reason Sanvaunt never runs out of stamina. The whole place forgets what we let him do to us.'

I wrinkled my nose above my grin. It was half-true. Sanvaunt was being teased, but in that department, he didn't exactly seem to mind.

'What you *make* me do,' he said. 'And it's not like you seem to get tired of—'

'Shush,' I said. 'It's funny when we say it. You're a boy. It's not the same.' Sanvaunt grunted, but he wasn't displeased. It was as much reminder as any of us needed of that one beautiful thing that we'd found between us here. Here, of all places. Love defies.

It always felt good to remind each other of that bond, and the lack of jealousy between us for having experienced it in a way that convention would have cursed at. Not that such things were on the table for us any longer— and we'd made good use of a table. We'd all had to recognise that in some ways, our lovemaking had been a way of saying goodbye. We'd taken what we could when time permitted.

None of us expected to escape the Fault. We didn't say it. Didn't even breathe it, even told each other that we'd make it. But we knew. I'd tried, and it had cost me my Gates. The creatures of the Fault were swarming through the tear in our reality, but we had no way to control it, no way to push ourselves through or ascend in that light. No. We weren't there to escape—we were just there to take whatever last chances remained to us. We'd chosen to seek the Queen of Feathers because we'd found a fallen standing stone with a picture on it, and we'd chosen to believe that it represented her, and us, and that in some impossible way that connected us. It didn't. It was stupid to imagine that it did. We'd needed something, anything to focus on. Anything to give us a purpose in a purposeless land. I didn't begrudge our silent refusal to acknowledge the truth to one another. It had given us each other, in the end.

'Look there,' Sanvaunt said, his pointing finger leading far off to the city's—let's just call it west for now. 'New arrivals.'

A double line, perhaps two hundred strong, approached the city. My eyesight had always been good, but I missed being able to trance into Eio and see things clearly so far away. They were Faded, that much was obvious. Here and there I picked out a pair of antlers, boar's tusks, backwards-jointed legs with hooves. Spears, polearms, shields. They walked into an opposing wind, cloaks and clothing billowing as the gusts tore at them. More than one of the Faded slipped and fell on their causeway, ice-panes shattering as they went down.

'It's like the city doesn't want them,' I said.

'It doesn't want them to leave the Fault,' Esher said. 'It's this place, isn't it? The Fault has a mind of its own. If everything leaves, if Iddin has his way, then it's left alone here. Isolated, empty and silent for eternity.'

'You think a place can be lonely?' I asked.

'I think anything can be lonely,' Sanvaunt said. 'Everything has been, and will be again one time or another. That's what life's for. Finding each other, for however long we get to hold on.'

'Then hold on to me tight, because I don't intend to let either of you go. Not until they pry you from my dead and frozen hands.'

We stalked onwards, into the wind. The temperature dropped further. A howling gale that had never bothered us across all the Fault flung flecks of ice into our eyes. It whirled and drove around the City of Spires in spirals, ever pressing down on us. Asking us to turn back.

'Isn't there something you can do about this?' I asked Esher.

'Changing a room, making some statues dance, lighting a few fires, those things are easy,' she called back. 'But even Maldouen's Gates have their limits. You're asking if I can change the *weather*. That's a big ask. I'll try to think of something.'

She carried on talking, but her words were lost in the growing gale. The moon horses plodded stoically onwards. They didn't like it, but they wanted us to go onwards. They were more limited here than on our own world, heavier.

'You could take us back right now if you wanted to,' I grumbled into my horse's ear. 'I know you could. But you won't, will you?'

The moon horse did not dignify my complaint with a response. They had their own agenda. The wind grew stronger. We practically rode into a blizzard. Ice crystals formed so swiftly they cracked away from the earth each time the horses lifted their hooves. I didn't know whether we could ride into this for much longer.

'Up high!' Sanvaunt called out. He drew his great sword and a ripple of warm shimmered around the blade, banishing the ice that threatened to form there. I followed his gaze. We weren't unaccustomed to looking up. A winged creature descended clumsily through the sky, as if unused to its own flight. I reached for my bow, but there was no way I could get her strung in the blizzard. The creature that came down was roughly humanoid in shape and pale as off-milk, but its legs were too short, and in place of arms it had huge, bat-like wings, massive bunches of hunched muscle on its back to drive them, a bald head on which half a dozen eyes blinked at odd angles. Its mouth was toothless. This creature didn't feed—I doubted it had existed very long.

'It's Iddin,' I said. 'Some part of him, anyway.' My lovers just nodded. There was something in its presence that felt the same, radiating out from the ugly, ungainly thing that skittered as it sought purchase on a sheet of ice.

'I did not expect you to build such a lead,' the pale creature burbled, a surprisingly wet voice. Its many eyes were the green of a stagnant pond, yellow slits widening and narrowing as it switched its focus between us.

'Is there something you want?' I asked.

'Yeeeeeeeeessssssssssssssss,' the thing hissed. 'Of course there is something I want. I do not expend myself idly.'

'Get on with it, then,' I said. 'I take it you're here to surrender.'

It didn't laugh. I hadn't expected it to.

'I'm curious,' Iddin said. 'What brought you here, of all places? My Faded Lords have control of three of the five Crowns, and the last remaining Crowns in Harranir and Ithatra are untethered. It is I who controls what passes through them. It will not be you.'

'You wouldn't be bothering us now if you thought we hadn't a chance to break you,' Sanvaunt said. 'Maybe things aren't going so well for you back in our world, is that it? Not getting enough bones from Ovitus's table.'

'My victory has long been inevitable,' Iddin hissed. The thing he spoke through stalked forward, the tips of its wings acting like arms. Maybe it had been a creature in its own right and he'd claimed it, or perhaps it had been made just for this occasion. 'Maldouen held me back for a long time, I will admit it. But you are not Maldouen. You don't even possess the knowledge of the Riven Queen. None of it. But Maldouen is gone, now. And you will follow him soon enough.'

As if his words were pulling at something inside me, my head seemed to want to turn of its own accord. I looked back the way we'd come, if indeed that had been the place we'd started from. Hard to be sure, here. The darkness that gathered across the horizon was little more than a black smear of dirt across the wasteland, but it caused me to grit my teeth, swallow, and not show my fear. That's where he truly was. This flapping, ungainly thing was just a mouthpiece. On the horizon, that black cloud was coming for us. We couldn't outrun it. We couldn't fight it. Maldouen's preparations had unleashed massive forces of magic, but even they hadn't stopped it. Now that we knew what Iddin was, to even attempt to challenge him on his own terms seemed like the greatest of arrogance. We would oppose him. We would die opposing him, in all likelihood. That was probably our best out-come. Still, there's value in trying. It's not all about the outcome.

'I just want to know,' Iddin said again. It was like he'd read my thoughts. Perhaps he had. 'Why you're still trying?'

'Because people deserve to live,' Sanvaunt said sternly. He shook growing icicles from his sword, vaporised the few that continued to cling. He was losing patience.

'But they don't matter,' Iddin said, his gurgling hiss betraying him for a moment. 'None of them matter. Even the Faded, they're just—they're all just temporary. It all ends for you, one way or another. What's the point of any of it?'

'He doesn't understand,' I said. 'He actually doesn't understand what it means to live.'

'Then I hope he can still understand what it means to die,' Sanvaunt said. He pointed his sword and a pulse of blue-gold fire sped from the blade. The leathery winged creature didn't last long in it, the flame intensifying. There was hatred in Sanvaunt's eyes. He was willing the fire to hurt Iddin, to cost him something. I didn't think less of Sanvaunt for that. Those who can't hate can't love either, and the line between them can be thin as cobwebs. The flying thing died, flames sputtering out as its carcass collapsed to the wind, and the ice began to settle across it.

That would have seemed a spectacle to me once upon a time.

'Let's go,' I said. 'Every minute wasted is a minute that thing gets closer.'

It was only a little further on that the moon horses stopped. They had never been driven by our heels, but by their own wants and desires. As one, they bowed their heads, and refused to go any further. Just ahead, stone slabs across the ground marked the beginning of the city proper. Our mounts, our saviour-steeds, wouldn't set foot onto them.

'I guess this is as far as we go together,' I said to my pale, silver-white moon horse. It gave little indication of having heard me. I patted her neck, and she didn't seem to notice. When the last of us had dismounted, they turned, and it only took moments for them to streak away, too fast to see, leaving a silvery miasma in their wake. It was much faster travelling in any direction but the one we'd needed.

'They waited until we knew where to go before they came to us,' Esher said. 'It wasn't until I'd learned the Queen of Feathers' name. There's much more to those horses than their form suggests. I don't think they're related to real horses at all.'

'Still not going to tell us her name though, are you?' I said. I shouldered what had until recently been my saddlebags, and were now just bags. Esher didn't tell us, but I hadn't expected her to. She kept her secrets to herself. I doubted that I'd enjoy the answer once I knew it.

I pointed towards the great pyramid-topped spire at the city's centre.

'Sanvaunt, can you take us there? Through the fire?'

He looked off across the city.

'I don't know the target, or what the distance is,' he said. 'It would be risky.'

'How risky?'

'Like "we could appear inside a block of stone and be merged with it" risky,' he said. 'We've got feet. Let's move.' Sanvaunt shouted to be heard over a sudden billowing cloud of snow.

The City of Spires held the Queen of Feathers' tomb, but far more had been buried here. There were creatures—the Hidden Folk, as I would have called them once—marching into the city, just as the troop of Faded we'd seen earlier had been, but they had been caught in the icy tumult. A row of creatures no higher than my waist with long noses and butterfly-like proboscises stood like glass-cased statues, frozen solid as they advanced between the towering blocks of stone. Here on the fringe, the fallons were low and squat, mimicking featureless buildings, empty window holes glazed over by the storm.

'We'll freeze to death if we push on,' Sanvaunt yelled, and his voice was barely audible over the howl of the wind.

'Inside,' I said, gesturing to one of the outermost structures. My words were lost, but they understood my pointing. The empty doorway, wide enough for five people to walk abreast, was solidly glazed with ice. Fingernails had broken off in it where something had tried to claw its way in; old blood lay inches into the ice. Sanvaunt summoned his life-fire and clouds of steam billowed outwards. The ice was dense, several feet thick, and the hot wet steam was whipped away as soon as it hissed out. We stepped through the hole as soon as it had formed, glad to escape the wind's fury.

Somehow it seemed colder on the inside. The building was near a hundred feet tall, square, featureless. It was a hollow, empty thing, a stage-play setting and nothing more. Halfway up the wall, a staircase led from nothing to a solid ceiling. Other inhabitants of the Fault who'd made it this far had crawled inside to escape the fierceness of the storm, where they lay, or stood, frozen solid. Dead? I didn't think so. I didn't think the Hidden Folk died from a flash freeze. A circle of Faded sat around what they'd hoped could have been a fire. Several of them looked entirely human, one had bovine features, short, blunt horns. Another almost entirely resembled a kingfisher. I couldn't understand what could have made them want to transform themselves that way, but they hadn't started out all mixed up with animals. It was a reminder, if one were needed, that the Eldritch Kin were not human, and they never had been. We might have looked similar, but we were different. Utterly, unendingly different. Some of these Faded were armoured in a style that only the memories of long-dead queens could recall, but most wore simple clothing, like they'd worked with a plough or a chisel.

'This ice isn't natural,' Sanvaunt said. 'It's like it's grown over them. Like it finds living things to cling to.'

'Just one more unnatural thing to worry about,' Esher said. She pulled the scarf-mask from her face. It had become solid, moulded to her, and she winced as she peeled it from her reddened skin.

'We won't make it far through this,' I said. 'Can't you do something to keep us warm?'

'The Third Gate needs the energy to come from somewhere,' Esher said. 'Fire's just heat and light. To keep us warm I'd have to take it from somewhere.'

'Sanvaunt?' I said. 'You're practically half fire these days.'

'You want to make a bonfire mannequin out of me?' he said, forcing blue-tinged cheeks to a smile. 'This cold is relentless. Let's burn anything else we can before we burn me.'

He ventured to the fire the Faded creatures had laid out, thin, brittle sticks from the stunted trees of the Fault. He was saving his strength, every last tiny drop of it. He knew he'd need it before the end.

Steam fled from the piled wood and Sanvaunt pried it loose. Esher knelt beside him, and I got the sense that her Third Gate was open and she was helping him, channelling that flame from within him, the raw energy of life itself, into ordinary heat. I'd watched them do all kinds of things to each other—I'd enjoyed watching, in fact—but watching them working together in this way was different. This wasn't a thing I could help with, wasn't even something I could sense. I'd never thought I could feel jealous of the two of them, but in this I did. I'd given up my Gates, or had them taken from me, or lost them—whatever the truth of it, the result was that I was inferior now. I had no power. Nothing that made me special. While they worked at providing us with warmth, I walked around the big, empty building, looking at the other unfortunate things that had made their way into this death trap.

There were dozens. They'd been drawn here, to this dreadful, false place, dreaming of ascension into the sky and the freedom thereafter. I wondered what they must have thought, ploughing onwards into the unrelenting cold, questing for that light in the sky, only to find themselves here amidst the frozen bodies of those that had come before. How long had it taken them to find a path here through the Fault? The realisation, as it struck them, that they were doomed to become icy statues here just like the rest?

One in particular took my interest. She looked no older than me. Her hair had been brown, with flashes of metallic copper running through it. An even-featured face, a shopkeeper you might never think on again, a girl carrying a bushel of wheat you could pass in the street. Her hands seemed much older, though. They were stretched out towards a fire that had never lit, fingertips tinged black, though the rest of her was in perfect condition. Her long tunic was decorated all over with coloured beads. But it was her expression that drew me to her most. Her eyes were closed, lips slightly parted. I could feel the final shiver that had run through her as she exhaled, and then the cold had wrapped her completely and taken that last breath with it.

How long had she knelt there, that final breath caught between her lips? It could have been days, or it could have been centuries.

I wondered how the creatures of the Fault had entered our world. It would be easy to have imagined that they were sucked upwards into that whorl in the sky, like they were being torn from the ground by some kind of inverted whirlpool, but that wasn't how things worked in a place like this. The city, the vortex above us, all of it was just for show, just as directions were relative and time failed to obey reason. I suspected that to escape through the Crowns was more a matter of will and understanding than of place. We hadn't come to the City of Spires to ascend into the sky, after all. We'd come to find that ally who had fallen strangely silent. Come to find her and release her, so that she could show us the tricks of the world's fabric that would enable us to find a way home.

Or to close that pathway for good.

We hadn't spoken of it on our journey here. I didn't know whether Esher and Sanvaunt understood that in the end, the best option might not be to go home at all. They were clever. They should have seen it. The Crowns had bound the Fault, had prevented its inhabitants—had prevented its very essence—from seeping into our world. But I had to wonder whether that bleed might not just be slowed by restoring one of the Crowns but instead, we might cauterise it at its source. The Queen of Feathers was ancient, she'd existed for thousands of years. If there was a way to cut the Fault off from home at this end, then we had to take it, even if that meant that we too became trapped, as Maldouen had become trapped. I hadn't dared voice those thoughts. There'd been a part of me that would have said no. A part that would have insisted upon my own survival over everything else. But that part, that selfish essence, had abandoned me. I'd do what had to be done, even if it cost me everything.

I sat beside the frozen Faded girl, hugging my legs as she had, and watched Esher and Sanvaunt bring fire to life. I loved them with a fierceness I'd never felt before. And it was that love that would let me doom them to this place if I had to. They cared too much about the world to see it destroyed in their names, even if they didn't know it yet.

In the deep cold, tears don't form.

23

A ball of fire had appeared in the sky a week ago.

'The world is ending,' young Dinny LacDaine had said on the first day. The tremors, the demons animating the trees, the calls of hideous laughter that floated sometimes on the wind, none of that had shaken him. Not with Castus around. But actual fire in the sky—that was doing the job.

'He could make peace and stop all this,' I said, though by now, I didn't really believe it. I looked up between the trees on the forest road. 'If Ovitus could just find one moment in his life to acknowledge that he might not know the truth of everything. He could let me take the Keystone from the Blackwell. I could enter the Crown. I could put this on hold. For a while, at least.'

'I think any chance of that disappeared when you slaughtered half his army,' Draoihn Palanost said grimly.

'You'd rather I'd let them finish you off?' I said. I had grown tired of her quips.

'They had it coming,' Hallum LacShale, the big clan leader who seemed to have sworn himself into my service without being asked, said. 'The rest of them still do. Every one of them. Every damn one.'

'It's life we're fighting for. Not more death,' Castus said. When had he become the gentle one? He shielded his eyes as he looked up towards the orange-tinged star that glowed even by day. 'What do you think it means?'

Through the long years of history, my queens and I had peered through the veil and gazed back from beyond it, had summoned the night and released it into day, had brewed plagues, burned cities, devoured souls innumerable. Through wars that had lasted centuries, many unusual things had been deemed to be portents in that time. After Serranis, Lady of Deserts, rose to power, droughts and famines were taken as signs that the oracles had missed, as though the weather had known what was to follow. It was nearly four thousand years since the so-called Quern-Stone of the World, the once-great city of Avontar, had been sacked by displaced tribes from the north, and its doom was heralded by swarms of biting insects that lasted three summers. Long after the age of the Eldritch Kin, the great war we'd fought against them was known to have been prophesied in the rise of the fallons, the great, unnatural spears of rock that pierced the land from shore to shore, even though they'd been raised long before. Ever did people look for a signal that some greater power was watching over them. Our gods had names, back in the Age of Bronze. Over time those gods had separated, merged, been regurgitated in different forms. It is always easy to find super-natural meaning after the fact.

Famines were famines. Insects came and went. The fallons rose because Serranis and Maldouen had tried to bind the Fault with them, and Avontar burned because people want what other people have. I had never believed in portents, but the ball of light that trailed through the sky for over a month had to signify something. The road north from Aberfaldy was long, and made longer by the trudging pace of Castus's army. 'Army' was a grandiose name for a couple thousand weary men. Our ranks had swelled as word had spread. Perhaps it helped that we moved north away from Redwinter, fleeing danger rather than marching headlong into it.

Did I know where the Lance was buried? That's what Iddin had to wonder.

Did the orange fire in the sky signify the end approached? That was for the rest of us to consider.

In all the bygone memories of the queens of the past, I'd never seen its like. I took it personally. Wasn't it enough that I'd seen the devastation in Loridine? That I knew that the Faded had breached our world? That fire had been distant at first, just another bright star, but it grew daily. It burned brighter, and people were afraid. They were right to be. If I let myself look deep inside, I'd have seen my own fear, but I couldn't afford it. Someone had to stay focused. Someone had to do what needed doing. I would make my own omens and prophecies.

'It doesn't mean anything,' I said. 'Think on anything long enough and you'll tell yourself your own story. It's a comet, or just another of the Fault's manifestations. But it's up there in the sky, and we're down here, so I'm not going to worry about it until I have to.'

'We're only a mile from Tintandal,' Palanost said. 'Perhaps it would be better if Raine made her presence less . . . obvious.'

Palanost had taken to speaking about me as though I couldn't hear her. She really hated me, but grudgingly I acknowledged she had a point. The absolution house was one of our waypoints on the long road north to Draconloch and the holy sisters who lived there would be well aware of our approach. We didn't know whether they'd welcome us, or we'd find their gates closed. I was tired of sleeping in a cold tent. I would have valued some of that holy hospitality which religious types are always so surprisingly able to provide—vows to abandon worldly possessions somehow seemed to generate them—but even I had to concede that I was anathema to their spirituality. I might not be responsible for the plague of calamities befalling Harranir, but I'd probably look like it to them.

'I'll rein it in for the good holy sisters,' I said.

I altered the Witching Skin. The fan of spines shrank away and disappeared. My attire, which after feeling a little outdone by Mathilde I'd rather enjoyed making more glamorous than it needed to be, remoulded itself to become chaste, with a high collar and a double row of buttons. My skirts extended down to my feet and I took away the gold embroidery, but all of it remained plain black. My hair was loose, and I summoned a page girl to get up on my horse behind me and coil it up into braids.

Once upon a time, I'd have been appalled at the idea of asking someone else to do something as simple as bind my hair as if my own two hands were too good to do it themselves.

Tintandal was huge by the standards of an absolution house, on a par with Valarane in the LacNaithe lands. She stood apart from clan structures, though technically she lay on Clan LacSpurrun soil. The clan pretended to forget about her so as not to have to worry about her upkeep, and the holy sisters of Tintandal pretended to forget about LacSpurrun so they didn't have to listen to a man telling them what to do. A decent arrangement all round, really. Nestled up against rising mountains, she boasted well-tilled farmland, heavily felled woodland, a solid perimeter wall beyond which a bell tower and numerous spires rose. I thought briefly of that other me I'd left behind in the Fault, Esher and Sanvaunt, all endlessly trying to find a way to spires of their own. I hoped they'd make it somehow. I missed them, when I let those thoughts intrude. There was just me, now.

Relying on yourself is the worst. There's nobody to blame if it all goes wrong.

We broke clear of the forest an hour past noon and Tintandal's quiet land spread before us, dark mountains rising at her back. The fields were ochre with wheat, awaiting autumn's scythes, well curtained with drywall. A woman paused at her weeding, a babe in a basket on her back, to watch us go by. A man rested his barrow and hurried off towards the absolution house.

'It's peaceful here,' I said to Castus. I had never been a farmer, but for a moment I was filled with false nostalgia for this quiet life. 'Maybe we'll survive all this, and I'll go find a farm somewhere. Somewhere quiet. A place I can sleep. Maybe I can live here.'

Cottages, single-story dwellings of rough stone and old thatch, lay scattered across the land. The forest continued on to the east, fields of stumps telling the tale of its harvest. Little clouds played with one another in the sky.

'You'd be bored out of your mind,' Castus said. 'I can't see you taking vows. Raine the holy sister, giver of alms, praise-giver to the Light Above.'

'Do you still believe in it?' I asked.

'Not sure I ever did,' Castus said. 'I just said the words all my life. Doesn't really matter, does it? There's a Night Below where the demons dwell, that we know for sure. And there's the Fault, that lies somewhere between us and them. But a great presence beyond us that wants good things for us, but does nothing to intervene? I don't think anyone really believes in it. Even the people who claim to, even the priests and the holy brothers and sisters. When they see a cow running at them, they don't pray for it to stop, they just get out of the way.'

'What's the point of it then? Why do we all claim we believe in it?'

'Loneliness,' Castus said. 'In the dark there's still something to hear us. Sadness. So that when we think about our loved ones dying, and we think about dying ourselves, that there's been a point to it all.' He turned and looked at me, a soft, gentle look on a face that had become drawn and hard. 'Who's to know? Maybe there is.'

'There isn't. Not really,' I said. 'There's no point to any of it.'

Hallum LacShale gave a grunting laugh, the kind you can only do in front of people younger than yourself.

'If you need a purpose greater than the vengeance we'll wreak on Ovitus LacNaithe and his bastard followers, you're looking for more from life than I.'

I smiled at that. I'd come to like Hallum. He was a big old bear of a man, simplistic in how he saw the world. Us good, them bad. After I saved them all, his loyalty had flowed to me and I don't think it had crossed his mind once to question it.

Our small group of commanders, along with the people who oversaw the everyday tasks like getting our new-sewn field of tents erected, herding live-stock and ensuring we had enough to drink, rode ahead of the main force as we began to emerge from the forest. We were met by a group of women in the lemon robes of the Order of Our Lady of Fire. A frieze above the absolu-tion house's gates showed similar women with radiant flames around their heads. Their hair was shorn to stubble, their eyelids painted cobalt blue. They were mostly composed of wrinkled skin and stiff bones.

'I am Matriarch Iohne, the abbess of Tintandal,' the youngest of them said, a woman of fifty or so. She wore a cobalt blue stole over her shoulders and a golden chain with a garnet-studded sun around her neck. Her face was impassive, but there was a tightness to her lips.

'Van Castus of Clan LacClune,' our leader began. 'This is Van Hallum of Clan LacShale, and—'

'I know who you all are,' Iohne said curtly. 'War snaps at your heels. We live by a code of peace here. We want to take no part, and can offer no ally-ship in the struggles of our land.'

'My father often spoke well of you,' Castus said. Iohne interrupted him again.

'He most certainly did not,' she said. 'Your father was known to me be-fore I took my vows. He never spoke well of anyone. But for his faults, he never made war upon the Crown, or upon Redwinter.'

Iohne's eyes turned to me. She looked at my hair, assessed what she saw in three seconds flat.

'This is the one they call your queen, then. The living abomination you bring to my gates.'

'If they call her a queen that's news to me,' Castus said.

'I'm Raine Wildrose,' I said. 'It's an absolute delight to meet you too.'

'Is it true what we've been told?' she asked me directly. 'Are you what they say you are?'

'They say a lot.'

'They say you're a soul eater. That you tear the spirits from men. That you're Sarathi, a new witch queen in the making.'

'Oh. Then yes, that's all true,' I said. Momentarily it occurred to me how once upon a time I'd have cowered before Iohne, abbess of Tintandal. That I'd cowered before Braithe, before the sooth-sisters, before high and low noblemen alike, before just about everyone. Redwinter had taken much from me, but it had given too. Castus was right. A quiet life now would have bored me from my mind.

'You may not enter our holy grounds,' Iohne said. 'You look to be no more than a girl, but you are blasphemy walking. The names of LacClune, LacShale and all those others that follow you are forever tarnished by their allegiance to you.'

'Raine doesn't have our allegiance,' Castus said, peeved.

'I doubt I can convince you of anything,' I said. 'But for what it's worth, you've nothing to fear from me. I won't harm anyone. Believe it or not, I'm trying to put a stop to all these terrible things that are happening across the country.' I looked up at the glowing fire in the sky, a tiny second sun. 'The world is dying, Matriarch. Someone has to keep it alive.'

'I need not cite scripture to you for you to know that what you do is anathema to us,' Iohne said grimly. 'We cannot drive you away, but neither will we bend before a foul wind. You will not enter our grounds.'

It was predictable.

'I won't,' I said. 'But I ask that you give what you can to our warriors. You may despise me, but Ovitus LacNaithe betrayed his country and his people. You're an educated woman. You know what the Crown does, and why the world is rotting. LacNaithe is the cause. If not me, then let our people draw water from your wells, and take what they need to carry us to Draconloch.'

Matriarch Iohne's eyes narrowed.

'Draconloch? There's nothing there but myth.'

'The Lance of Maldouen is buried there,' I said. 'We intend to use it to defeat the enemy.'

'Raine,' Castus said warningly. 'I don't think we should—'

'The abbess needs to trust us,' I snapped at him. 'She should know our quest. As Maldouen once drove the Riven Queen into the Fault, so too will we drive the traitors of Redwinter from our lands.'

'The Lance was shattered,' Iohne scoffed. 'Draconloch is a death trap. There is but one pass you can take, and nothing bigger than a hovel. They will come for you there, and you will have nowhere to run. You know that.'

'And that is why we stay but one night,' I said. 'I don't need to be loved here, but when the land's corruption ends, when the dark things go back to their holes, then know that it was I, Sarathi Raine Wildrose, who drove it away.'

The greeting party of ancient holy sisters clutched at their talismans, their unease spreading to their horses, nervous hooves stamping the grass. Matriarch Iohne held herself together. She'd come from some kind of clan prestige to have this role. I doubted she could control this domain by herself without some granite in her spine.

'We shall provide succour as we can,' she said. She turned to address Castus LacClune. 'I know what you intend—to take our grain, our livestock. Every army does it, and we cannot stop you. We can't even protect ourselves from the horrors that now plague the world.'

'Among your farmer tenants there must surely be some stout hearts?' Castus said. Iohne closed her eyes and placed her forefingers against the lids, a silent prayer. When she opened them, sorrow lay deeply within.

'There were. A group of young men and women, volunteers from the farms, who served to guard what wealth we have against robbers and the like. But something dark now haunts the forest to the east. When our men ventured there five nights ago, only three returned. We trust now only in stone walls and holy prayers. You'll raid us for what you will, and I will not have my people oppose you merely on principle. What I ask in return is that you leave ten of your men to guard us. Your enemies will come here in your wake.'

'I can spare no men,' Castus said. 'I'm sorry.'

'How many men did you lose to the forest?' I asked.

'More than a dozen,' she said. 'Young, eager bright fools, as men often are. But good men. Good hearts.'

'We'll leave you ten,' I said. I looked towards the forest. 'Point me in the direction of this darkness. I'll take care of it for you.'

'We can't spare ten,' Castus said. An edge of anger entered his voice. 'I'm in command here, Raine. We can spare nobody.'

'Let's discuss it when you're rested,' I said, and that only annoyed him further.

·   ·   ·   ·   ·   ·

I hadn't been alone for a long time. Yes, I'd been alone in a tent, or alone in a room, but that wasn't the same. There's something about being under a forest canopy, nothing around but the birds and the scuttlers in the undergrowth, that empties you out. For a while, you can let go of all the human stuff, and just exist apart from everyone else.

I was disappointed to find that even walking off into Tintandal's forest, I still wasn't alone.

There were snatterkin here. Those little sound-making things, free from substance, just living sounds, clicked and whispered among the foliage. I passed an old, ivy covered stone where a group of spriggans, wizened little goblins with overly large heads, watched me pass without breaking from what I had to assume was a stolen keg of mead. Their language was indecipherable. The Hidden Folk weren't so hidden anymore. Maybe they'd always dwelt here, but maybe they'd broken free of the Fault. They had nasty little knives made from flint, or shards of broken glass. One of them sought to show bravado by brandishing it towards me, but when my eyes switched towards it, it ran away howling. The other spriggans thought it funny.

I followed the trail easily enough. Braithe had taught me to hunt what felt another lifetime ago, but I didn't need much skill to follow the tracks of men laid clear in the mud. We'd had plenty of rain lately—it's always raining in Harran. That last summer I'd been in this world had been uncharacteristically scorching hot, but even that had ended with rain as well. The footfalls of the dead remained imprinted in the mud, a trail laid out to lead me on to a final, dismal resting place.

The ground was uneven. A rock wall rose forty, fifty feet, down which water fell into a pool, slithering off as a shallow stream. People had come here in the past to make offerings to the Hidden Folk. The remains of a small shrine, not much more than a waist-high stack of piled stones, had become the resting place of one of the young men. He lay crumpled, stripped naked. His friends were scattered around, similarly devoid of clothing. Some of them looked as though they were just sleeping, but their chests neither rose nor fell. One of them was propped beside the waterfall, his eyes a blank stare.

A small, rotund woman had her back to me. She sang a death dirge for them as she laundered. The men's clothing was piled at her sides, some wet, some dry. She dunked a shirt into the water, then spread it across a stone

236 and beat at it with a wooden bludgeon. Her hands had turned white with

and beat at it with a wooden bludgeon. Her hands had turned white with cold, running with blood where her chapped skin had cracked apart.

I knew her, or her kind at least. Hallenae had made use of the Nigheag at times. The washerwomen of the dead had been women once, the unacknowledged mistresses of men who'd fallen in battle. Old myths said that if you caught one and suckled at her breast she'd grant you three wishes, but they had no such powers. As unlikely a thing as the Nigheag was, granting wishes was beyond anything, even me. But there was one element of truth to their sad story. It was definitely better to take them by surprise. I picked up a smooth oval stone a little smaller than my palm.

I drew souls from my chest and sent them down around my feet, lifting me a few inches above the ground as the Sixth Gate's drone radiated around me. I felt the death in this place even more strongly. Death could have flavour, could taste bitter, tragic, fearful, even peaceful. This grave-place left sorrow across my gums. I could feel it in the air, a shimmering colour to the tunnel. You'd think sorrow was blue, or grey, but for some reason in my tunnelling mind it was lilac. My feet didn't touch mud nor undergrowth as I glided silently up behind the Nigheag, the raps of her bludgeon against the stone clacking out across the glade. She muttered as she worked.

'Cellum LacBrone, dead as a stone. Dead in a ditch, covered in pitch. Dead in a barn, unspooling like yarn. Dead on a lane, his face all a' pain. Lessie LacNell, died where she fell. Dead in the straw, breathing no more.'

I clamped a hand around the fat little woman's mouth, and another around her arms. Thick, meaty arms, heavy with flab.

'Enough of that, you little death-singer,' I hissed.

The Nigheag was flabby, and she resembled any old peasant grandmother, but for two things. One was her single wide nostril at the end of her nose, and the second were the five long, flesh-rending teeth in her mouth. In sudden anger, she lurched back against me, her strength surprising for such a small thing, and her dagger-teeth seeking my hand. We were flung backwards, my hovering feet having nothing to hold on to. She managed to get her teeth around the blade of my hand, but the Witching Skin flowed down over it, encasing it in night, and the serrated yellow fangs slid from my hand. She shook her head free of my hand and screeched.

'Raine of Dunan, dead in a—'

Before she could finish I stuffed the stone into her mouth.

'Bound by me, bound by the Sixth Gate, bound to serve,' I hissed and the light from my eyes illuminated her matted hair, sending crawling fleas diving to deeper recesses. My objective achieved, I stepped back from her.

'Who do you think you are?' she managed to say around the stone. Now that it was lodged there, she couldn't get it out. The Hidden Folk follow stupid rules.

'I'm the undying,' I said. 'I'm Raine Wildrose. But I'm also Riven Hallenae, and Serranis, and Song Seondeok. I'm two dozen others, whose names never made it to history. And I bind you to me, Nigheag. You will obey my commands, as your dead sisters once obeyed.'

The Nigheag looked me over, unimpressed with what she saw. Slowly she acknowledged that I was right, her flabby, slightly too-long arms falling down to her sides.

'Aye,' she said around the stone. 'I shuppose I will.'

I pushed the man's corpse from the piled stones of the shrine and sat down upon it. It wasn't like he needed it. The Nigheag sat down at the stream's edge, fat legs splayed wide, the way a child would sit.

The Nigheag's power came from their songs, and their deep knowledge of the world. Even with the memories of the Queen of Feathers at my disposal I didn't always know how things worked, and where that deep knowledge came from—how the Nigheag knew our names, or why they had to sing their rhymes, had never been known to the living. That was the difference between the magic of people and the magic of the Hidden Folk. Ours had to make sense, while theirs followed rules seemingly laid down at random.

'You can sing a woman dead, but you can craft a night's-eye stone and keep a soul trapped within it too. I have need of such stones.'

'How many?' she asked. Her single nostril flared wide.

'As many as you can craft for me.'

· · · · · ·

It was dark when I returned to our army. Hallum LacShale and his men had cleared a family out of a comfortable farm cottage for me. Most of our people would erect their tents outside Tintandal's walls. Those with pedigree would be given rooms within the absolution house itself, provided they weren't required to be present among the army. For once I found the peace I sought.

It's a strange thing to sit alone in the home of a stranger. The cottage was simply made, a wooden A-frame with a bark shingle roof. Its builder had done well, as had its occupants in subsequent days, keeping the drafts out, keeping it clean. The floor was only dirt, but they'd laid down plenty of dry rushes. It was in the details that I saw the story of the people who lived here. The bunches of herbs hanging from the central beam were neat, trimmed to size. A wooden block housed knives with varying handles of bone or wood, each of them well-ground to sharpness. The beds were neatly made. Somebody cared for this house. Somebody loved it. I would have felt bothered by that, only the bed was too comfortable, too soft. Unusual to find that in the commoners' world. I knew that Hallum would have left some of his men to watch my borrowed house during the night, but I charged a spirit with the task as well, tied it to the chimney stack with its own tail. It wouldn't tire or fall asleep, and it could see further and better in the dark. Nothing was going to surprise me.

I contacted Mathilde with the mirror as I made ready for bed, as I'd taken to doing most nights. We didn't speak of anything that mattered. It was mostly just chatter. Neither of us was going to give away anything that could give the other's side an advantage. I don't know why we both did it, other than it's lonely at the top of things, and there's a thrill in not getting caught.

I'd altered my Witching Skin into a nightrobe when someone started banging on the door.

'Open up, I know you're in there.' It was Castus. I was weary, but I opened the door to him anyway.

'What is it? Has something happened?'

'A lot has happened, but not today,' he said, stepping inside before I had a chance to tell him to leave. He wasn't impressed by my lodgings, but then, he'd been born to greater things.

'All ready for tomorrow? I'd have thought they'd have given you a room in the abbey,' I said.

'They did,' Castus said. He took off his sword belt and rested the scabbard against the wall. He didn't ask my permission as he kicked off his boots.

'There's clearly something you want,' I said. I stood with my hands on my hips, unimpressed. Castus shrugged and pulled a small flask from his pocket.

'Figured we could enjoy this,' he said. 'It's the last of the red my father laid down.' He pulled the stopper free and took a swig. I shook my head. Drink didn't have the appeal it once did. I took a stool and watched him, standing there by the window, drinking.

'What do you need from me?' I asked.

'I don't sleep so well,' he said, looking out of the clouded window glass into the blackness of the night. 'That was one of her things, wasn't it? Grand-master Robilar. She used to say that getting a good night's sleep was worth three days of preparation. It's just so hard these days.'

'Is Dinny keeping you awake?'

A little of the weight drifted away from Castus's face. He even managed a smile.

'I wish he was,' he said. 'But he's young. He's so young.'

'You're barely older than he is.'

'But I feel it, you know?' He sighed, tipped the last few drops of his father's vintage into his mouth and tossed the flask onto a table. 'They made us grow up so fast. Do you think she foresaw this? The grandmaster, I mean.'

'She was no prophet,' I said. I wanted to sleep, but I sighed and went to stand beside him. 'Just a woman with a mission. With a vision for who and what we should be. She believed in people, you know?'

'I guess so. She was someone you could believe in.'

'Just spit out whatever is on your mind,' I said. 'We've a long march to-morrow.'

Castus rubbed at tired eyes. I'd missed seeing it on him, the cloak of weariness. He didn't look at me. Wouldn't look at me. Just stared out of the window. Wrapped up in his own little world.

Weak thoughts, Hallenae whispered. I quashed her down.

'I just want to sleep,' Castus said.

I took him by the hand and led him to the bed, where he shed his Draoihn oxblood, his chain of leadership, all the trappings that made him who he was to everyone else. We climbed into the bed together, and he lay facing the wall, and I lay up against his back. And we lay, and we breathed, and within minutes his breathing changed. Became even. He slept.

I found a deep and easy sleep without dreams.

When I awoke, the commotion had already started outside, as I knew it would have. I was glad not to be part of all that fuss, but soon someone was hammering on my door.

'Ugh,' I grunted.

'I think you made them angry,' Song Seondeok giggled from the last vestige of a dream. Her laugh was so annoying. She sounded like a child. The banging on my door continued.

'Sarathi Raine!'

Matriarch Iohne had some balls on her to call me that. I yawned sleepily and opened the door.

'They're looting the absolution house,' Iohne declared. 'Your men are robbing us blind!'

'Yes. Sorry,' I said. I blinked a few times. It seemed very bright outside compared to the dimness of the cottage's interior. Iohne had been followed by a couple of the old crones but a small gaggle of younger sisters as well.

'What do you think you're doing to us?' Iohne demanded.

'Well. I ordered all those gold plates, all those silver candle holders and relic boxes and whatnot all taken with us,' I said. 'We've need of money, and quickly. And you have money. Sorry about that.'

'These are the treasures of Our Lady of Fire,' the abbess said. She was half-aghast, half-horrified. Really it should have occurred to her that we might ransack the place. 'This is an outrage.'

I leaned an arm against the doorframe, rubbing sleep from my eyes.

'Maybe you should take your grievance to the king?' I said. 'Maybe that neutrality of yours will pay off. I don't blame you for being mad at me, Matriarch. I can't prove to you that I'm trying to save you all. But that's the size of it. I'm just doing my best, and we need to hire miners up at Draconloch. We need to hire every miner from here to the sea if we're going to dig enough tunnels to find the Lance in time to put a stop to all this.'

'The king *will* hear of this,' Matriarch Iohne said. Her fists balled in fury.

'Oh yes,' I said. I smiled. 'I bloody well hope so.'

'Raine? Wake up. We need to move again.' Sanvaunt's voice was gentle. There was a little warmth here. Not much. Barely a whisper of heat. But it was enough that I didn't want to stir. I pried my eyes open one at a time. I'd imagined mornings where he'd wake me up back in Redwinter, only it had been so very different in my mind. The sun had slanted through half-drawn curtains, and the smell of warm bread and hot tea had filled the air. Here the air was so cold it burned my nose.

We three, we last three, moved quietly about the cavernous mausoleum. Esher had looted frozen clothing from the fallon's other occupants as I slept and they'd thawed out by the fire. We cut them into rags and stuffed them under our clothes, then put on the suits of Maldouen's armour. I winced and pressed my eyes shut each time my skin brushed against the metal and I had to pry it free.

'I can't do this. It's too cold here,' I said as my jaw quivered uncontrollably. My fingers wouldn't move right and my legs felt as agile as tree trunks. Sanvaunt placed a hand against my cheek.

'I'll give you enough to keep us going,' he said. I nodded eagerly, gritting my teeth to stop them chattering, and as I looked into his molten eyes they swirled and heat radiated through my body. It wasn't without pain, but the good kind. Places I hadn't realised were numb were coming back to life. I sagged against him for a moment, savouring the flood of warmth.

The entryway had frozen over again, but the film of ice wasn't thick enough to warrant melting. Sanvaunt just hacked it into panes with his sword until there was enough of a hole to climb out of. As the cold spilled in and what little warmth we'd made was stripped away, I bade farewell to the mute, solidified creatures who'd shared their grave with us, and headed out beneath the brooding red sky.

'No wind,' I said. My breath hung in the air where I'd left it, motionless steam. The world was unnaturally still. The rime crunched beneath my armoured boots.

'No anything,' Esher said. 'You could hear a baby's heartbeat out here.'

Silence, so deep and heavy that it threatened to blot out my other senses, hung across the world like fog. Every movement, every foot's shift against the cracking frost, was audible with perfect clarity. I'd never heard a sound like it, so distilled, so pure.

'This makes things easier,' Sanvaunt said. Ever pragmatic. Ever keen to move on. His gaze, ever more shadowed of late, led deeper into the City of Spires.

'I think I know why,' I said. 'Look there. Back into the swamp.'

Back beyond the buildings-that-weren't, darkness had grown to cover the land. A wall of blackness approached the city. Its movement was indiscernible to us, but it was coming. Iddin was coming. He was coming here, at monstrous speed, crossing that same vast distance the moon horses had carried us over as a tidal wave of malice.

'However this is going to end, it won't be long,' Esher said. She shielded her eyes as she looked back towards the ink-black cloud. 'I hoped we'd outrun it for longer. I hoped we'd have time to try to figure something out.'

I reached out and we linked fingers, gently, loosely. Iddin would reach us, his black wave would break across this city, and then we'd be gone. All the love we'd found between we three would be snuffed in its infancy. Evaporated, not even lasting as long as our breath in the air.

'I'd hoped for a lot of things,' I said. 'Now I just want us to make an end of it. Anything we can do to help the people back in our world. I'm tired. We've been running for so long. The fighting never ends. The fear never goes away.'

'It's me who's supposed to be afraid all the time, remember?' Esher said. She squeezed my fingers. Despair was swamping me, and I couldn't find the strength to return it.

'No more fear. No more dread, either of you,' Sanvaunt said. It was reassuring, but it was also a command. There was something fun in being bossed around sometimes and it made me smile. Maybe I enjoyed it because it wasn't real. It was just play. Just make-believe. With Esher I could splay open my ribs and show her the slow beating of my heart. With Sanvaunt I could play at being all the things I wasn't. To anyone else my loves might have seemed similar in many ways, competent, clever, athletic. But they were so different to me.

'How do we not fear that?' I said.

'We've already done the impossible,' Sanvaunt said. 'We've run for months. So we keep running. We don't give in to that thing, we don't give in to this place, and we don't let anyone take what we have from us. Not now, not ever.'

'I won't give up,' Esher said. 'Even in the face of destruction, I'll be fighting.' Her hand slid further into mine, her grip becoming firmer. Harder. 'Nobody takes it from us!'

'Nobody takes it,' I said.

'Nobody could,' Sanvaunt said. 'Let's move. Maybe today's the day we find her. Maybe today's the day we go home.'

I wished that it could have been that simple. I wished we could find the Queen of Feathers and she'd transport us back to our world. But even if she did, our world was doomed. That other broken half of me I'd recklessly hurled out of the Fault had a plan now. I'd felt it in my sleep. A single day here was worth nearly a week there. Maybe she had the time, where I didn't. She better. There was too much I still wanted. I wanted to feel Sanvaunt and Esher's spirits flowing through me like fire. I wanted to be swept away on fierce claims and a surge of love. I worked my facial muscles against the cold until my expression resembled the way that I felt. I began to walk deeper into the City of Spires, repeating the same words over and over through the steam of my breath.

'No surrender. Don't back down. Fight to the last, until the sun fails.'

. . . .

When Maldouen tore the Fault free of whatever poor place it had blighted before, he could at least have tried to retain a little logic. How it remained as a place at all was incomprehensible. The Fault didn't believe in time, or distance, or the division between one thing and another and as we pressed into the frozen heart of the City of Spires, it seemed to be forgetting rules altogether.

A mural splayed across the wall of a vast fallon, big enough to have been a castle, but here, just an empty shell of seamless stone. We thought it was a dull-coloured mural at first, at least. It showed some of the Faded, marching in a procession, heading deeper just as we did, only it wasn't long before we realised it wasn't a mural at all. There were slight signs of motion within it, almost imperceptible, but the occasional twitch of a finger, the flutter of hair caught in a wind we couldn't feel was there if you looked for it.

'Light Above,' Esher breathed. 'What happened to them?'

'Nothing good,' Sanvaunt said. 'On. I don't want to linger here.'

We left them behind. I almost offered a prayer for them, but I didn't believe in praying, and I'd seen the things the Faded had done in Loridine, and when I thought on that I didn't pity them anymore.

The path we followed changed from smooth to blocky. Cubes of frozen rock were missing from the ground, or else hung suspended in the air. None of us touched them. They defied the rule of falling down, sitting suspended in nothing as if the air itself had frozen around them. We passed more doorways leading into darkness, simple rectangles, the holes closed with ice. The bones of a dragon lay fallen beneath them. Perhaps its death had shattered this last bit of reality. There was power in creatures. Power in life. The Fault didn't always know what to do with it.

'It's endless,' I muttered. 'An endless city of nothing. Home to nobody.' I looked up at that vortex in the sky, the whorl of whiteness that led up from the city's heart like a great tree reaching for the heavens.

'Raine, move!'

Esher had sensed it long before I could. She lived in Eio now, her First Gate trance open day and night, maybe even when she slept. As I looked left and right, seeking the danger, Esher threw herself into me and knocked me flying. We clattered to the frost-hard street together in a tangle of limbs and ringing armour.

'What . . . ?'

The ground on which I'd been standing had turned black, gleaming with oily orange tints, and then it erupted upwards like a geyser from what had been solid ground only moments before. The jet of blackness spiked fifty feet into the frigid air. We scrambled further away before it could rain down on us. A rotting, congealed blood stench hit me like a wave. My throat clamped shut even as the heaving started. There was nothing in me to vomit.

'Again,' I managed to gasp between retches as what had been blanket-white snow beneath us began to turn. Esher was faster to her feet than I was mine, and she hauled me up. We staggered a few steps together and then with a whoosh the ground boiled through, sputtering then blasting a jet of rancid filth into the air.

'What is it?' Sanvaunt called. He took a few steps back from another jet spraying into the air.

'Bad shit,' I said. 'Let's move!'

Between the city's vast blocks of not-stone we ran, boots crunching the frost—until ahead of us, at the end of the street, the ground blackened and began to boil. The foulness suddenly billowed up, a wave of frothing rot and pestilence, hot and stinking and filling the way, a wave five feet high that surged towards us.

We turned to run, but there was no way we could be fast enough. The wave, black and foul, rushed down the passage with unnatural speed.

'Raine, window!' Esher shouted, pointing to a small opening fifty feet or more up on the smooth, ice-scarred side of a fallon. She turned her back to it and cupped her hands. There was no time to think, only to trust her. The Second Gate changed something in the nature of her muscles, magnified her strength, and when I set a foot into the stirrup her hands created, she hurled me upwards.

I launched, I flew, up, up high and I reached for the window. My fingers found the ledge, but Esher's calculation wasn't quite right and I threw my arms over the edge as the rest of me slammed against the smooth stone wall, ice shards raining on the torrent below.

I scrabbled against the stone. I'd done my training on the practice court and the months in the Fault had turned me hard and lean, but I was carrying a lot of extra weight in my armour, the extra clothing against the cold, my heavy pack filled with bedroll, bowls, the things I needed to live. Now they might be about to be the death of me. I heard the roar of the torrent passing below, couldn't see what was happening. My shoulders howled as I tried to force myself up. My fingers screamed as I tried to find purchase. After all this, after everything, the indignity was that I wasn't going to fall back down, shatter my bones and likely drown in the river of filth filling the street.

A hand latched around my wrist, hot enough to scald. Something else was already inside! Before I had time to make a choice about it I was hauled upwards. The steel encasing me protested and squealed as it was dragged over the lip of stone and into the space beyond. I tumbled down into a dark room beyond in a clatter of purple steel scales and lay gasping, my body taking a moment to remember how to work.

No time for that. I scrambled to my feet, drawing my sword and levelling it at the monster before me.

She was terrible to behold, her skin blackened and cracked like charcoal. Her lips were drawn back exposing broken teeth, her eyes stared bold, pale and lidless. Her whole body was a mass of terrible burns. A burned, dead thing.

'I am not here to harm you,' she said, her words grating, distorted. She seemed unimpressed by my sword. 'If I wanted you dead I didn't have to intervene.'

I had no time for this. I thrust at her and the sword's point drove into her chest where a human heart would lie. She looked down at the blade, unimpressed.

'Really? I save you, and you respond so?' she said. 'It would take more than that to hurt me now.' I drew the sword out and took a few steps back from her. My wrist was red, burned where she'd touched me.

'Who are you?'

'See to your friends, little flea,' she said. Thin wisps of smoke trailed upwards from her, and there was warmth there. She emitted heat, as if this dreadful damage had only just been inflicted. She took a few steps further back from me, holding her arms out slightly from her sides, as if touching anything would cause her pain.

She didn't *seem* to want to hurt me. The urge to look back was too great. The streets had become rivers of the roiling, orange-black liquid, choppy with waves. I saw Sanvaunt first. On the opposite side of the street, he hung from a square protrusion above the seething liquid that filled it. He'd once bet me a date that he could run up a fourteen-foot-high wall. He hadn't been lying, the arrogant, beautiful bastard.

Of Esher I saw nothing. Panic welled, but then—there, in the midst of the river as a wave subsided—I saw the gleam of gold. She was there, still as a statue, gleaming like a polished chalice.

'She's much too good at this,' I muttered as the poison washed around her, leaving her unscathed. She'd turned herself to gold, arms braced across her head, leaning forward into the crashing liquid. My heart surged for her. Mastery of the Second Gate, Sei, the Gate of Othering. She knew what she was doing, didn't she? She had to. She had to still be alive. I felt a thundering in the world around me, as if the air had grown so heavy it could crush me.

Sanvaunt heaved himself up onto the stone. It only jutted a couple of feet from the vast fallon's side, a random feature on a random wall. I saw his burning eyes go to Esher, then frantically search, and I realised he was looking for me.

'Hey,' I called to the other side of the street. 'I'm up here.'

A look of relief passed across his face even as his mouth set into a hard line. He said nothing. He was stuck there on a ledge four feet wide and half that deep.

'Esher's down there still,' I called out. The broil of orange-black filth had filled the streets. It had calmed, the waves quieting, leaving umber smears down city walls. 'Is she all right?'

'I don't know,' Sanvaunt called back. The fear encased his words. 'How did you get up there?'

'She threw me,' I said. 'Can she turn back?' Sanvaunt shrugged his dragon-styled pauldrons.

'If this subsides? I'll do what I can for her,' he called. We could only see the top of Esher's shoulders, her head and braced arms above the swells. 'Is there a floor up there?'

'Yes,' I called. I spun back to face my rescuer and to take in the building's interior. We stood in a low-ceilinged room that in every other way resembled the building we'd spent the night in. Featureless, cold. But there was a door. Not every building was utterly devoid of feature, then.

'Who are you?' I asked. My heart was pounding, blood surged through me in a torrent. I wanted to draw steel. The creatures of the Fault weren't to be trusted.

'This is not the place for the speaking of names,' she said. 'Names have great power here.'

'Light Above,' I said. 'It's you. You're the Queen of Feathers.'

She laughed, a ruptured, ugly sound, as if her throat were trying to remember how to do it.

'Should I be amused or insulted?' she drawled. 'You won't find her here, little flea. Her existence here ended many months ago now. You don't happen to have any chewing tobacco on you, do you?'

'No,' I said. The Queen of Feathers had called me 'little flea' in the past, and I hadn't liked it any more then. It was strange but I couldn't help but be relieved that this charred and burnt-through woman—if she had ever been a living woman—was not the key to our salvation. Most things in the Fault were threatening, but despite her disfigurement, she had saved me. I wasn't about to play at being mysterious. There wasn't much time. My friends were trapped, Iddin was coming, and back home the world was burning.

'I'm Raine of Dunan,' I said. 'Raine Wildrose, if you'd rather.' The charred woman eyed me up and down in a way that made her seem more human, and somewhat more discomforting than she'd been before.

'We're always pretty to begin with, you know that?' she said. 'Maybe it's just luck. Maybe it's part of why we get chosen. Maybe the Queen of Feathers, as you call her, just likes pretty girls.'

'Oh,' I said. We're always pretty. 'What do you call her?'

'I called her Nightlark. Did you ever sleep with her?' A ridiculous question. It might have seemed improper, but she was burned, I was split in two, my friends were either elbow-deep in black tar or clinging to a ledge, so what did it matter? If I could find any common ground with the stranger, I had to reach for it.

'I don't think she likes me that way. She's more like a ghost, anyway.'

'I know,' the burned creature said. 'I did, though. Before all this. It's all a bit messed up when that sort of thing starts happening. She would have wanted you, I expect.'

I was growing more uncomfortable by the moment. Yes, I was thankful to the charred woman for saving me but still, this wasn't the conversation I'd been expecting to have right then. She smelled like morning's ashes, the odour rising as the thumping in my chest started to quiet, giving other senses a chance.

'I'm not for the wanting,' I said angrily. This was not the time. 'I need to find her. I have to set her free. Everything depends on it.'

'That isn't going to work,' the burned woman said. 'Like I said, she's not here. Do you have any alcohol? Olatte leaf? Rose-thistle?'

'No,' I said. 'Sorry.'

'More's the pity.'

'How do you know she's not here?'

'Because she can't be. You'll understand when we get there. Come. I'll take you to the tomb.'

'Wait,' I said. 'Why are you helping me?'

The scarred woman stopped mid-turn and paused, her eyes going somewhere else as if she needed to think deeply. She was searching her memory, I realised. Seeking something in there.

'I don't want the cloud to win,' she grated. 'And I want my torment to end. I've burned here for too long.'

'I can't leave my friends,' I said.

'They are done for,' the scarred woman said. Her face went blank, and I knew I'd seen her before. I'd *met* her before, but her nose was mostly burned away, her ears entirely gone. 'Certainly dead soon. You don't need them. A witch queen stands alone. Your Queen of Feathers should have taught you that.'

'Don't count them out yet,' I said. I turned back to Sanvaunt and yelled across at him that there was someone else here, and I was going to try to find a way down and over to him.

'No,' Sanvaunt called back. 'Keep going. Find the Queen of Feathers. You can't help us here.'

'I can't leave you,' I told him. 'I can't leave Esher.'

'She's fine,' Sanvaunt called back. He pointed down to the golden statue in the swill. 'She's managed to move at least a foot so far. She's alive.'

I spun back to find the charred woman standing alarmingly close to me. I looked down into her eyes. There was so much colour in them, so much viridian, like nobody's eyes I'd ever seen. Despite all their colour, I'd never seen a person's eyes so unblinking, so devoid of a soul. A shiver passed through me, but I couldn't look away.

'Do you know a way out of this place?'

'There is no way out. I have searched for one here for a very long time,' she said. 'But you should be here for the ending just the same.' And she began walking away towards the door again.

I turned back to Sanvaunt.

'I'll find her,' I called to him. 'I'll do it. I'll get us out of here. I love you.'

Sanvaunt just nodded.

'I love you too.'

'When Esher gets out of there, tell her for me.' I didn't even have to say it.

'She knows.'

We nodded at each other, and I followed a half-dead woman into the darkness.

The black comet had crashed far away, east and south of us. We all heard it, felt the tremors run through the ground. Something momentous had happened. I hoped that it had landed squarely on Ovitus LacNaithe's head, but that might have hit Mathilde as well and I'd been enjoying our pointless, stolen conversations. They mostly ended with her imploring me to surrender, to let Ovitus focus on putting a stop to the horrors that were emerging across the land, but that was never going to work. I liked her vim, though.

We had reached Draconloch. I would make my final stand here. I remembered it, vaguely, through the Riven Queen's memories. It was all I could have hoped it to be.

A loch stretched miles through the mountains of the north. A lone gorge provided access to its narrow, stony shores before the rock walls reared upwards on either side.

It felt right that we be in Harranir's north. It had all started here for me. Birth. Death. Rebirth, and death again. The monastery at Dalnesse. I'd awakened there in more ways than one. I'd learned I had the potential to use the First Gate. I'd first seen the Queen of Feathers there, much use though she'd turned out to be in the end. I'd learned my true value, or at least as it had been then. How I was seen by others, how they sought to use me for their own ends, how to some I was merely a body, and to others a tool to be used. I remembered Ulovar fondly, though he'd sought to use me too. He'd given his life to defend Redwinter from his own nephew, and to deny Ovitus the power he craved. If he hadn't, Ovitus would have taken the Keystone and opened the Crown himself. It would already be over. So yes, Ulovar had used me, but I forgave him. Mostly because he was dead.

There is great beauty in a land of rain and fog. It still clung to the hills, even in the middle of the day. The loch extended on and on for miles, and it was on the banks of that still, silent water that I would bring Ovitus and his dog to battle. Or the dog and his Ovitus, more accurately. Legend had it that during the Age of the Faded a great dragon had died of a broken heart and fallen from the sky, and the crater it left filled with its tears, and those tears became the silver water. It seemed everything was about crying these days. Mine shafts dotted the mountainsides like pockmarks, though the workers had abandoned their homes and sought caves to hide in as we approached. An army seldom works out well for the local populace. Honest Harranese miners had cut ore from the earth here for nine hundred years. Anywhere you walked, there was likely a tunnel deep beneath your feet. Veins of copper, lead and tin flourished beneath the mountains. Snow capped the peaks above. Where better would one think to hide the shards of a broken Lance than in tunnels already carved? A lone fallon stood silent on a small island, standing firm against wind and time. Draconloch was a place of history. It was fitting that I end things with the eyes of the past upon me.

'You really think it's here?' Castus LacClune asked. We two stood on the loch's shore, a sloping plain of gravel. The falling drizzle was so light it didn't even impact the loch's surface.

'This is where we dig,' I said. 'Have we had any luck locating the miners?'

'My boys will find them,' Castus said. 'And when they hear we're offering gold for strong arms, they'll come to us.'

'How many?'

'The ones we've found say there were more than four hundred before they all ran off.' He blew out a breath, and I expected it to steam, but it didn't. I'd been feeling cold lately, as if winter had hit us early, but it was still months away. 'Do you really know what you're doing, Raine? What we're doing, here? You're gambling the outcome of a war on digging through solid rock.'

'Four hundred is not enough,' I said. 'Send your men out to every mine within fifty miles. I want thousands of them working for us. They need to be cutting my tunnels *exactly* where I say to. I don't have a map, there's no X marking a spot. But there are only certain places where it *could* have been buried, where the earth would hold it. I understand where it *might* be, and these tunnels will wind through all of the possibilities.' I ground my teeth. It sounded like nonsense, but then a lot of what I said these days probably did. 'Redwinter will mobilise against us soon. Ovitus knows our plan and he's not going to let us fulfil it. Not now when he's so close to victory.'

Castus surveyed the land.

'Not even you know where it's buried. It might not be here at all. It might not even exist.'

'That's why they must dig exactly where I tell them. There's a method to it all. I know things from the past, Castus LacClune. So we dig. This is where we force Ovitus to battle, on ground of our choosing. Without me, you're lost already.'

'And if we don't find the Lance? Or if it's shattered and broken, as every history tells us?' He shook his head slowly. 'This is too big a gamble, Raine. There's no fortification to stand behind. We don't have the supplies to last through any kind of siege even if we did. If Redwinter comes for us, there's no way out of this.'

I pointed south and east.

'The mountain pass we came in by is the only way to reach the loch with any kind of numbers. They've no choice but to come at us that way. We bring builders, every strong hand we can conscript, and fortify it. We raise a series of walls if we have time. The pass is narrow. It'll serve us better than any castle wall. If it comes to it we can always pull the mountain down and seal ourselves in.'

'I liked you more when we used to go drinking all night and waste the days away,' Castus said.

'A different me,' I said. 'I didn't have a world back then.'

'A world to save, or to take?' Castus asked.

I stopped watching the ripples across the loch's surface and faced Castus. He had a short beard coming in. It suited him. His doubts about me had grown over the weeks spent on the road. How could they not? He had Palanost harping in one ear, Suanach chattering in the other. I made decisions without consulting him, because he didn't need consulting, or because I forgot to, or because he wouldn't—he couldn't—understand. I asked my people to take a lot on faith, but they followed my commands because they had no choice. Castus was a rebel. There was no reconciliation to be had for him. He won or he died, no other options. I was his best bet, even though the way I was doing things burned within him. The others, the dozen Draoihn who remained with us, they all felt the same. I was monstrous. I was evil made flesh, but I was evil on their side, and that counted for a lot.

'Let's see what's left of the world when this is over, and whether we're the ones able to claim the pieces,' I said. 'You can be a duke if you like.'

'And what would that make you?'

'Victorious,' I said. I grinned. I'd used an incantation to turn my teeth whiter and my lips darker. It unnerved people.

'Aye, well that's the goal,' Castus said. 'I hope you know what you're doing.'

'Oh, I know it,' I said. 'I've known it for thousands of years at this point, even if I wasn't aware.'

·   ·   ·   ·   ·   ·

Our men found miners, and when word spread of the bounty in gold and silver we'd plundered from every church and absolution house along our route, they came on their own. My instructions were very clear, foremen were assigned specific shafts and given intricate plans showing the routes their tunnels had to take. They looked at them, bemused.

'You don't want us to follow a seam?' one of them asked. 'Just make tunnels? Do they join up?'

'No,' I said. 'Just dig down. If you find anything strange, you tell me. That's all.'

'And you'll pay in gold, just for this? Whether we find anything or not.'

'Just this.'

I paid them up front. Word spread further. Sons and daughters left the harvest to come and build walls across the gorge. The gold and silver they received up front made them think we had enough to keep paying them as the year wore on.

I listened for that other Raine in that time, and occasionally I dreamed of her. She travelled fast, her face pressed into a mane of white stars. She seemed happy, her thoughts on Sanvaunt and Esher. I didn't like to think of them. When I did, I grew jealous. I'd distanced myself from those thoughts as best I could; jealousy does not befit a witch queen. Yet still they pressed in, and though my work was constant, it wasn't enough to keep them from my thoughts all the time.

As another month passed by, Draconloch became our home. I made tunnels, I made walls, and I crafted magic in the dark of night.

On an autumnal evening, the twilight soon drawing close, I summoned those that mattered to come to me at the loch's shore. Draoihn Suanach and Draoihn Palanost led the way for a team of recruits carrying the incantation I'd been working on, a five-foot-tall sheet of thin steel panels riveted together, but covered for now with canvas. Beneath fur-lined caps they squinted against the drizzling rain. I'd been working on it ever since we reached Draconloch, night by night. The darkness was my time. I could craft things there that wouldn't be spoken of in the light. Suanach had been master of artifice in Redwinter, and Palanost had taught us incantation, and while they didn't like what I did, I wondered how much their loathing warred with their desire to know what I'd been making. Did they wonder, in those black hours when I was scraping sigils into the steel, when I filled the rivulets with drips of molten copper, silver and—for the central sigil—gold, what it would be like to command power like mine? What it would feel like to work magic on this level? They were jealous, even as they decried what I could do. They had to be.

Everyone of rank gathered along the water's edge, along with any warriors who weren't out stripping the countryside for people to dig the hills or join us in steel. Dinny LacDaine, Hallum LacShale, a bunch of thails and warriors with kills to their name stood at the fore.

The steel canvas found its place in front of the lake. A single sheet of steel would have been much stronger, but finding that even in a city would have been impractical, and out here, impossible. I was fortunate enough to have found an armourer able to make me this. Beneath the cloth covering I'd worked marvels. I'd shown nobody but my apprentice, Ranitha. She didn't understand it yet, but she stood alongside it as it was propped upright for them to see, her blue-and-black Sarathi coat worn proudly. She was going to play a major part in this spell when the time came. Loyalty must be rewarded.

'How are my thunder-stones coming?' I asked her. She was excited to see what this spell would do.

'There are twelve now, master,' she said. I nodded, pleased. She was crafting by night as well.

'Sarathi Raine,' Palanost said, her throat-punching voice a bold staccato in the cool mountain air. 'Before you do this. Before you show us what you have been working on. I feel we must speak to you, as Draoihn of Redwinter.'

She looked to Suanach for support.

'Yes, Raine,' he said. Where Palanost threw my title at me like a poisoned barb, he couldn't bring himself to say it. He opted for patronisation instead, even as he quivered. The weakness of men was so evident to me these days.

'We are thankful for . . . some of the things you have done for us. But there
are limits. Even in these hardest of days, there are limits. There are things
we cannot allow.'

I smiled at him. It was petty to enjoy their discomfort so much, but people are petty and I let myself play at being one of them sometimes.

You should kill these two, the Riven Queen whispered in my ear. *They will
betray you.* I ignored her. I'd got better at shutting them out lately. They'd
become something of an irritation. Nothing functional is ever designed by
committee.

'What would you say was beyond acceptable?' I asked the Draoihn with
a smile, showing my newly white teeth. I might have made them a little
sharper than they should have been too. Suanach couldn't find his words
again, even if he'd worn his oxblood coat and worn a sword.

'Raising an army of the dead to do your bidding,' Palanost said firmly.
She glowered at me. I really did like Palanost. She spoke plainly, and that
had to be admired.

'An army of the dead would take a bit more magic than just one incantation, Draoihn Palanost,' I said. 'Maybe if I was standing in the centre
of the Crown I might be able to do that. But no. If I could do that, don't you
think we'd be winning this war instead of getting cold and wet in this poor
excuse for rain?'

Palanost did not seem convinced.

'You used steel,' she said. 'You want this to hold power.'

'Oh yes,' I said. 'Don't worry. I think we'll all like it. Some of it, anyway.
Just close your eyes at the bits you don't. Ranitha? Where's Ranitha?'

'Here, my lady.' She stepped out from the group. Ranitha had a matronly
face, broad and round, carrying a little extra weight. Her skin had that lush
richness that said her blood was half Murrish, half home. Sometimes I wished
for that skin. It would have made a beautiful contrast with my hair, but
despite what people said about me, I didn't wear other people's skins. Not yet,
anyway. Ranitha had watched me working. She was highly proficient at
incantation, but I taught it differently to Palanost. She'd taught it through rap-
port, Ulovar had taught it like it was book-learning, but I taught it like picking
up a new language just by being around it. Which is to say I let Ranitha watch
me, didn't explain any of it, and hoped she'd just kind of pick up how to make
sigils of her own. Sarathi symbols were different to those the Draoihn usually

used in a way I'd never thought to explain. It was intuitive to me, the same way I knew that I wore *damp, crusty old boots* and not *old crusty damp boots.* Some things are just right even if you don't know why.

'Here. Take this stone, and go wade out into the loch a bit,' I said. I handed her the stone. It was inscribed with a few of the sigils, and she'd watched me inscribe it two nights before. Ranitha was dutiful, but provided a good lesson on why the young are better as apprentices. She looked annoyed at having to go out and get wet. She had more than twice my years, and even if she didn't do it openly, I knew she questioned me. I'd have preferred someone who ran around after me the way Dinny LacDaine ran after Castus, though I'd begun to see that chase was less one-sided than I'd thought, and they were catching one another most nights.

'Hallum, go with her,' I said. I didn't bother calling him Van LacShale. He seemed to prefer it that way. He was solid, reliable. When I began having suspicions that one of the serving men was working his way up to poisoning me, Hallum made him disappear overnight. It was a shame to lose a man who could have swung a pickaxe, even one, but better not to smell that almond tinge in my wine again. The big clan leader removed his sword belt, laid it on the shingle and marched straight out into the water. Ranitha didn't have any choice then and followed him with her nose tilted proudly upwards.

When they were outside easy earshot, I turned to Palanost and Suanach.

'I know I don't always sound like I take you seriously. But I do. It's just you're so annoying.'

'To be Draoihn is not annoying,' Palanost said.

'You know you need me, but you try to get in my way. Take me seriously now. What I'm about to do is for all of us. Interrupt this, whatever you see, and I will not hesitate to strike back. You cannot hurt me. None of you can. But you all need to see this.'

I didn't think my words would stop Palanost, but Suanach at least took a few steps back.

I pulled the wrappings from my steelwork and showed them my metal canvas. It was a beautiful thing in its own right, to me at least. The world was at the centre, in gold, written in a sigil that made sense to me and nobody else. Jagged, lightning-bolt lines radiated out as the Queen of Feathers' memories of Song Seondeok had taught me. Every inch of it was covered in intricate diagrams. I'd sigil'd the familiar and the unknown there, poured molten copper and silver into the grooves. I breathed in, smiling, enjoying my handiwork. For one passing moment I wondered whether Palanost was proud of what I'd advanced into, before quashing the feeling hard. Of course she wouldn't be. I might just as well have taken a shit in her rocking chair and kicked it wildly into motion.

I opened the Sixth Gate, welcomed its bass-note drone as the grinding of great iron wheels turning filled my world. I looked out across the lake and saw those that it had claimed and not released, greenish ghosts swimming below the surface.

As I intoned the words that matched the incantation, I began drawing souls. Deep beneath the water, three hundred feet deep, bones began forcing their way through the silt, pulling themselves free. The souls came easily, the loose-limbed bodies rising gradually, like smoke trailing a torch. There were many, more than I'd expected. They passed through the pictogram and into me, and I turned them back as I reached out into the world, into time, and into their lives. Many had drowned here over the long years. The loch was uncaring.

The loch's surface rippled momentarily, then cast back an image as though its silver surface was a vast mirror, but instead of reflecting the sky, it reflected another time and place.

It was a difficult spell, and I hadn't been totally sure I could pull it off. The silver hand mirror had given me the idea, but my queens had worked these spells before. Even Song Seondeok had bungled it more than once, so to get it working on the first try was really something. I suspected that I had the capacity to be greater than any of them.

I looked for Redwinter in the loch-mirror. The first soul I used showed me Grandmaster Robilar, and a man who I suspected was Ulovar, but young, and I felt that momentary pang for something that deserved to live longer, but I rifled forward and back and knew this one was no good. Whoever this unfortunate drowned person had been, he'd died before my time, and I needed someone who'd died recently. The place, the people didn't have to link to him—but time, that mattered. I was looking back into the past, and time—that, we're bound by. I discarded his soul, let its remains flutter back to his slowly rising bones. I drew the next. This one was even older—far older, in fact. This poor bastard had been rotting in the loch since the Age of Bronze by the look of things, and when I looked for Redwinter it wasn't even there.

I was aware of the muttered awe and gasps of astonishment around me. The loch's surface was quite a show, even if it wasn't what I wanted. I tried a dozen more. Some were more recent than others, the ghosts that dwelled trapped beneath the water answering the call eagerly, as if they thought I might be able to send them on down the tunnel. We saw some woolly rhinar being herded, and a battle that had to have been part of one of the rebellions against our Brannish oppressors—former oppressors anyway, now that Loridine was gone. I needed to find someone whose life span had encompassed recent days to see the events I needed to show them—events I needed to see myself. Unfortunately, none of these ghosts seemed to have died in the last month. But I was a wily Sarathi now, and I'd planned for that eventuality. I broke off my chanting.

'Ranitha, put that stone in your mouth,' I called out to where she and Hallum stood waist-deep. She alone of all the observers could see the souls as they drifted towards me.

'Why?'

'Just do it!' I commanded her, putting a little soul into making my rasping voice resonate a little in her bones.

Perhaps this was a moment for her to regret her recent decisions. Perhaps a life of artificing hadn't been so bad after all. Maybe she should have been content being Draoihn even if that meant hiding from everyone that she saw the unquiet dead. Too late now, Ranitha. She'd made her grave and now she had to lie in it. She put the stone, the night's-eye stone the Nigheag had crafted for me, into her mouth. I felt a little thrill of excitement. I hadn't done this in centuries.

'Ranitha, someone's daughter, dead in the water.'

She dropped like a stone, disappearing beneath the surface. This was the best way to do it. I needed the soul of someone who'd lived during the recent events I needed to see. The chances of someone having accidentally drowned in the lake in the last few months had been slim. Not impossible, just slim. Better to use someone who'd sworn into my service than not.

I chanted again as I drew Ranitha's soul from the night's-eye stone. It was a clean death, at least, no drowning, no lightning strikes as we'd done it in the old days. She should count herself lucky she hadn't been run through by a Faded Lord; that had been the worst. As I melded reality with my words and the soul in my grasp, the lake's surface shimmered and changed again. I sought Redwinter. I sought the fall of the black comet. It all sounds very conscious, but magic is more like speaking than thinking. It just happens without choice, just comes out of you, processed in the mind faster than waking thought can follow.

Ovitus wasn't in Redwinter when I found him. He was giving a speech in front of the masses of Harranir, outside one of his great labour homes. Things had gone well there—for him at least. The place was immense, dominating the Northbank that Sanvaunt had accidentally burned down when I stood him up. More people wore the labour home uniform than not, a dusty pale blue tunic and leggings. They had work, but I thought there was something missing in their spirit. They didn't control their own lives, and that takes a toll on anyone.

Ovitus stood there with Waldy at his side, that fucking dog that had tried to savage me when I scryed from the Fault. My former friend was orating about the need for more men and women to take up arms, to join the fight against the traitor. It quickly transpired that I was the traitor, rather than Castus, which my friend probably didn't like but I was rather proud of. Castus was probably well-remembered in Harranir, and in fairness, it was me who'd ruined Ovitus's army.

The black comet grew larger overhead. A shadow appeared over the assembled throng. People screamed as suddenly the purple-black shadow in the sky became all the more real. It wasn't just some celestial phenomena, it was real and it was coming for them all.

'Do not be afraid!' Ovitus called out to the panicking crowd. Where were they running to, after all? He stood, expectant, firm-jawed, looking up towards that dark mass. 'People of Harranir! I know you are afraid. But as your king, I will save you. I will protect you. I have called on the Light Above, and it has answered. Do not be afraid!'

He braced himself. Balled his fists. Bared his teeth.

For a moment I'd thought perhaps I was wrong, that the comet was going to come down on them and obliterate the lot of them. It would be a shame for all those labourers, but it would certainly have been a shortcut to winning the war. But no. Ovitus stood firm. He wasn't afraid because he'd been expecting it. He'd known it was coming. He'd called it.

He'd called it from the Fault, drawn further on that power. And that could only mean one thing.

Waldy, his familiar that was itself part of Iddin, slunk up to him and wound itself around his legs.

'Watch the dog!' I interrupted my incantation chant to tell the watchers at the lake. 'Watch the dog!' I was only half-conscious there, caught up in the spell, caught up in the lake.

The comet cast a large shadow, but it was much smaller than it should have been. Queen Mathilde tried to stand firm even as her ladies, Willdem the bodyguard, everyone but that dog abandoned them. She knew there was no point in running. Harranir would be wiped away, gone in a flash when the comet struck. But then the shadow grew smaller, the comet condensing and I realised it was not a comet at all, but a beam of terrible dark light traversing time and space, and it came down upon Ovitus and his hound.

A massive flash of light, an ear-blasting boom, and in place of dog and man there stood a block of glassy black stone, uneven and light-drinking, ten feet tall, resting in a crater in the earth. The screams had been silenced by the blast that had knocked people askew. As people picked themselves up they stared at the glossy black block.

Wails of fear and anguish continued unabated.

'Where is the king?' someone began yelling. Despite all his folly, people love to have a king. They want to be ruled. They love to think there's someone better than them, a regression into childhood where a father can watch over them. Both king and dog were gone. I watched Mathilde pick herself up, dusting down her skirts. A trickle of blood ran from a gash on her scalp where debris had struck her. She approached the obsidian block, swallowing her fear, and placed a hand on it.

'It's warm,' she muttered. The people of Harranir stared in wonder, but even I, the crafter of the great incantation that could look back through time, through space, felt the welling of fear.

Ovitus, what have you done?

The moment the obsidian cracked, they felt it. The wave of wrongness that pulsed out from the crumbling stone. It was only fleeting—the dark seldom shows its true face for long. That's how it wins, how it works its plans in plain sight for all to see. It shows itself and then cloaks itself in gold.

Flakes of the glassy stone fell clattering to the ground as the whole block began to disintegrate.

'Contain it,' Mathilde demanded of a gaunt-faced man in red-and-gold robes whose hair ran in a single thin stripe down the centre of his head. His hands were stained a number of different colours. A Brannish magician. Harranir put trances in our blood, in Brannlant the land made Artists. 'Whatever it is, destroy it!'

The Artist shook his head.

'It is not an enemy, Queen Mathilde. It is a gift. It is the king.' He bowed his crested hair.

'Ovitus is gone. I am queen here. And I'm ordering you to destroy it,' Mathilde snarled angrily.

'No,' the Artist said. 'Loridine is lost, but the kingdom is made anew today. The king comes.'

Mathilde's face turned stony, her jaw falling open. I doubted she'd ever experienced such defiance from a subject.

'Be not afraid,' a great voice intoned, booming over the square, deep and reverberating as if it spoke into a cavern. And then it shattered, collapsing around the figure within.

A man rose from the shards as the last of the obsidian flaked away. He was naked, wet with oily orange-black fluid, but as he stood it ran from him like rain down a windowpane. His hair was long and silver. His body was chiselled muscle. Big old cock, but that wasn't really the point. At his back, folded, feathered wings glowed in iridescent, metallic beauty, all the colours of the rainbow reflecting the light. It was only his eyes that were black. Black as a starless night sky, staring out from a face that had been Ovitus's. Oh, the fool. The absolute terrible fool. He'd begged help from his familiar, had offered more of himself than ever before. He'd drawn more of Iddin into himself.

Before the assembled royals, the figure slowly stood.

'Be not afraid,' he intoned in that deep voice that seemed to come from all around. 'The Light Above has answered my prayer.'

Those who hadn't fled the square, Mathilde, the Brannish Artist, warriors and courtiers stared in awe. He was otherworldly, more reminiscent of the stained glass in a cathedral than any true man. His body was beyond ide-alised, a caricature of masculine perfection, but there was still a hint of

Ovitus about him, in the cast of his face. Of Waldy the bastard dog, there was no sign. Gone. Merged with its master—or rather, the one who believed himself to be that.

'I am your king. I am Ovitus LacNaithe,' he said, his wings flexing behind him. They were beautiful, but too small to lift him. Decorative wings. 'The Light Above has made me its champion in our darkest hour.'

Mathilde stared in horror and awe of the gigantic man. Her tall body-guard seemed puny by comparison. The silver-haired being's wings flexed and she flinched backwards but she steeled herself. The Artist fell to one knee and bowed his head. Another pair of Artists had joined him, and to-gether they spoke in unison.

'My lord king. My master.'

Ovitus looked upon them and nodded with satisfaction. Obeisance. How he loved it. He should have adopted a regal, arrogant look, but instead he was filled with a childish wonder at how marvellous this all was.

Mathilde was not to be outdone. She stepped past those who should have been her vassals. She dipped a deep curtsy. Ovitus didn't even look at her. His black eyes swept out onto the assembled crowd.

'The Light Above seeks an end to war,' he said. 'To bring peace back to the holy land of Harranir. I have the power to destroy the witch who stands against you. The Sarathi whore who dares to defy the Light Above.'

Mathilde didn't enjoy the language. I was coming to read her little facial expressions, and this one meant she was tolerating nonsense. She used it with me sometimes when I could get her to speak to me through the mirror and said grand things about myself. But she was frightened as well.

'Can you be a champion of the Light Above and still a mortal woman's husband?' she asked. Hoping that he'd say no, perhaps.

The amalgamation of the usurper of Harranir and the king of the Fault turned to regard her. I wondered if she could read the hatred in its eyes. How they despised her, Ovitus and Iddin both. The hate of a mortal who, even in this incarnation, even having claimed a crown for himself, still felt belittled by a woman. She was beautiful, and that angered him, for he would always feel inferior. She was intelligent, and that angered him, for he could never own her. But now it wasn't just a petty, fearful man's hate. His eyes carried the hatred of an immortal, who despised everything that did not bow to him. Somehow, the patheticness of Ovitus's loathing was worse.

'My lady queen, I am ever your devoted husband,' he said, because appearance was more important to him than even his passions. 'We have work to do. The servant of darkness and her traitors must be stopped. She must not unearth the Lance of Maldouen. Mobilise every force at your disposal. We march for Draconloch come morning.'

Back in the real world, I heard the gasps and hisses of fear from my council, from my friends, from my almost-enemies.

'The Light Above opposes us,' Suanach said, his voice a reedy wail.

'If that is true, the Light Above has taken a long time in showing her hand,' Palanost said. 'The world has been burning long enough. I looked upon Ovitus's new incarnation, and I do not find it convincing.'

'Good,' I said. I released Ranitha's soul. Hallum had dragged her lifeless body out and laid her down on the pebble beach. I took hold of the soul like I was gripping an eel and forced it, wriggling and squirming, back down her throat. She was mostly still there. I'd burned some of her up in the casting: she'd not remember much of her childhood, and her life expectancy was probably down by a few years, but I'd been conservative with it. If the Riven Queen's demise had taught me anything, it was that you betray your own people as little as possible.

Ranitha choked out water, eyes fluttering wide and terrified. But I wasn't done yet.

'Watch carefully now,' I called out. My incantation stuttered. Most of the steel plates glowed with heat by this point, the lower-melting-point metals running in streams to drip on the pebbles. And this time I burned a little of myself. The lake changed to show the audience my memories of that twenty-times cursed dog. I showed them Waldy sheltering Ovitus from my Soul Reaper. I showed them Waldy tearing at me with his astral fangs. And then I showed them Iddin, the king of the Fault, the being of terrifying darkness who'd pursued me through the Fault. People actually screamed. Why did I go to those lengths?

Perhaps, despite everything I'd become, I wanted them to believe in me. Human weakness. No wonder the Faded blended themselves with wolves and eagles. A true predator doesn't care what the rest of the world thinks of it.

I blacked out momentarily as the steel of my incantation board suddenly gave way in a molten rush, liquid metal sloughing away to hiss in the shallows. It had been a great working, the like of which no living Draoihn had managed in this Age, but the world wouldn't hold together long enough to start another.

When I came to, there were a lot of bones floating across the surface of the loch. I didn't think bones were meant to float, but these ones did. A half mile across the silver-black water, something big momentarily broke the stillness, sending out waves that rocked the silence.

'The darkness you showed us comes for us,' Draoihn Palanost said. She stood above me. 'It comes for our world.' I managed to raise a softly clenched fist, a humourless smile. A little punch in the air for her finally being able to understand. I'd wanted her on my side all along, even if I hadn't admitted it to myself.

Lying alongside me, Ranitha's lovely skin was gooseflesh top to bottom.

'You killed me,' she said. She spat black tar, the remains of the night's-eye stone.

'Now you've died twice,' I said. 'It's the third that really gets things going.'

'Do not forget to watch the sky,' the burned woman said. 'Some of the things that linger here fly.'

There were stairs within the buildings after all, but like everything in the Fault, they chose to make no sense. The stairwells only started up high, on unreachable floors, or that would have been if not for Esher's Second Gate. The burned woman had made it up here. That said something. My guide had brought me up onto a fallon's top. Walkways spanned the gaps between the buildings, gaps now filled with the oily sludge the surging water had left in its wake. There were dead things down there, in the mire. Esher and Sanvaunt would find a way through it. If anyone could find a way to the central tower, it was them.

I hugged my cloak around me, Sanvaunt's dose of warmth still keeping the freeze at bay, though it wouldn't last forever. My guide went unbothered by the cold. She wore no clothing, but there were no real features to her body, all of it fused and melted together. I didn't trust her, but that was normal these days. I kept my bow strung as we traversed the arching gantries over the city, an arrow always at the ready. My sword hadn't done much against her, and I was far from convinced she was human. Tiny flakes of ash, scar tissue or char, something black and noxious, fell away from her as she walked. She stopped midway across one of the chasm-spanning walkways.

'The sky will sing now,' she grated. 'Any time now.' She looked up expectantly towards the circling vortex.

'How do you know?' I asked.

'I've been here a long time,' she said. 'The Fault is not as random as it seems. You should hold on.'

She didn't heed her own advice, but I crouched down beside the low, frost-encrusted wall that lined the curved bridge and rested an arm to it. A great tremor struck, and the sky howled, a racking peal of high-pitched thunder rolling out across the Fault. I gripped hard to the wall, one arm thrown over it, the rest of me hunkered down. The structures groaned and trembled, icicles dislodging to descend like snakes' teeth, tinkling as they shattered below. The howl, the quake, lasted half a minute. All the while, the burned woman stood there, casually upright, looking up at the sky as though the bridge was entirely stable.

'Well, that's done, at least,' she said, and strode on.

I'd tried to get her to talk, to figure out who or what she even was. How she'd come to be here. That was the only question that had brought a single speck of emotion to her face. A momentary, involuntary flinch.

'Doesn't it bother you at all?' I asked her as I got up. I wasn't asking to know why, I was just protesting at having shown myself to be afraid. Embarrassed. For all that she was hideous in her burning, there was something about her. A presence. A confidence. She reminded me of the Queen of Feathers, but I'd grown confident this wasn't some kind of trick being played on me. The queen was haughty, proud and arrogant but this burned woman was so *undignified*. She ignored my question.

The vast tower at the heart of the City of Spires lay before us, just a few bridges away. It was the only structure Maldouen seemed to have bothered to put any real detail into. Its outer walls boasted windows. There were actual doors. Gargoyles leered down from balconies, odd-looking stone warriors stood stonily in alcoves. The towers soared into the sky, impossibly tall, but why not make them that tall when they were carved from magic? Maldouen hadn't laid the foundations. He'd just brought it into being through magic. The sheer power of it was breathtaking. Perhaps if Ovitus had understood it all, been able to comprehend it properly, he'd have seen his folly. Nobody who could wield magic, not even those with altruism in mind, should have access to power on that level. We aren't made to be so grand. Our lives shouldn't change any world to such a degree. Eat food, drink water, make a little shelter, leave things slightly better for those that follow after. That's all we're supposed to do in our time. We try and prolong things, we try and shape the world to our will, but none of it makes anyone happier. I'd been given the world on a silver platter in Redwinter. Wealth I'd never dreamed of, waited on, educated, and what had I done with my time? I'd moped, I'd pitied myself, I'd blotted reality from my mind with rose-thistle and alcohol.

We reached the edge of the bridge, which led onto a flat-topped roof, bridges and stairs leading up or down. Only four more to go. Four more, and then I'd find her and learn whether anything we'd been doing had held any purpose at all. I had to believe it would. The Queen of Feathers had to be the answer. She was the anomaly, the link that was missing. She was here, she had to be. If she could stop being so infuriating for just one moment, perhaps she'd tell us how to end this. How to trap Iddin here in this plane of misery, to cut him off from our world. I couldn't bring back the people who'd died when the Faded escaped, but I could avenge them. I could protect their children, if any still survived.

'Ah. Some old friends are coming,' the burned woman said. She raised a flaking hand, trailing soot, to point into the sky. I followed her gaze.

'Shit,' I said.

They looked like women. Sort of. Three of them drifted down from the tower above, tattered dresses billowing and translucent, arms stretched wide, long hair fanning out in the cold air.

'What are they?' I asked. I drew a few arrows alongside my bow stave, nocked one to the string.

'They are the Fetch,' the charred woman said. 'They were like you once, but punished for their misdeeds. For their betrayals. They crave life. You should shoot.'

The women drew closer, drifting over the false buildings, feet splayed wide.

'They mean us harm?' I said.

'Only you,' the charred woman said.

'Why only me?'

She didn't smile, but raised one burned hand and curled her fingers. Charcoal skin cracked and fell away.

'They did this to me, after a fashion. But they paid for it. They will not make that mistake again.' Her scorched hand brushed against the low wall that surrounded the rooftop and she hissed, grunted in pain. I would wonder later whether the souls of her feet burned with every step she took but just then I had immediate problems to worry about.

The Fetch sang as they drifted through the air. It was a ghostly song, a sound of lost love and forlorn wanting. It had come from another place and another time, but some things translate wherever you are. The thin fabric of their dresses clung to their bodies, and they could have been beautiful if not for the rot set into their faces, the exposed bones in the crook of their elbows where skin and flesh had tattered away, and the thick iron nails through their wrists and ankles. I saw their decay as their gentle descent ended. They bent their heads forwards, arms thrust back like the wings of an osprey on the dive, and rushed through the air towards me.

Fear had become such a constant companion in the Fault that it embraced me like an old friend. I wished I had more of those stone-tipped arrows. I drew breath deep, drew the bowstring deeper, sighted by feel rather than eye, and sent an arrow lashing towards the leader. She swerved aside, and rushed down on me all the faster.

The song had changed. Gone the loss, gone the sorrow. It was a unifying cry of hate, pure and malevolent, burning with a desire to rip and rend. I hadn't seen the talons from afar. I'd have started shooting sooner.

Maybe she thought she'd been clever dodging that arrow, but there was a reason I had more in my fist. The draw on Maldouen's bow, the bow made from the Queen of Feathers' own staff, was far lighter than its power demanded and I had two more arrows in the air before the plunging, undead thing reached me. She dodged the second, but the third I launched as if I was in Eio, predicting her attempt to dodge it before it launched. The arrow drove into one rotten eye and out the back of her head and she dropped from the sky, her song ended. Her sisters came on.

The second Fetch whipped by me, slashing at me with double-length fingers. Claws that tapered into alabaster hardness drew a row of jumping yellow sparks from my armour as she shot by. The force of the blow spun me around, and my heel skidded on ice. I went down on my side, but I was already drawing the bowstring and shot her in the back as she arced upwards again. This one didn't fall, but a stream of clear liquid ran from her, like I'd punctured a waterskin, a shower through the sky as she banked. I shouldn't have stopped to look. The third Fetch caught me from behind, hardened ghostly talons jarring against my helmet and I felt the sharp pain, the wrench in my neck, as she went past me too, veering right where the second had gone left. They were circling me.

I found my feet. The charred woman just stood there, unmoving.

'Help me,' I growled.

'I have done enough to them already,' she said. 'It's not me they want. You'll have more luck using your Gates than that bow.'

'I don't have any Gates!' I snarled as the third Fetch swooped down on me. I ducked and her claws slashed overhead as she flew past, a gurgling sound in her throat. I chanced three more arrows as the Fetch wheeled in the sky, but there was no hitting them at that range, not without Eio, not with their speed.

'To the Night Below with all of you,' I said. So I began to run headlong towards the bridge.

'The bridge is suicide,' the burned woman said after me. I skidded to a halt. She was right. One of the Fetch whipped over the bridge at colossal speed, right where my run would have taken me. Even a glancing blow would send me spinning to break below.

'If you're going to show up out of nowhere and save me, now would be the time,' I said to Sanvaunt and Esher, but they weren't there, and the burned woman wasn't going to help me, that was clear. Another fistful of arrows followed the previous into the air, to miss and disappear into the city.

'They're toying with you,' the burned woman said. 'They were always fickle. It's in a Sarathi's nature to betray those above them, unfortunately. We all do it one way or another.'

I heard the scratching, scraping sound of nails against stone, spun around to see the first of the Fetch clawing her way up onto the roof with us, my arrow still through her face. I saw her up close now. Thick, square-sided iron pegs were driven through her wrists, and a gag of thick rope was wrapped around her head, chewed between yellowed teeth. Her death had been cruel: she'd been punished by being nailed to a tree, or a wall. Her rotting face was a mass of bruises. If I'd been put to death in that way, I'd have come back to haunt people too.

There's always a way. There has to be. There's a rule that you can follow, and as I saw the other two Fetch beginning to glide around, their arms and legs spread as if still nailed in place, my mind raced. Every dark being has a weakness. Had I still possessed the immense knowledge of those dread queens of the past I would have known it. There had to be a way to stop them.

The bow wasn't doing me any good. I dropped it and drew my sword. I didn't have Sanvaunt's inner fire, or Esher's newfound Gates. I didn't even have my own. But I'd been me before I had any of that. I'd become myself somewhere without any of it. There had to be a way to stop them.

The first of the Fetch, the fletching of my arrow jutting through her eye socket and the rest of the shaft jutting from the back of her head, sang a cruel, mocking song behind her gag. She tried to gain her feet, but the same heavy, black iron nails had been driven through her ankles, so she crawled towards me on her knees instead.

'Do something,' I said. 'Help me?' My voice came out thinner than I remembered it.

'Do it yourself,' my guide said. 'You need to remember how if you're to change anything.' When I looked at her blankly, she took my sword from my trembling hand, walked up to the Fetch and almost casually ran it through the chest. *Almost* casually. The Fetch ignored her. Clear liquid sputtered from the wound, viscous gobbets raining across the frost-rimed rooftop. She gurgled something at me from behind the gag. Probably something filled with hate. Probably something about wanting to suck my blood or devour my life. Probably. She ignored the charred woman, didn't seem to notice her at all. She crawled towards me, talons digging into the tiles as her sisters circled us, waiting for their moment to descend.

It was her one remaining eye that did it. I knew of the other me, off somewhere in my world, blasting apart our enemies, using the gifts I'd been given, but she wouldn't have seen what I saw there. A person's eyes show us more than we'll ever really understand about life, but we know it, we feel it anyway. And in that one remaining, cloudy eye, I understood. The hateful lash out because they're afraid, because they're angry, because they despair. This creature was all three. She'd been a person once, but her soul had been sent here, banished into inconstant isolation and loneliness. Into torment and pain, just as the charred woman had been. I knew what I had to do.

'I forgive you,' I said. 'You did what you had to. You didn't deserve this.'

The two in the air slowed in their circling, and their song rose higher and higher. The crawling Fetch stopped. One claw was reaching for me, the talons of her other hand scored half an inch into the stonework. The grasping hand quivered, then slowly lowered. My throat was blocked, and I wasn't going to get out any more words just then. I had to take a risk. I took a step towards her and she didn't move, only watched me with her remaining eye.

The two other Fetch had stopped their circling. Unmoving, floating on the wind, their arms and legs splayed back out into crosses as if that was their natural form. Another step and only the eye tracked me. A rough gurgle escaped her throat.

The gag had been tied without mercy. The flesh there was slick, swollen and puffy around the ropes, which cut deep. I was breathing fast, as if I were tending to a wounded animal that might turn and snap at me at any moment. The burned woman just watched, the piece of shit. I knelt beside the Fetch, and drew a knife. The rope was old, if age really mattered here. It was too deeply embedded to cut, so I pried at strands of it, picking them away one by one. Esher had sharpened our knives to a fine edge, but the going was slow. As I worked, I listened to this creature's laboured breathing.

She'd been a woman once. She'd died in terrible pain, her torment extended beyond nature's mercy as her soul was bound back into her, time and time again by the one who took vengeance. She'd been a traitor, this Fetch, had turned against her dark mistress on the eve of a great battle. She and her sisters broke down the Witching Skin, the Soul Shield, the Spirit Wards the Riven Queen had layered over herself, and when Maldouen's Lance blasted that tyrant into the Fault, her vengeance had lashed out. In a final act of spite, Hallenae had brought them with her, and taught them to suffer, as she suffered.

Perhaps they all started out this way. Perhaps the demons of the Night Below were the monsters we'd made ourselves. *Snick, snick, snick* went the knife, and with each strand I cut away, something in the air shifted around us. Finally the circle was broken. I eased it out of her flesh.

The Fetch arched back as if struck by a bolt of lightning, thrashing. Something went skittering away: an inch-wide, black iron nail. Her tattered body forced them out, discarding the pain, the past. My arrow was ejected. Past agony rose like a stench around us, thick and withering, cloying and burning. And then the cloud evaporated as she dissolved into clear goo, her body giving up its shape and spilling across the flagstones.

She would have destroyed the world, a voice whispered through me. *We were heroes!* And then it was gone.

I climbed to my feet. The other Fetch were drifting away. They didn't sing anymore.

'Why don't they seek release?' I said, stepping back from the spreading puddle. 'I could have helped them too.' The charred woman gave an ugly-sounding chuckle.

'Because they are the same witches as they always were,' she said. She handed me back my sword. 'They were traitors. But before that, they were not good people. They practiced the blackest rites, took lives as a farmer reaps wheat. Do not pity them, Raine Wildrose. Between them they devoured more children than all the wolves in the world have ever done.'

'So did you, Hallenae,' I said.

For a moment the charcoal woman closed her eyes and tilted her head back. Breath hissed through her burned lips.

'Say it again,' she whispered.

'Hallenae,' I said. I levelled my sword at her. 'You're the Riven Queen. The one who forced the building of the Crowns. The one who tore the veil, and summoned demons and the deathless to walk the land. You tried to take the world.'

'I had wondered what it would be like to hear my own name again,' she said. Her torn eyelids didn't quite close. 'It was not as gratifying as I had imagined.' She turned to look at me, green eyes bright in her tortured, hairless head. 'Yes, I did all those things. I did them under the guidance of the same spirit that has watched over you, that has guided you into your power. Do not think you are better than me, Wildrose. You'd have done the same.'

It should have felt more momentous to find myself face-to-face with the tyrant queen of legend. Hallenae, the Riven Queen, defeated by the Draoihn at Solemn Hill when her Sarathi coven betrayed her, destroyed by Maldouen's Lance. But not destroyed entirely, as it turned out. Banished here, alongside Maldouen, and the demons, the Hidden Folk, and all the rest of the creatures of the Fault. But there was no great moment for me. I was tired. I was drained beyond my resources, and all I had left was pity. Pity for the world, for me, for all of us who'd suffered so much. I could have struck her down, but this living, smouldering burn was a greater punishment.

A part of me feared she was right about me.

'Why did you do it?' I asked. 'Why did you try to destroy the world?'

'Because I wanted it,' she said.

'You allied with the Faded,' I said. 'It's your fault any of this happened.'

'You think you know so much,' Hallenae said. I amused her. 'You're just another of Nightlark's women. Do you know how many of us there have been? Do you know why she drives us to become the dark? No. I never discovered it either. Before us, in the Columnic War, she used Empress Seondeok to stop the Eldritch Kin from activating the fallons. In my time she believed that it was Paladeir who would destroy the world with them. She never mentions them, does she? Do you even know what they are?'

'Fallons?' I said. She hadn't answered my question. 'They're just standing stones.'

'Of course they're not,' Hallenae snapped. 'No wonder you managed to trap yourself here. The fallons aren't just blocks of stone, young princess. Serranis raised them long ago. They are conduits that bridge the gaps between worlds. They channel magic not just from your world, or this one, or Maldouen's, but all of them. Each world that builds them becomes connected. They bring creation together, focused and raw. In my age the Draoihn sought to use them to close the Sixth Gate, to become immortals themselves, as were the Kin. But they exist half inside it, not within the Fifth as people do. To break the Sixth Gate would have shattered the bond of the Seventh—Creation itself. So I defied them. I am the Riven Queen, but it was the world that would have shattered.'

'Mankind had always warred against the Faded. You sided with our enemies,' I said. There was such vehemence in her words, so much belief. I didn't know if I believed her.

'Mankind always wars with everything!' she snapped. 'I wanted the world, and the Draoihn, the Artists, the Serpent Mages, the Hexen and the Tharada Taan, they sought to break it. They had already captured the major fallons by the time I rose into my power. So I took the world from them. That's why I fought them. That's why I sundered their power. But in your tales I am the villain, am I not? You learned your history and forgot that important rule—history is written by the victors.'

'Everything is built on lies,' I said. I did not believe her. Not fully. Maybe there was some truth in there. But atop this frigid rooftop words seemed cheap. Discardable.

She began to walk away from me, onto the bridge. I could have abandoned her. I could have gone my own way, picked another route. I gave a self-pitying, despairing sigh as I realised that Hallenae, the Riven Queen of legend, nightmare tyrant and enemy of all life, had in fact saved my life by dragging me to safety. I looked up into that swirling vortex, and it was only now that she'd put it in my mind that I realised it.

The spires of the City of Spires were fallons. Gigantic, towering fallons. A link to another world.

I gave the pile of congealed sludge one last look before I followed her. It didn't matter who this burned wreck had been fifty generations past. I didn't need her. Not now, not so close to my destination. So close to the end. A few more crossings, a few more monsters, and I'd stand before the Queen of Feathers. I'd take my answers. I'd finally know what I was for.

Besides the occasional shake of a gargoyle's wings, nothing else came for me. It almost seemed too easy to walk into the great central tower. A bridge led to doors that stood cracked open, just wide enough that I'd be able to squeeze through. As Hallenae disappeared through the crack I paused to take one more breath of the Fault's tainted air, and to admire the craftsmanship. They were decorated with iron, images of a war that Maldouen had fought in some other place and time, perhaps. Much of it made no sense, the warriors armed with tools that didn't look much like weapons, but clearly fighting some kind of fish-like creatures with them. Magic, perhaps. I got the sense that Maldouen hadn't laid this image to celebrate those past battles as much as to honour this spire, this ungodly tower that pierced the sky. There was a depth of sadness to it, even here. He'd crafted this, never intending anyone to see it, a masterwork unintended for mortal eyes.

The dark beyond beckoned me closer, and as ever, I followed where it led.

27

Within the mountains that surrounded Draconloch Loch, the clatter of metal and stone died away. The mine shaft was alight with the pale blue glow of cadanum orbs.

'You need to backtrack twenty feet and dig in that direction,' I said, gesturing to my right. 'My instructions were specific and clear. And all that spoil you've taken from here? Put it back. Pack it right in.'

The forewoman was short, stocky, with the hard physique and stooped spine of one who'd spent her youth working with mattocks and picks, made into hardness through toiling beneath the ground.

'Begging your pardon, lady,' she said. 'We ran into a copper seam. We've already cut five cartloads of ore. If we keep going this way . . .'

'I don't care about copper. Keep the ore for yourself, but fill that tunnel. You dig where I say you dig,' I said. A number of other miners stood a way back in the narrow tunnel.

'But the value, the work we're doing,' the forewoman protested. She didn't look up at me in the dark. Down here in the tunnels, my eyes had a pale glow to them. I unnerved them. I'd borrowed some plain worker's clothes to make this less of a scene, but my eyes I couldn't do anything about. I avoided coming down here. I was above all this muck and dirt, but my plans had been specific, and they were not being followed.

'I'm paying you in gold to dig up a lance,' I said. 'Gold, not copper! That should be enough for you.'

The forewoman removed her iron-reinforced cap. She'd retired from the trade some years ago, had set up as a trader in a town twenty miles away. Her return to the tunnels hadn't been voluntary, but I needed every good hand I could find.

'Begging your pardon, lady, I don't mean to question your decisions, but there ain't no way that there could be a lance where you said to dig. It's solid basalt. It's been here since before there were people. We aren't going to find what you're looking for down here.'

'Are you saying you don't want the gold I promised you?' I said. 'I have fifty teams digging these mountains. If you don't want to get paid, there are others who can work here.'

'I beg your pardon, lady,' the forewoman said. She didn't look up at me. 'You're paying us well, but—some of the miners have been asking questions about that. Where it's coming from. Some of them feel—they're worried about their souls.'

'Ah,' I said. 'Because I stole it from churches?'

'I didn't say it was stolen, my lady,' the forewoman said, despite that absolutely being her meaning. She was right, of course. Castus had just over five hundred men at his disposal, and over the last weeks they'd not only been rounding up anyone who could wield a hammer or a mattock, every engineer who could devise a water pump, even youngsters who could haul buckets. They'd visited every church in the north and stripped them bare. It's surprising how much wealth a church can accrue. It had upset a lot of people. The new Van LacAud was especially unhappy about my raid on the cathedral at Dulceny, and that was understandable, but he cowered in his fortress rather than come to the aid of his priests. I needed miners, and I needed them working twelve hours a day if I had a hope of beating what Ovitus had become.

They called him Belphior now, we'd heard. He'd taken the name of one of the Light Above's servants, a winged avenger. I would *not* be calling him that.

'Well, the gold was stolen,' I said. 'But now it's mine, which means it's not stolen anymore. Your men need paying. Your children need schooling. This is the way the Light Above has presented to us.'

If Ovitus was going to play at being a servant of the heavens then I didn't see why I shouldn't call on religion to push people in the direction I wanted. It didn't seem quite as convincing coming from me, perhaps, not compared to the silver-haired, iridescently winged giant who now issued the orders. I should get a priest, I thought. A nice loyal priest. Or one of those girls who claimed to have visions. People loved those.

'As you say, lady,' the forewoman said.

'So you back up to there. You dig in that direction,' I said.

'Yes, lady.' She paused. There was more for her to say. I had to go correct three other tunnels after this one, where the miners had taken it upon themselves to choose their own directions. I'd been very specific about where I thought they needed to dig; every foreman at every shaft had a specific set of instructions. The insubordination was wearying, but I was trying to guide them with carrots rather than sticks.

'Out with it,' I snapped.

'I was wondering whether I could see my grandchildren this evening,' the forewoman said. 'We've not had a rest day in three weeks.'

'There's no time for rest days,' I said. 'The enemy will be here in under two months. There's no rest for anyone. The children are well cared for. I can assure you of that. Think of the gold, forewoman. You'll need to reinforce your pockets before you leave here.'

The gold argument seemed to be more convincing to the miners, less so to the forewoman. I sighed. I supposed there had to be some give in me or even the prospect of riches wasn't going to keep the work moving at the pace I needed.

'I'll have the children sent up from the school encampment,' I said. 'You can write? Good. Have a list of names drawn up. Someone will escort them up and your people can spend an hour with them at the end of your shift.'

That seemed to brighten her face more than any digging-talk would do. My school encampment was not popular. Children couldn't be left behind as we stripped the land of those able to work, but caring for them got in the way of actually working so they all lived in a big enclosure of tents and makeshift shacks on the other side of the gorge. I'd heard the word 'hostages' used more than once, but I'd put Draoihn Palanost in charge of them and she'd always been good to us back in Redwinter. She seemed to prefer that. The forewoman wasn't the only one who thought my methods of digging up Maldouen's broken Lance weren't going to be effective. It didn't matter. They all had to do what I said regardless, because with the pigs' legs growing to improbable lengths, the wheat laughing as it was scythed and the complete lack of babies in the world, they needed to believe someone could sort this whole mess out.

Three days back one of my teams of miners had unearthed something they shouldn't in the darkness. It had killed two dozen of them before it escaped into the world. It had lain buried since these mountains grew from the earth. After I took onboard the ghosts that had lingered, fresh recruits had been sent down that shaft to clear the bodies and continue the work. Those men were on triple wages.

I'd plundered every church and hoard that hadn't been hidden and dug up those that had, but the gold would run out soon. Food was even more of a problem. I'd put Hallum LacShale in charge of bringing in supplies, because he was an old hand when it came to raiding, his men were loyal and I knew he wouldn't flinch. We needed grain, sheep, ale. Without it my grand plan would grind to a halt. It would be a hard winter for a lot of people, but at least we'd actually see winter. Maybe.

Time falls away in the tunnels. I emerged into evening, and seeing Dinny LacDaine waiting for me didn't bode well. He looked tired. His face was wet, his eyes red.

'It's Van LacClune,' he said. He didn't need to say any more. I called for my horse.

. . . .

It took more than half an hour to descend the mountain paths, to track the loch's shore down to the army's encampment at the mouth of the gorge. Most of the camp was empty, our warriors away foraging, stripping grain from towns, herding back livestock or upsetting the clergy, but those that had remained as a garrison, some four hundred men, had all gathered around the empty, muddy circle of cooking pits. Not uncommon for warriors to linger near food, but nobody was eating right then. Castus's party had returned, and there were far fewer of them than had set out.

The man himself, my friend, my drinking companion, my onetime lover, was propped up on a stretcher. His face was awfully pale, and his hair was slick against his head. Bandages wrapped his shoulder, his chest. I dared not even look at what lay beneath the blanket that covered his left leg. The stench told the story well enough.

My heart screamed, a sound I didn't think it could make anymore.

My face remained flint.

Castus grimaced when he saw me. It wasn't the pain. I could see he'd been prescribed a variety of different intoxicants and medications by the surgeon, who had chosen to stand well back. It was the indignity. To be looked on by a friend, and to feel the shame of being broken. He was a fierce, proud man, and all his golden splendour had been reduced to burnt, torn flesh. I looked around at his men, looking for those I'd come to know in the five months since I'd rescued this army. Blood-spattered, dented, bruised, their own injuries were bound with stained rags but none were as heavily wounded as Castus. Maybe only one in three had come back. Those as badly injured as their lord had been left behind. Castus had often complained about the responsibilities and injustices of his birthright, but it was the reason he'd made it back, for all the good that was going to do.

I couldn't show him I cared. Not before his men. I stalked forward.

'Report, Van LacClune,' I asked, as though he'd just vaulted from his horse. 'When?' The gathered warriors scattered back from my approach like insects running from the light.

'Three days ago,' Castus said. His voice was weak.

'Where?'

'Some forest town. We were loading grain when they came on us.'

'Advance forces?'

'Redwinter men,' he said. 'The Artists were with them, I think.'

I took a deep breath, steeled myself. Time was escaping us. I couldn't afford to lose my war leader. Not now. Not with Ovitus bearing down on us. We only had weeks now.

'Are you dying?' I asked.

'Think so,' Castus said. 'Doesn't seem fair.'

I didn't know what to say to that. Every life ends with death. Bleak as that was, it was probably the only fair thing about life. Perhaps the unfairness was in his youth, but he was a warrior, and that was a risk they all took. In the Queen of Feathers' memories, my forerunners had sent thousands to die on boggy fields, on ships that burned and clogged harbours with broken hulls, to perish attempting mountain crossings, to fling themselves at castle walls or fall defending them. There had been so many. There had been few friends among them. A true witch queen cannot afford friends. They are the beginning of weakness. I thought I'd left all of that behind me, the tragic, whimpering part of me that needed other people. The craters in my spirit that need had once filled were gone. I'd left them behind with all the weakness, with the tears and the fear. But maybe not quite enough.

Maybe not all.

'No,' I said. 'It doesn't seem fair at all.' I looked around. 'Someone get him under a roof. I'll not have him lying out here.'

'No,' Castus said as his men responded to his command. 'No,' he said. He slapped a hand away, but the exertion cost him a lot. He fell back, his breathing coming in huge hoarse gasps.

'Can't you do something?' Dinny LacDaine asked. There it was, in his eyes, the weakness, but I felt it too. He must have known it was hopeless, but we hope against hope.

'The only Gate that can mend flesh is Vie,' I said. 'And no Sarathi can have the Fifth Gate as well as the Sixth. There's nothing I can do. He needs to be somewhere private.'

'No,' Castus said. I saw he was deadly serious. This was the last of his authority. His last command. 'I want to be here. Under the stars. With the moonlight on the water. Better to pass on to Anavia looking at something other than some miner's smoke-stained ceiling. There's nothing can be done inside that can't be done out here.'

It wasn't a good idea for his men to watch him die. The queens within me told me it would be better to keep him hidden, pretend that he still lived. Give them hope they'd see him again. But the craters, that damage we all carry that tells us to have pity, to be merciful, warred with them. It was the last time I would allow it, I thought. This one time, in honour of the times we'd shared together. Of the times we'd used each other's bodies to blot out the pain of our living. Of the times we'd been there for each other. For that, I'd allow it.

'Take him down to the water,' I said. 'Make a good fire to keep him warm. Point him towards the sunset.' Thankful for something to do, Castus's men leapt to do his bidding. 'Not you, Dinny. I need you to tell me exactly what happened.'

Dinny watched Castus being taken away.

'I should go with him,' he said.

'He has a few hours yet,' I said. I couldn't know for sure. I only had enough pity for one person. 'I need a report from you. How did it happen?'

'They knew we were coming,' Dinny said. 'We were headed to a town called Natherly. Just some stupid nowhere place along the forest road, running east into Clan Malbraic's land.' He pressed his eyes tight. I knew that look. He was remembering, recalling the terrible things he'd seen. The arrows flying, the spears punching into guts, the screams of dying horses. 'They were on either side of the road. No warning, just came down on us. We might have stood a chance but they were mostly Draoihn. Led by Winterra, I think. Your old friends.'

'I don't think they remember me that way.'

'No. There were only a dozen of them, but they thought that enough. They cut us to pieces like we were nothing. Normal men aren't made to fight that. Castus managed to wound one, and another couple got dragged down, more by our luck than their skill. And then they hit us with something. I don't know what. Our men just started laying into each other. It seemed like—like there were enemies all around us. Only there weren't. Everyone started attacking each other.'

I nodded. I'd been expecting this sooner or later. But they'd arrived far more quickly than I'd expected, and well ahead of the army.

'The Brannish Artists are in play,' I said.

'Aye, I think so,' Dinny said. He turned his eyes towards the ground as they glazed with tears. I wondered who he'd killed. How many of his own people he'd killed. How many Castus might have killed.

The Brannish magicians were different to us. They repainted reality somehow, made lies of truth. The rage was coming to wash away the grief. It was easier that way. Purposeful.

'Who took Castus down?' I asked. I feared the answer. Who else would have been closest to him but Dinny? The boy loved him.

'It was his uncle,' Dinny said. 'Haronus LacClune.'

'That green-faced piece of shit.' I grimaced. I'd put an arrow in Haronus LacClune's shoulder once. He'd tried to arrest Ulovar for trying to stop Hazia. But he'd also stood for Jathan at the Testing. That was the problem with wars like ours. Unless you understood what Ovitus really was, it was easier to choose his side. That was why we were outnumbered ten to one, relying on tunnels beneath a mountain to win the war for us rather than taking them head on.

'They've sent out their best to weaken us before their army makes it here. A risky little strategy.'

'There must be hundreds more on their way,' Dinny said. 'And if we can't tell friend from foe—how can we fight that?' He looked off to where Castus LacClune, beautiful Castus, was being stretchered away to die looking at pointless, ineffective stars. I'd needed him as my war leader. What a terrible waste.

'Be strong for me, Dinny,' I said. 'I need you now. I'm running out of commanders and I can't spare you.'

'I'm no commander,' Dinny said. He groped for his sword hilt, then realised his scabbard was empty. 'I can't do anything.'

'You'll do it when you need to,' I said. 'Failing that, you'll do it because I tell you to. Now go to the loch. Hold his hand. Tell him he made these last years of your life bearable. Tell him you wish you could have had more time together. Tell him you love him. Nothing else matters for him at this point.'

Dinny hung his head.

'I wish we'd had more time,' he said.

I sighed. There were still sighs in me as well as craters. Who knew?

'Me too,' I said. 'I wish there was more time for all of us.'

* * * * * *

I left Castus to his death, surrounded by his men, by his love. It wouldn't have been right for me to be there. I didn't need to see his ghost rise. I'd be seeing plenty of ghosts soon enough.

28

I had traversed a world of chaos, of madness and inconstancy, and all it had brought me to was this.

The tomb of the Queen of Feathers lay at the centre of a dark, twelve-sided room. Dim light filtered through narrow windows, casting beams into the dustless air. Pointed archways decorated with languages unknown and weeping faces ringed the chamber, rising up towards a ceiling that was impossibly far above me.

The sarcophagus stood upright. The lid bore her stony effigy. Her demure pose, hands folded before her, looked calm, serene, but there was anger around her blank stone eyes. She was remarkably lifelike. I wondered whether Maldouen had made this, or if it had been brought here from his old world. Now that I was here, I didn't know what I was supposed to do. The rest of the room was featureless. I hadn't expected this. I'd thought, despite everything, that I would find her here alive. That I would find the answers I so desperately needed. That things would be made right, if only I could pass the burden on to someone else.

I'd been carrying it for so long now. I didn't know enough to do this. I wasn't old enough to have to take these responsibilities. I wasn't big enough to carry the fates of so many across my shoulders. My back was close to breaking. It was here that, more than ever, I just wanted to be Raine again. Just wanted to be myself, but I'd torn myself in half. I wasn't even myself anymore either.

'There has to be something more,' I said. The archways took my voice and cast it back and forth, carried it upwards. This was what lay at the centre of the great fallon at the heart of the City of Spires. This, and nothing else at all. Somehow the Queen of Feathers lay at the heart of the Fault, and was at the same time absent. It didn't make sense.

'There's nothing more,' the Riven Queen said. Hallenae stood beside me.

'I pondered on it a long time. She used to be here, sometimes. It's why I stayed close, I suppose.'

'You were angry with her,' she said. 'You hated her, at the end.'

'She led me wrongly,' Hallenae said. 'She made me believe that I would be the one to do whatever it was she believed had to be done. And then came the Draoihn, and my Sarathi betrayed me, and Maldouen and his Lance. I really believed I'd made myself invulnerable. She was so certain that it was me.'

'She spoke like that to me, in the past,' I said. 'That there was some great purpose for me. Something I had to do.'

'Only she didn't know what it was? Yes, I remember those days.' Wisps of smoke trailed upwards from Hallenae's cracked, charred body.

'I guess it wasn't me either,' I said. I approached the cold, grey sarcophagus and put my shoulder against the lid again. I heaved against it, but I might as well have been pushing into a solid block of stone. Maybe when Esher and Sanvaunt arrived we could crack it open. If they arrived. I was doing my best not to think about that. Outside, the sky was darkening. The world was growing black. Iddin was coming, and he drank the world in his approach. I had no time left. It wouldn't be long now. I could only wait for the world to give me something back, or to end.

This was supposed to have been it. The big idea. The solution to our imprisonment in the Fault. The way to stop what was happening back home. It had been the slimmest of hopes, but we'd latched onto it, held it tight because we just didn't know what else to do. The Queen of Feathers had been with me since that day on the slopes of Dalnesse. She'd taught me. She'd helped me, had told me of her great purpose, of my great destiny. But there was nothing here, just a cold hard tomb. She'd been dead all along and the dead seldom know what they should be doing.

'Dry your eyes,' Hallenae said. 'Enough of this whimpering.' I hadn't realised I'd been crying. 'You stand before a queen. You should have been one yourself. This is unbefitting of our kind.' She glowered at me. 'You believed in yourself once, or you'd never have made it this far. So believe now. Be what you were born to be. Be what you made yourself into. I need Raine Wildrose, High Sarathi of Harran now, not some self-pitying girl.'

'It's too much for me,' I said. 'All of it. It's too much. I just want to be free of this. I just want to go home.'

'This is as far as I got too, and I cried and whined for a while as well,' Hallenae said. 'You don't really have the time for that though. There's no home to go back to unless you solve the riddle that has bound us all here. And we *all* end here, Raine. Not just you and I, but each of the great queens. Serranis, Lady of Deserts. Song Seondeok. Their tombs lie in the other spires, but now they're just as empty as this one. Where did they go? Why do we get brought here when we're wiped from the earth?'

'I don't know!' I cried. The arches cast my voice back at me, *know, know, know.* I slumped to the floor and buried my face in my hands. I was empty. I had nothing left to give. I could feel Hallenae's scorn burning down on me. She found me very annoying.

'I'd thought you would be different,' she said. 'But they were mighty. I was supreme. You're just a broken girl.'

She was right. After all of it, she was right and I was just me. Just Raine. I wasn't Serranis or Song Seondeok, or Hallenae. They'd all ruled kingdoms, empires. I'd never ruled anything. I'd never had a title, or destroyed armies, or carved out a name for myself that would live on through an Age that bore my name. I was just me. Cold, alone, and doomed to die.

'I never wanted any of this,' I whispered. The echoes took my voice and made it larger.

'Perhaps that is why you will be the one to succeed,' Hallenae said. 'Perhaps that is the point.'

'How can it be?'

'This was not my riddle to discover. There are four great tombs in the spires of the city, Raine. One of them is mine. They have always been here, since long before our arrival. Since before we were born. They hold on to us, but we should not be here. Look at me, Raine Wildrose. I am dead. I have been dead for more than seven hundred of your years, but I am bound to the Fault. Why? Why is it you who have no tomb?'

'Because I'm the only one still alive,' I said. 'The tomb predates you. How is that possible?'

'Everything is a mess here,' Hallenae said. 'You're lucky you didn't arrive ten years before you were even born. This place is chaos, raw and undiluted chaos. It was only Maldouen's magic that has kept it from spilling wholesale into the real world.'

I stared at the dull grey sarcophagus. The Queen of Feathers stared back from the stone, that constant anger around her eyes. Maybe it was more frustration than anger. I felt like it was personally directed towards me. She'd always been annoyed with me too.

'Do not fear. This is not the end,' she said to me that first time, when she protected me from Ulovar as I dragged Hazia through the snow. 'This is only our beginning.'

She'd been right, then. It hadn't been the end. And in truth, it had been a beginning. A beginning that had caused me a lot of pain. A beginning that had saved my life. A beginning that allowed me to be who I was, what I was, without fear, without judging myself—for a time at least.

'You've arrived,' she told me later, after I killed a man.

'What is she?' I said. The question was posed to the darkness, maybe to myself, though I didn't need to hear it. Hallenae said nothing.

'I am many things, Raine, just as you are, and have been, and will be,' she said to me that day, as the blood dripped from my hands. 'I'm exactly what we need,' she'd told me. 'You'll see, eventually, if you're the right one to see it. We both will.'

But she'd been wrong on that front, maybe on all of them. What I needed was to escape this place. I needed to undo what had been done to my world. I needed to be there, but it was already too late. What difference could I make there now, powerless and weak as I was? I couldn't stop the Fault from disgorging its horrors, not even were I there. I couldn't stop Iddin. To fight back against the rampant, uncontrolled chaos of this place, a place he was bound to, part of—I would have needed the power of the Crowns them-selves, would have needed Creation itself to answer to me. But the Crowns were lost to us, three of them in the hands of the enemy. There was no feat I could perform that would enable it. Not with the Sixth Gate, nor Sanvaunt's Fifth, nor Esher's four.

My head jerked upright. No. I had to be wrong. I had to be. I racked my mind, scoured it for the Queen of Feathers' words.

'They learned that ultimately, it was standing alone that brought them the greatest power.'

'That's why she always fails,' I said. 'It's because she's totally bloody wrong.'

The world began to shake. The whole great structure rumbled as vibra-tions coursed upwards.

'He's coming here,' Hallenae said. 'He's nearly upon us.'

'You can't help me,' I whispered. 'She was right, and she was wrong. You stood alone. That was her error. *That's* the great mistake. *That's* why none of you could do it.' I spun to face Hallenae, suddenly more aware of the life that filled me than I ever had been before. Was I mad? Was this idea that had struck me utterly, completely insane?

'Only when you stand alone do you have complete control,' Hallenae said. 'How would you know? You never achieved anything.'

'No,' I told her. 'I achieved more than any of you. I got to love, and I didn't bow to the darkness. I didn't let it eat me and isolate me. I need my friends.'

'What good will they do you?' Hallenae demanded. 'What good have *friends* ever done you?'

'They made me who I am,' I said. 'That's the riddle, isn't it? We're apart, but we're never apart. *Everything is one.* Me, Esher, Sanvaunt, even those who've gone before us and died. Somehow we're all still here. In the tunnel, in the sky, Anavia or Skuttis. When you break everything down, what lies between the things that make us up? It's nothing. And if you're separated by nothing, you're part of the same.'

'Worthless philosophy,' Hallenae said. 'A child's dream.'

'You can't see it because you don't want to,' I said.

The ground shook, more violently now. I turned and marched for the corridor, back to the city. As I approached the archway that would lead me back beneath the vortex-torn sky, a wave of heat struck me. The ice that cloaked the great fallon was melting, splashing down over the doorway. I stepped through a wall of warm water. It was hot outside, hotter than any summer's day I'd known.

The world outside was shadowed, a wall of night swallowing the horizon as far as any eye could see. Iddin was come. He was black and purple, vast, an embodiment of terror and destruction. Inner lightning lit the cloud from within as he began to consume the edges of the city. He was annihilation, come to consume all in his path. I'd spoken brave words, but they felt smaller now. Seeing his approach nearly brought me to my knees.

The creatures of the Fault fled his approach. Great Trow feet thudded against the streets as they ran, freed from their icy imprisonment. Fetch rose from the buildings, their songs discordant screams. The Faded clutched at their ears against the cries of the sky as they scattered through the streets.

Even monsters know how to fear. I'd let my fear rule me, but no longer. Not anymore. The creatures that had made it to the higher levels were coming here, seeking shelter.

A humanoid figure dressed in armour of bronze scales was crossing the bridge that led to the fallon-tower. He was one of the Faded, the Eldritch Kin that had been, his features vaguely feline, his hair tabby. I drew my sword, shook my head. He stopped and drew his own weapon. This was not a place for both of us. This was not his refuge. I shook my head again more slowly, warning. The Faded raised his own sword in a salute. Only one of us could have this place. Then he came at me.

He was very old, but I'd been cutting a path through the Fault and I'd been taught by the best there was. I struck first, slicing down from my right and he was surprised by my speed, but quick enough to parry. Not quick enough to see the reverse, the second cut rising from my left and clipping him in the jaw. He staggered back spraying blood. I did not relent. He sprayed more.

'Nobody passes,' I said as I kicked what was left of him from the edge of my sword. Along the bridge, another pair of them were coming. 'Nobody,' I said.

I would hold the door until my friends arrived, and then we'd see. We'd see about doing something so colossal, so impossible, so insane that it would change the world.

But first, the killing.

29

Men stripped the battlefield dead of their valuables, tugging rings from fingers, brooches from cloaks, shook out the cloaks themselves if they hadn't been pierced. It was the way, after a skirmish. They could keep what they found. Only fair, really. They'd done the hard work.

Hallum LacShale approached. A big grin spread ebulliently across his broad, blood-spattered face. One of his pauldrons was dented, but other than that he'd come through unscathed.

'How many of ours for the crows?' I asked, biting at a piece of raw mutton. The blood must have made a hideous contrast against my skin's pallor. I didn't care. There was blood everywhere and on everyone.

'Sixteen, Lady Raine,' the big southerner said. 'A score wounded.' He'd stuffed his axe back through his belt without cleaning it, a tenacious scrap of viscera resolutely clinging to the blade.

'How many do you think we got?'

'There are near two hundred enemy dead out there. Double that escaped.'

'Didn't go as well as I'd planned,' I grumbled, though the outcome was good enough. Our side of the wooden bridge was strewn with bodies. The water was choked with them, where men had fallen, where they'd leapt in terror, where they'd been harpooned like fish. No ghosts remained among the floating bodies. I'd breathed in, taken my fill, and I was heavy with them. Now and again a dead man's memory forced its way through into my waking thoughts. A bracelet being carved beside last night's fire. A sad, pining lust for a man sitting next to him who couldn't return his feelings. Anger at a child whose crying wouldn't cease.

'The bridge was the objective, not the men crossing it,' Hallum said. 'My men are already at work on the supports. We'll have it down within the hour.'

'They can still swim it. Maybe float their gear across on platforms. The river's not deep.'

'Aye, lady. But that would take an army days, and that's before we factor in their supply train.' Hallum was pleased with himself. Killing Ovitus's men muted the pain at his own losses. I hadn't known until recently that it wasn't just Liara he'd lost but a cousin, a sister-in-law and an adopted son. He'd have killed all day if I'd let him. He gestured over the river where we could still see the last stragglers limping after their fleeing comrades. 'An army moves as slowly as hunger forces it to. To reach Draconloch, they have no choice but to take track sixty miles west, cross at Ansford, maybe. The road's barely worthy of the name, and the ford is deep. We've won ourselves a victory here.'

'We've won time,' I said. 'That's good. We did well.'

It was our second victory over the royal forces, and the men needed it. We were one up now. Five days back we'd caught a scouting group in the night, camped upon Bovey Tor. They were inexperienced, some of them too young to be fighting. Ovitus had emptied Harranir's youth into his services. There was no way to know that before the attack on their encampment began, and it wouldn't have changed matters if we had. War was war. I'd fought so many of them down the centuries, or the queens who filled my mind had, that one terrible thing ended up blurring into the next. It had bothered the warriors, though. They didn't feel their victory was earned. Slaughtering kids of fifteen wouldn't bring Castus LacClune back from the dead.

There had been just two Draoihn among them. One I recognised from Redwinter, the other identified only by his oxblood coat. I'd turned my power on them, released a Banshee's Wail that should have torn them apart. The grass around them had withered and died, two unfortunate warriors were caught in the howl and their bones broke, eyes burst, but not the Draoihn. In fury I intensified my barrage, burning through gathered souls and eventually the sigil-worked shield the lead Draoihn was carrying cracked down the centre and my Sixth Gate tore him apart. The second managed to beat a retreat before I could get to her.

They have ways to counter your power, now, Mathilde had told me. *'Just as Draoihn did when they fought Hallenae.'*

I kept the pieces of the shield to give to Ranitha. Maybe if she could explain how it had held back my powers, I could do something they wouldn't expect. We were so outmatched in men and resources, my magic was all that held Ovitus in check. He feared me. How much did he need to fear me now that he'd melded himself to his dog? I didn't know what powers he could call now, but he hadn't rushed across the world to engage me personally. He was still Ovitus, after all.

I stared at the corpses floating in the river. The current was already trying to take them away, but there were so many, jammed between the banks like pickled fish in a jar. I'd done this. But then, as Serranis reminded me, I'd seen all this before. Over and over. The world repeated itself. When Serranis took the city of Amal Thray, the river had run brown with blood. She'd expected it to be red, but it just looked like mud. The night before Solemn Hill, Hallenae had put every prisoner to the sword, or the claw. She'd known the end was coming and her creatures were too distracted. And so I watched the dead men on the water, and I knew that what I'd done here today wouldn't even make it into a history, if any was written.

Here lies a dead man. He fought on the wrong side. He didn't know what he fought for.

.   .   .   .   .   .

Our battle—if that was even a fair name for it—had been over swiftly. There had been prisoners, but we had no means to keep them. The most vengeful of my people wanted to nail them to the trees along the high-north road, a warning to those who followed after—and a way to slow them. I couldn't allow that. Hallum hadn't balked when I told him the swift action I required.

I stared at the corpses floating in the river.

Not my doing. The doing of Ovitus LacNaithe.

'The enemies' gear's loaded on the wagons,' Hallum interrupted my thoughts. 'Light'll be gone soon though. Time to eat. I'll open a bottle of red as well.'

I liked Hallum. He had an earthy simplicity, muscle and single-mindedness. I liked that he followed my orders without whining about it. When he looked at me he saw a general. Twice my age, he was big and rough around the edges, and on nights when I'd felt cold and alone I'd thought about taking him to bed, but it would have been far too human of me. He saw me as something else, an ethereal thing. Showing him my bruises would have sent a ripple through the illusion. Since I brought myself back into this world, I'd been a distant, otherworldly creature to these men and women who now fell under my command. I had to remain apart. I had to be alone. There was no other way to rule.

We made a camp upwind of the dead. There was only one tent among us, and that was mine, small and easily carried by a single horse. Not much room to stand. As the world slept I practiced the blackest rites, drew incantations in the dirt, in the air, across my skin with a needle. The droning of the tunnel had become as commonplace as the chirping of grasshoppers, the whistling of the birds. I could stare into it without even hearing it at times. One foot remained in the world of the living, but I had been changed by my exposure to the tunnel. I no longer felt the cold, though I was cool to the touch. I only ate once a day, the hunger rising suddenly in a tide. I only ate meat, raw and dripping red, but it wasn't the meat I wanted. What I wanted was blood. Hot warm blood, filling my mouth, my throat.

Ranitha arrived with the dawn, travelled alone through the night on a wagon drawn by two mules. Her Sixth Gate was open now. She'd sensed the slaughter on the wind and found us easily. Her face was cold and stony now. She had not enjoyed her second death, but it had been necessary to bring her further into her power. What had she expected, that the path of the Sixth Gate would be easy to walk?

'You could have just broken their hands,' Ranitha said. 'Then sent them home as cripples.'

'No,' I said. 'I needed their ghosts. My reserves were running thin. You need to start drawing from them if you're to be any use when the battle comes. Two deaths should be enough.'

'I've tried, Lady Raine,' Ranitha said. She looked uneasily across the bodies in the water.

'You saw the ghosts? Saw how I drew them?'

'I'll try harder, Lady Raine.'

'See that you do.'

She pursed her lips, her brows furrowed.

'It has not been easy to keep the miners on the paths you determined for them,' Ranitha told me. 'They do not respond well to me. They still see me as Suanach's underling.'

'It won't be long before I return,' I said. 'They'll listen to you if I tell them to.'

'They should listen to me anyway.'

It had not been an easy decision to come out here leading men in the skirmishes that run ahead of the battle to come. I needed to be back at Draconloch, supervising the tunnelling. Without me present, things could go wrong. Without the memories I possessed, five thousand years of Sarathi knowledge, my methods couldn't make sense to somebody. Only I understood why our Lance-seekers had to dig the tunnels as they did. When Castus fell, my people needed someone at the front, a figurehead. They had to win something back.

Truth be told, I chafed at the bit back beside the loch. I saw knives gleaming behind every curtain, heard an assassin's footstep in every creak of a wooden beam. On war's path, the tread of marching boots sounded clearly. I had to give them a new leader, someone they could follow unreservedly. Someone with utter loyalty to me, but who had the humanity that I'd purged six months ago. Someone who could ask for sacrifice and be obeyed through love as well as fear. It was a hard thing to ask. Hallum LacShale was loyal and knew the business of war, but he excelled at following orders, not inventing them. Dinny LacDaine was too grief-stricken to make rational choices. He'd fallen into a frenzy during the day's bloodletting. I could have given one of our loyal Draoihn a command but I didn't trust them not to break, to return to Redwinter. So for now, it had to be me.

I let Ranitha sit beside my fire that night. She and I shared something I'd never thought I'd be able to share with someone else. She did not like me, I thought, but I didn't like her terribly much either. She disliked my youth. I disliked her unevenness. She wanted to know all about the Sixth Gate, but baulked at using it. It may not have made sense, may not have been fair, but I'd suffered in order to earn my power. Maybe she'd been gifted it too easily.

'If we see more fighting before we return to Draconloch, you'll take a ghost,' I told her.

'What if I can't?' Ranitha said. She held her hands out to the crackling little camp fire.

'You can,' I said. 'You will.'

'Perhaps I'm not that powerful,' she said. She'd been so keen that first day, but her enthusiasm seemed to have waned. She liked to learn about the incantations I wrought, the theory of it all, but actually *doing* it was something else entirely to her. All theory, no practice.

'I will teach you,' I grated. 'You just do it. Like raising an arm, or breathing.'

'What happens if I cannot?' she asked.

'Then I'll make use of you in other ways,' I said.

'How did you learn so much so quickly?' she asked. 'Even with the second death you gave me, I barely conceive of how to hold the Sixth Gate. It feels it would take a lifetime to learn what you just seem to know.'

She was not wrong. I held the knowledge of Serranis, and her five centuries of rule. I was filled with two hundred years of Song Seondeok's war against the Faded, and though Hallenae had been a mere one hundred and thirty-three when Maldouen's Lance blasted her from the earth, she'd been a fast learner. I was completed with the imperfect recollections of others who'd never quite become dread powers: Unthayla the Damned, Alianna Robilar, even some bone witch whose name was barely a word, living in a cave, gutting vultures for entrails. The Queen of Feathers had gifted me this knowledge, or these queens had. It wasn't always clear who the memories belonged to, like they were all the same thing, the queens, the cave dweller, the fallen grand master, and dozens of unhappy farm girls all blended together. Their lessons burned within me. I could tell Ranitha none of that. I had not forgotten how my Sarathi betrayed me before Solemn Hill, hungry for the power they thought I withheld from them. Well. They'd learned their lesson, that was for sure.

'The Sixth Gate takes as long as it takes,' I said. 'I have decades to teach you. If we survive.' I looked over to the wagon Ranitha had ridden in on. 'Leave that here. Did you bring what I asked for? With the necessary . . . adjustments?'

'I did,' Ranitha said. And she stared off towards that wagon with haunted eyes, and I wondered whether I had made a mistake in my choice, or whether every leader begins to doubt every subject when the price of failure grows so large.

· · · · · ·

It was nearly noon the following day when a messenger got through to us.

'I'm come from Cavercail,' he said. 'A huge force of royal soldiers are heading straight for Draconloch. At least a thousand, riding hard. They know you're not there, Lady Raine.'

'Didn't we have people holding Cavercail?'

'Not many,' the message bearer said. 'They abandoned it the moment they learned of the enemy's advance. It's a Brannish contingent. Fresh fighting men, borderland veterans of the expansion.'

'They're just men,' I said. But they'd be good.

'A force that size will have Draoihn of the Third Gate as well,' Ranitha said. 'And Artists.'

'It doesn't matter.'

'Shall I return to Draconloch? Have them man the gorge wall?' Ranitha asked.

'No. You're going to get your chance to draw ghosts. You stay with me. Dinny can go get the wall prepared in case they get around us.' I looked back to the messenger. 'We can intercept them?'

'You could head them off before they reach Cavercail if you move fast,' he said. 'But they outnumber you two to one.'

'The numbers are not a worry,' I said. 'Ranitha, you ride in the wagon with me. There are things I will show you, and there's no time better to learn new things than at the end of them all.'

Ranitha nodded solemnly.

'The world dies,' she said. 'Better to walk with death than quail before it.'

That raised an actual smile from me. Our warriors climbed into the saddles of weary horses and turned them west. I went to inspect what she'd brought me on the wagon. I'd not known how I'd feel when I saw it. I'd wondered whether it might call back to that part of me I'd abandoned to the Fault. Would tears burn in my eyes, or worse, spill down my face? Would I find that old version of myself welling up to reclaim control? But when I looked down on what I had made, lying silent and still, all I found was pride. Determination. Surety.

I'd come full circle. Hallenae would have been proud of me.

. . . . . .

Two days' ride back west. One night we lost two sentries to something that came out of the dark. Nobody saw it, and we hadn't time to follow the trails in the mud where the bodies had been dragged. Someone said a prayer, probably, and when dawn broke we rode on without them.

Swelled with recruits and a contingent of three hundred Kwendish bowmen, the rebel army now numbered nearly two thousand warriors. Not bad, given we'd started with five hundred, and the bowmen made up somewhat for our lack of archers. Some were our countrymen, others had come for the promise of the gold flowing from Harranir's churches and absolution houses. The north had exhausted itself with infighting after Onostus LacAud's death—one I was proud to say I'd personally delivered—and the clans were largely left in stalemate. In some dim political philosophy class in Redwinter I'd been told that when civil strife affects a land, it is easier to bring in an outsider to rule than pick from the disputing candidates, and so it was for us. The north had been ready to war with Harranir for years, and when the thails become weary and their domains fractured, warriors need work. Would they stay when Ovitus LacNaithe's army arrived? Part of our recruitment efforts revolved around lying about how many men Ovitus had. A huge Brannish contingent had swelled his numbers before his decisive battle with Castus. Ovitus's forces had numbered sixteen thousand before I'd gone to work on them, and despite desertion, the sicknesses that follow armies like midges, and the losses we'd managed to inflict, he still had to have twelve. Without something to turn the tide, my warriors would take their pay until the enemy were a few days away and then mutiny. It was inevitable. There were those who'd prefer to die hard, but there weren't many. The majority of my battle force had been pressed into hauling rubble back at Draconloch. Smiths worked day and night hammering out picks and mattocks, carpenters strapped together crates and carts to carry away spoil and warriors hauled rocks to raise walls across the gorge. It would all last until the money ran out. They didn't know it yet, but the wealth of the north already lay in Draconloch's pockets. I'd begun offering thaildoms to the commanders if we won, but those promises likely wouldn't steel men's resolve.

Castus had been right. Draconloch had some natural advantages to be defended. The enemy had to advance through the southeastern gorge, never wider than a quarter mile. Defensive positions didn't get much better, but that wouldn't be enough. Not against the numbers we faced. And if I couldn't deal with Ovitus himself, then it would all be for nought anyway. He hadn't come against us himself in person. He wouldn't risk his own safety over a campaign, and why did he need to? He wouldn't put himself face-to-face with me, but then, I was just one Sarathi. The Lance was the only thing he feared, and he didn't know whether we had it or not. He'd let his underlings do the fighting for him until he was certain he was safe—or until enough of Iddin's power had bled through to make him invulnerable. Eventually the Fault would spill over and vomit the creatures of the Fault through Harranir's Crown, and that would be it.

'There it is,' Hallum said as we crested a hilltop. Across the valley, over the purple heather that blanketed the moor, Cavercail sat atop a hill. It was cut from the black stone from the Age of Strife, just like the ancient city of Delatmar, whose memory still lay beneath Harranir, but like everything from that bygone era, it had long since crumbled and fallen. Most of it had been scavenged away. The stones that remained were similar to the dark substance of the night's-eye stone the Nigheag had made me. I had one left in my pocket. If another apprentice Sarathi presented themself I wouldn't hesitate. I needed every dark hand I could muster.

The road to Cavercail was open on both flanks, moorland heather rolling away, studded with grey-black breaches of bare rock. The wind was fierce out here.

'What's that smell?' Hallum asked. A grimy odour flensed the air.

'Worry about what's on the road, not caught up in the wind,' I said. 'We have to stop them reaching the fort or we'll never dislodge them.'

'That wasn't the plan, lady,' Hallum said. 'We were to hold them from taking the old fort.'

'Plans change,' I said. 'Your outriders reported the advance on Cavercail comes beneath not just the LacNaithe wyvern but the Brannish hare.'

'Different flag, same men to kill,' Hallum grunted.

'No,' I said. There was only one person who could put herself beneath that banner. 'It's Mathilde.' One corner of my mouth allowed a slight smile, the other refused to find it amusing. 'I didn't pick her for a warrior, but I don't know why I thought she'd sit idle. She's taking her Artists to claim it. Clever girl.'

'And if the Artists are there, then that means Haronus LacClune has joined up with them,' Hallum growled. 'I see. So it's vengeance, then.'

'It's along those lines,' I said. 'We form up down there at the foot of the hill. Once we set up in Cavercail we're trapped on the hill. We have a chance to take something back from Ovitus here. Castus will have his vengeance.'

'Will you be the one to give it to him?' Hallum asked. He waved his hand in the air a little. 'That thing you did back when you first appeared. Will you do that to them?'

'It takes a lot of death to cause that level of damage,' I said. 'And Redwinter has had a long time to prepare for me. They've started finding counter-charms, protections against my magic. I'll do what I can. Don't worry, I'm still dangerous.'

I was telling Hallum the truth, but I couldn't give him all of it. I couldn't tell him that even with the souls I'd taken two nights ago I was drained again, running empty. Every night I worked on the rites. Every night I poured myself into my spells. It was the big picture that mattered.

'Outnumbered two to one. We beat this and we'll be legends.' He grunted a laugh to himself. 'How many dead men have said that down the years?'

'Then this is our chance to firm up resolve, and show our people that the numbers don't matter. We fight them here. We put an end to the fear their Artists have put into the men.' I bared my teeth and for a moment a hiss escaped me as I glanced back at Ranitha aboard her wagon. 'I've got something new for them to worry about this time.'

. . . . . .

It's considered fair to give your opposite number a chance to surrender before battle is joined. I wasn't going to miss an opportunity to have a bit of banter with Mathilde in the flesh. Our mirror conversations had ended a while back, and I supposed this was why. Our line looked strong. We were low on archers, good on spears. Hallum's battle plan was a simple one: to let the enemy crash into our line, hold it, break them, then our horsemen reserve would run them down. Such things are seldom simple, but we had a good number of renegade Draoihn of the First Gate to hold the front line. They'd come from the west and the north, those who hadn't been packed off to join the Winterra, those who thought a little more deeply about why any of this was happening. We'd lost too many of them in the ambush that killed my friend.

The Brannish forces seemed like they wanted to obligate Hallum. Moor-scouring wind turned the drizzling rain horizontal. Arrows wouldn't have been so much use here anyway, what with the wind blowing back down towards them. But they had the numbers, and our scouts had been wrong.

Not a thousand. At least two thousand, and an even number of LacNaithe warriors. A great snake of orange-and-white checks, banners showing the rampant hare of Brannlant, advanced along the road.

'Eight to one,' Hallum muttered. 'I said we'd be heroes. Beat this and we'll be literal gods.'

'You take the first thousand,' Dinny LacDaine said, coming up alongside him. 'I'll take the next.' I hadn't wanted Dinny to be part of this, but he'd refused to return to Draconloch. He was looking for things to kill. Hallum looked to me. He trusted me. It's a lot to bear, that level of trust.

'You better have something special planned,' he said. 'You want my advice, we should withdraw to the hilltop.'

It's good to be confident, but sometimes you're not always right. The memories of ancient queens told me to damn it all, unleash the Banshee's Wail on the column and plough bone and viscera into the earth. But Mathilde hadn't been lying. They'd had months to prepare to face me. The Draoihn among their number would have more of those shields, amulets, maybe even incantations tattooed into their skin. I well recalled how the tide had turned against Hallenae when she relied too hard on her own powers. There was a reason she'd begun bringing forth the creatures of the Night Below to do her fighting for her, why she'd allied with the Faded. Those flashy, flesh-from-your-bones spells were brutal and efficient, but they were like a cavalry charge: if you know it's coming you can stand behind a row of defences and see it sputter out before it becomes dangerous.

'Withdraw,' I said. 'Withdraw to the hill. Sound it. Up on the hill!'

Shit. This was not good. I'd been careful. I thought this was a good place to take some of their better troops down, but that's the problem with field information—it's wrong half the time. Fighting a war was like trying to put socks on in the dark, only you have to rely on other people telling you where the socks are, and either they might be too big, too small, or there might not be any socks at all. Our people were well disciplined. They moved in good order. The Brannish trumpets followed us.

'What *is* that stench?' Dinny asked. It was foul on the air. Like an open bog. But I'd spent long enough in the Fault that such things barely touched my senses anymore.

'Something bad, I expect,' I said. I saw Ranitha was already at the top of the hill, her tattered shawl blowing out in the wind. The ancient blocks of black stone provided a defensive wall that varied between being barely more than flagstones to rising over head height. I hadn't wanted the enemy to have this position for precisely the reason that we were moving back to it now.

'Not too late to mount up and make a run for it,' Hallum said.

'No,' I told him. 'I want those Artists. I want them dead. If I don't take them down now they'll interfere when I have to face the monster.'

'Castus LacClune was a brave man,' Hallum said gravely. 'But not worth dying for.'

Was that true?

'Enough complaining. Have the men take positions. We'll hold the top of the hill tonight. We'll see what change comes with the dawn.'

Neither Dinny nor Hallum looked convinced. Nobody was happy.

30

The Fault was collapsing as Iddin devoured everything in his path. The rush of pale energy surged up around the tower.

My arm was weary, my breath laboured, but they were afraid now. They saw the bodies lying scattered before the arch. They saw the red sprayed across me. Perhaps I was as feral to them as they were to me. The Faded began to cluster at the far end. Some looked like people. Others were strange combinations of animal and man. I'd cut a goat's head from a creature with the legs of a rabbit. A thin, spindly thing had tried to drop down on me on dragonfly wings. None of them were the most terrible thing before me.

The rumbling black cloud crawled across the city, massive and terrible. It devoured whatever lay in its path. Its size was incalculable. It was a storm on the land, an ocean sweeping in to wash away all that lay before it. Iddin, king of the Fault, was come. In the orange-black water down below, faces formed, crying out in terror, before disappearing into the swirl.

Hope waned.

Where are you?

Blood ran down my leg where a spear had pierced my side. It hadn't got through much of the armour, but it had broken in. The twisted metal ground against my side when I moved, shredding more of me, but I needed it too much.

Blood dripped from my left hand where I'd lost my little and index fingers. They'd been cut away by one of the Fault's creatures—which one I couldn't say. Where they'd gone, I didn't know.

Blood was leaking from beneath my armour in other places. I didn't know why, or where I'd been hit. I didn't feel any pain. There was too much battle rush in me for pain, too much for me to think about the blood I was losing, the injuries I'd sustained. My body felt heavy. Standing upright required concentration. Was this it? Was this how it ended?

We do not escape the Fault, I realised then. Not just realised, but felt it, deep within me. I knew somehow, with utter certainty, that Sanvaunt, Esher and I did not get away. This was where our lives ended. It was the way it had to be. We'd sought the impossible all this time, but there was no god available to step in from the wings and bear us away. The dread cloud knew it too. It swallowed the world it ruled. As it approached, one of the Faded, unarmed, looked between my sword and the encroaching devourer and hurled itself from the rooftop, falling hundreds of feet to a swifter death below. Two creatures, skin striped like snakes, hugged one another before they followed it.

Where are you?

Not all were so quick to admit defeat. A warrior in rusted armour charged towards me. He was half-dead, his fleshless skull exposed as the visor bounced up and down on his reckless approach. He swung a sword at me, the blade pitted, jagged and turned orange-brown in the muck of the Fault's swamp. I parried and my enemy's blade snapped at the first blow. My arm was all but spent, but I managed to bring it back up and smash it into his helmet. Once upon a time that helm would have stopped my blow in its tracks but now it was brittle as old paper and I knocked the skeletal warrior's head clean off. Its body staggered around. I directed it off the parapet and it stumbled its own way off into nothingness.

We'd come so far. We'd fought so hard. None of this seemed fair.

'You'll kill yourself here,' Hallenae said from behind me. She had plenty of commentary for my skill with a sword.

'Maybe,' I said. 'Probably.'

'They're not worth this,' she said.

'Worth dying for?'

'Exactly.'

'They're worth far more than that,' I said. 'I don't expect you to care.'

Ripples of purplish lightning arced through Iddin as he swallowed the city. The vortex above swirled faster, a constant wail echoing out across the world. It would only be minutes before it reached us. Minutes.

Where are you?

'What is there to care about?' Hallenae asked. 'You're the one who matters. You're the one the Nightlark trained. There are other men to heart-bond to. Other women who can master the Gates. You don't need them. You can find more.'

I rounded on her. My rent armour ripped against my waist, a fresh wash of hotness coursing down my side. The effort, the rapidity was nearly enough to bring me down. The pain was. I clanged onto one knee, gasping. Sweat dripped from my face to spot the ground alongside the red.

Across the bridge, a Trow, already raggedly wounded from fighting its way up onto the adjoining building, made for the bridge. Its vast feet shook the masonry.

'You know *nothing*,' I snarled. 'There's nobody like them. There's nobody like anyone. We're all individual. We're all apart. Everything is one, but they *aren't*. I'm not. We're not all together. Imagine what we'd be like if we were? We'd have all six Gates to command. But that's not how this works. And that's how it has to be. The Draoihn are *wrong*. Everything is one but people are separate. That's the truth. That's where their philosophy fails. I might have had your memories inside me, but I'm not you.'

Hallenae regarded me unblinkingly. She couldn't blink, not without eyelids. But her stare was cold.

'You don't need them. Live for yourself, you fool,' she snapped.

She turned to the Trow who was nearly upon us. I couldn't have fought it even if I had the strength to lift my arm. Hallenae flicked her hand and the Trow crumpled to the ground. It tried to lift an arm, but it was dissolving, melting into rot.

'Please,' I begged her. 'I can't do this without them. If they're there. If they're still alive. Help me. Help them.'

The charred, blackened form of the Riven Queen bared her teeth at me. There was no pity in her, but she did want something from me.

'Fine,' she said. 'Try it your way. I'll go and find them, but you see whether it helps. But go inside. If you're torn from the battlements by a panicked gargoyle, I lose you for nothing.'

'But—' I tried to plead, but she pushed me back into the tunnel. I hadn't the strength to resist. My sword fell from my grip, fingers no longer strong enough to keep going. Hallenae, the Riven Queen, shut the huge door on me and left me in shadows. The door cracked closed with the sound of a final, falling hammer.

I drew air in uneven gasps as I staggered along the corridor and into the sarcophagus chamber. Greater waves of pain started filtering through. I fumbled at buckles and straps that had become familiar, but seemed alien now. Slowly, fingers tingling and numb, I yanked them free. Steel clattered, thin and tinny, sending its echoes away to find corners and alcoves to trap themselves in. Piece by piece I shed the shell that had protected me in the outside world. There was a strange sound coming from my throat. It contained no words. It wasn't a scream, or a sob, or a cry. It was just the last sound I was able to make that could enunciate what was happening to me. The grief, weighted and maroon. The physical pain, rising knife-sharp and gouging. The shuddering sense of loss and failure. So I pushed that sound out of me, just a gargled throat-cry as I lay amidst the battered, dented steel, and stared wet-eyed into the shadows above me.

A voice scratched its way through the dirt around my mind and into my thoughts.

He doesn't have enough strength left to travel through fire, little flea.

I sat upright. My side screamed in white agony, a fresh run of blood pattering onto the mosaic tiles.

Hallenae? My thought seemed to find echoes of its own within me.

He's spent all his strength and the silver-eyed girl can't travel. Hallenae's commanding voice scraped against the insides of my mind. *You'll need to bring them through. Do it now, the dark is upon us.*

I don't—I can't. I don't have my Gates anymore.

Stop being such a whining fool! There's no time! Think! Back when I had to escape from Ettis Kar I linked to one of my vassals. We joined the tunnel from both sides. You know this. Hallenae's thoughts snapped at me like a knotted rope.

'I can't do it,' I cried into the darkness. 'I'm not her. I gave it away. I'm not her, I'm not, I'm not!'

You ARE her, Hallenae roared into my mind. *You're both of you. You split your soul but you can no more deny what you are, what you've always been, than you can give up caring about these two soon-to-be very-dead people. Do whatever you have to but remember who you are!*

I felt the fury of the Riven Queen, hammering down on me through her Fourth Gate. I looked for the tunnel, but it didn't answer. I strained. I strained and searched the world but though death was everywhere beyond the door, there was nothing here with me. I was alone, even with a voice in my head.

I gave that part to her, I said. *I didn't want it. I didn't want to be that person.*

Hallenae's snarl sounded desperate.

Then take it back. Take the pain back into yourself, you self-pitying wretch. Find it. Pain makes you strong. Use it!

The whole world shook. Iddin approached and I could hear the crashing of falling buildings, muffled beyond the walls. Screams rose, so many that they formed a single voice as he obliterated everything in his path. I needed my friends. My lovers. My heart of three. I needed them so badly. I would do anything. Would be anything, if only it meant I could have them back.

I clenched my fist and drove it into my wounded side. I screamed without shame. I screamed and I reached now not for the Gate, but for that part of myself to which I'd spoken. She might not want to listen to me, she might not always be there, but she would feel this. I became nothing but screaming agony, ice-cold raging pain ripping through all that I was and she would listen to me now. She had no choice. I demanded her attention, and took it.

JUST A DREAM

'Where are we?' she, I, ask. We're both here now. We're together, and we float in a luminous void of starlight. Drifting. It's peaceful here. We know that time is meaningless in this space that is not a space. It's just she and I, we, both and the one of us, together inside ourselves and in the separate places we occupy across worlds. It took a lot to get us to be here together. We hope that we'll survive it.

'We're within us,' she, I, we say. It's hard to tell which one I am, but then, we're both me anyway. It hasn't been so long we've been torn apart for one of us, only a month. For the other it's been nearly half a year. The disconnect is heady. It doesn't make any sense to me, or her, or both of us.

Within us it's beautiful. There are lights, beautiful lights. There are tiny things that whirl around other things, and within those things are things that are smaller still. It's all so still. We've never known peace like it, even though the fracture line runs deep. We can see ourselves, opposite but the same. Like reflections in a mirror.

'This is confusing,' we say. 'What are we doing here?' And we realise that we aren't quite together. We aren't quite one. We name the two halves of the whole differently, because in a name there's a kind of structuring to the world. We name things and think we know what they are.

'I'll be Raine,' I say. 'You can be Wildrose.'

The other half of me, the half that went back to our own world, accepts this. The naming works. It firms up the concept of our identities, that they're more real to us now that we've chosen what we want to be.

'I need them back,' Raine says. 'I need the Gates I gave you.'

'The Gates I took with me, you mean,' Wildrose says. She's a brittle thing. I gave her my cruelty, my wrath. I kept my gentleness. My love.

'Yes,' I said. 'I need them now. Esher and Sanvaunt need me. They'll die.'

'Why ask me this?' Wildrose says. 'I have no time for it. I took none of your *compassion. Nothing that would make me weak. Why would I care what happens to you?'*

'You do care,' I said. 'I know you care. You need me. You know you need me.'

'I am our vengeance,' Wildrose says. She sounds like Hallenae. 'I've sent men to die. I've done terrible, terrible things. You think I could have done it, committed atrocities if I'd hoarded your weakness? I've worked men to death, Raine. I've sacrificed them on battlefields. I've executed them and worse. And now you want me to give up my power?'

'You think I haven't suffered?' Raine spits back. 'You think I haven't feared and burned inside every day? You took the easy road. You split us apart. I'm the one who has to feel my friends die.'

'And I'm the one who has to watch the whole world burn!' Wildrose is no less angry. 'I'm the one who bears the weight of every life on the surface of the world. It's me that has to do it. If I don't succeed in our plan, the world dies. You didn't want it. You didn't want to have to bear all that suffering on your shoulders so you spat me out like I was refuse. The parts you didn't want. You're the one who gets to know love. You're the one who gets to have them. So you're the one who loses them too.'

There are stars within us. Or perhaps everything is a star when you burrow down deep enough. Bits of me, bits of her, of us, drift silently between us. Raine reaches out and touches one of them. Wildrose does the same.

We relive a few moments of the past, as well as we remember it. It's a sunny day. We sit with some of the LacNaithe apprentices. A retainer has brought iced apple juice after we finished training on the practice courts. We weren't very good back then, in the days before we trained with Lady Datsuun. We're all there. Liara is there, and Jathan, Adanost, Gelis. Colban too, the first of us to die. Ovitus laughs at a joke. We all look so happy.

'We lost so many people,' Wildrose says. She's forgotten to be angry with Raine. 'It felt like we barely started, and then everyone was gone.'

'We'd lost people before, but it was different,' Raine says. 'Redwinter felt like home.'

'Stop it! I don't need to see this again,' Wildrose says. She drags us away from the memory. Raine reaches out and presses us both into another one.

We're in bed with Castus, in the LacClune greathouse. He's inside us, we're teasing him above. We're playing, it's meaningless, but that only gives it more value. It's freeing. It's a respite from everything we've done wrong. He doesn't need me and I don't need him. He laughs as he tries to hold on. I've bet him that I can break him. I'm going to win. There's such joy in it, in the sex and the coming together. It doesn't matter that we're not in love, or that we're using each other. It's friendship. It's real.

'He's gone,' Wildrose says. She's quiet now, even if there's really no such thing as sound here. 'He mattered a lot. He was important to us. Gone now. Dead.'

'Oh no,' Raine says. It's a stupid thing to say, but it's what comes out. *Many must be dead. Many certainly are. We hadn't thought that Castus would be one of them. He's too full of life, too sure in the world. Or he was.*

'I know,' Wildrose says. And that's when Raine sees it. That's when she sees the silver sliver of pain in Wildrose, a crack in that armour.

'Oh,' Raine says. *It's coming down on her hard. It's heavy, angled, shaped like a battering ram. She's been able to do things in the Fault because she was finally rid of the corruption, of the darkness, of the raw brutality it called out from her. All the things she'd used it to do in the past, the murder, the slaughter, the shattering of bone, the flaying, the reaping of souls. All the screams, the blood, the souls that Wildrose—that Raine—has taken. All of it.*

But they don't belong to Wildrose. They belong to us both.

We're no different. We've just chosen which parts we want to put first. And we needed this. We needed to be able to love, and love freely without the weight of self-loathing. Without the hatred of what we've become. Without fearing what those we love see when they look back at us. But we needed to be that monster as well. We needed to embrace the power, to revel in it—and to number ourselves. We need to not care that our plans are horrifying. We needed to commence them without knowing, so we could give ourselves to Sanvaunt and Esher. It's all suddenly clear now.

The love that Wildrose feels isn't separate from it. She did those things because of love, not despite it. It seems so obvious now.

'I think I have what I need,' Raine, I, we say.

'You just have the weakness!' Wildrose, both of us, yells back. *But she knows. She understands it too, much as she doesn't want to. We were safe this way. Now we both have to feel.*

'I think this is the last time we see each other,' Raine, I, we, the two, the one say into each other's hearts. And then, we separate for the last time.

31

There was no call to parley. We had nothing to say to each other. We occupied the hilltop and the warriors of Brannlant and LacNaithe gathered at the foot of the hill. The wind howled hard around the ancient hilltop fort of Cavercail, and it would be a cold, sleepless night for the men who stood ready behind walls that had not stood against time.

I tore at a piece of horseflesh, the meat slippery, stretchy. One of the mounts had gone lame after a nesting bird startled it and it stumbled into something's burrow. Tonight it fed us.

'I could have that cooked for you, my lady,' Ranitha said.

'Better like this,' I said. I sucked at the juice, the blood. The meat had lost its warmth. The men were cooking the rest of the meat on spits in the middle of the fort. I could smell it, but that roasting meat smell had lost its appeal.

'Will I come to crave it this way too?' Ranitha asked. 'Does it give some kind of power?' There was always an intensity to her questions. She saw me as something she might become, and wondered at every aspect of me. Would her hair turn white, would her eyes take on that luminosity? I didn't know. Perhaps the Sixth Gate changed us all in different ways.

'Eat it however you want to,' I said. I'd sucked away all that I needed and tossed the rest of the meat over the low wall for the night scavengers. Perhaps I should have thought better of it. There were other things that roamed the dark looking for flesh these days.

Ranitha picked at scabs that had formed on the back of her hand where she was always scratching at herself. She was nervous. Everyone was nervous. By morning we'd beat a retreat down the other side of the hill. Mathilde would try to harry us, but our smaller force would be much fleeter, and I'd been dreaming through a number of nasty surprises I could leave in their wake. Spirit-snares were particularly good, and any man who tripped them wouldn't pursue us any longer. The further he went from it, the more it would constrict around him. They would only catch a few, but nobody would understand what was happening, and fear is the best way to slow down any pursuer. When hunting, you have to believe it's the prey who is at risk.

'You should retire and sleep, Master,' Ranitha said.

'Tonight there's no sleep for anyone,' I said.

'We need you strong and well rested for the journey,' my apprentice continued.

'Rest if you want to. I'll be here.' I said. Ranitha scratched at her hand and bowed her head.

'No sign of anything or anyone moving down there that we can see,' a warrior said, completing a circuit of the perimeter. It was a clear night. The rain had faded away and the moon was nearly full, fat and gibbous. A stroke of luck for once.

I stayed watching the front for a while longer. Six hours to dawn. I walked through the hilltop encampment. Women and men nodded at me as I passed their positions, put down their skewer of horse meat and wiped the grease from their faces. Many of them saluted me. They served me now. I had no words for them. I had moved beyond conversing with the common man. There was an importance to how far I remained apart. I spoke to Hallum briefly, and Dinny, and a few of the other high-ranking warriors, but they had nothing of importance to tell me.

I was lonely now. I had to admit that. Something felt like it had changed inside of me that night. It had only been a flash at the side of my perception, but a great sadness had welled up through me. I'd made myself this. I'd turned away from the road walked by other people, and I'd revelled in the authority that an otherworldly fear can bring. I enjoyed the power. But there were times, like then, when the world grew quiet and we had nothing to do but wait, that I'd still been able to speak to Castus. We'd started growing apart, but he'd been able to speak freely before me. Our shared history had mattered. What I'd done to him had seemed necessary, it was necessary, but in those silent, moonlit moments, I didn't know if I liked everything about what I'd become.

I thought about her, too. That other Raine I'd left behind. I felt we'd communicated again somehow, but it was more of a feeling than a memory. I wondered about Sanvaunt and Esher, and I hoped they were all together. I hoped they weren't all dead, or dying. I needed them to succeed. I needed them to find the Queen of Feathers. Without her, everything I'd prepared for, every part of my grand machination would fail. Without her I had nothing.

'Lady Raine!' One of my warriors approached me holding Mathilde's silvered hand mirror. The surface was rippling with jagged light. I'd not thought it prudent to carry around a means by which Mathilde could have a look at our defences so I'd left it in my tent.

'She wants to talk, does she?'

'I found it down the hillside,' the warrior said. 'I saw the light.'

'Down the hill?'

'Lying in the grass, lady.'

My brows drew in, fury masking sudden fear. How had it got there?

'You did well,' I said, taking it from him. Always affirm good work. The warrior was glad to be rid of it, and disappeared back to his post. The mirror's surface was dark but shimmered with rolling lines of crackling white light. How had it left the small travelling chest I kept in my tent? Could it have fallen out? It didn't seem likely. Traitors, traitors everywhere. I stroked the mirror's back.

Mathilde's lovely face appeared, the mirror up close to it. She was in a dimly lit tent of her own.

'You want a bedtime story?' I said. My voice rode on wasps. I'd enjoyed our bedtime conversations, and finding her leading the charge had made me angry.

'There's no time,' she said urgently. 'I've been trying to reach you for an hour. The Artists are nearly at the top of the hill. They're leading the Lac-Naithe men into your position.'

'There's nobody on the slope,' I said. 'We have eyes. This is a poor trick.'

'You can't see them,' Mathilde warned. She sounded frantic. 'That's what they do. They make one thing look like another. You have to trust me, they're there. They're almost on you. You can't fight them if you can't see them.'

'If it were true, why would you tell me?' I asked.

Mathilde spun away from the mirror as the tent opening was flung open. A man advanced on her from behind, Willdem of Thurstown, the big, bowl-haircut killer who'd travelled with her from Brannlant. He had an axe in his hand and that dour, watchful expression was gone. Here he was, the killing-man I'd always known him to be. I shouted a useless warning as Mathilde spun, the mirror falling. With a loud crack the glass in my own mirror fractured and left only darkness behind. Steam and sparks spat from the broken mirror as its power bled away into the night. Mathilde was my enemy but I felt a surge of sudden panic for her. Her own bodyguard had come for her with a cleaver in hand and murder in his eyes.

Rivers of Skuttis, was she telling the truth? I ran back to the wall, undignified but uncaring, coming alongside Hallum LacShale.

'Anything?' I said, my rough voice cold in the night.

'Still nothing,' he said. In the moorland valley below, the camp fires of the Brannish-LacNaithe forces spread, small but bright. I stared. There was nothing to see, but if Mathilde was telling the truth, if they were coming and the Artists' power had turned our minds—why had she warned me? She was my enemy. She was the one who'd led them here.

I kept staring. I listened, and the wind blew cold against me. I heard nothing. No clink of riveted armour. No thousand boots working up through the heather. No hissed curses as a man got his kilt caught on a thorn. Nothing.

'It's so quiet,' I said.

'It's *real* quiet,' Hallum agreed. 'Even the wind's holding its tongue.'

Even the wind was silent.

That decided me. I looked down into my chest, gripped hard on two dozen souls, and drew breath.

'Cover your ears!' I yelled into the night. 'Cover them now and get on the ground!'

My people, my warriors obeyed me as I drew a vast breath and unleashed the Banshee's Wail down the hill.

I saw them, caught in the howl. Ranks of armed men, barely twenty feet from us. They were outlined like ghosts themselves in the sudden blast of death, but the front rank carried shields embossed with sigil wards and runic charms. Shimmering like white-spun spectres, I saw their armour, saw that these weren't just warriors of LacNaithe. They were Winterra, Redwinter's elite fighting force, and the shields they carried had been worked specifically to stop me. To stop this.

Not everyone was saved. Seven, eight men went howling into death as shields cracked and splintered, bronze-cast sigils spinning away into the night, and the men behind them crumpled and broke apart like dandelion seeds. But as the breath left me, they disappeared from sight. Only now we heard their charge, heard them roar a battle cry.

'Fall back!' I cried, but it was no use. There was nothing there to fall back from. I drew souls up from my reservoir, but then a spear slammed straight into my chest. It appeared from nowhere but had the force of a Draoihn's throw behind it. The Witching Skin took the impact, but souls burned for it.

'Protect Lady Rai—' Hallum bellowed and then blood was erupting from his face as a sword hewed into him. I stumbled back, let fly another frantic killing spell and the man who'd cleaved into Hallum exploded, sheared in two. I looked for someone, anyone to kill, but there was nothing to fight. Screams erupted along the wall as my warriors fell. They routed almost at once. There was no way for them to fight this. Our fortified position was abandoned, but men were falling. Dying. Butchered.

I ran. Me, Raine, the High Sarathi of the North, ran away. I felt something hard and sharp slash against my shoulder. The Witching Skin held. I jumped over a dead man, one of my men, felt an impact against my back. The Skin held strong, but every strike was costing me. I ran straight into someone, like running into a pane of glass, and suddenly I was bound with hard-muscled arms around me and a voice in my ear yelled, 'I've got the witch! Finish her! Kill her!' I put my arms around my unseen captor, found a head, a face, put my fingers into his eyes.

Forgot I was trained by Lady Datsuun, didn't you, you little Winterra bastard!

Eyes burst beneath my thumbs. I squirmed free of him as he fell back, free of the grasping hand that tried to latch on to my ankle and ran on. Slaughter ruled the hill. We were done for. We were all so very, very, royally done for. It couldn't end like this, I couldn't afford me to die. That other Raine, that distant, complaining cousin of mine I'd left in the Fault, needed me too. We didn't win without each other.

In the centre of the hill fort there lay the wagon Ranitha had brought me—where was that bitch? I hadn't had the time I needed. Hadn't been able to plan, to make a ritual, so this was going to have to be fast and ugly. But then, maybe that's how it always was.

I vaulted onto the wagon. The screams all around me were brutal, but they were generating ghosts, which staggered around trying to fight things they couldn't see, unaware that they were dead, trying to save us. I was glad my men were spared that sight as they ran, and died. I threw back the tarpaulin, and another underneath. The stench that had followed us hit me square, watering my eyes. There he was. Cold, skin white as snow, but mottled and discoloured. Light Above, but he'd been beautiful.

'You're not getting away from me that easily,' I said. 'You think dying was going to keep you from helping?'

I widened my Sixth Gate. I stretched it further and wider than I'd ever dared to before. I saw the souls escaping into it, and I reached down through it. I'd ventured around the tunnel, I'd stared into it, felt it rage around me, but this was different. This was throwing part of myself into it, and I needed to bring something back. I knew it wouldn't be the same thing that had gone in. But it would work. It had to work, or it was over.

I needed to find him, in another place, another plane of our existence, or maybe it wasn't existence, it was something else. I needed to link to him, to show him why he was needed. I had to give him something to hold on to.

The first time we met, in a tavern, and you invited me to drink beside you like we held equal rank. The same day, seeing you stab a drunk to death, then fleeing together into the colour storm.

A spear, or a sword point, or something smashed into my back. The Witching Skin held. Blows fell like hail.

Watching you smash down Ulovar's apprentices like you were a bull among lambs. The drinking, the rose-thistle-fuelled lost days, the sex, the quiet intimacy, watching you stand helpless as I was sentenced to die.

Swords, hammers and axes rose and fell on me now. Souls escaped one after the other as they stopped those blows, and my reserves began to falter.

Meeting you years later on a battlefield, making plans with you, annoying you, being your friend. You being my only true friend. Leading beside you. Seeing you on your death bed. Letting you go.

They hacked at me, yelling, screaming their rage and their vengeance. My head rocked to one side, my neck jarring painfully. The tip of a blade forced its way through into the meat at the small of my back.

I can't let you go.

I need you.

I pressed my eyes closed and I screamed into the tunnel of death, and I held my hand forth. And something took it.

A shock wave rippled out across the darkness atop the hill. A dry thump of air followed by the clattering of armour as iron-clad men went tumbling across the ground. The rain of blows stopped hammering at me. I panted for breath. A cut I hadn't known I'd taken dripped blood into my eye.

'About time you pulled me out of there,' he said, and his voice was the drip of old water into a vast, empty cavern. 'Frankly, I'm amazed you lasted this long without me.' I slumped forward into the bed of the wagon. I couldn't hold the Witching Skin anymore.

A heartbeat trance opened back onto the world. *Dhum-dhum. Dhum-dhum. Dhum-dhum.*

Castus LacClune rose from the wagon, unfurling like a flag. His sword was in his hand. His leg was new, forged from iron and Draoihn crafting. Iron plating worked with arcane Draoihn sigils covered the places where his wounds had taken away flesh and skin. His hair was a rippling mane that shimmered like fire. He was changed, modified, a creature of war. But it was his eyes. Burning pits of night, roads into oblivion that swept the world. He had the look of Ciuthach. I'd expected that, but I'd not known just how afraid of him I'd be. He reached out, seized an unseen man by the throat and lifted him like he was a toy. There was a crunch as he squeezed, blood burst into the night.

'What's it to be, dark lady?' Even as a deathless creature from Skuttis, Castus could mock with half a dead-lipped smile.

'Kill them,' I whispered. 'Kill them all.'

The thing that had been Castus LacClune obliged.

A terrible pulse of oppression emanated from him, a cascade of invisible stone, a wave to crush the mind. It was the same power that Ciuthach had unleashed all that time ago in Dalnesse, the same that the Faded Lord Sul had turned on Grandmaster Robilar. I had brought this back into the world. I had raised my friend to be a creature of annihilation.

The Artists' spell faltered as the force hit them. Suddenly men were visible all around us where none had stood before. At least ten of the enemy had crowded around the wagon. They fell to their knees, clutching at their heads. They arched their backs and crumpled to the ground, heels scraping dirt. It was not just the enemy who fell. I felt it and it wanted to crush me too, but I seized hard on the ghost that emerged from the ruined body at Castus's feet and wrapped it around me like a hood. The dead man's spirit took the force instead of me. It wouldn't last long, but it would do.

Castus stalked through the hill fort, a longsword in one hand, a bearded axe in the other, and each foe he came to he hacked into with inhuman force, sundering armour and sending bodies bouncing across the earth. I summoned a shadowed blade to my hand, a rippling length of purplish darkness, and I went with him. We felled men as they tried to force themselves back to their feet. I found one of the Artists, a fat man with that same single stripe of hair down his head. His face dripped perspiration as he tried to work some kind of countercharm, but there was no stopping us now and the shadowed blade carved half his skull away.

A man, a brave, powerful man of terrible determination, managed to make it to his feet and loosed an arrow at Castus. It bounced from him. My creation, my servant, my champion was not going to fall for such pitiful tricks. I recognised the warrior. I didn't know his name, but he'd been at my Testing in Redwinter. He'd cheered for me. There were many Draoihn here. Many Draoihn had to die. Many did.

The hill became red with blood. I took each ghost that I could. Castus tore the arms from the second Artist, and I stamped hard on the head of the last, the one I'd seen through the lake, hard enough to break his skull apart. I was exhausted long before Castus was done. This was what I'd brought him back for, after all, to be this terrible thing. It was little wonder the likes of Hallenae and Serranis had brought wraiths to their aid. Castus would only become more powerful over time.

There was a moment, of course there was, when I looked at my new lord of war and wondered just what I had done to the world. It was a transgression. It was ugly, much as his remaining hair caught gold in reflected light. War is an ugly business, the ugliest, but there should have been rules. There should have been some kind of restraint. But there was to be no holding back in this terrible world, this grimmest situation. The killing lasted a long time. Even an avatar of the Night Below can only move so quickly. I tired of it. I sat and watched, hearing the gibbering, insane shrieks of the ghost I'd wrapped over my head as it bore the brunt of Castus's oppression field. Eventually the world grew quiet. The emanating power ebbed away and Castus was the only one still standing, looking out over the tumbled walls towards the camp below. Those who were still alive found their feet. Not all my warriors had perished. I saw a few dizzy enemy warriors stagger out onto the hillside on unsteady legs. I let them go. They weren't a threat anymore.

'Wait,' I called as Castus started to advance. 'Wait for me.'

He turned to look at me. His face was a wet red mask.

'Still more of them to kill,' he said. 'I should thank you for bringing me back.'

'No,' I said. 'You shouldn't.'

Together we advanced down the hillside.

Something had happened at the foot of the hill. The enemy camp was in disarray, some of the tents aflame, casting long shadows in the night. We weren't the only ones who'd suffered chaos. I'd shed the insane ghost I'd used to armour myself against Castus's power. The onslaught had driven it mad, and I let it flutter away like a rotten leaf on the wind. Not everything should live within you. We trudged down, my legs aching. My arms felt as if they'd never have the strength to swing a sword again.

'Did Dinny survive?' Castus asked. I hadn't expected him to. I hadn't known he would care. But why shouldn't he? Death didn't mean oblivion. When Alianna's ghost had ridden around in my head, love had been one of the first things in her mind.

'I don't know,' I said. 'I don't think Hallum did.'

Castus's cold, bloody face became blank. I may have summoned him back, but those eyes were hard to look at. Ciuthach had looked that way. Despite everything I'd done, everything I'd become, I could still shiver at the vileness of it.

We strode unopposed to the enemy camp. No arrows, no shield wall. They were waiting for us. I'd been expecting that we'd launch back into another slaughter, but instead Mathilde stood with a few of her people of rank. She'd changed her clothes, luminous now in a gown of white that left her shoulders bare, more bride than battle. None of them carried weapons.

'Do nothing until I say,' I told Castus. 'But be ready. If you feel a Third Gate opening, hit them with the oppression field.' He still had his sword and axe in hand. He showed no sign of sheathing them.

Mathilde walked out from her people. She had to be terrified, but she had it under control.

'You're beaten,' I said. 'You failed.'

'Did I?' she asked. She held her face proudly. She met my eyes squarely. Didn't even look at Castus, horror that he was. Only a slight tremble of her fingers betrayed her.

'Why did you warn me?'

Mathilde bowed her head.

'I surrender myself and my people to you, Lady Raine of Redwinter. My forces are yours.'

I looked across her captains. None seemed to disagree. Castus had to be loosening their bowels. He could halt the waves of oppression, but he couldn't diminish the terror of his eyes.

'You've left it late in the day,' I said. 'What reason could you have to join us now?'

'I didn't come to Harran to marry a creature of the Night Below. I am not fooled by silvery hair and wings,' Mathilde said. 'If I'm to marry a demon, then I ought to choose which one. Ovitus LacNaithe made me a queen in name only. But if I'm to be queen, then I will rule as a queen.'

I couldn't find a lie in her tone, her face. Pride can make us do strange things. There was more to it than that though.

'Your people attacked us.'

'The Artists had to go,' Mathilde said. 'They switched their allegiance from me to Ovitus as soon as he sprouted feathers. They were my jailors. You have freed me from them. My beautiful Loridine has already fallen to the dark. Harranir will be destroyed in turn, and you, Lady Raine, are the only one standing in the night's path.'

'Finally, someone understands,' I said. It wasn't true, of course; I'd swayed many to my cause. But I smiled at it all the same. Mathilde wasn't just someone who was cowed by my power, or for whom I was a necessary, despised ally. She was coming to me of her own volition.

'What terms do you require?' I asked.

'Let us discuss that in private,' she said. 'The night is long. There are many wounded on both sides. Not all of my retinue were so eager to turn. My own bodyguard was among them.' She didn't go into how she'd survived him, but it didn't seem all that important. There'd been a lot of killing up the hill and down.

'Send a man up the hill to let them know that there is peace between us,' I said. 'Castus, go with him. Put Dinny in charge if he's still alive.'

'Haronus LacClune,' Castus said. His voice was deathly. 'Where is he?'

'Not with us,' Mathilde said. There was a moment that I feared Castus was considering killing everything he could see, but eventually he turned and started back up the slope. I was left alone. I was trusting someone. But I'd feasted on ghosts and I wasn't the one who'd be in danger if they turned on me.

Mathilde's tent was ten times larger than mine and bore some of the furnishings one would have expected of a princess. Piled cushions to sleep on, a campaign desk, a wooden chair and even a mahogany vanity. Braziers warmed the room, lanterns gave low light. The broken mirror lay where it had fallen. Blood streaked a white fur rug, a long wet stripe where a body had been dragged away.

'So,' Mathilde said as I closed the flap behind me. 'I have terms.'

'I'm sure,' I said. 'But why should I listen?' I stood five paces from her, hands planted on my hips.

'I gifted you a thousand men of your enemy's soldiers,' she said. 'I gave you my Artists. I warned you they were coming. I don't know what more I could do to assure you my offer is genuine.'

Her words were strong, her voice bold. She had to be afraid of me. She'd have been mad if she wasn't. Speaking to a monster through a mirror was different to standing alone with her in a dimly lit tent. The sounds of people moving about the encampment continued on outside, muffled, a separate world.

'I'll hear you then,' I said. 'I like you, Mathilde, but don't think me weak.'

'I know,' she said. 'I like you too. I like you a damn sight more than I like Ovitus LacNaithe, who is the worst of men. I didn't know, not truly, what I was marrying. I thought him spoiled. Naïve. Malleable, certainly. He seemed a good match. Through him I could have wielded great power. I was born to power, Lady Raine. I will not be kept from it.'

'You think I'm the better chance at it?'

'I think you're the chance to keep the world from burning,' she said. 'I know you alone can open the Blackwell and retrieve the Keystone. Ovitus should have made peace with you, but his vanity and spite have made a fool of him. You aren't the one causing the great collapse. So I offer you my warriors and their service.'

I smiled at her. One of those wolf-smiles, a little cruel, a little fun.

'But not your own?'

'I do not serve,' Mathilde said.

'Then what do you do?'

'I stand as an equal beside you,' she said. 'We rule together.'

'The princess and the girl from Dunan,' I said. 'Like a children's tale.'

'You're more than that and you know it,' Mathilde said. She took a step towards me. Her eyes were dark, the lids coloured green with glamours. The braziers did a good job heating the tent. Far hotter in here than I'd expected a few glowing coals to generate.

'We're rebels,' I said. I swallowed a lump in my throat. After everything that had just happened, everything that had made me afraid, the dirt and the lives on my hands, I wasn't going to be cowed by this. It was a challenge. I took a step towards her, taking back control of the distance.

'The world has fallen apart,' she said. 'What better place for two queens to rule together?'

Her turn to take a step. There was my heart, that battered block of flint I thought I'd lost somewhere along the road, reminding me it still worked by pounding, pounding in my chest. It was so hot in the tent. And fear. I could still be afraid of this. Somehow that was good to know. My turn to take a step, but my feet moved willingly, without thinking. A foot apart, practically face-to-face.

'You're already married,' I said.

'Never consummated.' Mathilde spoke into my face and her breath was warm, a little sour, and I wanted more of it.

I reached for her white, shoulderless gown and pulled it down. I was not gentle, my arms less tired than I'd thought. She gasped, chin tilting up, breath catching, and her hand caught hard to my waist. I looked down into her eyes.

'Then we take what we want and make the world ours.'

And then, we separate for the last time.

I opened the Sixth Gate and the tunnel yawned wide. I found Sanvaunt, I caught hold of him, and Esher, and Hallenae the Riven Queen, and dragged them through the breaths between worlds.

Dark fire erupted above me, not gold but furious, black and red. The world howled at the intrusion, and then it tore. Sanvaunt and Esher fell through the rip, trailing yellow flame, dropping ten feet to hit the ground hard, battered armour ringing against the stone. Hallenae descended through the hole more gracefully, floating like a wisp of dandelion on the breeze, her feet touching the tiles noiselessly. She still winced.

'Well done,' she said. 'Just as we did in Ettis Kar.'

Sweat seemed to fall in waves across my eyes. It's no easy thing to be in so much pain. I dragged myself across the floor. My legs had no strength. I left blood in my wake.

'Esher?' I croaked. 'Sanvaunt?'

They lay still, but they were breathing. What horrors they'd had to endure out in the city must have made my own pale by comparison. There wasn't an inch of their armour that wasn't scored or gouged. Their weapons had been lost along the way. That didn't matter anymore. Blades were no more use here.

'Raine,' Esher breathed. There was a rush of love on her voice, like she'd just crested a rise to spy home across the valley. She lay on her back without moving. 'Where are we?'

'We're in the central spire,' I said.

'Is Sanvaunt alive?'

My man, my beautiful man, had lost consciousness. He was breathing, but weakly. I made a committal noise as I pushed myself up onto my knees. My finger stumps dripped blood.

'Raine,' Esher said again. Her voice was distant, almost dreamy. 'Raine, I can't move my arm.'

I crawled over to Esher. I hadn't seen it straight away in the clatter of bodies falling through the dark fire. I choked. For several moments I couldn't breathe. From the elbow down, Esher's left arm was gone. I went to work without emotion. No time to feel things now, just act. Where was a scar in the mind when I needed one? I emptied myself of what I felt, just for now, just so I could do this. I cut straps with my knife, got Esher out of her harness. Took my belt, made a tourniquet as best I could, dragging hard, harder than I'd ever put strength into anything. A wail escaped Esher's lips.

Sanvaunt dragged himself across the floor. His legs didn't help him. They lay like dead things, clinging to the part of him that still lived. He scraped his way forward on his elbows. There was something wrong with the way his body was twisted. Something very, very wrong. He reached out for Esher's stump.

'Sanvaunt,' I said. The choke grew stronger, constricting my throat. 'Sanvaunt, can you move your legs?'

The briefest, tiniest flicker of blue-gold flame crackled, so tiny it barely existed at all. The blood stopped running from Esher's arm. And then Sanvaunt's face fell down to lie on the floor.

Silence descended again. They were both alive. There was that. I'd just been so late in reaching them. Hallenae said nothing, stood apart from we crumpled, broken three. I lay still too for a while, even as the tower shook, rattling to its very foundations. Iddin had arrived. I could only imagine what lay outside of here now. The Fault was smothered in him. There was nothing but darkness out there. The stones of the spire growled and clicked as the oblivion cloud picked away at them.

We were trapped. Trapped and isolated. There was no way out of this place. The tower was shaking, groaning at the foundations. No way home after all. And there never had been. There was just a monument to a dead queen, silent and sealed.

No. Not sealed. Not anymore.

I forced myself to my knees. The Queen of Feathers' sarcophagus lay open, the lid swung smoothly aside.

Oh, no.

There was no body inside. No tomb. Instead, within it lay the tunnel. Grey and black, droning as it turned, the tunnel of death reached away into the land of the dead. I was too tired, too blank to feel the disappointment that should have come. That's all it had ever been, then. A portal into death. We were so close anyway. It was fitting, I supposed. The Queen of Feathers had been dead all along.

Perhaps I could bring her here through death. But I could have done that anytime, were she a spirit to be summoned this way. I'd tried. So we'd fought our hardest, we'd come here, and there was nothing. Nothing at all. It tasted so bitter I could have spat. Esher had lost an arm. Sanvaunt—I didn't want to know just how badly he was hurt. Not yet.

I did what I could for the two of them. Took away the scarred and broken armour. These two, these once-beautiful two, the loves of my life for now and always, lay inert in a kind of sleep. Even with Hallenae standing nearby, watching, quiet, the loneliness swelled over me. If I'd had the strength, I'd have wept. But I didn't have the strength. Instead I lay down between my friends.

'There's no time,' Hallenae said.

'There's not anything,' I whispered.

A crunch and a crack from outside, as Iddin battered against the walls of the spire. Maldouen had crafted it well, had made it to withstand the assaults of the Fault's foulest creatures. But nothing lasts forever. Entropy takes everything in the end. Life, death, it was all just a fleeting pass across the page, a flick of a storyteller's tongue. It would not be long before every strand of success we'd ripped from the Fault's bones, every bloody wound we'd suffered, even the love we'd found in our most desperate hours, was washed away. It only existed here, within these three minds. Perhaps my loves dreamed of me, or us, or maybe they dreamed of nothing but the black void.

Sanvaunt's back was broken. I spotted Esher's missing arm, lying a few feet away, still encased in its gauntlet. The bleeding from my side had slowed, but I was a wretched, torn thing, leaking away onto the floor.

'With Maldouen gone and the spires destroyed, little will stand in Iddin's path back to the world,' Hallenae said. 'I did not fight my wars to see such a thing as he dominate my world.'

'That's why he hasn't gone to face Wildrose directly,' I murmured. 'He's waiting for his true power to flow through. He's the last thing that escapes here. When there's nothing but him, the vortex will sweep up the rest of his power.'

'He is halved, just as you are halved,' the Riven Queen said. 'Stop feeling so damn sorry for yourself. Agh!' She stamped her foot, howled as her tortured flesh connected with the tiles. 'Stand up, girl. Stand and fight.'

'With what?' I muttered bitterly. 'We came all this way. And there was only death waiting for us. There's only death waiting for me, everywhere I go. Was I a fool to think I could stand before it?'

'The Nightlark believed in you,' Hallenae said. She crouched down beside me, wincing. Seven centuries and more, and she still smouldered. At least when Iddin broke through the doors, our deaths would be swift.

'She should have put her faith in something else,' I said. 'Where is she, Hallenae? I believed in her. And I was wrong. She was a ghost, and then she was a book. And now nothing.'

'I don't think it's anything.' Alianna's words floated back to me, down the months, along eddies and breaks in time.

'I refuse to believe this is the end of us all,' Hallenae said. 'I will not have it. That feathered bitch didn't do all this to us, didn't make us into what we are, just to disappear at the final hurdle.'

'Then where is she?' I asked. 'Where's our saviour when we need her? Why isn't she here anymore?'

Hallenae stared into the tunnel within the upright sarcophagus, stretching impossibly to nowhere, impossibly into the realm of the dead.

'You arrived here, and she was gone,' the Riven Queen said.

'I summoned her to me, once,' I said. 'But I tried here and there was only silence. I thought she was trapped here. I thought she was buried, locked away. That if I could free her, she could show us the path home. That she could tell us what to do. She has the knowledge of millennia. She taught me these tricks, these powers. Why would she do all that only to vanish?'

'Why are you here?' I asked her once. It felt like another lifetime ago now.

'I'm always here,' she'd said. *'Even when you don't acknowledge me. I've always been here.'*

I was acknowledging her now, but she'd lied to me. She wasn't here at all. She wasn't anywhere. She hadn't been anywhere ever since we'd entered the Fault. Not back home, helping Wildrose fight her war. Not with me, fighting to escape the Fault. Just gone.

I blacked out briefly. Maybe only for a few seconds, until a thunderous crash shook the spire. The king of the Fault wanted to come in.

'You need to hurry,' Hallenae said. 'Whatever it is you need these two for, do it now. Your time is up. I hope they were worth it. I will hold him in the corridor as long as I can.'

'You can't hold him,' I said. Her blackened lips cracked and split, revealing red-raw flesh below as she made a hideous smile.

'Watch me.'

'Thank you,' I said, but whether Hallenae, Riven Queen of legend, heard my croak or not I couldn't tell as she walked slowly, painfully towards the corridor.

Sanvaunt stirred. His breathing was laboured. He had a cut above his left eye, another below it. He'd lost teeth. His face was covered in blood.

'Help me sit,' he said. It was no easy task. I was weak from the loss of blood, and my fears about his back were confirmed. I managed to prop him up, and held him upright. He struggled to breathe. I faced him away from the sarcophagus, looking down the corridor as Hallenae began scribing sigils directly into the air.

'Is there much pain?' I asked.

'All of me hurts,' he said. 'But that's not what you mean. No. I can't feel my legs. I don't know what it was that got us. There were so many of them.' He coughed, and I realised from the blood that came away on his fist that his wheezing was more than exhaustion. 'How is she?'

'Passed out,' I said. I rested my head on his shoulder and he put a hand on my hair. Such a long damn way, through such fear and pain and bloodshed, only to die like rats in a trap.

'I don't regret any of it,' Sanvaunt said, as if he could sense my thoughts through the tears that dripped onto his shoulder. The spire gave another great shake.

'Neither do I,' I said softly. 'I hoped, you know? I hoped that love like this existed. That it could exist. There was so much in my life that was painful and dark, and filled with disappointment.'

'You never disappointed me,' Sanvaunt said. His hand closed over mine.

'Liar,' I said, thinking of the times I'd let him down, over and over.

'We fought hard,' he said. 'We fought well. We tried.'

'We tried,' I agreed, and in the end, maybe that's all anyone could ask of any of us.

'Light Above,' Esher gasped behind us. I turned to see her. Sanvaunt couldn't. She was staring into the sarcophagus.

'I know,' I said. 'That's what we came all this way for. It's just the tunnel. There was only death here all along.'

'Death?' Esher said. Her right arm clutched to the stump of the left, but its absence seemed almost forgotten as she took a step towards the Queen of Feathers' tomb. 'It's not death. It's the world.'

'I've seen the tunnel a thousand times,' I said. 'Don't go near it.'

'That's what you see here?' Esher asked. 'A tunnel?'

'What do you see?'

'I see the moors,' Esher said. Her voice was lost in wonder. 'I see the sun rising. I see dew on the forest leaves, and the wind blowing through mountain valleys.'

I looked into the open sarcophagus but saw only the revolving grey-black walls of the tunnel. Perhaps it was the blood loss. Better that she had a peaceful vision at the end, maybe. A piece of a statue fell a hundred feet to shatter across the broad room.

'Show me,' Sanvaunt said. With great effort and little dignity, I swivelled him around. He exhaled softly.

'What do you see?' I asked.

'It's the sky,' he said. 'The clearest sky that ever existed.'

'Do you see now?' Esher said. 'This isn't a tomb. It was never a tomb.'

'Then what is it?' I asked. She was smiling. Lost her whole damn arm and she was smiling.

'It's a Gate.'

33

The losses atop Cavercail had been significant. Three hundred of our best had perished, but in turn we'd gained two thousand Brannish veterans, and so on balance we'd come out up. It was hard to feel we'd won a victory, but when you're fighting a war, you don't have the luxury of mourning.

I made Castus put a full-faced helmet on. Dinny LacDaine had come out to greet us. I didn't think it fair for him to see the truth of what I'd done to the man he had so clearly loved.

Work had gone well at Draconloch. The entrance to the valley was heavily fortified. The wall could have been higher, but it was backed with a bank of mud and fronted with stone. It could have used some towers. There was no gate. The only way to enter the loch's valley from the southeast was a single-file path that led up the hillside south of our newly raised wall. We could climb up, a hundred feet above the wall and then descend, but the wagons we'd returned with had to stay outside. We took them apart so they wouldn't provide cover on the half-mile approach along the valley, and hoisted the supplies we'd returned with over the wall with rope. As we dismantled the wagons, many a warrior's face set gravely. They weren't entering a fortress. They entered a dead end, and both 'dead' and 'end' were equally potent in their minds.

'Are all passes that approach the loch suitably fortified?' Mathilde asked. She mounted and rode beside me on a shimmering, silver-coated desert horse as we came down from the over-path and proceeded towards the loch shore and the mines that decorated the mountainsides like festival decorations. Distantly I could hear the sounds of labour, the snap of wood on wood, the clank of metal, the groan of pulleys at work.

'There's only this one,' I said.

'And what if Ovitus's scouts find another way in?'

'There are mountain trails, but too far west and north for him to have time,' I said. 'He knows he has no choice here. He has to come at us directly.'

'He's that fearful of the Lance you seek?'

'He knows it's the one thing that could hurt him,' I said. 'For all he knows, we have it already.'

'It seems a scant hope to find some buried, broken thing now,' Mathilde said. 'I know the old legend, but even if we find it here—do you think you can wield it?'

'We'll find out, I suppose,' I said. 'In some ways the Lance is more about hope. We've gathered here every man and woman of fighting age, and made it as hard to get to them as we can. The being that has melded with Ovitus and turned him into this false god is on the cusp of its victory. It won't allow us to stand.'

'Is it real?' Mathilde asked. 'The Lance? Or just a way to rally the hopeless?'

'I'm sure it *was* real,' I said. 'This is where it's said to lie. That has to be enough.'

I'd sent men on ahead to warn the people in Draconloch of our arrival and our new allies, but that didn't stop the stares. The people of Harran were familiar with the Brannish, who'd been our overlords and whose governor-houses had stood in every major town across our country for centuries, but the Brannish soldiers had been recruited from across their empire and beyond, people of all races and creeds. There were Murrs, Kwends, Porienti and Hyspians. There were Faralanti with beads in their hair and Russlanti with stone rings on their fingers. Some people's origins I couldn't tell at all. But they all had the look of the kind of soldier you wished you had at your command: lean, hard-faced, well-armed. What they made of our makeshift bastion I didn't want to know.

I left Mathilde to take charge of billeting her men along the riverbank as I headed to find Palanost, who I'd given charge of the digging after we sent all the children away. She was stony-faced as ever, her mouth a grim-set line. There was rock dust on her cheeks.

'Does it all go to plan?' I asked.

'They've found nothing,' she said. 'These tunnels they're supposed to find have not proved to be there.'

'But they're doing the work?'

'They are. More of the miners slip away every night.'

'Did you make examples of them?'

Palanost was a good deal taller than me. Her heavy-lidded eyes were only ever filled with judgement these days. She'd changed a great deal over the course of the war. Back when I was an apprentice, she'd been the patient one, the one who let us come to understanding on our own. She was someone else now, as were we all. Nothing unmakes you like war.

'I let them go,' she said. 'I am not a slave driver. The church silver ran out a week ago. There is little food. Rations are halved. Those who remain do so because they are afraid.'

'I do not like to be disobeyed,' I said. My anger rose. The work here was essential. Without it we were lost. Didn't she see that?

'Then punish me, if you will,' she said. 'It was my decision to let them leave.'

I glowered, but it struck home that I wouldn't punish her, because I needed her, while I would have flogged and hobbled those who'd sought to escape because they were just numbers. War may unmake us, but we have to choose what to become as it does.

'You did as your soft heart tells you to,' I said, unwilling to concede that she'd been right. 'Show me the tunnels.'

A retainer brought me meat as I'd asked for, raw and bloody, and I sucked at it as Palanost showed me the map of the pathways that had been cut through the mountains flanking the loch. They were mostly where I'd specified, their depths and gradients marked in Palanost's clear hand. It took nearly two hours to examine them all.

'This plan never made any sense,' Palanost said. 'Why would we look for an ancient tunnel by cutting new ones?'

'Because Maldouen sealed the shards of the Lance away in separate chambers, then melded stone over the top,' I said. I discarded the last scrap of meat to a dog that had nosed its way into the tent. It sniffed it, confused as if it found something about it unclean, then whined and snuffled off out of the tent, my scraps untouched. 'Here,' I said, pointing to one of the tunnel diagrams. It followed my instructions to a point, and then changed angle. Incorrect. 'This isn't where I said to go.'

'They hit a pocket of gas,' Palanost said. 'I rerouted them this way, at a twenty-degree angle down. Then worked the opposite direction, upwards five degrees for twenty yards, then down again with a split here.'

Her decisions had taken the diggers in quite the wrong direction. But as I looked over the map as a whole, I saw her working.

'Yes,' I breathed. 'Yes, the correction works.'

'I don't know what this is,' Palanost said. 'I'm trusting you.'

The words touched me in a way the words of so many others hadn't.
'Why?'

'Because I remember the girl you were,' she said. 'Not this terrible face
you present to the world. You were good. You were sweet, and kind. You
loved your friends. Whatever all this is, it's no maze to find a lance. And I
have to believe that as death bears down on us, you're giving us a fighting
chance.'

I half choked. Where had this influx of weakness come from? I wasn't
quite myself anymore. Or at least, maybe I was more my old self. I needed
that girl gone. I needed to be the jagged edge on which Ovitus and Iddin
would gouge themselves and bleed out. There could be no softness, no
round edges.

'I can use you more than I do,' I said. 'How would you feel about a second
birth?'

'If it comes to that, leave me dead,' Palanost said. 'I'm Draoihn unto
death. I will never be Sarathi, Raine of Redwinter. I could *never* be Sarathi.'

'Shame,' I said. 'But we all say that in the beginning.'

·   ·   ·   ·   ·   ·

Ovitus was coming, and at pace. Our information was patchy at best. Our
bravest people were our outriders, travelling long distances in pairs, trying to dodge those in Ovitus's service. Only one in five made it back to us,
losses we could ill afford. Of those who had made it back, we had word that
Ovitus's army would be upon us in just a fortnight with ten thousand men.
His cavalry were of no use to him here, but he had plenty of archers and
crossbowmen. Hoardings were being erected on our paltry wall, even as
one hundred yards back along the gorge men worked to erect a second wall,
this one higher. Men packed roughly mined stone with earth into steadfast
banks. When the enemy made it across that first barrier, they'd find a second beyond, and if we had time, a third. All of this would be moot against
the power of the Third Gate. I'd seen Ulovar bring down the gates of the
Dalnesse monastery, alone. I hadn't the Draoihn at my disposal to stop him.
I needed something special to go to work against them. I had ideas. I didn't
know if anything would work.

Truth be told, I didn't know if any of this would work. It was all just blind hope, in the end.

Only I understood the scale of my plans. Ultimately it didn't matter whether we survived this or not. The world was falling apart. Loridine gone, Ithatra gone, Khalacant, Osprinne gone, and Harranir uncontrolled. Five Crowns to hold back the Fault, four in the hands of the enemy and one left fallow, uncontained. Had Iddin's Faded Lords managed to take ours—had the Remnant Sul succeeded and not been frozen in the Blackwell by Grandmaster Robilar—he would already be here in his full power. While he was torn between two worlds there was a chance to defeat him. We clung to life by a thread, and that thread frayed daily.

Only the threat of the Lance held him at bay. But I saw on the faces of every one of my people, those brave souls toiling for twelve hours a day beneath the earth cutting meaningless pathways through solid rock, or raising walls that wouldn't hold, stewing vegetable peel to serve weak broth, training fourteen-year-old kids how to raise shields too heavy for them to hold for long, splinting broken bones before packing their patients back into my mines, on every face I saw the hope tattering and spilling away into the uncaring mountain wind. They needed something more.

I gave orders to slaughter the horses that weren't being used in the mines. It was a terrible waste. We kept ten palfreys in case we found a need for them, but horses were no use to us here. We had no cavalry. There was no real way out, and we had all the information we were going to get. The butchery sounded out across the loch's surface, travelling over the water in its ripples. The blood was drained. We could make that into sausage. The rest was roasted. That night I sent great steaming baskets of the stuff up to the mines, while everyone who wasn't smashing their way through solid rock was summoned down to the loch's shore. Miners who worked the northeastern side crossed over on punts and small boats. Lanterns shone on the surface as the dusk fell. We raised bonfires along the water's edge. A woman with a beautiful voice began singing around one of them, and soon someone brought out a wooden flute. Before long, buoyed by bellies full of meat, souls stirred by music and tongues loosened by the last of our ale, people were singing folk songs and there was even dancing.

I didn't feel right among them, so I kept apart. They knew me, they served me, but I was a creature of fear and night. I didn't belong.

'Make yourself look different, my beauty,' Mathilde said. She had changed her gown into the shoulderless, virgin white she'd donned back at Cavercail. I had fond memories of that dress. I had fond memories of it hitting the floor.

'How?'

'More queen, less witch,' she said. She had a smile for me now. It changed her face altogether. It changed who she was to me, or at least, changed what she was prepared to show me. There was humour in it, and something shared. It made her more human. That frightened me a little. It was one thing to fall into bed together in the aftermath of woeful terror, another to share your blankets night after night, waking up to each other's sleep-crusted eyes or a strand of your hair in her mouth. To find midway through the day that you scratch your lip and smell her on unwashed fingers. To find her looking sidelong at you across a group of horsemen, share the moment and glance away. I liked it. It scared me.

I changed my Witching Skin. My gown of gold and black became silver and midnight blue, with trailing sleeves, a black choker that looked like lace at a distance, long gloves. I let Mathilde weave my hair up around my head in a way that I was sure would look foolish, if not for her confidence that it didn't. Suitably gowned in souls and frippery, we walked through the revelry together. Many of those gathered hadn't seen me before, and none of them had seen Mathilde. A few of her countrymen tailed us ten strides behind, ostensibly to protect her, although bodyguards hadn't worked out so well for her the last time. The Brannish princess's presence was like a spark of joy among them. People even looked less scared of me.

I looked for Dinny LacDaine among the fires, but he'd avoided me ever since Castus fell. I couldn't blame him, and this was no place for him tonight. I doubted he had much more than vengeance on his mind right then. Mathilde and I stopped eventually on a platform I'd had my carpenters raise along the shore. We ascended it and her soldiers got people to quieten down. The drums, flutes and pipes sputtered out. The two of us commanded attention, utterly out of place in our finery, but then, that was the point. I took a deep breath.

'We all know why we're here,' I called to them. My voice was less raspy than it had been. There was a little more of the old me in there. 'Times are hard. Our lives have been uprooted, turned to tumult by powers beyond our control. The sky rains snails on us, or spits up wolves that stalk on two legs. The world is not what it was. Nor will it be the same again. But I want to thank you, all of you, for the great sacrifice you've made in being here with us.'

'We're with you, Lady Raine!' one of my warriors called up at us. A few voices followed him, but not many. I waited for them to subside.

'Things have gone upside down,' I called. 'But you and I know that they cannot go back to what they were. Even if we win this. If we complete our task here and send the usurper of Harranir running, we cannot go back. So today we go forward.'

'Forward!' Mathilde shouted alongside me. It was a good sentiment. Her voice rang crisp and brimmed with that natural authority that had formed within her since birth.

'Forward to the future!' Others took up the cry. By the light of the fires, heads bobbed in agreement, even if the sentiment was largely meaningless. Even if there was little future remaining for most, if not all, of us.

'My mentor, Ulovar LacNaithe, a good and noble man, died to stop his nephew Ovitus from taking the Crown for himself,' I continued. They likely didn't get the difference between Crown and crown, but it didn't matter. 'In these dark years Ovitus has named himself king. King! A usurper sits upon our throne of Harran. But with your help, we shall see him unseated, and a new Age will dawn. No more will the rich men of parliament hold their elections to place puppet kings on the throne for personal gain. No more kings. Instead, you will give your allegiance to those who have fought for you. Those who have bled for you. Those who died for you.'

'No more kings!' that warrior called, and I was beginning to think Mathilde had a plant in our audience. Maybe a few.

'What about queens?' someone else called out, and my suspicions were entirely confirmed. I took Mathilde's hand and smiled at her. I was going to smile no matter what, even if it felt like a rare use of the muscles of my face to do so, but I found it was genuine. I even showed teeth. Less sharp now, just normal teeth. Mathilde's cheeks bunched, her eyes narrowed as she returned my smile.

'Behold,' I called out. 'I present you with Queen Mathilde of Harranir.'

'And behold,' Mathilde matched me, raising our hands together. 'My lady wife, Raine, Witch Queen of Redwinter.'

It is the most curious thing about people, that they desire to be free, yet offer them a royal noose and they'll often thrust their heads right through it. There is a need in some to be ruled. One of those ancient scholars of the Haddat-Nir had theorised that it calms men to believe that someone, anyone, is in control of things. A royal line lets people believe that there are those who are actually suited to such things, that they must have some mystic power to be good at it.

Mathilde and I kissed one another then. It wasn't very decorous, but then, these weren't courtroom courtiers with their faces buried in silk handkerchiefs. There was a lot these honest, hard-working common people would never understand about what we did here, but there were some things they could. Kissing someone beautiful was one of them, and we *were* beautiful.

'All hail Queen Mathilde!' people began shouting, and they weren't plants at all. 'All hail Queen Raine!'

It was a simple calculation really. Mathilde had the royal blood of more than one kingdom, so that was secure. I had the power, and had been leading them for half the year, so that made sense too. I'd not intended to be queen, but it seemed fitting, and Mathilde had been destined to lead, so that fit just as well. Someone started up notes on the bagpipes, an old Harran song called 'The Maids of the Isle,' which had a suitable title even if the namesake maids ended up hanged for doing precisely what Mathilde and I had been doing to one another the last few nights. It didn't matter. Ours was a song that wasn't likely to get to the end of the seventeen verses anyway.

'They seemed to take it well,' Mathilde said quietly as we stepped down. There were plenty of shouts of 'Health to the queens!' as we walked back through the camp. The statement was made. We'd leave them to their revels now.

'They have two more days to enjoy it,' I said. 'And then we find out whether we hold, or if we're overrun in a day.'

'How much longer do you need?' Mathilde asked.

'Four days,' I said. 'That's my hope. Four more days and we stand a fighting chance.'

34

We three, we last, desperate, holy three sat quietly in a triangle before the Gate, knees touching. One final gateway. That's what it was to each of us, differently yet connected. None of us experienced it the same. To me it was death, grinding and dragging the living onwards. To Sanvaunt it was life, an open sky to be explored, to be revelled in, to fly. Esher saw it as the world, all of its constituent parts from the world within to the world beyond, both the hard and the intangible.

Esher and I held Sanvaunt upright. With Esher's maiming, I did most of the holding, but it was important that we all be there, in contact with each other. It was late in the day to have realised that it was, in fact, the only thing that really mattered at all. Late, but also early, perhaps, because this wasn't the end. It was only the start.

'We begin,' Esher said, and through incalculable pain she managed a smile at her double meaning. She was leading us. She'd figured it out before the rest of us had, so it was natural for her to take charge. Her hair was knotted and matted with dried blood. Some of it was hers, most not. There was no sadness in Esher. I was afraid. I was so afraid. If she felt it, she didn't let it show.

She didn't need to tell me the Queen of Feathers' name. We all knew her names now. I understood now why Esher had kept this knowledge from us. It would have been too much for us to deal with together, too frightening. We might have tried to change the course, might have had questions when the answers could only be found here. She'd held that knowledge for us, taking the burden as one of the whole.

A block of stone fell hundreds of feet from above and shattered against the floor, dust and shards of black stone flung across the hall. They clattered around us without striking.

We began. Six trances radiated out from us. The First Gate made the drums, and as they joined and intertwined, the second, third, fourth, fifth and sixth trances made the music. I could hear only the drums and the drone of the tunnel. Sanvaunt must have heard something different, Esher something else still. That's the reality of existence, isn't it? We're all there together, and we all see, perceive, feel something totally different.

There are six Gates. Six circles lie within six circles, the spheres of the world, and through them we perceive everything we come to know through our lives, whether they're brief, or long—if any human span of years can be considered long. There's the self, the first thing we know. That interiority, that feeling that we ourselves exist, that there's something at all. We call it Eio, and the Draoihn name it the First Gate. Understanding of the self, expanding it out into the world so that we connect with all the things that lie beyond that quiet knowing. That voice running around inside my head, the one that was filled with bad ideas, the one that feared the past, the one that feared the future, that wasn't Eio. The voice was just a trick, something I'd invented through my years to keep me alive. It was pushing beyond it that mattered.

Iddin roared his fury as he strove to enter the spire. A great crack ran through the door as his venom crushed against it. As my Sixth Gate radiated outwards I could feel the death beyond our walls. Spirits flickered and fluttered, uncertain, afraid.

Beyond the trance of Eio lay Sei, the trance of the Other. If we exist, it only stands to reason that other things must. The roots of mountains will outlive us all, and no matter how iron is reshaped, heated, broken and hammered it will always be iron. That was the trick, understanding that we're iron too. Malleable, changeable, battered and bruised by the things that life throws at us, but at the core, we're still iron. We're the roots of mountains, the essence of stars, the drift of water. We might change, we might be destroyed, or reforged by the hammers of the world, but there is something that makes us individual. Everything is one, they say, and it was almost true. It would be soon.

Taine, energy, I had understood least of all of the trances. Fier, the trance of the mind, was closer to the Sixth Gate than any of the others, perhaps. It's the part that goes with you when you pass through the tunnel after all. Esher used it now. She slipped it forward so slowly, so quietly, that I was unaware of it until we were all there together. Sanvaunt, Esher and I, all three of us gathered in a space that was apart from our torn and broken bodies. There was no pain here. We three stood naked before each other, and a beam of light connected us all, heart to heart. A heart bond. A three-way heart bond. What we'd done here in the Fault hadn't just been the soothing of our hearts. It hadn't just been youthful, joyous lust. It hadn't merely been succour from a world intent on ruining us. It was love. It was love so powerful that it tied us, bound us, made us one with each other in a way that had never been accomplished before. We had bled into one another, had suffered for one another, had loved so hard and so fiercely in our desperation and our need and in the acceptance of each other's bodies and minds that we became more than the sum of our parts. We were not just Raine and Esher and Sanvaunt, not just human. We joined our trances together and the music began to rise in my mind.

It was beautiful. It was us, individual and apart. It was the world around us, the mud and water, the stone and the air. It was the warmth of fire and the light spat from a storm. It was every feeling we'd ever experienced, every tear that had rolled across a cheek, it was each jealousy and each wry smile, each moment of laughter and each gasp at the beauty of the world. It was the joy of life, the pain of hurt. It was the mending of a cut, the growth of a child. It was the changes we'd experienced as we aged, and the absence of them from the ages we would never see. And it was the ever-looming shadow of mortality, the droning endgame that awaits us all, that precious, vital knowledge that we have only a short time in the world to do something, to be something to someone, to become part of the greater story told across the world, day after day, good or ill. We only exist once, and the impression we leave impacts everything and everyone forever.

And in all that, time is the one thing that tricks us. We think of the past as having happened, the future something yet to come. But there is only the present. It's all one. Time is an illusion. The Fault had taught us that.

The music rose through me and around me, lifting me, carrying me, tuneless but ascendant and glorious. It was praise unto itself, though it carried itself without value.

DESIST! Iddin's vast voice roared through the hall where our bodies still lingered. I felt so little attachment to that weary, broken flesh now. I'd left it behind. *YOU CANNOT WIELD THAT POWER!*

'No one person,' we said as one. Our Gates coiled through and around one another, crossing that heart bond that made us into what we were. Not just one being, not any longer. We were becoming more than that. More than a person. More than three.

YOU CANNOT DESTROY ME WITH THIS, Iddin roared. It was a voice from the heavens. It ushered upwards from the darkest depths of caves untrodden, reverberated from every surface.

'We don't destroy you here,' we said as one.

THERE IS NO WEAPON THAT CAN HURT ME, he bellowed. *I AM IMMORTAL. I AM A GOD. IT SHOULD BE MINE!*

'Not here,' we said, our voices music, our resonance powering out into the Fault. If anything else lived out there, it would have been deafened by it. 'And not now.'

The music rose. Six trances joined together, the rhythm of the drums, the chorus of life and death, the magic of the parts that made up the world and all of it deep within our minds, where we now existed. Our minds rose away from the bleeding flesh and shattered bone. I sensed downwards, and there our physical forms had collapsed. Sanvaunt had sprawled backwards, an arm outstretched. Esher had fallen across my knees. Where I'd been sat cross-legged, I sagged slightly forward, one hand on Sanvaunt's leg. It was right that the bodies ended this way. Right that we finished this way. We'd entered the world alone, but we left it together.

'I love you so much,' Esher said. 'I love you both so much. I know we have to do it, but I'm scared. I don't want to go.'

'This is what we do,' Sanvaunt said. 'It has to be this. It's the only way we can be together.'

'I know,' Esher said. I felt her pain even through the glorious music that surrounded us, that was us. 'I'll miss you both so much.'

'We'll always be together,' I said. 'That's how this works. And we have to. Because I need her to teach me. She has to teach me how to do all these things that I've done, or I couldn't have learned them in time. This is how we do it. This is how we save them all. It will feel like a long time.'

'We'll have each other,' Sanvaunt said.

The doors to the spire collapsed and Iddin boiled through, a venomous cloud of purple-black inky darkness, flickering with inner light and rage. Hallenae met him in the corridor. She flung what power she had against him, a deathly howl rising from her. And for five glorious seconds, she stood alone against the power flung against her. And in that moment, amidst all his rage, all his blind fury, I felt the tiniest flicker of doubt pass through him.

I hope she smiled. For five seconds, the Riven Queen defied a god. And then Iddin smashed through her magic and she disintegrated into black dust.

Iddin filled the chamber, surrounded our bodies. Our trance held him back, but would not for long.

'We have to forget each other,' I said. 'We have to forget it all. She can't know what she is. The grief would be too much. We have to let her be her own person.'

'It all ends here,' Esher said. 'The love we found. It ends with us.'

'All love ends,' I said. 'What matters is that it existed.' I wrapped them in what I had, every wicked, selfish part of me, and there were other feelings within it, and they hadn't been mine. But they were me now, as mine were theirs. Coils wrapped with coils. Memories of things I'd never done, places I'd never been, interlocked with my own.

Below, my body was torn apart. Sanvaunt and Esher too. Iddin painted the walls with us as he exulted in his victory. Nothing remained of what we'd been.

HOW ARE YOU STILL HERE? Iddin rumbled with the growl of ten thousand collapsing stars. He sought for us, furious. *DO IT. DO IT, SHOW ME WHAT YOU THINK YOU CAN ACHIEVE. I'LL DESTROY IT. I'LL TEAR YOU APART. I'LL REND YOUR SOULS FROM EACH OTHER.*

Bodyless we swirled.

'We can't make her here,' Esher said. 'This place is doomed.'

'We have to,' I said. 'We just don't make her *now*.'

It had to be this way. It had always had to be this way. The Fault didn't obey the laws of time. Slower, faster, backwards. We held six trances together. Impossible, they'd said. Nobody can hold the Fifth Gate, Vie, the Gate of Life, alongside Skal, the Gate of Death. And they'd been right. No one person could hold both. But three working together? Life and death, the self, the other, energy and the mind, we brought them together through an almighty heart bond that bound us tighter than an oath.

'*I would have life,*' she'd told me once. It really was that simple. She needed to live, and I needed her to come before me. What my other Wildrose self was doing to save our world couldn't have been learned over a single nineteen-year lifespan. She needed centuries of learning, needed the knowledge of queens, needed the power she wielded to be derived from the magic of the great warriors of the past. She had to become the book that taught me, had to become Sanvaunt's master. She could not touch Esher: some part of we three had to exist without her entirely. We knew all this and more, as we looked back over five thousand years of existence and were, finally, what we needed to be.

The music roared as Iddin crushed down on us. I clasped the last parts of Sanvaunt and Esher and together, we fell into the final trance.

Our song opened Gei, the Seventh Gate. The Gate of Creation.

'Maybe we've become like your Queen of Feathers,' Esher had said to me atop a fallen head once. But that wasn't it. We weren't *like* her.

'The stories of this age begin and end with birth,' we whispered to one another. 'And ours is no exception.'

We *were* her.

Five thousand years in the past, in a primal age when humankind was in its infancy, we manifested anew, together, a being born of raw Creation, an impossible, millennia-walking spirit. We made her from us. We thrust everything back through the years, power and life, walking between different worlds, and after that all we could do was leave it to her.

Iddin sensed it. He sensed the making of the shift in the world, in time, in creation. His howl was incandescent. His fury was the scream of every soul he'd consumed, a tidal wave that swamped the entirety of the Fault. It didn't touch us.

'Goodbye,' I said. 'I love you more than anything.'

'I love you,' Sanvaunt echoed, fading.

'We love each other,' Esher said, as her voice died to a whisper, and we three, we three who had loved and fought and died for each other, disappeared from existence altogether.

Sunrise came as a series of bands of colour, rising upwards across the sky. At its base lay a bruise-deep purple, before a hard break into orange, a soft glide to yellow-green and then finally the sky began to shift from night's dark to blue. For many, it would be the last dawn they saw. I felt sad for those who hadn't risen in time to see it, and sadder still for those who'd not had that last bit of sleep which they'd desperately need in the days to come. That's if we lasted days.

I had taken a small boat out, across the silver water, to the island in the middle of the loch. I rested my back against the cold, lonely fallon, stained all over with bird crap. Fisher birds had settled back down on top of it, scanning the water for fish. It seemed the right place to start the day. I felt the weight of expectation upon me, the baton of responsibility weighty in my hand, and I would run with it for as long as strength allowed. The sun had only just broken the horizon when the forces of Ovitus, usurper of Redwinter, unwitting servant of Iddin and traitor to his own kind, began their last march towards the Draconloch gorge.

I was surrounded by the incantations I'd hastily drawn through the night. They were weak things of paper and ink, but they would do what they needed. Only one I'd carved into the ground, and it had taken two days. It was old, and I hadn't tried it in many centuries. The queens' memories were excited. Not even they had tried anything quite so audacious. But I needed something that would level the score a little, that would buy me more time. I didn't have the power I needed yet. I would soon, but not yet. Time, and lives, were what mattered now. Out beyond our wall, the enemy snaked across the world, an iron-black mass interrupted by ripples of colour where larger banners forced themselves to the eye. There were a lot of them.

Castus stood beside me. He was a terrible thing, now. There was great power in him, but I couldn't use him on the wall. His oppression field would bring down every man standing around him, friend or enemy alike, and he'd be a sitting target for the Draoihn of the Third Gate who'd be coming to bring our wall down. They were the biggest factor in all this.

'You understand what I need of you for this?' I said.

'I understand,' Castus said. His voice steamed death in the mountain cold. A heavy pack hung from his back, but he didn't feel the weight.

'There's nobody else,' I said. Castus looked at me, and I was reminded for a moment of the horror of what I'd done to him, what I'd made him into. I tried to put up a wall. Nothing about what I had to do was going to get better until it became so, so much worse.

'I understand, my queen. I'll kill them all, when the time comes.'

I'd had a similar conversation with Mathilde before I came out to the island.

I hugged my knees up against my chest. Something had changed last night. Something momentous. The certainty, the force of will I'd been driving myself forward with all these long months, had faltered. Doubt had emerged within me, unwanted and malevolent, crawling up from cracks I long thought I'd sealed. When I looked at Castus now, a great sorrow filled me. I remembered the way he used to make me feel, the freedom of his company. He wasn't merely a piece to be used in this horrible game. He'd been my friend. My last friend.

They were all gone now, I knew that. Esher and Sanvaunt too. I'd had to steel my heart against this, knowing that it was an inevitability, that it had to happen eventually. But it didn't make any of it easier. It didn't reduce the impact of the loss. I'd known already that I'd never see them again, had tried to force them from my mind in the cut and thrust of directing a war. I hadn't had a chance to say goodbye to them. It didn't seem fair.

Winter was on us. I could taste it in the air.

'It's time,' I said, gathering up my scrolls and cutting canvases free of their wooden frames, rolling them and stowing them into a waxcloth sack.

'I'll see it done,' Castus said, bowing his head to me. The dark voids of his eyes swirled with endless hatred. I shivered at what I'd created.

'I'm going to try,' I said. I got up, went to push my skiff back into the water.

'Queen Raine,' Castus called after me. I turned back to find him staring off into the sky. His gaze found a bird, and it dropped, spiralling with rag-doll wings, to bounce from the slope below. 'If you can save Dinny LacDaine, he is worth saving.'

'I'll try,' I said, though of all those who might survive, Dinny was low on the list. There was no point in telling him that. Castus knew too.

'Even if we don't win,' he said. 'We'll give them one hell of a fight.'

'We will,' I told him.

                    . . . . . .

As I paddled across the quiet water, the mines were deserted. They dotted the mountains that surrounded the lake like the burrows of great serpents, pulleys, carts, shacks, crates and barrels arrayed around them, abandoned now. I hadn't given the order that they could depart, but I didn't begrudge them. There was no more digging to do. I'd thought about putting out a rumour that we'd succeeded, that the Lance was found, but if it had ever been here at all, I doubt our tunnels had come anywhere close to it. I couldn't pretend anymore, and I couldn't ask them to trap themselves in warrens while the knives drew in.

It was peaceful here now that the work had stopped. I rowed myself across the shimmering silver surface of the loch, the paddle strokes breaking the morning quiet. They said Draconloch was filled with the tears of the dragon who'd fallen from the heavens here. Tears seemed right about now. I wished I had some left. Maybe I'd find some again before the end. It was a quiet, lonely journey through the barely risen light of the day.

I could have escaped then, of course. Could have rowed myself north and west up the loch, taken one of the steep mountain paths and disappeared into anonymity. Could have given myself more time to combat the evil that came for me. There was no more time, though. It wasn't just Ovitus, or Iddin's swelling strength. Our world itself was dying. This was it. This was the final battle. This was the last stand.

I saw fewer warriors than I'd liked. Men snapped to attention to salute me as I strode towards the wall. Mathilde stood at the entrance to the pass. We kissed once, briefly, and I had nothing to say, and she had nothing either. Her pack looked too big at her feet, but she was stronger than she looked.

I walked through a corridor of men along the mile-long gorge that led to our outer defences. Harranese, Brannish, Murrs, they all bowed their heads or struck a fist to their hearts. Some fell to a knee. Different cultures, different customs, all had come together here. It wasn't just me they fought for.

They'd looked for hope, and somehow, somehow, in this tiny, undisturbed corner of the world we'd found it. Together. There was strength in that.

I strode up the smooth, boarded bank that led to the wall. No need for steps, no drop on our side. The hoardings looked good, wooden shelters along the parapet that would hold any number of arrow-falls. We had two walls across the pass, separated by one hundred yards of killing ground. I'd hoped for six, but two was good. Two was enough. I stood atop the wall, the rising sun at my back, dressed once again as a witch queen of legend in black-and-gold spines and runes. My warriors were ready, faces set grimly, spears clutched hard, shields freshly painted. We were all ready.

Dinny looked at me. He wore a general's brooch on his cloak. He was young, much too young for this, but after Cavercail, he was all I had left. He didn't nod, or salute me. Any love he'd had for me had gone when Castus fell. He must have heard rumours about Cavercail, that Castus LacClune had appeared and destroyed the enemy single-handedly. He hadn't asked. I hadn't told. This wasn't some romantic fantasy in which the undead and the living find a way back to one another. Castus was not some lonely immortal. He was a wraith, a death-bringing lost soul. The older part of me hoped Dinny didn't know what I'd done. The part that was fighting a war knew he did.

'Looks like it's all of them. Fighting men by the thousand,' Dinny said. He'd lost half an ear somewhere through the months. I hadn't noticed it before.

'Ovitus is nothing if not a student of history,' I said. 'They have the numbers. Our fortifications are few. A direct assault is the right strategy here. He'll lose a thousand men in taking the wall, but he has more than that to lose.'

'The Lance was never here, was it?' Dinny asked. I thought about it before I answered him.

'No,' I said. 'Not that I ever heard of.'

'Then what was the point of all this?' he asked. 'You have some other plan?'

'There's always a plan, General LacDaine,' I said. 'I need you to hold the wall for one day. That's all we need. We need to show Ovitus that he won't break through easily. We need him to commit. Then I'll deal with them.'

'I heard they have wards against you now.'

'They're not wrong. But I'll deal with them nonetheless.'

Dinny nodded. He was resigned. It might sound strange, that these warriors of mine would commit themselves to a plan they didn't even understand, that they'd fight this way not knowing why, or what they could hope for. But that's the nature of war. Men don't know where they're going, or whom they're fighting, and honestly most of the time they're doing it for pay. But in this case, I think that most of them just wanted to fight. They wanted an enemy they could see clearly. They wanted to come to blows with the warriors who'd slaughtered their friends and kinfolk across a bloody civil war. I hoped they'd come to terms with knowing they were going to die. Unlikely, but there it was.

'You should say something,' Dinny said. He gestured towards the men clustered along the wall, and stood back beyond it. I wasn't much one for speeches, but I thought I'd give it a go.

'No surrender!' I shouted. Then louder, 'We can break them here! No surrender!'

That was it. Those were my words for them. The last free warriors of our world took up the roar. They hammered spear hafts against shield rims. They stamped their feet. I turned to look out across the open ground in a swirl of skirts and cloak and awaited those who would meet us.

* * * * * *

I knew Ovitus. He would not take the field today. His form might have melded with that insufferable dog, but I had figured out two things. In this realm, Iddin was powerful, but he wasn't totally invulnerable. Not until the rest of him crossed here from the Fault. He had no reason to risk himself when he had innumerable underlings at his command. Secondly, though there may have been a merging, Ovitus was still Ovitus. He was not under his dog's sway, and at heart, he was a coward. Ovitus LacNaithe had once sent the rest of his uncle's apprentices to kidnap Castus LacClune. He'd organised a revolt from the shadows with Onostus LacAud in an attempt to give himself greater power. Only once had he ever been forced into direct action himself, when Esher had challenged him at my trial, and in that trial, he'd been beaten despite it being his ground, his advantage, and he being the one with the power. That kind of defeat sinks deep into the bones. No, Ovitus may have been the strongest among the host that came to tear us down, but he would not show himself. He believed in the Lance. He'd wait to see if I had it.

Ovitus sent Haronus LacClune to do the pointless exchange of words. Age had come on Haronus in the years since I'd last seen him. The furrows cut into his scalp still glowed with a faint luminous green tinge, the mark of some demon's claws many years gone by. He brought a few younger men and women with him, some in oxblood coats, others in the most expensive steel a clan leader's coffers could stretch to. But Haronus sat a little lower in the saddle than he once had, and I thought one of his shoulders slumped slightly. The same shoulder I'd put an arrow into all that time ago, before I'd ever laid eyes on Redwinter. They approached beneath banners turned upside-down, the LacNaithe wyvern and the LacClune rose, lashed to fresh-cut branches. The parley flag. They came nervously. They knew I had no ne-gotiating to do. They didn't come near enough to be heard, but I pulsed in Eio, and my senses were beyond human in that thrumming trance. When Haronus spoke, I heard.

'Sarathi Raine,' Haronus said. 'I am given licence by my lord to offer you a chance to surrender.'

'Did you know it was me who put an arrow in your shoulder?' I said back. To those around me on the wall, it must have seemed like I was talking to myself.

'I knew,' Haronus said. His expression was unchanged. 'You were just a pup. Just a clan girl Ulovar had dragged down from the north to clear his name. I could hardly blame you.'

'Then you know that our confrontations have gone poorly for you in the past,' I said. 'This one won't go any better. What's it like serving under Ovitus LacNaithe?'

'Kings come and go,' Haronus said. 'How does it feel betraying your country, your people, and Redwinter itself?'

'You all betrayed Redwinter when you betrayed Grandmaster Robilar,' I said. 'I always thought you were a piece of shit, but I didn't take you for some lickspittle.'

'You're Sarathi,' Haronus said. 'You're the enemy we've always prepared for. You've no lectures for me.' His lip bunched in disdain. 'I'm not here to fling insults. I'll give you the offer, which you won't take, and then we'll start killing you all.'

'I'm listening.'

'Surrender yourself to us, and all others are pardoned,' Haronus said. 'You can save them all. Every man, woman and child you have holed up in the loch with you. You have to die. You can do it yourself, if you wish, King LacNaithe will accept your body. But no Sarathi can be tolerated on Harran soil.'

'My,' I said with a sardonic drawl. 'What a fine offer you bring. My counterproposal is this. Ovitus LacNaithe can drop his trousers, bare his arse, bend over and back towards us slowly. If he makes it from your lines to ours without anyone putting an arrow up there, I'll accept his surrender. Moreover, I will rule Harran as queen, alongside my wife, Queen Mathilde of Brannlant.'

My coarse insult to Ovitus didn't faze him. Mention of Mathilde did.

'You have the queen?'

'I've had the queen for days,' I said. 'Make sure you tell your shit-eating, golden-skinned leader that as well. He might have failed to consummate his marriage to her, but she and I have been consummating the hell out of each other.'

'Childishness,' Haronus said. But even if he was serving him, I knew that Haronus LacClune hated all things LacNaithe and he wouldn't be able to resist mentioning it. That would spread like wildfire through the enemy, and when Ovitus heard it, his rage would make him stupid. He'd tried to have me, tried to buy me, tried to bully me, to entice and pressure me to be his and I'd said no. That I'd taken his wife as well might be enough to make him lose his mind completely. I enjoyed that.

'It's childish to offer pointless terms I'd never accept,' I replied. 'Snivel your way back beneath your lord's robes. Tell him whatever you wish. You'll find nothing here but death.'

Haronus nodded.

'Then this is how it ends.'

. . . . . .

I left the canyon and took a mule up a steep path that gave me a clear, distant overview. I watched from afar, my senses enhanced, a coarse woollen cloak flapping around me in the mountain wind, as the killing started.

The battle for Draconloch began with a rain of arrows. Ovitus was predictable. He'd spent so much of his life studying ancient philosophy, the machinations and battles of the past, perhaps he saw himself as part of a greater canon of military work. If you have sufficient missile troops, you begin with a barrage. Weaken the enemy, dispirit them, make them understand that this is only the first step. Bowmen and crossbowmen advanced. Our own archers—we had few—sent arrows in return. The hoardings raised over the battlements did good work. The enemy had marched hard and fast, no pavisses to protect them. Black rains of arrows filled the sky, thudding and hammering home into the wooden shelters erected along the wall. Here and there an unlucky man took a wound. Ghosts appeared, green and waxy, confused as ever ghosts seemed to be, and I reached out and called to them. I disrupted them from their path. I tore them from the tunnel, and brought them to me.

The first man to die saw the arrow that was coming for him. He thought, *There's no way that's coming for me,* and then felt the relief when it whipped by him. A light touch on his neck, and then blood, so much blood. The frantic calls of others as they tried to save him, knowing he was done for. And then he slipped from his body and heard my call, and he came to me.

As each man fell I claimed him. I built. I grew. For every one of my own men whose spirit I called to me, I took ten of the enemy. They drifted across the surface of the lake, bidden to find me as I whispered spells into the wind, unknowing the prison that would befall them when they came to me. But in truth they were a tiny amount compared to what I needed. That would come. That would all come in time.

By noon, Ovitus had tired of sending volleys that weren't hurting us. He did the wise thing, and sent in his heavy infantry. The gorge wasn't wide, but they could still advance one hundred men abreast through most of it. Of course, they came slowly. They carried planks of wood with slats nailed onto them as makeshift ladders. Some at the front bore tower shields, huge things that a man could fully hide behind. Our archers sent what shafts they could, but against steel-plate armour they could achieve little. My train of souls dwindled to the occasional morsel. But I knew it would start again. This had all been preliminary. It was to begin in earnest soon.

I was glad to be so far away. I stopped watching it after a time. There were only so many men you could see being crushed by chunks of thrown rock or smashed back down with hammers and spears, so many eyes to be seen gouged, so many swords finding a weak spot before the sight of it can sicken even someone like me. I'd seen terrible, awful things. I'd done them, too. But the men and women dying on the wall or falling down below? They weren't bad people. They were just on different sides. Ovitus had sent what was left of the Winterra in first. That's what his books would have told him to do, send your best veterans, your most heavily armoured, while they're freshest. Smash through with the opening attack. But the Winterra's advantage had always been Eio. It made them fast. It made them sense attacks as they came. But the press of warriors moving up behind them penned them in, crushed them, and there's little that the First Gate can do to save you from a basket of rocks falling on your head when you're stuck between two other men on a rickety, makeshift ladder. One of Ovitus's commanders had made an error. Though it was only a vanguard of two thousand men he'd sent forward, the press of bodies pushing hard along the canyon crushed those ahead between the wall and the press of men behind. We got over a hundred of them for free for that dreadful error as they suffocated in the vise. I sang my spell to myself, fingers working little patterns in the dirt, as I called the spirits across the quiet water. Paper incantations burned up around me as I called them to me. Called them on to serve.

One by one they came to me.

36

I am born in an age before man knows how to work metal, before empires have been conceived, when a woman can be queen with just fifty subjects. I scream as I am born, as all of us scream as we are born, but where most babes scream with need and terror, mine is a cry of loss. I am formed of three parts, but we are one, inseparable, and in our becoming we have lost each other forever. I want all the separate parts of myself, but I can have none of them, and for three hundred years I am nothing but grief and rage, laying waste, shattering rock, hiding myself in darkness so deep I seek to banish these feelings, these thoughts that run through me with every step of my being. I don't understand where I have come from, only that I have been brought into being, and so much of who and what I was has been stripped away from me. There is work to do, that much is clear, but what that work is, who it is for or why I should care are beyond me. I am so much more than anything that exists. I know nothing, but I am not like these other things. I have no physical form. I seldom appear to the stone-chippers, the flint-workers, the rhinar-hunters. They are afraid of me. They don't know what I am. I do not know either.

There are four species vying for dominance of the world at first. There are the Eldritch Kin, the Lucara, the Humans and the Neander. They strive and battle for resources. The Lucara are possessed of a single mind. They think as ants think, communicating with wisps of scent they leave as trails on the air, consuming all in their path. They start as the dominant people, spreading swiftly, but are ill suited to a world of conflict. Their pheromones are too slow to direct them to act in unity. The Neander are the biggest and the strongest, reminiscent of the great apes of the south with their hair-covered backs, pale fur and flat faces. I know I have to choose one of them. Even now, in what my fractured mind knows to be the Primal Age, I have to choose a side. I do not belong here in this world. I am not like anything else.

I can fell trees with a word, I can unfreeze the snow and turn it to rivers. I am so deeply alone.

I desire companionship, but I am too different, so I take animals and change them. I take a horse for my steed, and I make him stronger, faster, and through our bond he begins to become like me. He sires offspring, and they too are fleet and beautiful. They are *my* horses, their flanks glimmer like moonlight. When we ride, we cross land and sky. They are beasts, but an essence of my will passes down, through their blood. They will always be mine.

Gods come to the world. They choose the Neander to be their people. I choose the Humans and the Eldritch Kin, because they are losing and I dislike the interlopers. They came from far away, another realm. I play my first trick on them, show the Humans that the berries of the mandrake plant are death to them. The gods are poisoned atop their mountain, and their bodies sink in the sea, meaningless and empty. I find that I am victorious. It feels good. I have done something that mattered for the first time in six hundred journeys around the sun. I have desired nothing from these hunting tribes, but now I see what I could be were I to control them. But I cannot be one of them.

There is another world alongside my own. When I tire I find myself there. It is a place of confusion, of twisted land and uncertain time. It is dangerous to stay there too long, but as time passes I find myself drawn there more and more. I do not like this other world, but there is one there who I can speak to, a boy of iron and steel. He is not afraid of me, and he watches over a great dark presence that sleeps deeply, an ageless slumber, a banishment. On occasion it stirs, but cannot wake. The presence is stronger than either of us. We know what will happen if it regains itself. The child and I become allies. I ask him what I am, but he cannot tell me. He doesn't know either, but it is he who tells me that I have a task to complete. I arrived too fully formed to be meaningless. I may not have a body, but I have will, and will must always be directed. My wandering is over. No longer guided by whim I seek meaning. I cannot do it alone. There is only one thing that can bring about my destiny.

It is a thing that the Humans and the Kin understand all too well, and it is called power.

I am torn between two worlds, as if I were born in both, and so I need a mortal. Only a mortal lifespan is too fleeting to accomplish the great work I need. I find a slave girl, beaten for some imagined slight and tossed into the great river to drown. She is washed through the desert, but I hold the gateways to life and death as I have always done, and I pull her free of the water and I give her back her soul. Her name is Serranis, which is the name given to all girls born to serve in that kingdom. It takes me eighty years to teach her what we need. She learns so slowly, but I persevere. What comes naturally to me, what is part of me, is like showing her the cosmos. The Humans and the Kin are distracted, battling the last of the Neander, who are strong but reproduce too slowly to win a war that has lasted centuries. The last of them starve, driven into the desert. I teach Serranis to raise the dead. There are many bones beneath the desert sands. We take the city of Amal Thray and topple its statues. I have forgotten myself and my purpose. I enjoy the power she wields at my command. But the more of my power I expend for her, the more I find myself forced back into that shadowed world of inconstancy. I am ebbing. I cannot fight her wars for her.

I name the blighted land the Fault, for it is a crack that runs between worlds. I have come to know of the demon realm, the Night Below, which is a swirling place of chaotic energy and spirit. It has no substance. The Fault has appeared between the mortal world and the Night Below, and the iron child has confessed that it is his doing. It is unstable. Too much bleeds through. Serranis has moved beyond my control, grown more powerful than I, and she draws on the dark things of that void. As they cross the Fault its bonds weaken. Things that should not be spill across the void. With their passage, the sleep of the presence in the Fault grows lighter. He is trying to find his way out of the dreams that bind him.

The iron child and I make a plan. We must bind the Fault with the magic of the mortal world. Under his instruction I trick Serranis into raising the fallons, great pillars forged from the hearts of stars, and the motion of the planes ceases. The Fault is contained. It will not break through.

Even as we work, the Eldritch Kin seek to use my creations for their own end. The conduits I have raised harness the world's power, but could be turned to their own purposes. They betray Serranis, and King Paladeir casts her down. She escapes their judgement at the end, but her time is over. She chooses to relinquish her long existence, and I let her go. She was not the one.

Still, I remember her fondly, despite her failure. I remember sitting on a riverbank as she threaded beads to string, weaving a skirt. She taught me the names of the riverside insects in her language that day, and the sun caught the peaks of the mountains beyond the desert and seemed to make them glow.

The Age of the Bronze Kings sweeps in, and I am quiet for nearly two thousand years. I put much of myself into the fallons. They are part of me, in a way, like children I will never have. They mirror me, ageless and knowing, their origin forgotten, watching out over the world like sentinels. Only I am not guarding this place. I need to rule it. I find others—sometimes men, but they cannot learn the way that I have to teach them, and they do not trust me. Most of the women do not trust me either. I took eighty years to teach Serranis the powers she needed, but I grow impatient. I try to speed up the process. I have already existed too long, and I am weary and I grasp with increasing desperation. Most of those I find are caught, and killed, for after Serranis, Human and Eldritch Kin alike have learned not to allow those with the power of the Sixth Gate to live.

Paladeir of the Eldritch Kin does not give me the time I need. He is powerful beyond any of his forefathers and he seeks to use my fallons to commit a great work. I do not have long, but one prospect arises. Song Seondeok, a merchant trader from a land once called Akora, which lay east of Dharithia but is no longer remembered, has taken two deaths before I find her. She learns at a colossal rate. It is not long before I have her at war with Paladeir. The war lasts a hundred years, and as he comes close to losing, Paladeir attempts to activate the fallons. At the last Song reversed his spell, but that collision awakens the dark presence in the Fault. The tiniest sliver of its mind knows where it is. It wants to escape. It begins its plotting.

Song I remember perhaps most fondly of all my dark queens. She was good, at her core, which I do not know can be said for any of the rest of them. When she looked back across the centuries of bloody struggle, she regretted it all, though she had prevented annihilation. Only now as I flit between two worlds I sense the growth of the dark presence's power, and it names itself Iddin. It came from another world, but it wants ours. It wants that which all understand, just as I do, and its name is power.

Humankind has its own problems over the centuries. I am not the architect of every war, every disaster. The Nine Devastations are the work of the wizards of the Haddat-Nir, and I do not bury the city of Junath. But Halle-nae is mine, and she rises to be mighty. I use her to stop the Draoihn as they too lust for the power of the pillars I have speared into the world. Hallenae is terrible, but she is bleak, and she is evil at her core. I am beyond caring at this point. I fear the great darkness in the Fault, but I am grown thin. Much of what I remembered has faded from me. My power has grown weaker, weaker, with every passing day. I am a shadow of that cosmic being that was birthed in the Primal Age. Longer and longer I must rest in the Fault, and traversing the gap between realities takes its toll on my astral form.

It is only when I find Raine of Dunan, just a girl, but bruised and hurt, and so alone that she can turn to no other, that I realise that I may have one final chance. I no longer know what my task is. I only know that I need to exist. I need to be born. I save her. I give her the chance to be the one.

37

One by one, soul by soul, I drew them into me.

Draoihn Namuae cursed as something flashed by her face. She didn't see what it was, maybe a fragment of falling stone, maybe an arrow, but it had come close. Her helm would have taken it. It was good Redwinter steel, the metal diamond-forged, but she couldn't get her commands out. Couldn't shout them above the noise. They were packed in tight in this death-trap canyon. The defenders on the wall were experienced warriors, and by the look of them they were the Brannish contingent sent north under Princess Mathilde. Why were they there? What were they doing? She couldn't see backwards, couldn't see forward.

It had been fifteen years since her Testing. Fifteen years of grinding skulls under her boots as a warrior on the Winterra's front lines, of sleeping in ditches, huddling with her comrades to keep warm under freezing desert nights or sheltering from driving rain beneath creaking branches. The last few years serving under Ovitus had been like a dream, a reprieve, soft beds and a proper roof over her head. Fifteen years had been a long time to fight in the Winterra. But it had never been like this.

There was no time to think on it. Namuae forged ahead, pushing at the men in front of her. The best ladders were all broken, shattered by great blocks of stone the defenders had heaved out over the edge, but that stone and the piling bodies were forming a rampart of their own. Light Above but it was hot; she could barely draw breath. This was a disaster. Ovitus had claimed the defenders were half-starved, low on morale, the last remnants of Castus Lac-Clune's rebellion. Kill their witch queen leader and all the corruption would end. The winds that whispered lascivious desires, the spiders that erupted from diseased corpses, the eruptions of noxious orange-black tar, right in the midst of cities—slay the witch and it would end.

There was the Crown of course. There had to be a way to open the Crown, but—damnit, she couldn't breathe. Warriors crowded in behind her, pushing, always pushing. Ahead of her, a defender heaved a great block of stone over the parapet and it crashed down through another ladder, breaking apart three men. Namuae sucked in a breath, but it was stinking and boiling. She could hear something. Hear a high-pitched sound. Was that pipes? A signal from the rear? Was Ovitus ordering a retreat?

Would he ask her to dine with him again? Ask her to dance for him? He never touched her, but his words were always filled with sickly, obvious signs of courtship that he seemed to forget the next day. And now he was that thing. But she was choking here. She listened for the pipes. It had to be a retreat, it had to. She couldn't hear.

Namuae pulled her helm from her head. She sucked in an easier breath, but the air was hot and stank of sweat and blood and the screaming of wounded men only intensified. And then yes! There it was. A discordant, cat-screech blast on the war-pipes, three times. The attack was being called off. They had to retreat. The crush would end. Namuae glanced back up at the wall and a man was aiming a bow at her—

She came to me. Shouldn't have removed her helmet.

I was swollen with spirits. I no longer saw their containment as a cage. It was a pool, and they swirled together. Namuae was just one among many hundreds. The bloodshed had been horrific. Even now, with Ovitus's vanguard retreating back beyond bowshot, they died on the gorge's floor, bleeding out. My spell-song didn't end; I called them to me constantly as the wounded expired. Their stories entered me, and I tasted a little of each of them, even as I strove to blot them out. I didn't need their existences or their memories. They were just fuel to me, whether they'd fought on my side or the enemy's. Fuel for the great work.

The light was already beginning to fade. I'd expected it to take longer. Snow began to fall, beautiful, heavy flakes drifting like feathers. From my vantage point on the mountainside, back against a solid rock wall, I watched the retreat of Ovitus's finest. He couldn't know how much damage he'd done to our forces. It had been worse than I'd hoped, better than I'd accounted for. Three times the Winterra had made the walls, forced a breach through, but three times the reserves had pushed them back off it. It was senseless, as all war is senseless.

What mattered was that he believed he was getting nowhere. The wall couldn't hold, not indefinitely. It was just bait. I couldn't face Ovitus and all his Draoihn, not together. My brave followers were evening the odds with their lives. They would never understand the contribution they made. Nobody would. Not even the two who approached me up the slope.

I uncrossed my legs and stood slowly. I had expected them to wait for this moment.

Suanach LacNaruun approached in a coat of oxblood red. He was old, the kind of man who had always seemed to be old. Ranitha had abandoned her blue-and-black snakeskin, back in Draoihn red, as should always have been the case. Their longswords hung at their sides, but on their belts, on the metal cuffs at their wrists, chokers at their throats, bands of leather around their foreheads, they wore rune-worked charms of stone, bronze and silver. Their skin was painted with warding sigils.

'I wondered when you'd come,' I said. 'Better now than later.'

'It was inevitable,' Suanach said, his voice stronger than I'd ever heard it before. No quailing, no trembling. Second Gate. 'We are Draoihn. We have always been Draoihn.'

'And that makes me your enemy,' I said. 'Even among all this?'

'The battle will go as it goes with or without you now,' Suanach said. 'Ovitus LacNaithe is a tyrant and a usurper. But we have seen your darkness, and even he is preferrable to that. Perhaps LacNaithe himself will fall trying to break your wall.'

I rolled my head around, easing the stiff muscles. Rolled my shoulders back, loosening myself with clicks and cracks.

'He's sending in the Draoihn of the Third Gate,' I said. 'He won't risk himself.'

Ranitha drew her longsword. The fire of the sunset caught along its length, making it seem to ripple as if with inner fire. Her sword was runed. The artificers of Redwinter saved the best for themselves.

'You didn't want the path I offered you?' I asked her. She had enacted none of the teaching I showed her. It had only been a way to learn what I knew, to look for a weak spot, to see how to ward herself against me. She'd been a spy, of a kind.

'I can't help having died,' she said. 'But I can choose what I become.'

In another story, she would have been the hero. She'd died twice to try to unseat a dark queen, and refused the power I'd offered her. The charms, the wards, looked strong. Masterwork. She'd done well.

'It's traditional to betray the witch queen on the eve of battle,' I said. 'You gave yourself away throwing the mirror down the hill, though. Careless. Lazy, though doubtless you didn't think anyone would survive to find it. You must have realised I knew you'd turned on me.'

'I never turned on you,' Ranitha said. Proud. 'I was never *with* you.'

'Just biding your time until you'd made enough amulets to protect you, was that it?'

'Until we could resist your power over death,' Ranitha said fiercely. 'And until you were foolish enough to venture out alone.'

I lifted my own sword and flung the scabbard back and away. Suanach drew his own. I recognised the witch-killing blades the assassins had held, which hadn't gone into the forge after all, but which he'd empowered all the more. Every inch of the blade was rune-worked, the kind of sword a master artificer crafts for himself, the kind that no armour on earth could stop. The kind that could fell a witch queen.

The time for words was drawing to its inevitable closure. Away along the pass, the synchronised beat of dozens of trances began to emanate out as the Draoihn of the Third Gate moved to tear down the wall.

'I would have given you a chance to surrender,' Redwinter's master of artifice said gravely, his voice level, as though he were a judge passing sentence. 'But I have learned that mercy is not always right. You're too dangerous to be allowed to live.'

I smiled at them as they came into guard, side by side along the path.

'You've done me a favour,' I said. 'Dealing with those Draoihn of the Third Gate was going to take a lot of power. But the souls of traitors are a special currency where ancient things are concerned.'

'You're just a child without the Sixth Gate!' Suanach snarled. He didn't seem so old. His Second Gate beat from him in triple time. He would be fast. He would be hard to kill. Ranitha no less so. Wrapped in their wards, to them I was just a Draoihn of the First Gate, barely better than an apprentice. But they hadn't counted on Ulovar LacNaithe, or the fierceness with which he'd trained me. The resolution in him that I be as great as any Draoihn. The long hours, the beatings at the hands of Lady Datsuun's son Torgan, the aching bruises, and the long months of practicing those skills against innumerable enemies in the Fault—they had no idea who they were dealing with.

I didn't waste any of my soul energy trying to battle those wards. It might as easily have reflected back at me. Instead I launched my assault with blistering cuts that fell from on high and then rose back from low. They were no front-line Winterra. They were artificers, and they were far older and far less trained than I, and my onslaught drove them back. I caught Suanach across the hand, and cut away a jewelled ring but his Second Gate held and no fingers followed. I parried Ranitha's swift but obvious parting cut, wound it aside and redoubled my sword around to hammer down against her forehead. No time to check what damage I'd done, I twisted left to avoid a thrust from Suanach's sword, and then I had him where I wanted him. He might have seen everything coming through his First Gate, but that didn't mean he could stop my blows ringing down against him. His coat fell in tatters as slash after slash clove through them.

Ranitha came back at me again, another wrath-cut delivered from her right and this time I met it full force. That was a mistake; her Second Gate made her stronger than me and the balls of my feet skidded in the gravel. Suanach joined her, and together they cut and thrust at me, turned me around, forced my back closer and closer to the rising mountain wall. My opponents were breathing hard. Nothing about the First or Second Gate gives one unlimited energy and they weren't used to handling trances in the midst of battle. They were doing well, as befit a Councillor of Night and Day and his apprentice, but I was barely started.

Suanach swung down on me and as I parried his blow my sword blade snapped, but he'd misjudged his blow and the blade hammered into the stone behind me, slowing its arc. All Torgan's training came through me on instinct as I grabbed his wrist, and put all my weight behind the move, sent spirits into my legs, core, spine and arms to multiply my strength until it was more than a match for Suanach's own and his wrist snapped at a terrible angle. Suanach staggered back, his steel-hard bone flopping as I drew his sword from the rock. Ranitha looked from her master and back to me, breathing hard. She placed her feet carefully.

'I release you from your apprenticeship,' I said.

Ranitha knew she'd lost. She screamed and attacked. We cut together. Mine was better. She stumbled on a few more paces, then sagged to her knees. Suanach went to say something, but I'd heard enough out of old men for one lifetime and I ran him through with his own sword. All those runes he'd placed on it had been good for something in the end after all, though probably not what he'd intended.

The Draoihn's ghosts howled as I caught them, but I didn't draw them into me.

'I needed traitors' ghosts for this,' I said. 'This was good timing.'

I sent them down into the loch, trailing vapour like misty green comets, screaming.

It's time, I whispered through the tunnel. *It has been many long years, but your greatness must be seen again. Drive back my enemies. Take wing one more time, queen of the sky.*

There was an age when things were not so clear-cut between our worlds of living and dead. There were great things that could hear both sides of the veil, that knew of the tunnel of death and the sky of life, and all the hard things in between. Millennia ago, one of those great beings had fallen from the sky, and its tears had formed the loch.

The death-dragon erupted from the water, ancient unrotting dragon hide fouled by mud and weed. Its head was the length of two full-grown horses. It turned hollow, spirit-glow eyes in my direction.

What do I take from this service? she asked.

I give you the chance to take wing once again, I told her. *To be remembered not as the dragon that fell, but the dragon that felled the enemy.*

The black-scaled dragon dragged itself from the water and took wing. It took her a couple of attempts to get airborne but she managed it. I hadn't known she was here at Draconloch before I came here, but she was the surest bet I had for dealing with those Third Gate Draoihn. It was only a shame I wouldn't get to see it up close. They were too far down the pass for me to see the battle, even with my First Gate stretched to its limit, but I heard some of the echoes. I saw the flashes of light as fire and lightning erupted. The din went on for nearly an hour. Dragons do not die easily the first time, let alone the second. By the time full dark was upon us all was silent, my dragon downed, but I was confident that the Draoihn of the Third Gate were either dead or spent. At such a range my soul-song couldn't draw them to me. I needed them closer, needed them much further along the pass. But they would come. They had to.

It was nearly time. I left the traitors' bodies, half running down the mountainside, and rowed swiftly out to the centre of the lake, soaked my legs as I clambered out and up the gravel bank onto the island. Nearly time. I placed a hand against the fallon, felt its cool murmuring. Nearly time. Nearly time. I was bilious and sick with ghosts, but I still needed more. I still needed one last push over the edge.

Ovitus was a student of history and a tactician, but he was also arrogant, unwise, and in the face of humiliation, reckless. He'd lost the greatest part of his fighting force to a dragon of bone and lake weed, and he wasn't going to wait for morning. I could have used the extra time. War-pipes sounded the charge. He sent everyone. And this time, he would come in person.

The fallon was cool beneath my fingers. Covered in bird shit, but cool. I rested my head against it. Here it was. Here it came.

My people were well prepared for it. I'd given the order clearly. At the first sight of Ovitus coming in person, they were to retreat, abandon all walls and give it all up. I had to hope that they were obeying me. I had to hope that they were fleeing and retreating. I took the time to rest. Mathilde and Castus had their orders too. I hoped they'd be able to wait as long as possible. I hoped as many of our people as possible could get out. Hope on hope. Too much reliance on hope.

The enemy army advanced along the gorge. The second wall was incomplete. They'd take that as a sign as they scrambled over. I was sorry for them. They weren't necessarily bad people, though show me a warrior and I'll show you their crimes. There are few who dedicate themselves to a life based around hacking other people apart who'd somehow balk at lesser evil. Honour kept them in line, I suppose, that fickle notion that some things reduced one's worth in others' minds. We cared about it far too much, and sometimes not at all. And then there was the Othering. If we told ourselves *Those people have different skin, it's all right to take what's theirs,* then did we do anything wrong? *Those people live under a different king, why not raid their barns? Those men worship a different god, go by a different clan name, live in a different village. He's not in my family. Those women aren't men, why treat them as people?*

Excuses one and all to take, to hurt. Sitting alone on my island, the water of the loch gently lapping, oil-dark in the starlight, I felt momentarily romantic. I decided to allow myself one last thought of them, those two I'd left behind. Sanvaunt, straight-backed, dutiful, earnest, and honest where it mattered. He'd made me want to be like him, not by teaching, just by being.

Esher had opened me to a world of fun, had shown me that it was all right to be a woman. That I could be beautiful and revel in it, that I could be hard and make war with it, all at the same time. She'd been so full of fear, but so much courage too. I thought of them now, because there was no going back from this point. I hadn't wanted them to see those things I'd already done. I'd left the best part of me behind, the part that could love them without shame or self-loathing. What was left had come through into this world. I was half a person, but that's what I'd needed to be. No empathy. No compassion. No remorse, no self-examination for the things I was doing and the things I'd done. I needed to be this. For the world, I needed to be this.

I shed a few quiet tears for the girl who was gone, then dashed my sleeve across my eyes. She had to stay gone.

'It's time,' I said, and I entrusted my words to tiny glitternacks that had been drawn to the fallon and its magic. The little creatures buzzed away, carrying my words off to those that waited up the sides of the gorge.

For this great act, I had placed my faith in my most trustworthy, most ruthless commanders. Castus was ready atop the gorge's northeastern wall. Mathilde was ready atop the southwest. I didn't know whether they would survive it. They didn't know either, but they could be trusted. For each of them, it was win or die. This was our best chance. They would wait until as many of the enemy as possible were between the first and second wall.

Along the length of the gorge, Ranitha's thunder-stones lay in holes cut into the banks. Carefully placed beneath overhangs, into cracks where freeze and thaw had split boulders, into the gaps where tree roots had gouged away at the rock wall's integrity. And wherever the snow lay heaviest at the peaks, wherever we might disrupt the tranquillity of the mountain.

My winged messengers' words reached them, and a series of cracks ran out. They sounded small at this distance. For a worrying moment it seemed nothing had happened, and the souls in my chest felt my distress. A series of answering snaps and pops echoed from the gorge's southern wall. And then, the unmistakable sound of the avalanche.

It begins as a whisper. Like the first sound of a river in the distance. And then you see it. The pouring sheet of white, descending like water. It picks up speed as it goes. It rushes, impatient to meet the ground. A mountainside isn't smooth. Where it levels out or juts into a promontory the collapsing barrage leaps into the air, arcing in great trails. The snow above covers the cascading rock below. For Ovitus's army, marching through the gorge, expectant of victory, for a few moments at least it must have seemed beautiful. And then it wouldn't. Then it must have been terror and asphyxiation as the snow descended upon them, and then the rock and the rubble. Eight, nine thousand men and women, and all of them doomed.

The crashing went on, and on. There were no screams to hear.

I saw my warriors, what was left of them, beating the retreat back along the loch's shore. They didn't see me, alone in the dark on my island. There was cheering among them, exultant. They couldn't believe their luck. The entire enemy army, wiped out with one fell-handed blow.

Quiet descended on the world as the snow drifted around me. Nearly time.

A great beam of energy, purple, orange and black, erupted from the sky, boring down into the centre of the gorge. It writhed and crackled, wild and unprepared. The cheers of elation turned into cries of alarm, of fear, of terror. Ovitus had advanced at the centre of his men—perhaps I'd not anticipated all his moves. Perhaps Iddin's power had made him bolder than I remembered, or perhaps he thought he'd already won. The flares of purple-orange light within that serpent of energy could only mean one thing. Iddin was breaking through from the Fault. He was here, and he was protecting his puppet form. I doubted any of Ovitus's people would survive being near that. But he was here, coming here in all his terrible, majestic, cosmic terror and I wasn't done yet. I needed time.

My men routed along the loch's shore. They could go now. Their work was done.

I sang the spell-song of soul drawing, louder and clearer now than before, its words so familiar and well-worn on my tongue that I cried it out to every flickering, shivering, howling soul along the gorge and I demanded they come to me and my tunnel. They flowed from beneath snow and rock in a flood, escaping the obliterating, world-changing energy that had descended from above. It was a race now. Iddin's beam of power was neither small nor stable. This wasn't part of Ovitus's plan. Iddin was breaking through the final barrier that separated the Fault from our world, but he needed a vessel here, a shell. Ovitus would be that shell. Good. Two birds, one big fucking stone.

The green-white vapours flowed around me. I couldn't draw any more of them in. Thousands of them, a whole soul army, rippled and swirled, a vortex of the dead spun circles across the surface of the lake. They stretched all the way from my island to the shore on each side, howling, crying, screaming their need for release.

It's time now, the Queen of Feathers whispered to me across a vast distance.

Are you prepared? I asked her. *Are they all ready to do their part?*

We all know what to do, she told me. *It's time we retook the world.*

My name was Raine of Dunan, and I was born in a nowhere village somewhere in the northern mountains of Harran. I never knew my father, nor cared to. I abandoned my mother, and I loved, and I lost. I travelled to another world, and I returned.

My name was Raine Wildrose, and I was an apprentice. I became Draoihn, and I became a pawn, then a queen. I loved and lost, and I spoke with the dead and raised them up again.

My name was Raine, Witch Queen of Redwinter, and I was the greatest power the world had ever seen.

I turned and placed my hands against the fallon, and I made myself a tunnel between the souls around me and the conduits of power that ran through the bones of the earth. I felt them then, the fallons studded all across our world, mighty focal points for these titanic energies, and the souls raced through them in five directions, burning the world as they passed along the energy lines. And as I found myself in that rushing river of power, I sensed the other fallons beyond our world, those that the Blind Child had raised. Iddin came through them too. A whole city of spires, a whole city of fallons, offered him the road to our world and he was taking it.

It was time to close that gate.

'Arise,' I whispered into the seething mass of spirits that coursed through the fallon and across the world. 'Arise, and take back what's ours.'

38

They are no longer in her world, and so she is back. She didn't know it before, but whilst those three parts of her were separated in the Fault, split across three bodies, she could not be whole. They'd searched for her all that time, not knowing that they were looking only for themselves. But they are gone now, destroyed, and so she re-exists. She doesn't need the Fault anymore. The soul-river rushing through the world empowers her, fills her, gives her substance, and she steps out from reality's tearing onto a quiet hillside, to look over the ruins of once-great Loridine.

It is a city of monsters, now. Few humans remain, and those that do are degraded, chained and enslaved to serve the creatures that have spewed through the Crown's breaching.

She needs a name here. She has had many. But it is Raine who has completed the great task, Raine who has realised the great purpose, and so she chooses the name that Raine gave her.

She is the Queen of Feathers.

The way to the Crown is filled with her enemies, with those that have served the king of the Fault. Among them is one she despises particularly, a Faded Lord who wears a mask whose feathers spread like the sun. He was known as Paladeir once, and it was he who broke her plans in the past. She will see him fall. But not alone. She needs warriors. She needs allies. She needs an army. The souls well through her and around her as Raine sends them pulsing through the fallon network that Serranis raised so long ago, that Song Seondeok fought to keep, that Hallenae saved. The dead call to the dead. This is but child's play to a dark queen of five thousand years. She looks across to the mass grave—the rotting pit where Loridine's people were marched and put to the sword. There is her army. There are her warriors. The dead call to the dead. The Queen of Feathers smiles. Beneath the piled, rotting corpses, a finger twitches. A socket long scoured empty by worms blinks. The beings that swarmed across Loridine are fat and lazy, drunk and purposeless. None *watch. None see the dead begin to claw through the long grass as they heave themselves from the trench that was to be their deathbed.*

Loridine sleeps as an army of the dead approach it. They drag rusted bill-hooks and threshing flails behind them, implacable in their march to retake the Crown of Brannlant.

The Queen of Feathers goes apart from them. She finds the Faded Lord in his sun mask, and even the impassive gold quirks in astonishment.

'You?' he breathes.

'Me,' the Queen of Feathers says. She sends the killing spell at him. He is old, this Faded Lord. He throws his counterspell, tearing runes from the air, but the killing spell has been honed through five thousand years and it shears it apart. The Faded Lord tries again, and again, and again, hurling every protective charm and ward in its way, but the spell will not abate. The Faded Lord is hoisted into the air. Every bone in his body shatters, like glass struck by a hammer. He screams, and then the flesh is torn from him piece by bloody piece. A shudder runs through the world as the power of the Crown he has taken is freed and the Faded Lord's soul is sent howling into the Night Below.

The Queen of Feathers looks up at the hill. There are more things to kill before she can take it for herself. But nothing can stop her now.

* * * * * *

Iddin smashes through the door and rushes towards her, and Hallenae flings her power against him. Five seconds she holds. Five seconds she defies a god. She smiles.

The power smashes into her and—

She is somewhere else. It is dark here. There is little of her, nothing substantial. But the pain is gone, for the first time in nearly eight hundred years the pain of her burning is missing. There is something atop her. Earth. She flows up from it, leaving behind fragments of bone and the remnants of a jewelled gown. Glowing blue and white in spirit, she looks out across Solemn Hill. This is where she fell, where Maldouen's Lance bit her and sent her to her demise.

'How did you bring me here?' she asks into a current that flows around her. She can't keep the anger, the spite from her voice even though she was dying a second time minutes before. She knows it's unwise to always be on the attack,

but it has been her way. Her father taught her that. What did it matter that he'd died for it? We are what our parents make us.

Solemn Hill lies beyond the city of Khalacant, which had seemed a fitting place to die. The serpent queens raised mausoleums of bones from the remains of those they fed to the great snakes that dwell in the pits beneath the city. The practice of human sacrifice has been practiced here long before Hallenae was defeated.

'It doesn't matter how I got you here,' Raine says, and there is such command in her voice that for the first time in her centuries of existence, Hallenae almost takes a knee. 'But here is the power you need. Use it. Retake the Crown from the Faded Lord that controls it.'

Hallenae bows her head.

'As is your will, Empress.'

The mausoleums begin to shake. Bones look for matching sockets. The city itself begins to come down upon those who have worshipped death, as the buildings begin to form into new forms, constructs of bone that will rend the way forward.

. . . . . .

She had been the Lady of Deserts once, but the land changes, and even deserts and oceans can vie for dominion. Serranis's tomb lies deep beneath the waves, and is warded with spells and sigils to prevent exactly this moment. The enemies of the past couldn't destroy her remains, such was her power, but they never wanted to see her rise again.

Serranis remembers drowning. It's the first thing that comes to her mind as she awakens in the cold of the ocean floor. There is a heady rushing of power that connects her to everything else, souls being poured into her, and she understands her purpose. She has never met Raine, but somehow as she slept she has been with her, and nobody, not even she, has ever attempted an undertaking of this magnitude. Awe blankets all other feelings.

Raine has not just sent her the river of souls. She's sent her spells as well, spells that shatter the sigil wards and runic inscriptions that have bound Serranis to her watery prison. The sarcophagus shatters and the first witch queen floats free. This city was once Amal Thray in Ithatra, she realises. There were no Crowns in her lifetime, but Raine is telling her everything she needs to know. She rushes through the water like an eel. A great dome looms before her, and its lights glow bright from the crack running across it, where the pressure of the ocean has forced aside the entryway. No Keystone is needed here. The way is clear to one who doesn't have to breathe.

. . . . . .

The story is the same in Osprinne, far, far away to the east of the Dharithian Empire. The first the people of that city are aware of is the disturbances in the cemeteries. There has been plague lately. Those bodies return, jerking awkwardly upright and staggering out to grasp the people and crush them. The living who fall rise again, and their numbers swell.

Song Seondeok starts subtly, but within hours, half the city is hers. There is no fighting her deathless horde. They cannot be felled with normal weapons. Removing their heads doesn't stop them, for the spirit is bound to the heart. The Faded Lord who took Osprinne's Crown looks down from her palace and knows terror. Has she not secured it for her king? Has she not done enough?

By dawn, the survivors are fleeing the city in streaming lines and Song Seondeok walks between a double line of her warrior-dead as she stalks towards the Crown.

. . . . . .

The spirit that awakens in Harranir's Crown shivers at finding herself back in the world. She looks around the dome, at the winking star-lights that cover it. She has been here before. She did not expect to ever come back, not into the Crown, not to the world of the living. But somehow, she is not surprised.

The world is shaking. Trembling. Time is almost up.

She had faith in the right person. She sees that now. There was no prophecy to guide them, nor path to follow. There was no history to repeat. This is something new. She has no Sixth Gate, but she is dead, and she feels the flow of ghostly energy being directed into her. It has dragged her back from a land she has already forgotten. She smiles a spectral smile. Her sister would have thought this hilarious.

Raine appears before her. She seems a ghost too, though this is merely a projection.

'You're the only one who isn't part of me,' Raine says. 'This is Harranir's Crown. You have to take it.'

'Why have you chosen me, child?' she asks. Raine bows her head.

'Because I don't trust anyone else.'

'You could take the fifth Crown for yourself,' the ghost tells her. 'You could be empress of the world if you wished.'

'I don't want it,' Raine tells her. 'I never wanted anything like it. And you'll relinquish it when it's done. The others . . . I don't know. We're closing the doorway to the Fault, but what happens after? I've unleashed the most powerful witch queens the world has ever seen back into it. There has to be someone among them that isn't that. Somebody who is something else.'

'And you chose me? I'm flattered.'

'I can't stay here,' Raine says. 'The king of the Fault has almost made it through. Banishing the Fault means nothing if he escapes.'

Vedira Robilar, once Grandmaster of Redwinter, offers a ghostly smile. She can feel the presence of the other four great and terrible women, thousands of miles apart but linked through the standing stones that spear the land.

'Then go, child. Leave this to us. Fight your battle. Go with our love.'

'Go with our love,' Serranis echoes through the ocean.

'Go with our love,' Song Seondeok whispers as she tears the soul from the Faded Lord and rips a Keystone from his hand.

'Get on with it,' Hallenae growls through the spirit river, though it's the same sentiment.

'Go with our love,' the Queen of Feathers tells her. 'And kill the bastard.'

39

I erupted back from the fallon in a scatter of souls as a great crack split its surface. The blast flung me ten feet through the air to be caught in hard, metal-clad arms before I could hit the snow. I lay with my eyes closed, inhaling frigid air through numb lips. The world felt scrambled, as if nothing was in the right place, the wrong parts of me had attached themselves in some erratic array, my eyes were no longer in my head, my thoughts scattered in a wide spray across the world.

'Is she alive?' The voice seemed to come from far away, but it sent warmth into me. Mathilde. My Mathilde.

I was deathly cold. My body had forgotten to work, but now it sent chattering shivers through me.

I forced my eyes open, though they'd frozen shut. It was light now. Midmorning. I'd been five ways across the world all at once, had watched the fall of nations, the slaughter of thousands. I'd seen the retaking of the Crowns. I'd done the impossible.

I did it!

'I'm alive,' I said. I tried to make fingers and toes work. My limbs were unendingly heavy.

'Did you do it?' Castus asked, his terrible voice grating. After what I'd seen, what I'd unleashed, he didn't seem all that bad now. I avoided looking into his eyes. Better to believe a slight untruth while it lasted.

'It's done,' I said. I was hoarse. Had I aged fifty years in one night? I felt like it.

There were only the three of us. Everything else was silent. The snow had diminished, light but steady. The world was blanketed pure and white. Mathilde came to me, throwing a cloak around my shoulders, as if simple wool could ever ease the chill that had reached all the way into my bones.

'We have to get away,' Mathilde said. 'He'll be here soon.'

As if to punctuate her words, a hollow boom emanated from the gorge.

I batted at Castus's armour until he put me down, unsteady on my feet like a tottering child. I firmed my limbs up with one of the souls I still held inside me. I'd poured the dead through the fallon, but I still had reserves. A handful only. I looked along the loch's surface, to the shore and what had been the pass beyond and was now filled with the detritus of the landslides. Far above the debris, a great vortex had formed in the sky, through which that dread white energy bunched and coiled. We held the Crowns, it could no longer pour through, but the Crowns had not closed the pathway to that terrible void. Lightning crackled and sparked out from it, bleeding the sky, colouring the snow below in luminous shades.

'He's blasting his way out,' Castus grated.

'He survived the avalanche. It's impossible, but he lived,' Mathilde said. 'We've done all we can here. We have to run.'

'No,' I said. 'No running. I won't run from Ovitus LacNaithe. It's time to put him down for good, as I should have done long ago.'

'It wasn't meant to kill him, was it?' Mathilde asked. 'Just to kill everyone else?'

I gave the slightest of nods. Getting any part of my body to move was difficult. I was so cold, so stiff, so numb. But I'd done it. I'd taken back five Crowns from our enemy in a single night, and if I could do that, then I wasn't going to go down now. For the first time in my life, I was absolutely sure of where I was supposed to be and what I was supposed to be doing. I knew how I'd do it. It was a sure thing.

'You should both get away now,' I said. 'I don't know that I can protect you.'

'This is where a queen's queen should be,' Mathilde said. She had nothing more to bring to the battle, but I was grateful for her words.

'This is where a friend should be,' Castus said.

I didn't have the energy to argue.

A silence descended back upon us. The snow fell silently, crisp and white. Mathilde and I shared our cloaks, and her body fed the warmth back into mine. From time to time hollow booms rippled out from the gorge. And then finally, eventually, snow and rock sprayed from the gorge's entrance and the sun caught on a flash of gold.

'He's here,' I said.

I had not seen Ovitus LacNaithe in the flesh for more than three years of this world's time, but I opened my First Gate and watched him come. The comet's fall had changed him. He was taller, his golden-skinned body so overly muscled that he might have been a statue from the days of Delatmar. His hair, which had been chestnut brown and curling, flowed like a silver mane. No eyeglasses anymore. The remains of once-regal robes hung in tatters from broad, powerful shoulders. I wondered whether he'd designed himself this way, and if so was this his idea of what the ideal man would look like? Despite the changes, I could still see the boy he'd been when I first saw him on that hillside. The uncertainty of purpose had left him, but that deep, soul-aching need for approval was still there. Whether it was his own approval or someone else's didn't matter, but it was a thirst that could never be quenched. He'd never feel that he was good enough, no matter how high he rose, or how far he fell. And he'd fallen further than any that had come before him.

Ovitus unfurled iridescent wings behind him. One wing had snapped away. He stepped out onto the surface of the loch and didn't sink, though tiny ripples scattered in circles from his footsteps as he approached.

'The deaths of ten thousand men lie at your door, Raine of nowhere,' he said, and his voice filled the valley. It bounced from the mountains, disappeared into mine shafts.

'The number's a lot higher than that,' I said. I didn't feel a need to enhance my own voice. He could hear me well enough.

The world shook. Snow tumbled from the mountaintops, slews of scree cascaded as the sky flexed and groaned. The vortex portal to the Fault pressed down on the world. It wanted to bring forth all its corrupted power, to swallow us, to make us part of it.

Ovitus continued his steady advance across the icy water. Coils of purple smoke drifted upwards from his golden skin. As he neared us, I saw the cracks that ran through the outer façade. The king of the Fault had poured his power through that tear between worlds, into the bond he'd made with Ovitus through the dog-familiar that had, in fact, been more master than slave. His eyes were the most human part of him. Still anxious. Still mortal. He stopped walking fifty feet from us. I had souls ready at my disposal, prepared to shield us from whatever power Ovitus chose to wield. He had three Gates at his disposal, and their power was backed by the awful, corrupting magic of the king of the Fault.

'You couldn't get everything through before I closed the tear, could you?' I said as he drew closer, almost close enough for his feet to touch the dirt. 'You're still divided.'

'What are you talking about?' Ovitus asked.

'Not you, idiot,' I said. 'Iddin. The god who's riding in your skin. The god who you thought was a dog come to serve you. You didn't figure it out?'

'There's no god here but me,' Ovitus said. He raised a hand. 'The Light Above made me her champion.'

His Third Gate roared and lightning erupted from him. The same lightning that had killed my friend Liara. Castus stood in its way. The lightning burned against him, but he could take it. Not so easy to kill my friends this time. Mathilde wisely took refuge behind the broken fallon.

'A god?' I said. 'The Light Above? You really believe that of all people, the Light Above would choose a weak, self-serving creature like you? You've spent your life grubbing around other people's feelings. Manipulating them, deceiving them, crying to yourself that life isn't fair. This is the fairness you found, is it? The Light Above rewarded you for all your heartache. Look what you've brought us to. Look what you did to our country. To the world. For the sake of your stupidity, I've had to destroy thousands. I raised armies of the dead. But the deaths lie at your hands.'

'It's you who did it,' Ovitus spat. 'You who are the enemy. You who tarnish the name Draoihn. You and your miserable common blood. Look at me, Raine. I have fought for good. For right. I have spent my whole life learning, learning how to be the man people want me to be. And for what? So that you can defile us all with your rancid magic? Your lies?'

'My common blood,' I said. I smirked at him. 'I was good enough to pretend that you'd slept with. Good enough to tell me you loved me. But in the end, I'm just common blood. You don't believe in *anything*, Ovitus. You don't care about good or right, because they change to meet whatever suits you in the moment. You read five hundred books on philosophy and you learned nothing.'

'You know nothing,' Ovitus said. His eyes bulged with fury. 'You're just some northern whore. I did nothing wrong. I did *nothing wrong*!'

He brought raw force down on me, an invisible wave that fell like a hammer. Souls squealed and burst as I held it back. Castus raised his spear, took aim, and launched it. It sped faster than a crossbow bolt and hammered against Ovitus's Gate-enhanced, golden skin. The spear hung in the air, its point lodged in Ovitus's oversized pectoral muscle. Ovitus stared at it in horror as if astonished that anything could hurt him. A sudden wash of oily, black-orange blood burst free as he tore it out. He looked down at the ichor oozing from his body. Fear, the same fear of inadequacy that had haunted him his whole life, crossed his face. And in that moment, hovering over the shallow silver-black water at the edge of the isle, he looked up at me for help.

'What's this?' he said as the tar-like filth boiled from him. 'This isn't my blood.' He looked afraid. It was dawning on him for the first time, the first time since he'd launched a rebellion and murdered Liara LacShale, that he might possibly have been wrong. Hard to keep hold of your composure when you're leaking stinking blackness.

I TIRE OF THIS SHELL ANYWAY.

There he was. Iddin, the king of the Fault. The wound tore wider and Ovitus screamed as a torrent of the foulness surged out of him and into the water. It gushed as if a dam had been pierced, the liquid surging with fury into the lake, rivers of it, far more than any body could hold. Castus went to start forward, reaching for his great sword, but I held him back.

'Not yet,' I said. 'Wait.'

We all felt it then. The presence, the emanating force of will, so deep, so ancient and so powerful that where it didn't fill physical space it was still known by the universe. All things are one, but some things shouldn't be.

Ovitus deflated like a punctured wineskin. The imagined musculature sagged, the skin hanging loose as he splashed down into the shallow water. The silver hair lost its shine, turning brittle, and flaking away into the water. His broken wings fell from his back, turned to grey. He blubbered and wailed, splashing and clawing his way through the water.

'Should I finish him, my queen?' Castus asked.

'No,' I said. 'He's powerless now.'

'M-my Gates,' Ovitus stammered. The clattering, bee-stung-bull-covered-in-pots-and pans din of his First Gate trance was gone. The thunderous music of his Second and Third, stolen from his uncle, had died too. He was just a sorry-looking, tattered young man, thrashing his over-large robes in an over-large skin.

'It can't be that easy,' Mathilde said.

'No,' I said. I took a breath. 'It's not.'

'Help me,' Ovitus wheezed. There was real blood leaking from his chest now, but it didn't look serious. Maybe it was. I didn't care.

Behind him, where the darkness had poured into the water, something rose. It was formless at first, just a mass of writhing, twisting liquid and crackling purple energy. It rose twenty feet, forty, sixty, towering above the small island, taller than the riven fallon, and a body began to take shape, a rounded head atop it, great arms splitting from the torso.

I'd steeled myself against everything that could be thrown at us, but I staggered back against the standing stone. Needed something to brace myself against. Castus, terrible and deadly though he was, seemed a small thing in opposition to it. Sanvaunt, Esher and Maldouen had put themselves against this awful thing, and I'd launched red-runed, stone-tipped arrows into it and they had availed nothing.

ALL YOUR EFFORTS COME TO NOUGHT, MORTAL QUEEN, Iddin intoned, still growing. He didn't speak. His words ran deeper than that, hammering through the particles that made the universe. The stones at my feet, the perspiration on my cheeks, the snow that fell around him, all understood him. Everything is one. Everything is one.

He rose higher, a hundred feet tall, stretching up into the sky, and he bellowed. A roar that shook the mountains and railed out against us in a wave of destruction. I threw out every soul I had left to me, shielding the three of us on a spit of island. The souls collapsed one by one, and I fed more and more into it. He knew exactly what he intended. The wave of crushing power dissipated as the last of my reserves tattered away into nothing.

YOU FOUGHT HARD. BETTER THAN THE BLIND CHILD, Iddin thrummed through the world. Birds left the mountains in flocks. BUT NOT EVEN A WITCH QUEEN OF YOUR MAKING CAN STAND BEFORE A KING FROM THE DEPTHS OF TIME. THERE IS NOT A POWER YOU CAN CONJURE THAT CAN HARM ME. NOT AN INCANTATION THAT PAPER, WOOD NOR METAL CAN WITHSTAND TO BIND ME. YOU HAVE NOTHING TO BRING AGAINST ME. KNEEL NOW. KNEEL BEFORE YOUR GOD!

Ovitus cowered in the shallows, crawling, splashing. He looked from the monster that had spewed forth from him, back to me, and maybe finally, at this very last, he understood that the world did not revolve around him. He scrambled to his knees and dipped his head.

'Not paper,' I said. 'Not wood. Not metal.' I leaned back against the fallon. Needed it for support. 'What if I had a spell left to me. An incantation I'd been readying just for this moment. Something bigger, stronger than anything anyone had tried before. Do you think you could withstand it?'

I'd managed to surprise him. The black monstrosity's face was crude, pits for eyes, a hole for a mouth, nothing like a nose. But though it claimed itself fearless, it wanted to know. It didn't fear me. It wouldn't let itself fear me. Iddin and Ovitus were not so very unalike in that regard. His belief in his own superiority eclipsed reason.

A BOLD BLUFF. BUT THE BLIND CHILD MALDOUEN TRIED THAT. NO INCANTATION COULD BE BIG ENOUGH. NO MEDIUM COULD HOLD A SPELL SO POWERFUL. NO BINDING CIRCLE COULD BE . . .

His sound died away. I wished I could have experienced what it felt like. The moment of realisation. The thunderbolt-strike moment as it dawned on him. He saw the little holes dotting the mountainside all around, entrances into the dark.

I smiled. I showed my teeth. No more restraint. No more playing dead. No more denying just how truly powerful, how invincibly brilliant, how terrifyingly deadly a true witch queen of Redwinter could be.

'You're standing in the middle of it, you king of *nothing*!' I screamed at him as I activated the incantation with a slash of my hand through the air. 'I've carved it through the damn mountains!'

Hundreds of teams of miners, working twelve-hour days in shifts, carving through stone to my precise and exact specifications. Stone, the bones of the mountains, stone that endured aeons, stone laid down thousands, tens of thousands, millions of years ago. The lie of the Lance, which had never been here if it existed at all, to lure him in. A ring of mountains, each one burrowed through, each winding tunnel a part of a greater whole that only I understood. The mines running through the mountains of Draconloch, one gigantic incantation, a spell whose forces were so great that they required the weight of stone to hold them, that were cut so powerfully into the earth that they resonated and thrummed with magic that was new and great and awesome to behold. The Queen of Feathers had taught me this, through a book I hadn't understood, through every lesson she'd given to her dark queens. We had learned it together over five thousand pitiless years. We enacted it together.

Iddin roared in terror and fury and attempted to hurl his power against me, but nothing came. He stood within a binding circle, and all his fury and godlike magic was trapped within him, locked away. Great gouts of water exploded as he slammed his arms down, but he could proceed no further. The peaks of the mountains echoed with the sound of splintering stone as even those great peaks struggled to contain that which I'd drawn.

'Everything is one,' I said. 'Except you.'

NO!

'Go back to your empty realm!' I howled at him. 'Go back to your land of nothing. No subjects. No minions. You've emptied it or killed everything that was still there. And with the Crowns in my fist, I'm sealing you away. Forever. Enjoy your eternity in your own empty hell!'

I clapped my hands together. The tunnels within the mountains flared with light, dazzling, as Iddin, king of the Fault, screamed with a terror he'd never knew he could feel as his dripping, liquid form was torn upwards from the water. He thrashed. He raged. He tried to find some kind of purchase in our world but my incantation had cut him from it. Everything is one, but the power of my spell cut him out of it. And where it wasn't one, it had to go somewhere else. Swirls of Iddin's body streamed towards the vortex in the sky in long black streaks, but his rage-filled screams bounced from mountain to mountain. We watched them go, up into the sky.

'Is—is he gone?'

I looked down at Ovitus. Wet and bedraggled.

'Don't worry,' I said. 'You're going with him.'

I would always remember his face. The relief turning to sudden horror. Never to age. Never to go hungry. Locked away in a cruel and empty place where there was nothing and nobody, forever. It was the only fate he deserved. The tiniest flick of my hand modified the spell just that much, and Ovitus LacNaithe, the usurper of Redwinter, was lashed away into the sky, became one with nothing, lost so fast he was lost from sight in the vortex before I could draw a breath.

I fell to my knees.

Close it, I thought, and the Queen of Feathers, Grandmaster Vedira Robilar, Serranis Lady of Deserts, Song Seondeok and Hallenae the Riven Queen made the slightest adjustment within the domes of the Crowns, and the void above Draconloch snapped shut. The earth's shaking subsided. The land became calm.

It was over.

I held Mathilde's hand as we watched the snow fall. Her hand was warm.

EPILOGUE

The stories of this age begin and end with birth, and mine is no exception.

It was a beautiful, warm morning, eight months and two weeks to the day after the usurper was defeated, that a baby was heard crying in Harranir's streets. She was a healthy girl, and her mother named her Summer, as that was when she was born.

The snails no longer rained, the rivers had ceased boiling, and the pigs were back to their regular size. Not all was right with the world. There were strange things abroad. It wasn't wise to walk in the woods alone. But on the whole, the country of Harran had ended up in a place a good sight better than it ought to have been. The warriors who were so often at one another's throats formed the Order of the Blue Rose, and put their swords to battling the dark things that had escaped into our world. Their leader was a war hero by the name of Dinny LacDaine, and he faced the darkness time and time again. It was said that in times of great danger, a terrible, golden-haired warrior rose from the shadows to protect him, but people say a lot of things.

The Brannish empire was broken, and the civil wars continued across its former glory as tyrants and populists tried to claim the scraps. Brannlant itself was an inhospitable, monster-haunted wasteland. Refugees poured across the land, looking for new homes, new earth to till. They said the dead walked in Loridine, that it was a corpse city. Rumours had finally reached Harran that in Osprinne there was a new plague, swarms of corpses roaming the land, crushing everything in their path. The dark empress of myth, Song Seondeok, had risen again, they said. But people say such things from time to time, and Osprinne was a long, long way away.

I was crowned and more formally married to Mathilde in Redwinter's grounds, the day after Summer's birth. We'd sworn we'd not declare ourselves until that day and the Matriarchs of the church were not happy about it, but things were going to change in that direction. There were all sorts of questions about how the royal line would proceed, but we had decided that since I was barely twenty years old, that could wait a while. Bridges could be crossed when they had to be. We moved into Grandmaster Robilar's former home, and from time to time it showed us its secrets.

The Crowns were secure. After everything we'd been through, everything we'd done, the Fault was gone. Iddin was bound. For now, we were safe.

One morning I left Mathilde sleeping, slipped on drab clothes and slunk out and walked into Redwinter's grounds. A group of five youngsters were being trained in the First Gate by Draoihn Palanost, who still glared every time she saw me, but had at least accepted my offer of a position on my Council of Night and Day. The grounds were all but deserted now, the great-houses empty. I'd given Mathilde the task of filling them with the Brannish refugees and the poor from down in Harran. The clans weren't happy, but what were they going to do, find a bigger god to fight me?

'It was worth it all, in the end,' the Queen of Feathers said to me.

'It was, I suppose,' I said. 'I'm still sad that I lost them. I loved them both so much.'

'I know,' she said. 'But life goes on. We live, we love and we lose.'

'Do you love?' I asked her.

'There's always love inside me,' she said wistfully. 'I was made from love. What more could I ask for?'

I watched the apprentices at work for a while. They were so clumsy, so unsure of themselves. That had been me, not all that long ago.

'Hallenae's making war on Song,' I said.

'Of course she is,' the Queen of Feathers said. 'It's what she does.'

'I sent Castus to sort them out.'

'He'll make war of his own, eventually.'

I sighed. A problem for another day.

'I hear them within you, now. Sometimes,' I said. 'Sanvaunt's drive, his sense of obligation. Esher's passion, her desire for the world. My own stubbornness and cruelty.'

'There's more to you than that,' she said. She laid a hand atop my hand, ghostly and invisible to everyone else, but I very much felt it. Having left Mathilde abed, and I felt a slight sense of betrayal at the intimacy of the Queen of Feathers' touch. I was a married woman now, but then, I was probably going to live for an awfully long time. I felt almost shy as I glanced at the Queen of Feathers. She was very beautiful.

'I need to ride,' I said. The Queen of Feathers dissipated without me having to ask for solitude. I took a horse from the stable and headed out onto the moor. It was beautiful at this time of year, the low bushes swathing the rolls and folds of the land in yellow and purple. And there, distantly across the hills, a herd of perfect white horses galloped, their hooves barely touching the ground. They had escaped too. They'd wanted their freedom as we all had. I kicked my horse to a run, and I joined them and together we crossed the miles of this beautiful land.

I looked up into the sky, watched a bird wheeling around. There was sun on my face. It was all I'd ever wanted, a little sun. A little peace. Just for a little while.

Dramatis Personae

Rulers

Ovitus LacNaithe—A usurper, lord of Clan LacNaithe, married to Princess Mathilde of Brannlant

King Quinlan LacDaine—King of Harran, bearer of the Crown, father of Caelan LacDaine (deceased)

Prince Caelan LacDaine—Prince of Harran, son of Quinlan LacDaine, refused to take the throne and the Crown

King Henrith II—King of Brannlant, father of Mathilde

Princess Mathilde—A princess of Brannlant, daughter of Henrith II, married to Ovitus LacNaithe

Lady Dauphine—Princess Mathilde's cousin and her companion

Rebels

Van Merovech LacClune—Lord of his clan

Castus LacClune—Son of Merovech LacClune, heir to the clan

Suanach LacNaruun—Draoihn of the Second Gate, master of artifice

Dinny LacDaine—Wildrose (illegitimate) son of Prince Caelan LacDaine

Palanost—Draoihn of the First Gate, Raine's former tutor at Redwinter

Hallum LacShale—A warrior seeking vengeance, kin to Liara LacShale

Ranitha—A Draoihn of the Second Gate and an artificer serving Suanach

Of the Fault

Iddin—King of the Fault

Maldouen the Blind Child—Created the Lance and the five Crowns, which were used to defeat Hallenae and her armies, vanished thereafter

The Dryad—A twisted creature

LacNaithe Household in Redwinter, as it was

Ulovar LacNaithe—Van of the clan, Draoihn of the Fourth Gate, holds one of the seats on the Council of Night and Day (deceased)

Ovitus LacNaithe—Heir to the LacNaithe clanhold, nephew to Ulovar, cousin to Sanvaunt, holds the rank of thail as well as being an apprentice

Sanvaunt LacNaithe—Draoihn of the First Gate, nephew of Ulovar, cousin to Ovitus

Raine 'Clanless' / Raine Wildrose—An apprentice sponsored by Ulovar

Esher of Harranir—An apprentice sponsored by Ulovar

Jathan of Kwend—An apprentice sponsored by Ulovar (deceased)

Adanost of Murr—An apprentice sponsored by Ulovar (deceased)

Colban Giln—An apprentice sponsored by Ulovar (deceased)

Gelis LacAud—An apprentice sponsored by Ulovar (deceased)

Liara LacShale—An apprentice sponsored by Ulovar, youngest daughter of Kaldhoone LacShale (deceased)

Hazia LacFroome—An apprentice formerly sponsored by Ulovar, fostered at Valarane with Sanvaunt and Ovitus (deceased)

Tarquus of Redwinter—First Retainer, servant

Ehma of Harranir—Second Retainer, servant

Howen of Harranir—Second Retainer, servant

Bossal of Harranir—Fifth Retainer, servant

Patalia of Harranir—Fifth Retainer, servant

Waldy—Ovitus's loyal wolfhound

The Council of Night and Day, as it was

Grandmaster Vedira Robilar—Leader of the Draoihn order, head of the council, Draoihn of the Fifth Gate (deceased)

Kelsen of Harranir—The king's personal healer, Draoihn of the Fifth Gate (deceased)

Ulovar LacNaithe—Van of Clan LacNaithe, Draoihn of the Fourth Gate, usually at Redwinter, uncle of Ovitus and Sanvaunt (deceased)

Onostus LacAud—Draoihn of the Second Gate (deceased)

Hanaqin Clanless—Draoihn of the Fourth Gate

Lassaine LacDaine—Draoihn of the Fourth Gate, great-niece to King Quinlan LacDaine, commander of the Winterra (deceased)

Merovech LacClune—Van of Clan LacClune, Draoihn of the Fourth Gate, father of Castus

Kyrand of Murr—Draoihn of the Third Gate

Suanach LacNaruun—Draoihn of the Second Gate, master of artifice

Legendary Figures

The Queen of Feathers—A being of unknown origin who visits Raine

Hallenae, the Riven Queen—Made war against the world, defeated at Solemn Hill by Maldouen and the last surviving generals. Hallenae was imbued with the power of the Night Below, which was bound and stored in five Crowns. Slain more than seven hundred years ago, her defeat marks the beginning of the Succession Age.

Empress Serranis, Lady of Deserts—A dread Sarathi ruler, defeated more than 4,000 years ago

Empress Song Seondeok—A dread Sarathi ruler who brought the world to ruin around 1,900 years ago

Grandmaster Unthayla the Damned—A Sarathi, unmasked and defeated in the year 456

Sul, a Faded Lord—The most active of the Faded Lords, and a constant threat to the Draoihn. Sul murdered King Dern LacNaithe in the year 370, and fought the Council of Night and Day to a standstill in 456. He returned to fight Grandmaster Robilar in the year 681, leaving her permanently wounded.

Alianna—Grandmaster Robilar's sister (deceased)

The Mystic World

The Draoihn

The Draoihn enter a series of existentialist trances that allow them to expand their consciousness into the world around it, become one with it and then affect it. To do so, they open a Gate in their mind.

EIO: The First Gate—the Gate of Self. Allows exceptional sensory perception by expanding the essence of one's self into the connected world around. There are about one thousand Draoihn of the First Gate, most of whom are sent to serve the Winterra, supporting the king of Brannlant's territorial expansion.

SEI: The Second Gate—the Gate of Other. Allows the expansion of consciousness into non-living matter in the physical world around the trance holder, and the manipulation of the Other. There are only one hundred Draoihn of the Second Gate, around half of whom work under Suanach LacNaruun working on artifice at Redwinter.

TAINE: The Third Gate—the Gate of Energy. Allows the expansion of consciousness through energy, the transmission of that energy, and its redirection. As every scientist knows, energy cannot be created or destroyed. There are only thirty Draoihn of the Third Gate.

FIER: The Fourth Gate—the Gate of Mind. Allows the expansion of consciousness into the minds of living creatures the trancing Draoihn touches, enabling them to impact the thought processes of that creature's mind. There are only four Draoihn of the Fourth Gate—Ulovar, Merovech, Hanaqin and Lassaine.

VIE: The Fifth Gate—the Gate of Life. Allows the expansion of consciousness into the physical forms of oneself as well as other living matter. This is mostly used for healing. There are only two known Draoihn of the Fifth Gate, Grandmaster Vedira Robilar and Kelsen of Harranir, who acts as the king's personal healer.

SKAL: The Sixth Gate—the Gate of Death. The old power of the Sarathi.

Modern Draoihn are forbidden to even attempt to access it. There are no Draoihn of the Sixth Gate.

GEI: The Seventh Gate—the Gate of Creation. The Seventh Gate is purely theoretical, a concept used to understand how the Faded changed the world as they did thousands of years ago.

The Sarathi

Wielders of the Sixth Gate, they sided with Hallenae the Riven Queen, and enemies of the world, but are said to have betrayed Hallenae prior to the battle at Solemn Hill where she met her defeat. They are always enemies of Redwinter.

The Faded

A race of powerful and sentient beings, the Faded once lived alongside mankind. They were banished into the Fault by Maldouen at the beginning of the Succession Age. Very occasionally one of the Faded finds a way to escape that prison.

The Crowns

Prior to the Succession Age, the Riven Queen amassed such power that she could not be defeated. In their hour of need, the Draoihn were presented with an answer by the legendary Blind Child, Maldouen, who informed them of his labour to construct five great Crowns across the world, and that those Crowns could banish her most terrible allies—the Faded, the demons and dead things she had summoned. The Crowns lie in Harran, its imperial neighbour Brannlant, and the distant realms of Ithatra, Khalacant, and Dharithia. Vast domed chambers filled with magic, the Crowns' power must be ever bound to the mind of a mortal, or the dark creatures that were banished from the world might find a way to return. For the Draoihn of Harranir, the bond to the Crown is always forced on a would-be king, so that the ruler might understand that protecting the Crown is his greatest responsibility.

The Draoihn support the occupation of Harranir by its more powerful neighbour, Brannlant, because it leaves two Crowns under a single leadership. Khalacant is a realm ruled by the serpent queens, while the city of Osprinne lies in the distant empire of Dharithia. Ithatra lay beyond the western ocean, a voyage which has become too treacherous to make by Raine's time, and what has become of its Crown is unknown.

The Hidden Folk

Once, the Hidden Folk existed alongside the rest of the world, and this name was not given to them until after their banishment. When Maldouen created the five Crowns, most of the magical creatures of the world were banished into another plane of existence known as the Fault, while others were left in a kind of limbo, uncertain whether they belong in one realm or another. Those that do still have a presence were driven into the far-flung, wild places of the world and are seldom seen. The Hidden Folk encompass a wide range of creatures, from the deadly, mermaid-like 'Drowners' to the small and mischievous Powsies and harmless snatterkin. Some compose whole species, while others are singular, unique beings.

The Fault

The Fault lies between the mortal world and the dark terrors of the Night Below. Some of those creatures, such as the moon horses, have ways of moving between the realms, but little beyond that is known of it.

The Hexen

Destroyed by the Draoihn during the Betrayal War, they burned the Glass Library of Redwinter.

The Knights of Tharada Taan

The knights drew their power from the Everstorm around Tharada Mountain, until the Draoihn destroyed it and ended their power.

Acknowledgements

For their assistance in bringing this story onto these pages, I would like to thank:

My agent Ian Drury, for supporting the stories I've always wanted to tell.

My editor Claire Eddy, who saw Raine's potential and took her forward.

My editor Brendan Drukin, whose enthusiasm for these stories gives them momentum.

Gillian Redfearn, who helped Raine to grow and champions her still.

Sanaa Ali-Virani and the team at Tor, whose tireless work keeps the cogs turning.

The team at Gollancz, whose labours never go unappreciated.

Gaia Banks, Alba Arnau and all of the team at Sheil Land Associates who have sent my words around the world.

And finally, this book would never have got here without the assistance, suggestions, and ongoing support of my first reader and editor, my inspiration and companion: Catriona Ward, who is all the colours of my heart.

About the Author

ED MCDONALD is the author of the Raven's Mark and Redwinter Chronicles series of novels. He studied ancient history and archaeology at the University of Birmingham, and medieval history at Birkbeck College, University of London. McDonald is passionate about fantasy tabletop role-play games and has studied medieval swordsmanship since 2013. He currently lives with his partner, author Catriona Ward, in London, England.